SILVER WINGS GOLDEN GAMES

THE GODKISSED BRIDE
BOOK TWO

EVIE MARCEAU

Samaur: sah-MAR

OTHER NAMES

Basten: BASS-ten
Folke: FOHLK-uh
King Rachillon: RAH-shee-yon

PLACES & VOCABULARY

Astagnon: AH-stag-non
Volkany: VOHL-kah-nee
Monoceros: mon-oh-SAIR-ous
Tamarac: tam-UH-rak

PRONUNCIATION GUIDE

HOUSE DARROW
Sabine Darrow: sah-BEEN DAIR-oh
Lord Charlin Darrow: CHAR-lin DAIR-oh
Lady Suri Darrow: SOO-ree DAIR-oh

HOUSE VALVERE
Lord Rian Valvere: REE-an val-VAIR-ay
Lord Berolt Valvere: BEH-rohlt val-VAIR-ay

THE IMMORTAL FAE COURT
Vale: vayl
Iyre: EYE-ur
Artain: ar-TAYNE
Solene: soh-LEN
Popelin: POH-peh-lin
Meric: MAIR-ick
Thracia: THRA-see-uh
Alyssantha: ah-liss-AN-tha
Woudix: WOO-diks

THE ANCIENT IMMORTAL COURT

Vale the Warrior, *King of Fae*
Iyre the Maiden, *Goddess of Virtue*
Artain the Archer, *God of the Hunt*
Solene the Wilderwoman, *Goddess of Nature*
Popelin the Trickster, *God of Pleasure*
Meric the Punisher, *God of Order*
Thracia the Stargazer, *Goddess of Night*
Alyssantha the Lover, *Goddess of Sex*
Woudix the Ender, *God of Death*
Samaur the Sunbringer, *God of Day*

PROLOGUE

Hekkelveld Castle, Old Coros

Three men's breath clouded in the cold air around the breakfast table, though only two of them were alive. The younger priest—his skin the tawny brown of a Tiger's Eye stone, with a patch over his right eye—pressed his chapped hands between his knees as he gazed ruefully at the empty fireplace. The priest seated to his left, whose silver streak in his dark blond hair gave him the air of a man older than he was, drew his hands into the woolen sleeves of his robe. In the third seat, King Joruun of Astagnon wheezed a rotting breath that reeked of death.

"This has to stop," the young priest begged. "How much longer can it possibly go on? Look at him."

The elder priest reclined, kicking out one gilded boot, toying with one of the table's runestones. "It will go on until the King's Council agrees to turn Astagnon into a theocracy with me at the helm. If the king were to die before that time, our enemies would have the opportunity to invoke the Kinship Mandate. The monarchy would remain, and the throne would automatically pass to the closest blood relation."

The one-eyed priest sank his head into his hands, tearing at his scalp as if he wanted to crawl from his skin. The king *had* died. The first time was six weeks ago, when a bout of pneumonia stopped his lungs. The court healer and two nurses in attendance had been quickly executed to keep the news silent. Then, the young priest had been rushed in from the Temple of Immortal Woudix and told it was the gods' will he use his deathraiser godkiss.

The second time the king died, his heart gave out.

The third time, his spine snapped.

Now, the young priest laid his palms flat on the table between the runes. "His body is falling apart. Keeping it like an ice box in here will only preserve the flesh for so long. The rats have been at his feet again. The fae did not bless me with my godkiss so I could desecrate our benevolent king's legacy into a pile of rotting flesh—"

"I alone know the gods' plans." The older priest's fist slammed down hard enough to rattle the runes. "You are a sworn disciple of the Red Church; your godkiss serves the fae, not your own earthly whims. As Grand Cleric, I am your superior. I'll be damned if I let the throne fall into the hands of those Valvere devils instead of under my own shepherding."

The Grand Cleric stood, sweeping the runestones into his velvet pouch. "If the king dies again in the night, I expect to see him sipping tea at this very breakfast table in the morning. Or it will be *your* death written in the ledgers."

As he stormed out, the reanimated king slowly looked up with blue-cast, unseeing eyes as a strange hiss snaked up his throat. At the corner of his mouth, a maggot wriggled.

CHAPTER 1
SABINE

"After you, songbird."

Lord Rian Valvere, swathed in a cerulean cloak, swings open the gambling den's door and cocks an eyebrow as he waits for me to enter. Laughter and the sound of clinking gold pieces spill into the street, and I hug my fur-lined cloak around my neck. Back home, in Bremcote, it never got this cold in April.

Though the den's warmth beckons, I hesitate.

I never thought I'd be here. In Duren. Trapped by high city walls. Engaged to a man who forced me to ride naked across half of Astagnon—as a *political distraction*. And now? I'm about to strike a bargain with this angel-faced devil, binding our fates with iron shackles.

So, yes, I have every reason under the stars for pause.

A cough from the street steals my attention, and I squint into the shadow of a bakery's rear entrance, closed for the night, where a huddle of threadbare clothes coughs again. Two silver-dollar eyes lift to meet mine. It's a boy. He can't be older than ten.

From across the street, a cat meows.

"Sabine," Rian prompts with an impatient edge.

I scoff, "One minute, Rian. Surely you're wealthy enough to spare that."

As I jog over to the boy, Rian pinches the bridge of his nose and mutters a curse about strong-willed women. Ignoring him, I drop to a crouch beside the boy. "Hello. Are you sick? Hungry? Do you have a family?"

His watery eyes rise to meet mine, but he only stares as though he doesn't understand the Astagnonian words. His clothes are tatters—patched so many times over that the original fabric is a distant memory. It's no wonder he's shivering like a sapling in a storm.

"For the love of the gods," Rian groans. "Come *on*."

The boy shifts, and as the gambling den's light catches his cheek, I swallow a gasp. A curving burn mark mars his cheek from temple to jaw.

"He's freezing," I call over my shoulder, already untying the satin ribbon at my throat to give the boy my cloak, but as I slip it off my shoulders, Rian's hand clamps over mine.

"That cloak costs more than the boy's life is worth," he says in a velvety warning.

"Good, then he can sell it—"

"You don't understand. The first drunken riffraff to see him with something so fine will slit his throat and take it. Give the boy your cloak, fine—but you might as well twist it around his neck first to spare him a worse death."

There's a cool indifference to Rian's voice, like we're debating dinner plans. As much as I want to hurl accusations of callousness, a snag in the pit of my stomach tells me that, while heartless, he might not be altogether wrong.

As a vicious gust of wind whistles down the street, Rian

holds a gloved hand toward me. When I hesitate, he says in a tone with no trace of its usual mockery, "You can't save every street boy in Astagnon, Sabine."

I want to remind him that he, too, once took pity on a street boy. If he hadn't pulled Basten off the streets to become his sparring partner, Basten would likely have been beaten to death in the fighting rings. Even a top fighter can be brought down by dirty rules.

Though, of course, pity had nothing to do with it. Rian needed Basten for his heightened senses. And whatever Rian needs, Rian takes.

I squeeze the boy's shivering knee, exposed through a hole in his trousers, and whisper a plea to Immortal Solene, Goddess of Nature, to ease the biting wind. But if I relied on prayers to the fae gods, I might as well invest in a good rocking chair, because it would be one hell of a long wait.

So, as Rian taps his boot on the curb, I call to the stray cat across the street instead.

Come warm this boy, kind friend, I say to the cat. *Sleep beside him tonight, and he will warm you, too.*

The cat trots out of the shadows, slinking along the closed storefronts. Her tail is crooked—broken more than once. She blinks her marble-green eyes at me before winding her way to the boy in the bakery doorway, nuzzling against his bony knee.

All angles, no fat on this one, she sniffs.

But that's cats for you—always complaining. When she finally curls up in his lap, it's only seconds before she starts purring contentedly.

"There," Rian mutters, raking back his hair into its perfect style. "Can we get on with more pressing business?"

Inside the gambling den, the strong, smoky aroma of

incense burns down my throat. The clinking of coins echoes from the card tables, where silver pieces are traded between players. My hand goes anxiously to my short hair, cut just below my chin.

Popelin's Gambit is Duren's highest-class gambling den, catering only to those who can show five hundred coins at the door. A chandelier hangs from the two-story ceiling, casting a warm, dim light over lavish mahogany game tables. Gilded mirrors reflect the flickering candlelight. On the wall hangs a portrait of Immortal Popelin, God of Pleasure, the establishment's namesake. The artist has draped his slender frame in delicate chainmail and painted shimmering, golden fae lines along his pecan skin. He holds a pile of coins in one hand and a cup of wine in the other.

It's crowded. The wealthy guests are dressed in fae-style finery crafted of luxurious, colorful silks with asymmetrical hemlines. Guests and dealers alike wear fitted satin masks over their eyes. As far as disguises, the masks are woefully insufficient. I easily recognize Lady Runa Valvere, Rian's cousin, at the dice table by her glossy black tresses.

The masks aren't truly meant to hide anything, I think—they're just part of the ambiance.

"Your cloak, Sabine," Rian prompts. He hands his own to the door attendant, which leaves him in a simple black shirt, unbuttoned at the neck, flashing a triangle of warm, tanned flesh—and a lack of godkiss birthmark. He's the only Valvere not shamed by his lack of magic.

I touch the ribbon at my neck.

"Let me." His hands come around my throat from behind to unfasten the ribbon, close enough that I can smell a trace of sandalwood in his hair and saddle leather on his skin. Woodsy, masculine. It's easy to see why every woman in Duren wants to be in the High Lord's bed. I need to play the part of a willing bride, too, if I want to keep him from suspecting my secrets.

But my heart will never belong to Rian.

For better or worse—let's face it, *definitely worse*—it beats for the guard who promised me, in a cave with moonlight winking off a rushing waterfall, that we'd run away together.

But he lied.

Wolf Bowborn really should go by his given name, Basten, because it's such a perfect fit. *Basten the Bastard.*

Where is Basten? I wonder for the thousandth damn time.

I hate how much I crave the answer. When Rian pulled him off my guard duty and replaced him with dour old Maximan, he hinted that Basten had a side job that would occupy his attention for a few days. But it's been nearly a week, and I haven't heard so much as a single one of Basten's growlsome curses.

What I loathe most of all is how much I miss them.

"This is a discrete establishment, so masks are required," Rian explains, handing me one of the satin eye masks. "Though I have no illusion that everyone here will recognize Duren's famed Winged Lady's gown, mask or not." His fingers glide lightly down the length of my back, where Brigit has embroidered silver wings. The wings run from my shoulder blades to the small of my back, where Rian's hand drifts to the swell of my hips and squeezes.

Once we're masked, Rian offers me his arm like a perfect gentleman. "Now, songbird, let me introduce you to my smorgasbord of sin."

We sweep into the crowd, and he's right—all eyes shift

to me amid whispers and pointed looks. Elegantly dressed men nod to Rian, hoping to garner favor from the owner of Popelin's Gambit and every other gambling hall in Duren. Rian exchanges brief greetings as he leads me through the maze of tables. The blue smoke of pipe herb thickens the air, rising in snaking lines toward the high ceiling.

I feel everyone's attention on me like daggers. Duren's lower classes embraced me because I dared to defy the Valvere family, which puts me squarely in the wealthy class's ill graces. The looks I get are wary but also disdainful —these fine lords and ladies can't imagine a provincial girl is any threat to centuries of their rule.

One set of eyes across the room feels different, however. Less like pointed blades and more like a warm ribbon of sunlight. Intrigued. Ever watchful. When I turn toward the feeling, I find a tall, masked man with a mane of dark blonde hair studying me from the bar. A streak of white hair cuts down over his forehead. He seems too young to be graying —more likely the result of an accident. He holds a crystal glass of amber liquid, and though his clothes are as elegant as everyone else's, he stands out like a crow among swans.

"Hazard," Rian says, jerking back my attention. He nods toward a game of chance where a wheel is spun with a pendant that flaps against numbered pins. "There is little strategy with this game, so if you chose it for our wager, you'd better pray to Immortal Popelin for luck."

A triumphant gasp erupts from a woman in a maroon gown as the pendant lands on her stack of coins.

Rian skirts me to the next table, where four players hold hands of cards. "Perhaps a card game. This is Cipherian. It's a game of strategy. Not as much about the cards you hold, but reading your opponents."

One of the players tosses three silver coins on the table while a high-class prostitute wiggles into the lap of the elderly man across the table.

"It's a bluffing game," I say, trying not to wince as the gray-haired man slides his tongue in the prostitute's ear. "My father played card games. I remember from my childhood. His favorite game was—"

"Basel," Rian says smoothly, and I stare at him for a second before my cheeks darken.

Of course, Rian knows my father's game. He entrapped my father through Basel into debt—which is why his diamond engagement ring circles my finger.

A trade to settle debts.

At this reminder, anger sweeps through me like one of the puffs of cigar smoke. For as affable as Rian can be, it's all an act. As artificial as his black silk mask.

To steady myself, I curl my fingers around the table's edge. My eyes fall on a gilded wall mirror, and for a second, my breath runs cold. In my elegant clothes and mask, I don't recognize myself.

Instead, I see my mother looking back. Her swanlike neck. Her secretive smile. Her chin tipped as though daring the world to stand in her way. In that brief flash, the woman in the mirror looks like she wants to tell me something. Unlike animals, though, I can't speak to ghosts.

Gods, it steals my breath.

Lately, I've been thinking about my mother more often. At night, I toss and turn, memories trying to unearth themselves like wriggling worms from deep within my brain.

I was ten when she died; old enough to hold an image of her in my mind's eye, to recall her hugs and laughter and off-tune humming. Specific memories, though, are harder to summon. My mind smothered them to ease the pain, like a bandage over a fresh wound.

I jump as Rian lays a hand on my nearly bare shoulder, clothed only with a delicate lace strap. "It's warm in here with so many bodies," he breathes close to my ear. "Come. I want to show you someplace more private."

My heartbeat kicks up in warning. Privacy isn't what I want with Rian, but then again, I have to keep my enemy appeased.

"Trying to get out of our wager?" I ask as I turn, now the picture of a tantalizing young fiancée playing hard to get.

"Not at all. There are *other* games than these."

The secretive ripple in his voice prickles the hair on my upper arms.

He leads me to a staircase to an upper level. After winding through some dim hallways, we come out on a balcony that's curtained off from the gambling floor below with gauzy white curtains, closed now. Lamps blaze beside a mahogany desk and chair. A pile of books weighs down a stack of letters. Beside it, a long, pointed letter opener winks at me with the promise of violence.

My heart strums faster. I tug off my satin mask, shaking out my hair as I look around. "Your office?"

Still masked, he moves the desk chair to face the gauzy curtains. "Yes, technically, though my uncle Gideon handles the day-to-day business. Maintaining the books. Stocking the bar. Hiring the whores. Keeping a close eye on cheaters."

He returns to the desk and switches off the lamp.

The windowless room goes black. I blink, bristling at the sudden shadows, afraid of Rian's intention. But my eyes soon adjust to the glow coming from the wall of curtains. Whatever fabric they're made of is so sheer that I can see down to the gambling floor like peering through cloudy glass. From this angle, every player's hand of cards is visible.

Rian's chest brushes up behind me as he runs a slow finger down the curtain. "It's a type of gauze from Clarana. I designed this space so that we can see the players below when the lights are off, but they can't see us."

"For surveillance."

"Yes, though there are other benefits to being out of sight, of course."

"Other benefits?"

His arm hooks around my waist from behind, and with a smooth tug, he pulls me into his lap in the chair.

He brushes a curl of hair away from my temple.

"The other benefit is so that I can do this." His lips tease along the shell of my ear. His arm around my waist drifts up to graze the underside of my breast. The contrast of his soft lips and the punishing edge of his teeth on my earlobe make me stiffen, heart pounding.

Rian tilts his head back just far enough to sear me with a keen appraisal. "What, songbird, not in the mood? You liked it well enough when I had my tongue down your throat at our engagement party."

There's a challenge in his voice. Like this is all a game— only I'm the one he's watching for tells, not the cheaters on the gambling floor below.

This is a man who built his family's empire by reading people's slightest shows of emotion, so I have to be as stolid as the Cipherian players.

I twist in his lap to toy with the open uppermost button on his shirt, playing coy as I blink up through my long eyelashes. "Well, my lord, that was before I learned you kept helpless animals *caged*." My voice sharpens into a blade as I fasten the button, which does a satisfying job of choking him.

I give a withering smile.

His eyes flash—he likes it when I defy him, which is precisely why I did it—and makes a low chuckle as he unfastens the button again and adjusts his collar.

"A monoceros is hardly a helpless animal, darling. That monstrous horse could raze a forest to ash before you snap your fingers. It could decimate all of Duren with a single blast of funneled sunlight from its horn. It is the greatest weapon any kingdom could possess—and war is on the horizon."

"The monoceros is only a weapon against your enemies if you can tame it," I say steadily. "Otherwise, it's just as much a threat to us."

Uninterested in political talk, his hand slides along the outside of my thigh, his middle finger tracing the seam where my lap meets his.

His breath tickles my neck as he murmurs, "Exactly how sheltered were you in the convent, songbird? Have you only seen animals rutting? Illustrations of Alyssantha and her lovers? I can make you feel the most exquisite pleasure and pain that you've ever imagined . . ."

His hand wanders over my gown, and as soon as his fingers graze my inner thigh, I bolt to my feet.

Heart in my throat, I smooth the dress's fabric back over my legs, hoping he didn't feel what I was hiding there . . .

When I finally gather my wits, I paste a thin line on my lips. "You're trying to distract me from our deal. We agreed to play a game, and the winner takes all."

He leans back in the desk chair with that devilish grin

that's won him so many women, and lifts a shoulder. *Guilty as charged.*

I fold my arms tightly. "I've decided on the game, and it isn't any of the ones below." My eyes fasten to his shirt pocket. "A coin toss—that's all I want. Your Golath dime."

One of his dark eyebrows arches at the game's simplicity, as though I'm insulting his extensive gaming empire. But he simply says, "And the wager?"

"If you win, I'll train your monoceros to be the weapon you need to fight against Volkany. But if I win . . ." My throat bobs. "You let me go."

"Let you *go*? Are you in shackles, songbird?"

"Release me from our marriage contract."

He snorts as though I've asked him to turn the sky red. He reaches into his pocket for his Golath dime: a rare piece from a lost empire before the current Kingdom of Golath was formed, the only one of its kind still known to exist. He tosses me the coin, and I lunge forward, narrowly catching it. "Go ahead, then. Your game intrigues me. Deciding the fate of love and war with a coin flip."

I smooth my thumb over the dime's raised carving.

"I'll take the Serpent side." I pull a breath thick with lingering incense deep into my lungs. Though I may not be much of an actress, I've gotten this far in my plan. The last step, though, is the hardest.

As I smooth out my dress skirt again, I tap twice on the side of my leg, behind me where Rian can't see.

"I'll take Scepter," he replies.

His dark eyes haunt me as I pace in front of the curtain, balancing the coin on my thumb. My heart lilts so fast I'm afraid I might faint. The coin trembles on my thumb.

With a whispered prayer, I flip the dime.

The gesture is clumsy, and instead of flying high where I can catch the coin, it rolls under Rian's desk.

"Oh, hell," I mutter, dropping to my hands and knees to fish the coin out from under his desk.

Rian shoots to his feet so fast that the papers bluster off his desk. "Slow down, songbird. We'll check it together so neither of us can flip it to our side, eh?"

My heart thrashes like a trapped bird, its delicate wings beating against the cage of my ribs. I let my nerves show in the flush in my cheeks as if he's caught me mid-scheme.

He sinks to his knees and clamps a hand on the dime, then drags it out, caged under his palm.

"Love and war," he murmurs, his dark eyes hooking into mine, before lifting his hand to reveal the coin.

The Serpent.

Time seems to stall as we stare at the carving glinting in the faint light.

I tip my chin up in a dare and murmur, "I guess the house doesn't always win."

A triumphant smirk tugs at my mouth, though Rian's hand suddenly closes around my narrow wrist as I reach for the coin. He drags me to my feet with a punishing strength, then shoves me backward so that my bottom collides against his desk. He hoists me by the waist to sit on it, then leans forward, trapping me between his arms.

His hooded eyes are close enough to see tiny flecks of mica in the cerulean paint lining his lids—the only fae adornment he allows himself.

Finally, he rips off his own satin mask and lets it fall to the floor.

"You cheated, songbird."

A laugh escapes me. "Cheated? How could I have cheated? You checked the coin, not me."

"That coin is weighted to always land on Scepter."

Fear rises up my gullet like a tide before I can swallow it back down, where it sits heavy in my stomach.

I spit out, "A weighted coin? Then *you* were cheating!"

His head tilts. "Not really. It only would have been cheating if I'd picked the side. But I let you pick, which means you had an equal chance of picking Scepter as Serpent."

"But . . ." I sputter.

"Darling, I felt the mouse hiding in your skirt. I saw it dart under my desk while you were pacing so prettily, trying to distract me. You told it to flip the coin to Serpent, didn't you?"

The blood gushes out of my cheeks, draining to my toes until I'm numb.

Oh, blast.

Rian's roaming hands weren't after sex all along. *He was checking me for weapons.*

Sensing my fear, the forest mouse peeks out from under the desk, wiggling his whiskers at me.

The mouse and I planned this trick late the night before. I knew that Rian always kept his Golath dime on him, and it would be the easiest game for us to manipulate as a team. All I had to do was pick a dress with a layered skirt that the mouse could hide in, and sew a small pocket for it.

My hands ball, damp and trembling. I'm too furious to feel ashamed that he outsmarted me.

His eyes take their time reading the story in my face before murmuring dangerously, "Do you know what we do with cheaters, songbird?"

I swallow, forcing myself to maintain eye contact. "Give them a seat at the High Lord's table?"

This earns a dark chuckle from him that rumbles over me like the vibrations of a passing carriage. "Funny, but no. It's either the dungeon or the arena. Cheaters can enter the Everlast tournament for a pardon. Have you heard of it?"

I slowly shake my head.

"It's Duren's annual justice trial. Instead of a judge, prisoners fight to the death in the arena for a pardon. Of course, that's essentially a death sentence. Out of sixteen fighters, only one survives."

Fear knits up my spine, tying me in knots that all seem to be connected to Rian, like a beautifully dark puppet master.

He grips his long fingers around my throat, high at the base of my jaw so that he can tip my head toward his.

"I'll make an exception for you, songbird, because I reward cleverness. Not many sheltered lord's daughters could devise such a trick. Nor have the backbone to try it against a Valvere. It makes me wonder what else that pretty head of yours could plot." His velvety gaze settles on my lips. "Ask me—on your knees, groveling at my boots—and I'll spare you the death sentence."

I want to hiss at him, scratch and claw like a wildcat. I don't care that he's technically correct that I cheated. Because in this world, powerful men hold all the cards. Every coin is weighted in their favor. Women have to cheat for even a chance at an even playing field.

"And our wager?" I murmur between cheeks squished by his thumb and forefinger.

"Oh, you'll train the monoceros for me. We both know you never would have abandoned it, anyway."

I squirm my ass on his desk, pinned like a butterfly by his hand around my jaw. "I want it out of the basement. Somewhere it can move and breathe fresh air."

Finally, he releases my jaw and steps back. "Darling, if you can tame it, I'll build it a king's stable."

I pause. The laughter from the gambling den downstairs roars louder. The patrons are drunk on wine and winnings. Through the curtain, I see the jewel-toned gowns of prostitutes being shamelessly fondled by old men.

"And our marriage?" I ask.

"It stands. But to show my mercy, I'll move the date to Sairsach Eve."

It isn't much of a mercy—Sairsach Eve celebrates summer's end, only a few extra weeks past Midtane, the original date.

"Now," he purrs, stepping back to give me room to drop to my knees. "*Ask.*"

Gritting my teeth, I scoot off the desk and, throat strangled with rage, sink to my knees in front of him.

Fixing him with a searing glare, I spit out each word. "Forgive. Me. For. Cheating. *My. Lord.*"

His lips curve upward. He rolls his Golath dime once over his knuckles before securing it in his pocket.

I glare up at him as I remain on my knees and vow, "I won't ever love you, you know."

He reaches down to help me to my feet, brushing his lips across my knuckles before I jerk my hand away. "That's how it always starts, darling. The greatest love comes from hate. I wouldn't have it any other way."

CHAPTER 2
WOLF

"How is he?" I ask gruffly as I duck into the dungeon cell, where my prisoner has been recuperating for the last week. I'd rather him suffer, but I need him healthy so I can pump him for answers. The cell is dank and reeking, the meager straw on the floor steeped in the prisoner's mess.

Leaning in the doorway, Folke puffs on an herb pipe that's seen better days. "He can drink water without coughing up blood now. I'd say he's ready."

A cloud of bluish smoke drifts over the pathetic husk of the Volkish raider I know only by the name Maks, who is slumped against the wall, flitting in and out of consciousness. I'm lucky that I convinced Folke to stay in Duren to help with the prisoner—but then again, for enough coin, there isn't much Folke won't do.

I toe a dirty wooden plate resting near the bars. Brackish water and kitchen slop make for a poor feast, but if you ask me, it's still far too good for the likes of this prisoner's loathsome ass. This man tried to rape Sabine. He doesn't deserve pig slop.

I crack my knuckles.

"Easy, Wolf," Folke warns.

I bristle, irritated. Though I want nothing more than to wring the life from this raider, Rian wants answers from him. And answers require the ability to speak—which means no strangulation.

Not yet.

I pull my shirt over the back of my neck and hang it from a hook, then roll my neck from one side to the other. The cell's single torch makes my bare skin glisten, already lightly sheened with sweat. I run my palm over the constellation of scars on my chest and abs, then slap my muscles to shock some adrenaline into them.

I swore I'd never return to this. Serving Rian with my fists. The blood. The bruises. And yet, as much as I hate that I'm right back at the place I spent years digging myself out of, for Maks, I'm more than happy to oblige.

I have to admit that a piece of me feels like it's slipping back into a well-worn shirt. Whether I like it or not, my main worth has always been in my fists.

This is who I am.

A Bowborn? No. I don't merit the surname of a hunter anymore. Not even that of a Bladeborn, the name they give to bastard soldiers. *Bloodborn* would be a better surname for me now.

And damn if a smile doesn't curl my lips as I crack my knuckles in front of the prisoner.

"Maks of Volkany." I crouch down so we're at eye level, though he's so slumped forward to ease the pain in his broken ribs that he can't sit fully upright. He wheezes at me as hate winks in his one good eye. "I'd be lying if I said I wasn't looking forward to this."

I signal to the two guards flanking the cell to string him up. They bind Maks's wrists with rope, then thread it through the cell bars, lashing him against the metal beams so his arms are splayed.

His one working eye cuts into me.

"Now," I say, cracking my knuckles again, "I *could* tell you that if you don't give me every scrap of information you know about Lady Sabine Darrow, I'll turn your face into porridge. I *could* tell you that I'll bleed you from a thousand cuts. I *could* tell you all that, but we both know you won't give up anything useful until at least three sessions together. So today? Today is just a fucking meet-and-greet."

I slam my fist into the tenderest, most oozing bruise on his jaw.

His screams wouldn't sound good to anyone but a monster. But damn if they don't sound good to me.

It's as dark as the inside of a coffin as I pick my way through Sorsha Hall's hedge maze, but I don't need my heightened vision to know the way. All I need is memory, having wound through these paths so many times my feet know which turns to take. Water drips steadily from the castle's eaves, left over from the rainfall earlier in the day. The scent of a bird's nest crooked in the statue of Immortal Popelin hits my nose.

Adrenaline still spikes in my veins from the session with Maks, making my heart race, my steps urgent as my body craves release. There's so much need beneath my skin I could burst.

And then, finally, I'm standing in the rose garden beneath the southern tower.

Her tower.

Sorsha Hall is renowned throughout Astagnon as one of the finest examples of fae architecture. Its copper spires and elongated stained glass windows could be transported directly out of the Book of the Immortals. Decorative carvings cover every stone facade: round coins for Popelin, fae knots for Meric, twin axe blades for Vale.

Everyone else sees an architectural marvel when they look at the southern tower, but me? I only see the climbing path Rian and I used to sneak out of the castle every night as boys.

I tap my pocket to ensure the small, sheathed knife is secure.

I'm not here to see her, I tell myself for the thousandth time. *Only to deliver this knife to keep her safe.*

I couldn't commission a dagger from any metalsmiths in Duren without possibly alerting the Valveres, so I put Folke on the task of discreetly sourcing one from the black market that would fit a small hand the size of Sabine's.

This one put a hefty dent in my savings, but it's worth it. It's a single-edged, five-inch blade with a hardwood handle carved in intricate fae knots, and a supple leather sheath with an adjustable buckle that she can fasten around her thigh beneath her clothes.

It isn't that I don't trust Rian, but I feel better knowing Sabine has a knife on her that none of the Valveres know about.

Not even him.

I step onto a fountain ledge, then use its height to climb onto the statue of Popelin that sits beneath the tower's lowest window ledge. Popelin's marble arms—extended in welcome—make for an easy climb until I can hoist myself onto the second level's window ledge, where the stained glass pieces glow from the candlelight within, casting me in a prism of light. For a second, I'm struck by a memory of Rian and I as boys, huddling here, trying to silence one another's laughter as Lord Berolt scoured the castle for him. I can't help but feel a pang of loss for the joy of those days, now just an echo.

Next comes the tricky part of the climb. From this window, it's a matter of using the decorative carvings to scale the outer wall. Below, it's a straight fall of twenty feet onto the metal spires of the hedge maze's fence. I'm a hell of a lot bigger than I was at seventeen—the last time I attempted this climb—and what I've gained in strength is tempered by my added weight. It doesn't help that the carvings are still slick from rain.

Fucking gods, I groan as my left boot slips.

Catching myself with my upper body strength, I secure my footing and climb onto the second-floor rooftop extension. From there, I use the gargoyle rain spouts as handholds to ascend to the third floor. The final step is to skirt around the tower by clinging to the structural grooves. The only problem is, I've never climbed as high as Sabine's bedroom before, and there are no grooves on this part of the tower's upper portion. Just thick tendrils of creeping vines whose wooly roots hold fast to the bricks, and it's impossible to guess if they can support my weight.

Well, only one way to find out.

I keep my weight close to the wall and grip the vines,

using them as hand- and footholds until I can ease my way onto Sabine's windowsill.

Bracing my hands on the window's stone border, I take a moment for my heaving lungs to calm so I can hear anything above my own strained breath.

I listen, tapping into my heightened senses.

There.

That slow breathing with the hint of a rasp that I know so well. It tells me Sabine is inside and deep in slumber, which is hardly surprising. It must be well past midnight. Torture can't be rushed, after all. And Maks deserved the extra few hours of pain.

I pick up on the sounds of two more sleeping creatures —the forest mouse and a nuthatch. I'll have to be stealthy. If they wake, they'll alert her to my presence.

And the last thing I want is to wake Sabine.

I'm only here to deliver the knife. If I also happen to see her beautiful sleeping form? Hear her soft breath? Smell her flower petal scent? Well, that's just a nice fucking perk of protecting her.

I ease the window pane so the hinges don't groan, then slip into her bedroom.

Immediately, I'm enveloped by the scent of buttermilk soap and rose water, but beneath the perfume is *her*. My little violet. Her scent slams into me like a branch snapping against my chest, knocking the breath out of me.

My hand drags down my face, knowing with that one whiff that I'm fucked. It's been a week since I've seen her. Every one of those damn days, the craving to be near her has me crawling out of my skin.

Sabine is a beautiful addiction. I could fall and fall and fall into her, and it would never be enough.

The mouse twitches in its sleep beneath her bed. The nuthatch slumbers on a perch atop her tall walnut dresser. It's peaceful here, quiet. This room has sat mostly empty since Rian's mother died twenty-eight years ago. It's my first time seeing the famous Immortal Court painting that spans the domed ceiling. The furniture is exquisitely crafted, the carpeting plush underfoot.

Sabine rests her head on a pillow that holds the clean scent of goose down. Her coverings are silk, topped with fur blankets, though she's tossed them off in her sleep, and her graceful, exposed bare feet slide along the bottom sheet.

My jaw locks.

She's so fucking beautiful that she belongs on the ceiling with the rest of the gods. No mere mortal could sway a man's heart with just that glimpse of a bare ankle, the graceful curve of her foot's arch . . .

I huff as I turn away, dragging a hand down my face. It's wrong for me to linger here a second longer than necessary. She deserves a night of peaceful sleep. She's safe, guarded by that ill-tempered asshole, Maximan, on the other side of her door. She's dressed in the finest silk nightgown. She has everything a woman could possibly need to feel at ease.

A good man would leave her alone.

But fuck me, I can't stop my boots from bee-lining to her bed. With her asleep like this, I can take my time basking in her beauty. Her chin-length hair suits her so much better than her long tresses ever did. It's splayed over the pillow in tangles from fitful sleep. Her lips twitch hungrily as if she's dreaming of honey tarts. A breeze blows in from the open window, and goosebumps erupt along her exposed calves.

She shivers in her sleep.

Before my rational mind kicks in, I sink onto the side of

her bed. My hand drifts to her nightgown's lacy cap sleeve, which is decorated with a robin's egg blue ribbon.

There was a time when Sabine slept in nothing but *my* coarse shirt. On a bed of leaves. Beneath the stars.

By the gods, I miss those campfire nights with an intensity that burns a hole in my chest. There's little I wouldn't trade to turn back time to when it was just the two of us, a crackling fire, and the quiet of the woods.

The shirt I lent her on those nights is currently tucked in the back of my drawer, unwashed for fear of losing her scent. I'd rather not admit how many times I've pulled it out and buried my nose in the fabric—or how many times that's led me to fisting my cock, drowning in the scent of her perfect curves.

Fuck. Already, I'm hard. Filthy ideas materialize in my mind about what I could do to alleviate that current state. Sabine is deeply asleep, judging by her slow and steady pulse. She wouldn't wake if I traced her curves with the back of my hand while unfastening my pants to fist my cock once more . . .

Stop it, you ass.

Disgusted with myself, I banish that forbidden fantasy. Just how fucked up *am* I?

I smooth the coverings over her exposed feet and tuck them in gently to keep her warm.

Who am I kidding? There's no absolution for me. I don't deserve sympathy. Yeah, I sacrificed any chance of happiness with Sabine to save her life, but I couldn't let that be the end of it. I should have walked away. Gone fucking grouse hunting, like Rian said. But the memories of our time together keep drawing me back to her like bees to honey. And hell, what a dream it would be to taste her nectar over and over—a whole lifetime of it.

But that's me being a selfish asshole, craving more than I deserve.

I'm no good for her. In no world, even the realm of dreams, would I *ever* be good for her.

I'm a monstrosity. That's the simple, stark truth. Maks's dried blood on my knuckles proves the point. There was a brief time when I thought I could be something more. When it was just me and a bow in the woods, hunting quarry to feed hungry mouths, and I fooled myself into thinking I might be worth a damn after all.

But I was lying to myself.

Rian knew the dark heart beating in my chest—knew I'd eventually return to the darkness. Was that why he let me leave my former line of work, years ago, and take up hunting? Because he knew I'd never actually escape at all?

A church bell tolls in the distance. *Shit.* I can't stay here. I need rest, too, if I'm going to have another go at Maks tomorrow.

I shove myself off Sabine's bed while I still have enough decency to leave her. Trying to resist looking at her lips—failing miserably—I set the small, sheathed dagger on her nightstand.

It isn't only the Valveres I worry about. Sabine doesn't know it, but she is the daughter of King Rachillon of Volkany. The cursed kingdom. Our enemies. Right now, the public adores her for defying the Valvere family. But if they find out she's an enemy princess, they might turn on her.

Call her a traitor.

A spy.

She could be imprisoned, tortured for information she

doesn't have, or used as collateral. And I can't fucking allow that.

Only two people in Astagnon know her secret: me and Sabine's father. And that old drunk sure as hell isn't doing anything to protect her.

King Rachillon already sent raiders to kidnap her once. It's only a matter of time before he sends more. Rumors say he is godkissed with the ability to wake the sleeping fae beasts and gods, so I can only imagine he wants to use her power to further his aims. It's anyone's guess how far he's come.

Are the gods already awake? Do they walk the Volkish forests?

The church bells toll again.

Go, Wolf.

Now that I've delivered the knife, I have no reason to stay and every reason to leave. Regardless, my feet are so filled with lead as I climb back out the window that I slip three times on the way down and only narrowly make it to solid ground without impaling myself on one of the fence spires.

The whole trek back to my cottage, all I smell is violets.

CHAPTER 3
SABINE

"**M**y lady, I don't think High Lord Valvere would like you exploring on your own!"

Brigit plucks at her collar as she trots down the grand first-floor hallway behind me, peeking over her shoulder as though she's afraid Maximan is going to come at her with a battle axe at any moment.

"Oh, don't fret, Brigit," I say breezily. "We haven't even left the castle. Besides, I'm helping Lord Rian with a project that's of utmost importance to him—he'll forgive my wandering if I can find what I need."

Until now, I've only been able to explore the sections of Sorsha Hall that Rian permits me. He's careful never to state that any place is expressly forbidden, always emphasizing how "free" I am, but there are a suspicious number of locked doors for such "freedom." Not to mention the soldiers barring hallways. Servants appearing out of nowhere to guide me away from wherever I was headed. And of course, my bodyguard, Maximan—though I managed to slip him today.

A fact that still makes me smile.

The castle is laid out like a five-pointed star, typical of fae-inspired architecture. Four towers rise in the four directions, with the star's fifth point being the grand entrance. Besides the grand foyer and stairs up to the second and third levels, the entry floor houses the ballroom, a gentleman's study, and a library. Down a half-flight of stairs are the servant areas, mostly hidden from sight: the kitchen, the cannery, the laundry. Bedrooms take up most of the second floor. That's where Lord Berolt, Lady Eleonora, and Lady Runa reside, and where Rian has a formal office. The third floor contains guest rooms, including my southern tower suite.

But I've seen only a fraction of any of it. Between the servants' hidden passageways, the cryptic tunnels in the basement, and entire mysterious wings, Sorsha Hall is full of secrets.

After descending a set of stairs, we reach a heavy set of oak doors carved with a relief image of Immortal Meric, God of Order and Knowledge. As I reach for the brass knob, Brigit makes a small squeak. She's usually all sunshine and smiles, and the thought of chasing away her good nature with my own storm clouds makes me pause.

"Truly, Brigit," I say, tucking back a stray strand of her chestnut hair. "If Rian has any ill words for us, I'll make certain they fall on me, not you."

Relief eases her pinched face, and gradually, as she bites her lip, a spark of mischief lights up her eyes. "Well, I *have* always wanted to see the library. Only the downstairs maids get to dust it."

"There you go! That's the spirit." With a grin, I tug open the heavy door.

Immediately, we're eclipsed by a strange stillness and smells that are utterly new to me. Aged paper and leather. Binding glue and stale parchment. Lamp oil with a touch of frankincense. It makes my stomach tighten with longing for something I've never had.

Books.

It's rare for anyone to own more than one book. Most families consider themselves fortunate if they have one tattered copy of the Book of the Immortals, passed down as an heirloom from generation to generation. A country lord's household might contain as many as three or four books— usually fat volumes covering Astagnon's history. In my father's house, we had three titles: a Book of the Immortals with gilded edges that was left on display in the foyer; a hand-written account of the ancient Battle of Balaysia, and my mother's personal copy of the Book of the Immortals. It was a small, simple edition. How badly I wanted to flip through those pages, but whenever I asked, she would close it with a secretive smile and then sweep me up in her arms, tickling my chin in a flurry of giggles, and carry me into the kitchen for honeycakes.

"By the gods," Brigit murmurs, eyes round as silver coins.

Both of us hang back in the doorway as though afraid to enter the beautiful library, as though one step will shatter this spellbinding vision. The Valvere library is two stories high, with a balcony running along the second floor to access the highest shelves, and a spiral staircase in one corner. A massive mahogany fireplace is cold now, a chill snaking down the chimney to tickle my bare ankles. Busts of Immortal Popelin and Immortal Meric rest on the heavy mantel. A map table holds thick stacks of atlases and charts.

But it's the books themselves that my eyes drink in.

"There must be hundreds," Brigit murmurs.

"Thousands," I say in an equal hush.

My lungs feel tight, like I've forgotten how to breathe, the ability stolen by the library's promise of knowledge. My legs are weak as I turn in a slow circle, lips parted in awe.

The silence here feels reverent, yet nothing about this candlelit place calls to mind the convent I spent the last twelve years in, with its damp walls, heavy air, and droning prayers.

Here, dust motes dance in the air from one open book to another, like a playful promise of the stories found within. My fingers prickle, wanting to explore every page. To delve into each leatherbound book.

A brass clock chimes, and I snap out of my reverie.

"Quickly, Brigit, search for books about fae beasts. Cloudfoxes, starleons, monoceros—"

Brigit's rosy cheeks pale to the shade of parchment. "I cannot read, my lady."

"Oh." I forget that not every girl had a mother who patiently taught them to read, night after night, with slate and chalk, despite my father's grumblings that it was time wasted. "Oh—no bother, then. You keep watch, and I'll look."

While Brigit peeks through the keyhole, I rest my hands on my hips as I scan the shelves.

Political Discourses on the Kravada Border War

A Guide to the Spezian Military Conquests

A Compendium of the Royal Families of Clarana

Curiosity spider-walks up my limbs. I was never taught much about our neighboring kingdoms. The Sisters at the Convent of Immortal Iyre were far more interested in me learning to sweep and chop firewood. But now, I can fill in all the missing gaps in my education about the world beyond Astagnon.

One thought snags at me, however. There don't appear to be any volumes on the kingdom of Volkany. As our historical enemy—and given the current problem of raiders penetrating the border—that would be extremely useful information.

Though it pains me, I leave behind the geographical section, promising myself that I'll return for the books here when I have time. I scan natural history guides to the various regions of Astagnon, biographies of past kings and queens, and thick tomes on philosophy, then finally spot the section on the fae gods.

After thumbing past dozens of different editions of the Book of the Immortals, I find more specific stories about the Immortals:

Samaur and the Prison of Night and Day

The Illustrated Encyclopedia of Lovemaking Acts: Immortal Alyssantha in the Flesh

Immortal Iyre: Essays on Chastity

The Gift of the Godkiss

A Comprehensive Guide to Fae Flora and Fauna

I pull out volume after volume, hand trembling as the towering stack of books grows. No one could possibly read all this in a year, yet I can't stop myself from gorging on the buffet of literature like a starving person.

Arms straining under the precariously balanced books, I stumble to the closest reading table, though the book on Alyssantha slips off the top.

As I crouch down to fetch it, a book under the table

catches my eye—someone must have accidentally dropped it—and I cradle it in my palm.

It's small, the same muted scarlet color as my mother's treasured Book of the Immortals.

The Last Return of the Fae, the threadbare spine reads. The handwritten pages are so faded to the point of being nearly illegible.

"My lady!" Brigit's cry rattles me, and I nearly knock over the stack of books as I rush to my feet. She stumbles away from the keyhole just as the door sweeps open and Rian strides in wearing a scowl like a second set of eyeliner.

"Lady Sabine? What the devil are you doing?" His gaze fixes on my teetering stack of books. "Where is Maximan?"

I take my time inspecting my fingernails with a coy shrug. "Last I saw, he was chasing a polecat that *somehow* got into the castle and bit his ankle."

Brigit has to hide her snicker behind a fit of fake coughing.

Rian's dark eyes simmer. "You are supposed to keep your guard with you at all times for your own safety."

"And feel like a prisoner in my own home?" It's a stretch to call Sorsha Hall *home*—these opulent towers will never feel like where I belong—but I want to impress upon Rian that I am not powerless within these walls. "I'll take my guard when I leave Sorsha Hall, but while I'm inside, I want freedom to explore. Real freedom."

His eyes narrow, casting them deeper in shadows. "For what reason?" He picks up the closest book. " To read bedtime stories?"

"Maybe." I snatch the book out of his hand. "Or *maybe* I'm searching for *information* about the *potatoes* you're keeping in the *cellar*." I tap my thumb on the book's title—*A*

Comprehensive Guide to Fae Flora and Fauna—and then on an illustration of a monoceros on the cover.

Rian's head pinwheels toward Brigit—our audience—as the chastisement on his tongue melts away.

"I see. Brigit? Leave us."

She's still squashing a giggle as she goes.

I have to fight the urge to smile at Rian's obvious displeasure. I greatly enjoy irritating my future husband. From the day he announced our betrothal, I've seen him as the enemy.

How ironic that, given our deal over a coin flip, Rian and I are allied now.

And Basten? The first person I considered a true friend in over a decade?

He's no ally of mine any longer—in fact, he's managed to take the top slot on my list of most loathed men, which is rather impressive. There are a *lot* of men on that list.

Rian's gaze crawls down my ochre gown with its voluminous skirt and ankle-length hem, and I move the book casually to my front. I don't think the hidden knife strapped to my inner thigh is visible through the dress's folds, but I don't want to take any chances.

The dagger mysteriously appeared on my dresser a few mornings ago. It doesn't take much deduction to figure out who gifted it to me. Basten told me on our journey that he'd have a knife made to fit my hand, and for once, he upheld his promise.

Though I'm grateful for the blade, I don't love the idea of Basten climbing through my window unannounced. That's the only way he could have gotten in. Maximan or another guard is always posted outside my door at night, and I drag a chair to block the servants' door in case Rian—or worse, Lord Berolt—is ever tempted to drop by for a midnight visit.

Well, Basten won't be sneaking in unannounced anymore, I think wryly. I took steps to ensure that.

"It's just as well Maximan is off chasing one of your pets." Rian speaks plainly now that we're alone. "My family is across town, dining at the Silver Cup. No one will notice if you and I disappear to the basement for a few hours."

My stomach wrenches with both excitement and nerves. "We're going to start training the monoceros?"

It feels strange, sharing this secret with Rian. Feeling a hint of excitement with this man who's done such heartless things to me. But I can't help it. The thrill of using my unique power with the monoceros ignites an undeniable vibration within me from the tips of my toes to my throat.

"That depends on if you can ride in that dress," Rian says, his eyes on my curves.

"Who said anything about riding?"

"That is the traditional thing one does with horses, unless you plan on teaching it to waltz?"

I roll my eyes. "First of all, the monoceros is a *he*, not an *it*. Secondly, he isn't a horse. And it can take months to break in a naturally docile horse, so how long do you think it'll take before a vicious fae creature lets me on his back?" I shake my head. "The first few sessions are only to get him used to my presence."

I grab the top book on my stack—*The Race of Sun and Moon and Other Fae Tales.* "I want the rest of these books delivered to my room. If I'm going to make progress with the creature, I need to learn everything I can about it."

I brace for an argument since literacy is rarely encouraged among noble women, but Rian only shrugs. "Done. Now, put on my cloak. It's cold down there."

We plunge through a lower cold storage level full of potatoes, then down a set of half-stairs, then around a winding hallway blocked by an iron gate. Rian unlocks the gate and leads me into a neglected tunnel that's nearly pitch-black. It feels like ages until we finally see light coming from the former stable ruins ahead.

Hate this place! The beast's booming voice echoes in my head at the same time he smashes a massive hoof against his iron gate. *Stinks of iron. Stinks of man. The hay has fleas, humans. FLEAS!*

An unlucky Golden Sentinel perches on a stool as far back in the corner as he can from the monoceros's stall. I say "unlucky" because he must know how many of his predecessors the monoceros has killed—and that those who survived met their end at Rian's blade to keep knowledge of the fae beast's existence secret.

I clutch the leather-bound book like a shield as I dare a step closer.

Hello again, friend, I say to the monoceros.

His wild eyes roll, flashing the whites, as his massive head swings toward me. Since the first time I spoke to him, a little over a week ago, he's been calmer. Or at least, a little more coherent in his complaints. I can only imagine the relief it was to hear a kind, intelligible voice after a year of imprisonment down here.

Fae has come back, he says, eyeing me with wary disdain.

I don't bother to correct him. The only people to ever communicate with him were the ancient Immortals a thousand years ago, so he thinks I must be one of them.

That's right, I tell him. *I've come to visit you. I'd like to give you a treat, too.*

I take over the stool from the gangly Golden Sentinel, who is all too happy to scramble away. When I reach into my satchel and pull out a handful of strawberries—Myst's favorite—he snorts a burst of steam.

Not interested.

I drag the stool closer to the stall, careful to leave a good five paces of distance. Then, I open the book.

"The Ride of Sun and Moon," I read. "In the age of the second return of the Immortals, the twins—Samaur, God of Day, and Thracia, Goddess of Night—found themselves at great odds with one another. Over the course of a full year, they warred violently for possession of the sky. Samaur's sunlight bolts scorched the earth without end, drying out the lakes and streams. Thracia retaliated by casting eternal night, which withered crops and left humans scrambling . . ."

"What in the name of the gods are you doing?" Rian sputters, his jaw hanging open in disbelief.

I bookmark my page with my thumb. "The monoceros needs to get used to the sound of my voice. My real voice, I mean, as well as the mental one I use to communicate with him."

"So you're reading it fucking *bedtime stories*?"

I lean back on the stool, tracing my thumb over the book's cover. "Would you prefer I read aloud from ledgers of all the gamblers you've entrapped into debts, starting with Charlin Darrow?"

Rian's brows fall flat. He saunters over to take the book from me, flipping through the pages until he finds an illustration of Immortal Solene riding astride a monoceros.

He reads the caption. *"When I could ride the beast, I could control it, and we worked as one.* See, songbird? All the instruction you need is written in the ancient texts. Solene tamed the monoceros by riding it, not reading to it."

I pinch the bridge of my nose, tucking away my impatience. "How many soldiers have died so far trying to mount it?"

Rian looks up at the ceiling and murmurs, "None have lived long enough to try."

"Exactly." I snatch the book back from him. "This is necessary. I know what I'm doing. You have to trust me." I lay my palm over the book. "My mother . . ."

My voice breaks on that word. I've used it so infrequently that it's rusty on my tongue.

Clearing my throat, I try again.

"My mother, before she died, taught me three things: to read, to build a fire, and to ride horses. She said it was all a girl needed in this life. She never spoke of her past before marrying my father, but I gather she'd been taught the womanly arts of sewing, cooking, dancing—and she wanted a different life for me."

"Fortunately for you," Rian says evenly, "I don't give a fuck if my wife can darn a sock. I'd much rather she tame a monoceros. In that, your mother and I agree."

A strange tendril of pleasure unspools at the compliment. I continue, "She trained horses. I saw her do it dozens of times, with unbroken yearlings, ill-tempered old geldings, and even wild stallions captured off the southern plains. There's a process to earning a horse's trust."

He runs a finger along the cut of his jawline, and it's a minute before he says more measuredly, "I can be a patient man, songbird, but my father does not share that virtue. If he discovers that you're reading the monster fae tales instead of whipping it into submission, he will take measures to speed up the training. He already doubts the extent of your abilities."

I don't know what those "measures" might be, but Rian's warning tone is enough to chill me to the bone. For better or worse, Rian and I are partners now. He knows his father better than I do, so I have to trust him in this.

"How long will it take?" He folds his arms, his face tight, but his irritation doesn't seem directed at me.

"Six months."

"We don't have six months. We don't have *three* months. I've given the order to renovate an old army barrack into a training stable. It's made of stone, so there's nothing the beast can set on fire. My builders have designed a retractable roof to keep out sunlight until we want to allow the monster access to it. The monoceros must be reliably able to wield fey fire for us by Midtane."

I draw in a breath. "That's impossible—"

Rian drops his hand. "King Joruun is dying. The Immortals are awakening, if rumors are to be believed. Their creatures already walk our world. In the time it takes you to read bedtime stories to this monster, Volkany could burn Astagnon to the ground. All King Rachillon needs is to find and awaken one god, pledge Volkany's servitude to him or her, and he'll wield Vale's axe, or Artain's arrows, or Samaur's burning sunlight. Our king-dom's defenses are weak. Old Coros relies more on my mercenaries to safeguard the borders than its own royal army, which is poorly trained and untested. If Astagnon is to defend itself, it needs a weapon to rival the gods themselves."

Our heads rotate to the monoceros, who stamps his hoof and snorts.

You cannot start a story and not finish, fae! he scolds.

I want to shake my head at this obstinate creature— apparently, monoceros and horses aren't that different when it comes to stubbornness.

Soon enough, I say, shaking the book in the air like he's a demanding toddler.

He snorts a blast of steam, turns away, and mutters, *Your cruelty knows no end.*

I face Rian again. "The dangers you warn of may have merit, but how am I to trust that you want to protect Astagnon, and not just put yourself on the throne?"

There's something warm about Rian's smirk, as if he appreciates how easily I see through him.

"I won't pretend I don't wish to be king. No one has seen King Joruun in weeks, and my spies tell me he hasn't left his chamber. There's something strange going on in Old Coros. His death is imminent; when that happens, Astagnon will need a strong successor to face the Third Return of the Fae."

From what I've heard whispered about, Lord Berolt has already attempted to stack the deck for Rian to be next in line. According to the Kinship Mandate, the throne should pass to King Joruun's closest blood relation, which would be Lord Berolt, followed by Rian's older brothers, Kendan and Lore.

But Lord Berolt prefers to scheme behind the scenes. Kendan gave up his birthright when he joined the royal army in Old Coros. And no one's heard from Lore in nearly ten years—ever since Lord Berolt's vicious abuse drove him away.

Which leaves Rian as the natural choice. Still, no amount

of bribery can guarantee the outcome they want. There are dozens of others vying for the crown, making wild claims of blood ties, though they'll have to prove it by having their blood sampled by a godkissed bloodtaster. Their strongest challenger, however, has no blood tie at all. If rumors are to be believed, the Grand Cleric of the Red Church has launched a campaign among the elite of Old Coros to turn Astagnon from a monarchy into a theocracy—with himself as ruler.

So, king under a different title.

However, a weapon as deadly as a monoceros *could* guarantee the crown goes to Rian.

I shove to my feet and slam the book against the stool. "I agreed to help tame the monoceros because it can protect Astagnon, not for your own aims."

His dark eyes flash. "Darling, those are just different sides of the same coin."

As I step backward, frustration bubbling up my gullet, a shadow looms over my right shoulder.

Scalding breath singes the hairs at the back of my neck.

The reek of sulfur slams into me.

I can't move out of the way fast enough . . .

Rian lunges for me. He grabs my arm and jerks me out of the way a second before the monoceros's teeth clamp down where my neck had been.

We crash to the straw-strewn floor, where Rian shelters me with the weight of his body.

"Dammit, songbird," Rian murmurs. "Be careful."

He braces his arms on either side of my head, gaze painting over every curve of my face to make sure I'm not hurt. His chest rises and falls fast. I've never been this close to him—our bodies flush, hips squared against each other.

His thumb brushes a tender spot on my temple where I feel a bruise blooming.

This is new—Rian taking care of me—and I don't know how to feel about it.

"Get—get *off* me," I shove away his arm, then roll over to glare at the monoceros.

But it was my fault.

I was stupid, distracted. I stepped close enough to his stall that he could bite me. If Rian hadn't pulled me out of the way, half my shoulder might be missing.

It's a humbling reminder that the monoceros is *not* a horse like Myst. I might be able to speak to him, but that doesn't make us friends. I have a long way to go before I ride astride him, commanding his horn's fey fire like Immortal Solene.

The monoceros snorts, **Get out.**

For once, this comment feels directed at me.

CHAPTER 4
WOLF

Blood.
    Puss.
    Vomit.

A sigh grates up my throat as Maks lets out a hacking cough that spurts crimson blood across my shirt. Fuck. Again? It's getting really old to return home every night only to spend an hour washing Maks's bodily fluids out of my clothes. With my godkissed senses, every drop reeks ten times stronger, turning my stomach until I think I can't gag anymore.

Folke smirks from the dungeon cell's doorway. "Better ask the kitchen maids for more laundry soap."

"Or maybe your useless ass could scrub my shirts instead of standing there mocking me," I mutter as I tug the filthy shirt over my head and toss it in the corner.

I roll my neck from left to right. I could use a drink of water, anyway. After five days of this, Maks is looking worse for wear. I have to stop every three punches to let him regain consciousness. The kaleidoscope of stab wounds, bruises, and dented bones across his body makes him look more like a sack of kitchen scraps than a human.

"The bastard doesn't have much life left in him," Folke observes as he puffs steadily on his pipe.

"Good," I grunt.

Folke takes his time with another puff. "*Not* good. He hasn't told us anything useful."

That isn't entirely true. After I broke each of Maks's fingers, he admitted to being a bounty hunter for King Rachillon, as well as working with the godkissed spy who attacked me in Blackwater. But that isn't enough to satisfy Rian. He won't be happy until he knows exactly why the raiders were targeting Sabine—and if they plan to return for her.

As I chug a canteen of water, Folke looks me up and down. "So, how's your love life these days?"

I snort. "How's yours?"

Only Folke would make small talk while someone's blood drips onto the floor. I once saw him whip out his cock to take a piss in the middle of a bar room brawl.

He says smoothly, "Exceptional, thanks for asking. It turns out that extending my stay in Duren has meant more opportunities to meet the most beguiling women."

"Whores, you mean," I counter. "I've yet to see a high-born lady deign to pleasure your cock."

He shrugs, taking another puff of his pipe. "I like a challenge. But don't change the subject, you clod."

His tone is uncharacteristically serious. As I wipe my mouth, he lifts his eyebrows meaningfully. When I still stare blankly, he makes a gesture of fluttering wings—the symbol of the Winged Lady that the townspeople have taken up.

My face settles into a scowl. I toss the drinking canteen

into the water bucket and turn back toward Maks, stretching my fingers a few times before forming fists again.

"I told you there was nothing between me and Rian's bride."

"You did, you did. But then, on the night of the full moon, I saw you climbing the south tower into Lady Sabine's bedroom."

A punch of indignation hits my gut. "You were spying on me?"

"And that shocks you? I'm a *spy*, Wolf. I spy on *everyone*. You just happened to be in my line of sight that night." He casually digs in his pocket and then stuffs a fresh plug of herb into his pipe. "Risky fucking move, by the way."

He lights the herb with a match that deepens the shadows over his chestnut, pox-marked face.

I don't know if Folke means it was risky to physically scale a vertical wall, or the transgression of visiting my master's bride. It doesn't matter. Either way, he's right.

Coughing from the smoke billowing my way, I mutter, "From now on, don't spy on business that doesn't involve you."

He chuckles. "That the best answer you've got?"

I don't answer.

Now, when I return my focus to the prisoner hanging by his wrists, it's with fresh motivation. Irritation drips thickly down my back, prickling my muscles. *Damn Folke.* I've tried to keep any thoughts of Sabine out of this dank cell, but now all I can think about is how long it's been since I've felt the warmth of her smile. How much I ache for her.

She's the one bright spot I've had in years of darkness, and the more she slips away, the more I want to cling to that light. I need it—need her—as much as air.

I'm trying so fucking hard to keep her sheltered from the storm clouds on the horizon, but really, I'm cutting myself off from the sun, too.

My left fist lashes out in a straight punch to Maks's solar plexus. The strike connects hard against his already bruised ribs. I hear the bone's satisfying snap beneath layers of skin and muscle, feel the vibrations of his wheezing breath. A groan slides between his teeth as his head slumps forward.

I shake out my hand, grinning to myself like a kid. *Damn, that felt good.*

It's fucked up, but I've always gotten a sick excitement from feeling a bone shatter. It's almost as satisfying as sex, like when Sabine utters my name in her sexy little moan when she comes . . .

Wait. What am I thinking? Nothing could ever come close to having Sabine's perfect curves beneath me.

I swing an uppercut at the underside of Maks's jaw, slamming his head up and back against the bars. A wail tears from his lips. I take the time to steady his head with both my hands to line it up like a target, then pat his cheek with mock affection before winding my fist back for a hook to the temple.

His head blasts to the side as blood bursts from his lips. He moans in broken breaths, "No more . . ."

"Oh, we're just getting started."

And I go at him with all I've got. Striking with any part of me that's hard enough to leave bruises—elbows, knees, knuckles, forehead. My teeth ache with the need to distract myself—to pour my bloodlust into the fight, instead of craving Sabine. I've always thought that fighting and fucking aren't that different. The tangle of bare limbs. The back-and-forth tussle. The mix of pleasure and pain.

When it's time for a break, I shake my left arm a few times as I plot out the hammer fist I'm going to wail down on his collarbone, but as soon as my elbow swings up, Maks cries out plaintively, "*Enough!*"

It isn't the first time he's begged me to stop, but something rings truer in his tone now.

I pause my strike, licking my lips as I fight the urge to let loose.

Dammit. I was enjoying this.

I fist his filthy hair to jerk his face up, then shove my nose an inch from his. "Enough? Enough for you to finally give us the fucking truth?"

"Yes." He sobs openly, an utterly broken man.

I release him and step back to give his oozing, shattered, ruin of a body an assessing look. This bastard kidnapped Sabine. He tried to kill me with an axe. Any modicum of pity for him is entirely absent.

I mop my palm over the sweat dripping down my face and say, "Start with why King Rachillon put out a bounty for godkissed people from Astagnon."

Maks manages to get out, "Rachillon is—is godkissed himself. He can—can wake the gods."

I flash a look to Folke, who slowly takes his pipe out of his mouth and shakes his head back and forth as if to say this is a lie. The problem is, this isn't the first time I've heard this claim. Rian himself told me similar rumors that King Rachillon ordered the kidnapping of godkissed people with wayfinding abilities. He needs them to locate the ten gods' resting places, so he can wake them.

But there are only a handful of people who know that truth. Folke isn't among them, and it needs to stay that way unless he wants a target on his back.

I turn back to Maks. "That's fucking bullshit."

"It isn't."

I offer a derisive snort. "No wonder your people let a fraud take the throne if you're all so fucking gullible."

"It's t—true." Blood spurts from Maks's lips. "Rachillon p—proved it. He—he awoke the starleons . . ."

At the mention of the mythical birds that rain down pestilence from their wings, I can feel Folke's eyes like two hot daggers against my neck.

Sweat breaks out on my brow. When we were in Blackwater, fighting the Volkish spy, Folke passed out before he saw the starleon that appeared in the inn's back alley.

I dance my fingers in and out of a fist, prepping in case I need to shut Maks up quickly. But for the benefit of Folke and the pair of guards outside the cell, I have to make it look like this is an actual interrogation.

I bark, "You think we wouldn't know if starleons were awake? Hell, I'm not even sure they're *real*. It's been a thousand years since the Second Return of the Fae. Enough time for stories to get real fucking exaggerated."

"There—there are starleons beyond the border, I swear it," Maks coughs. "They're all over Volkany. Goldenclaws, too. And cloudfoxes. Rachillon is waking all the fae beasts. They'll cross the wall soon if—if they haven't already."

I flinch, thinking of the starleon in Blackwater, and the signs of a goldenclaw near the border towns.

They *are* already here.

He's fading. I can see the light dim in his eyes. Wetting my lips, I demand loudly for the audience of the other guards, "The border wall is impenetrable."

Maks gives a weak laugh that turns into a sob. "How the f—fuck do you think I got here?"

The bastard has a point, I have to admit. The only way anyone has gotten from Volkany to Astagnon in the last five hundred years is by ship, but the passage is notoriously difficult, with rocky islands and strong currents, not to mention that our ports strictly check the provenance of all inbound travelers.

"Tell me," I demand. "How did you get here?"

"Havre Peak." A wracking cough explodes from his throat. His eyelids flutter like a dying bee's wings. He's on the edge of losing consciousness—this time maybe permanently.

I jerk his head up again by his mop of dirty blond hair. "Havre Peak? There's a breach at the wall there? Hey, stay awake! Why does Rachillon want Lady Sabine? Tell me!"

"He ordered us to find . . .girls between eighteen and twenty-five, with light brown or blond hair, they had to be godkissed . . ."

"Why? To what end?"

The two dungeon guards drift up to the cell. They, too, can sense the end is near. Folke is silent, watching and listening with that attention that never misses any detail.

When Maks doesn't answer my question, I throw in some extra theatrics, slapping his cheek a few times, splashing him with his own piss bucket.

"*Why?*" I demand.

His voice is barely audible amid the blood bubbling in his mouth. "The orders—orders didn't say. But there were rumors. One of Rachillon's whores escaped—escaped tw— tw—twenty-two years ago—"

My hand flies on instinct to the hunting knife at my side, and before his next word, I slash a three-inch-deep gash from one side of Maks's throat to the other.

I step back, blood dripping from the blade onto my leather boots. Maks's body, finally sent to the underrealm, slumps from his wrists bound to the bars.

My lungs grab for oxygen. My grip is so tight on the knife that I don't think a charging stallion could drag it away. *That was close—too close.* Maks almost hinted at a truth that would put Sabine squarely into the bull's eye of every powerful man in all seven kingdoms.

The guards rush in to check Maks for any sign of life—which is frankly overkill, given that his head barely hangs on his shoulders.

The shorter of the guards exclaims, "The prisoner is dead!"

"*Fuck.*" I spit on the floor and give a frustrated growl like this fact annoys me. "I wanted to wring one more answer out of him. I only meant to threaten him—the blade slipped."

Folke makes a doubting sound in his throat, so soft only my ears pick it up.

"He was finally talking," the shorter soldier says. "What was it he said? About Rachillon? I could barely understand him—"

"He said Rachillon woke the starleons," says the other soldier, who has the unfortunate trait of smelling like baked beans.

"No, after that," the first one says. "Something about a whore who escaped twenty-two years ago—"

"*Two* years ago," I bark sharply. "He said two years ago, you idiot. Clean out your ears."

The other one furrows his brow. "I swear I heard him say—"

I interrupt viciously, "He could barely form words at all.

He was lucky to get as much as a stutter out. Or are you questioning *this*?"

I jab the butt of the knife against my godkissed birthmark on my breastbone. Every soldier in the Golden Sentinels knows that I have superior hearing.

But Captain Baked Beans has a backbone. "With all due respect, Wolf, I heard him say the number 'twenty-two.' Something happened twenty-two years ago with a royal whore."

It's a battle to keep my thundering pulse under control. Turning to Folke in the shadows, I demand, "Folke, what did you hear?"

The sight of a nearly-decapitated man doesn't faze Folke as he runs his fingers over one of his dreaded locks. He takes his time with a puff from his pipe before he laughs at the soldiers. "You two grog guzzlers need to clean the wax from your ears, as Wolf said. The bastard said *two*."

I grunt in satisfaction at Folke's confirmation, though I worry what his lie will cost me down the road, when he inevitably comes to collect. And Folke always comes to collect. Even from friends.

I say off-hand, "There's a whore at a King Street brothel who's rumored to be Volkish. Folke, go check it out. See if she's only been working there two years. Maybe she'll give some answers about what the prisoner meant."

He nods. "Consider it done."

I'll make sure Folke does nothing of the sort, but even if the soldiers do find Carlotte, there are plenty of people who can verify she's been in Astagnon for decades, and they'll drop that line of questioning.

I dump the remainder of the water bucket over my head,

shaking my loose hair like a dog, and then mop my balled-up shirt over my chest.

I skewer Captain Baked Beans with a cold stare as I order, "You two. Dispose of the body. Clean up this cell."

It isn't until I'm halfway down the hall, my heart still sledgehammering in my chest, that Folke catches up with me. Even with his limp, the bastard is fast.

"Twenty-two years." His voice is low and emphatic. "I know what I heard, Wolf. A Volkish whore escaped into Astagnon twenty-two years ago, and now Rachillon is scouring our kingdom for a girl the same age, with Volkish features and a godkiss? I'd bet my good leg that the escaped whore was pregnant with his child, and a godkissed sooth-sayer told him it would be a girl." He drags a hand along the stubble dusting his jaw. "*And* that I know who the baby is."

Muscles firing, I slam him against the wall by his throat before I can stop myself. My lips peel back like an animal. *Calm down, Wolf. He's a friend. He's no danger to Sabine.*

Slowly, I drop my hand from his throat, then drag it back through my own tangled hair. "You were always too smart for your own good, Folke."

He chuckles as he massages his throat. He murmurs, "A lot makes sense now."

I lick my lips as I slide my friend a warning look. I've intentionally not resheathed my hunting knife dripping with Maks's blood. We might have history, but Folke has to know that I wouldn't hesitate to kill him if he threatened Sabine.

He snorts as he lays a heavy hand on my tense shoulder. "I called it, didn't I? You lovesick bastard."

~

"Lord Rian," I announce with a dip of my head. "If I may have a word."

My hair, still damp from a much-needed bath, drips water down the back of my hastily donned sentinel armor.

Rian sits at the head of the High Lord's table in Sorsha Hall's ballroom, tearing into a roast turkey breast. Lord Berolt and Lady Eleonora are arguing over the arena's upcoming Grand Spectacle. Berolt wants to make attendance free to the masses, and Eleonora insists they charge.

"Berolt just wants to pack the stadium," Lady Solvig says with a sloshing wine glass in hand, "to show the public that his pretty future daughter-in-law is one of us, not them."

Lady Eleonora slams her withered fist on the table. "It's treasonous, the way they speak of her. Another mural went up in the Blacksmith District. And there's some hand gesture now, or so my servants tell me . . ."

"Oh! Yes, it's like this!" Lady Runa interlaces her thumbs and flaps her hands like wings. "Though I've never understood why they love her. It isn't exactly brave to sleep on silk sheets and wear crystal-studded gowns and eat Astagnon's finest mutton—"

She's cut off when Lord Gideon belches.

There's no sign of the Winged Lady that they're gossiping about. Sabine's chair next to Rian's is empty. For her sake, I hope that Rian is letting her dine alone in her bedroom instead of having to sit with these jackals.

Still—I'd hoped for at least a glimpse of her. Despite the venom between us, I'd take her hate, even if just to witness the beautiful chaos unfold in those stormy eyes.

Rian sets aside his wine goblet as his laughter tumbles to its end. There's a smile on his face, but his eyes are knife-sharp—he knows I've been in the dungeon and that there's only one reason I'd dare to interrupt his meal.

"If you'll excuse me," he says to his grandmother, Lady Eleonora. "I'm needed for pressing state business with our huntsman. Perhaps a squirrel has gone missing."

They all chuckle at my expense before switching to gossip about a wealthy man caught cheating in Popelin's Gambit.

Rian and I don't speak until we're in an alcove far enough down the hallway not to be overheard. With a start, I realize it's the same damn alcove where I pinned Sabine against the wall in her Winged Lady costume and ravished her mouth.

Focus, Wolf.

Tearing my eyes off the alcove, I say in a low rumble, "The Volkish prisoner is dead."

Rian takes the news casually as he picks at something between his teeth. "Did he talk?"

"I'll write up a full report. A few pieces of information may amount to something. I have Folke investigating one of his claims in the Sin Streets. And, I'd like a few days' leave to travel north to follow up on another tip about the border wall."

Rian nods. Disappointment that I didn't get anything more concrete is evident in the taut pinch of his lips, but he had to know it was a long shot that Maks would tell us much, anyway. "Understood. The leave is approved. Is there anything else?"

I hesitate. "I'll—be returning to service as Lady Sabine's bodyguard, then? Other than the few days' leave?"

He drags a hand over his shadow of a beard, nodding distractedly. "Take the rest of the week to plan your trek to the border. You'll take over her guardianship next week. She'll be pleased—she's no fan of yours, but she *hates* Maximan. I can't blame her. His breath smells like turnips." His eyes shift toward the titters drifting out of the ballroom. "Before you reassume guarding her, I need to show you something."

A catch in his voice makes my gut lurch.

I nod. "Now?"

He glances back at the ballroom once more, then grunts with satisfaction to hear his family all so inebriated that they won't notice he's gone. "Yes. Now."

The tightness in my stomach cranks up as he has me follow him to the stairs. We pass the kitchen's cold storage, then the coal shoot. My worst fears are confirmed when he turns toward the tunnel that leads to the dungeon.

Keeping my voice gruff, I say, "I already had Maks's body removed, if that's what you're after."

"We aren't going to the dungeon." His deep voice echoes against the damp walls.

He says no more as our boots clank on the stone floor, and at the end of the hall, he turns left instead of right. A chill climbs up the lines of my arms as we plunge into a dark tunnel. Most of these ancient underground passages collapsed decades ago, and as far as I know, house only rats.

When we reach an iron gate, Rian unlocks it with a key I've never seen before. He turns to me with a strange look in his eye. "What's the old prophecy the Red Church ends its sermons with?"

My stomach fills with ice at such a random question. I only lift a shoulder. "Hell if I know. I haven't set foot in a church in . . .ever."

He smirks in a way that doesn't quite reach his eyes. "Ah,

yes. I recall the phrase now. '*First will rise the fae beasts, blessing the land and wind and water. Fae vines will sprout from their resting places, and fae flowers will bloom in the beasts' footprints. Only then, the fae themselves will rise, and we human vassals will bow to our woken gods. Thusly, the Third Return of the Fae will begin.*'"

I stare at Rian with a terrible sharpness in my gut. First, Maks insists with his dying breath that fae beasts have awoken in Volkany, and now Rian is spouting off about the prophesized Third Return of the Fae?

His sardonic smile falls away as he opens the gate and plunges into the darkness, with only a faint flicker of lamplight far in the distance.

It smells strange here. Of old iron and sulfur. Of flea-infested hay. And beneath it all, a faint note of violets.

It hits me like a brick: *Sabine has been here.*

My pulse quickens as Rian says over his shoulder, "As it turns out, Wolf, you aren't the only one who's been occupied with a side project. Sabine has been busy, too."

We move toward the light like moths to flame, and I find myself stepping into a partially dilapidated subterranean stable.

How long has this been here?

Why haven't I heard of it until now——?

All thoughts are robbed when a hoof slams into an iron stall door hard enough to dent it. I jump back, my pulse in my throat.

"Rian, what the *fuck*?"

He merely toys with his Golath dime as I dare step close enough to peer within the stall. Immediately, a bolt of terror shoots down my spine, and I can only gape as I stare at a creature that no one has seen for one thousand years.

In that moment, I realize the depths of my miscalculations.

The secrets I thought were mine to guard from Rian were nothing compared to the ones kept by the Lord of Liars himself.

CHAPTER 5
SABINE

As the days pass, my attempts to win the monoceros's trust are as effective as a one-sided conversation with a brick wall.

On my second attempt to train him, I come out with two bruises instead of one.

On the third attempt, my tailbone aches from where he knocked me down.

On the fourth attempt, I leave covered in horse piss.

He's hot-tempered. He's unyielding. I'm not even sure he's totally sane. He keeps calling me fae, only to remind me then that he *hates* fae the same as he hates humans.

However, despite the monoceros's mulishness, the more time I spend with him, the more begrudgingly used to my presence he becomes. It's a matter of wearing down his will. Beating him at his own hard-nosed game.

I've read *The Race of Sun and Moon and Other Fae Tales* a dozen times, cover-to-cover, until every detail of Immortal Samaur and Immortal Thracia's deadly horse race runs through my dreams. I've swept the underground stable daily to get him used to brisk movement. I've even sung fae carols, though my voice is as off-pitched as my mother's was.

Day by day, he lets me inch closer to his stall door.

It's progress—but it's too slow for Rian.

Or rather, it's too slow for *Berolt*. As time rushes forward, I fear more and more what Berolt will do to both me and the monoceros if we don't produce results.

If you let me place a rope around your neck, I tell the monoceros, *then I promise that I can get you out of this dungeon. The humans who own this castle are building a stable for you. Room to run. Fresh air. A chance to—*

Sunlight? the monoceros asks sharply.

Because, of course, all he can think about is burning us to crisps with his fey fire.

I fight the urge to roll my eyes. *No sunlight until we can trust you.*

In response, he lifts his tail and drops steaming bricks of manure onto the floor.

After so many failed attempts, I need a pick-me-up. So, I find Myst in the royal stables, and together, we ride at breakneck speed around the dirt path that circles the Golden Sentinels' training grounds. It's outside the city walls, but Rian lets me come here to ride as long as Maximan is with me.

Besides, what could be safer than army grounds crawling with his soldiers? The view might not be the best, admittedly—latrines at one end, muddy formation grounds on the other—but the space is enormous. I can gallop Myst for wide stretches with the wind blasting away all my thoughts until it's just me, Myst, and the elements.

The soldiers cheer for us whenever we pass—in their

dreary lives, a girl enjoying a bit of freedom is as welcome as the first spring crocuses.

When Myst and I finally slow to a walk, we're both panting, but a smile pulls at my cheeks, and I swear there's extra pep in Myst's steps, too.

As I brush her down afterward in the Valvere stables, however, the thrill of the ride fades away to make space for worries to bubble back up.

Myst noses my shoulder as I comb her mane. *Sad?*

I run the comb through her silken hair, shaking my head. *I had a good ride. I'm just having trouble with the monoceros.*

The fire stallion? she says—her term for the monoceros.

That's right. He can understand me, but that doesn't mean he trusts me. At this rate, it will be years before I can even feed him an apple. Like you. Grinning, I produce an apple from my pocket for her, and her ears pop up in delight as she practically swoons.

Myst munches on the treat as I finish combing out her mane and tail, and then we switch to speculating about what the haggard old Sisters at the Convent of Immortal Iyre are doing without us to torment.

They need a good rut, Myst says matter-of-factly. *To pound some life back into them.*

I rest my head against the soft fur of her neck, shaking with giggles so hard my belly quakes. *Myst!*

What? A rut is good for the body. Look at how relaxed you were after rutting with the huntsman.

The laughter dies on my lips, replaced with a fiery burn across my cheeks. I clamp my hands around her muzzle. *Don't say such things! Basten isn't our friend anymore. We hate him now, remember?*

But he brings me apples every evening.

I roll my eyes. Of course, Basten has been coming to visit Myst and bribing her without my knowledge. For some reason, it irks me that the two of them continue to be friends when they wouldn't even know one another without me.

A bell dongs from a church spire in town.

I sigh. *I have to go.*

She stamps her front hoof. *But my braids?*

I groan, forgetting I'd promised to braid her mane. My pretty girl likes the braided fae style as much as any high-born Durish lady.

Next time, I promise, dumping the comb in the supply bucket and swinging open the stall door.

Wait. Myst stamps her hoof as I start to leave. *The fire stallion wants what you have not given him.*

I pause, looking over my shoulder, not sure I understood her right. *Freedom? I can't give him . . .*

I do not mean freedom. I mean a name. Animals cannot give themselves names.

I hesitate. *A . . .name?*

It cannot be any name—it must be his soul one. She snorts, ending the conversation.

I latch the gate slowly, working through her meaning like a tricky game of Basel with no obvious answer. It's true that animals do not give themselves names. If they need to refer to one another, they use physical descriptions: Broken-Wing Nuthatch. Chicken with Big Feet. Ash-Colored Cat. It's rare for Myst to use even my name, but she seems very proud to have one herself.

My mother named her, not me; but I wonder if Myst's name is why it's always been easier to connect with her.

Maximan is waiting outside the stable with his arms

folded. I flash him an apologetic grin for taking so long, but the brute is impervious to girlish charms. He merely jerks his head for me to follow him.

All the way back to Sorsha Hall, my mind tumbles over what Myst was trying to tell me. A soul name? I can only assume she means that animals have one true name, but how could I ever guess what the monoceros's is?

He leads me up the stairs to a third-floor hallway I never even knew existed. It's bare-bones compared to the rest of the castle, with simple oak doors. The last door on the right is open, warm light spilling out.

Maximan practically shoves me into the room, muttering about tardiness. I find my footing and discover I'm in what looks like a tailoring room. Measuring ribbons, hand mirrors, and an unclothed dress form fill the tight space.

A strikingly beautiful, raven-haired woman smiles at me, in welcome contrast to Maximan's gruffness. She wears a floor-length gown with a crystal-beaded bodice and matching gemstones studding her fae ear caps. The dress's neckline cut is deliberately low and square, drawing the eye to the godkiss birthmark on her breastbone.

I can't help but stare. Though she has the fair skin that is most common throughout Astagnon, her straight midnight locks and purple irises mark her as a Balaysian, from across the Panopis Sea. Balaysia is far outside of the seven kingdoms. Little is known about it, as the sea journey is so long that there are only a handful of Balaysians in all of Astagnon.

The woman pats a padded stool in front of three angled mirrors. "Please, have a seat, Lady Sabine. I'm Ferra Yungblood. Lord Rian requested that I work on you before tomorrow's Grand Spectacle in the arena. Half of Duren will be there, and the Valveres have invited wealthy guests from across Astagnon, so naturally, he wants you looking your best."

At my stare, she arches an elegant eyebrow, and I quickly shut my gaping mouth and slither into the seat.

"I'm so sorry. That was rude of me to stare. I've never met anyone from beyond the seven kingdoms. I didn't have a chance to meet many foreigners growing up. I was a ward of a convent."

Her warm smile says she isn't offended. She smooths an assessing hand down my chin-length hair, holding up a strand to examine the texture. "No need to explain, my lady. Everyone in Duren knows your history."

My eyes jump to hers in the center mirror as I blurt out, "They do? How?"

She squints closer at the strand of my hair. "Word gets around. Especially about you. Some days, it feels like all anyone talks about is the Winged Lady of Sorsha Hall."

She takes out a measuring ribbon. It strikes me that I was wrong about this room; it isn't a tailor's shop. It can't be, because there isn't any fabric. No sewing scissors. No skeins of wool.

I shift on the stool, stomach starting to knit itself into knots.

Ferra measures my hair in the front, back, and on either side, and closely feels along the ends where Adan coarsely hacked them off with his knife.

Clearing my throat, I say with a nervous laugh, "I appreciate that the Durish people admire me, but I'm not sure I've earned it. It isn't as though I've done anything for them."

Ferra side-eyes the door, where Maximan is occupied by

an argument with the head maid, Serenith. According to Brigit, they were common law married before Serenith cheated on him with a butcher—and judging by their raised voices, tensions still run high.

Ferra says in a low whisper, "You can imagine how much the people of Duren resent the Valveres. It's no secret they built their fortune on the public's backs: extortion, debts, taxes. Oh, they like to play at being benevolent rulers. Their sentinels keep the city safe, and every Mistlemass, they give away bread to the public. Pish. They aren't fooling anyone. So, when you showed up flaunting Lord Rian's rules for your ride, you spit in the face of the ruling class. And the public will *always* admire that."

She cackles, delighted by the idea of needling the Valveres.

I frown, eyeing her elegant clothes and ample jewelry. "Aren't you . . .part of the ruling class?"

"Me?" She tips her head back in a laugh. "Gods, no. My mother was a laundress."

"But your clothes—"

"Are just clothes. I'll admit that I enjoy the finer things in life, and my godkiss earns me enough coin now to afford them, but beneath these jewels beats the heart of a coinless peasant girl, I assure you."

She runs a silver brush through my hair in long, soothing strokes. With a pull at my chest, my mother comes to mind. She used to brush my hair every morning like this, humming an off-tune song, in the quiet hours before the household began to stir.

It's been twelve years, but I miss her like she died yesterday.

Ferra sets down the brush and rests her hands on my shoulders, giving a small squeeze. "Are you ready?"

"For what, exactly?"

"Rian didn't tell you the nature of my godkiss? How like him." Before I can ask what she has in mind, she coils a one-inch section of my hair around her index finger. As she works her way to the end, her hand simply keeps going. The lock, which was bluntly cut at my chin, continues longer and longer until it's unspooled down my back all the way to the floor.

She starts in on another section.

I sputter a gasp, because even though I have my own magic, watching Ferra work is so entrancing that it's hard to focus. It feels somehow sacred to watch it happen with my own eyes.

She smiles at my gawping reflection as she finishes lengthening my second curl and then sections off a third. Her fingers work with such deft speed that I can hardly follow their movements in the mirror.

"Beauty," she explains. "My godkiss lets me alter beauty. I've worked on nearly every highborn woman across Astagnon. Smoothing wrinkles, pinching noses, plumping lips. The High Lord only requested that your hair be restored to its original state. He didn't want any other alterations. I guess he finds you perfection just as you are."

She winks in the mirror as if to say, *lucky bride.*

I stifle a snort.

"It's true," she murmurs. "Lord Rian adores you. Everyone can see it. And from what I hear, the feeling goes both ways . . .at least in the bedroom." She winks in the mirror.

I blurt out, "*Pardon?*"

She teases, "The whole castle knows the two of you disappear nearly every night together. Listen, I'm not one to judge. Rian might be lacking in morals, but he makes up for it in looks."

My mind tumbles through a laundry pile of thoughts, and then suddenly, it all makes sense.

Oh, holy hell.

While Rian and I are hunkered in a dungeon working with the monoceros—decidedly *not* romancing one another —everyone thinks I'm fucking my betrothed.

The worst part is, I can't deny it without raising questions.

I give a weak titter, cheeks blazing.

As Ferra continues to length my hair, I toy with the idea of correcting her about Rian's and my relationship. Since the day I arrived, I've vowed never to go through with the marriage. The engagement ring on my finger is a necessary sham.

And yet . . .

In the few months that I've been at Sorsha Hall, Rian has been respectful in his unique Valvere way. He can be controlling, but he also let me fill my bedroom with animals, saying nothing of the constant vermin underfoot. He forced a ring on my finger, but he gave Myst the finest stall in the royal stables and encourages me to ride her as often as I like.

My fingers twist together in my lap like writhing snakes. Kissing Rian doesn't make my body come alive like when I kiss Basten, but I'm *done* kissing Basten. He might fill my dreams, but that's all they ever were.

So, I need to forget about him entirely. Let him ghost me as my bodyguard and nothing more.

Rian is clever, handsome, and ambitious. His sharp wit

makes me laugh as much as groan. Besides, a marriage doesn't have to be romantic. Hell, I'd wager most of them among the high class *aren't*.

And really, Rian and I already have a platonic partnership with the monoceros's training, so why not for a marriage, too? I would be High Lady of Duren, able to influence the town's prosperity, help the townspeople who admire me even though I've done so little for them. I'd even own that gorgeous library full of a lifetime of knowledge.

Would it be crazy to give it a chance?

"There," Ferra announces, pulling me from my reveries. When I look in the mirror, a slice of disappointment cuts all the way to the bone. My hair falls in honey waves down to the floor. Ferra's work was expert—but the last thing I want is to be weighed down by silken shackles again.

Someone clears their throat in the doorway. Lady Runa stands there, watching Ferra fluff my hair with a look that is hardly what I'd call reverent.

"I heard you were back," she says sharply to Ferra. "I need work on my nose. You didn't turn up the tip enough last time."

I can feel Ferra's warm energy change as her smile flattens. "I'll work on you as soon as I finish with Lady Sabine, Lady Runa."

But Lady Runa doesn't pick up on the dismissal. She sashays into Ferra's workroom, running a finger down the dressing form's curves.

"I saw a rat in the hedge maze," she says to me. "Perhaps you can let it sleep on your pillow, Lady Sabine."

I meet her gaze directly in the mirror. "I've had worse bedfellows."

Ferra smothers a snicker. A scowl flashes on Lady Runa's

face before she saunters out the door, vowing to come back later.

Ferra bursts out with a full laugh once she's gone. "What an ass."

I blink a few times, shocked. It's the first I've heard anyone in Sorsha Hall dare to speak an ill word about any of the Valveres. "I . . .have to say I agree."

Ferra tuts, "She's jealous of you. The people love you, so the elite feel threatened. Did you know that last night, Duren's arena held a horseback acrobatics show with a white horse and a performer dressed as you, costumed in paper birds and moths? You should have heard how the crowd cheered. Everyone, of course, except for the lords and ladies watching from the Immortal Box."

I wind a long lock of hair around my thumb, frowning.

"A word of advice?" Ferra finishes my hair by adding a few sunkissed strands among the honey-colored tresses. "The best way to deal with a Valvere is indirectly. Always smile to their faces. Then, find ways to needle them in the back."

I meet her eyes in the mirror and smile.

The elegantly dressed Ferra may be as capricious as the Valvere women when it comes to fashion, but maybe not everyone in Sorsha Hall is out for blood.

Hoot.

I stir awake groggily, not sure if I heard an owl in my dreams or if I'm back in the woods with Basten. Gods, I've wanted that so badly it burns my bones. The quiet of the road. Just me and

Basten and Myst. The roar of a campfire, the smell of his warming coffee, the chorus of animals in tree branches overhead, his thick arms blanketing me against the night's chill...

Then, it comes again.

Hoot.

Sleep tries to hold me in its grip, in that slumberous world where anything is possible. In my half-awake state, I toss and turn, trying to get used to the thick braid tangling around my knees again.

I trail a lazy hand up my arm, thinking of the last time Basten and I were in this bed together. An ache throbs at the base of my belly as I hazily blink up at the painting on my domed ceiling.

In the painting, the ten Immortals lounge on fae hills that bleed into a beachy expanse of the Panopis Sea. Immortal Alyssantha has one breast exposed in her lowcut gown as she clutches a bowl of grapes, and that trickster, Immortal Popelin, is reaching for her nipple instead of a grape.

But it's the other side of the painting that my eyes keep drifting to.

There, Immortal Solene, Goddess of Nature, and Immortal Artain, God of the Hunt, sit with a cloudfox kit between them. Is it just in my drowsy head that their hands touch ever so slightly as they pet the fae creature?

The more I fade in and out of half-sleep, the more I dream that Artain and Solene are Basten and me. That we're away from the crowd, tucked in a glen, sharing a secretive smile. Maybe we'll walk along that beach like I used to dream about. Basten and I in Salensa, him holding the seashells I collect in his big hands...

Wake up! the owl hoots sharply in my head. ***A man comes!***

Immediately, the remainder of sleep vanishes like morning mist. Two hoots. Blast, that's our signal!

Adrenaline bursts against my pulse points as I jump out of bed and replace my shape with pillows to make it look like I'm asleep. Then, I grab the heavy silver candlestick from the mantel and press my back against the curtains, on the side of the open window where the owl is perched as a sentinel.

The curtains reek of rosewater perfume so strongly that it burns my nasal cavities. I try to muffle the sound of my breathing until it's paper thin. I even try not to *blink* too loudly.

Slowly, a shadowy figure climbs over the windowsill in near-perfect silence. It's almost spellbinding to watch the man's massive frame move with such silent agility.

His shoulders are built as thick as a stallion's. His dark hair is secured in a knot at his nape, holding it out of his eyes.

As he pauses to scent the air, his head jerks an inch in my direction.

Now.

I burst out from the curtain with the candlestick poised high, ready to bring it down on his skull. The instant my bare feet scuff the carpet, the intruder whirls my way.

He sidesteps the candlestick hurtling toward his head, then lifts a massive arm to catch it before its heavy weight pulls me all the way around. We wrestle under its weight until, with an easy sweep of his leg, he buckles my knees.

We both crash to the floor, a tangle of limbs. Breath struggles in my throat as I scramble to get the upper hand, but he cantilevers me around to pin my back to the carpet. My nightgown rides up my thighs, flashing bare skin in the moonlight.

One of his rough hands clamps against my mouth while the other shoves the candlestick out of my reach.

Basten lowers his face close to mine in the darkness. "Dammit, Sabine, it's me!"

My chest heaves beneath his, my nipples brushing his chest with every rise and fall of my ribcage.

I narrow my eyes until they're paper-thin slits.

He finally releases my mouth.

"I *know* it's you," I spit at him. "Why do you think I was so anxious to clobber you?"

His hand moves down to lightly circle the column of my neck. There's a moment where his throat bobs with a tight swallow—a flash of hurt in his eyes so quick I almost miss it —but then his features reharden.

He gives a smirk, hiding his pain. "In that case, you should have used the knife I left for you."

I tilt my chin so that our lips are whisper-close. Slowly, I press the sharp point of the dagger in my right hand against his abdomen.

Ever since he gave the blade to me, I've slept with it strapped to my thigh. Just in case of a time like, oh, *this one.*

My lips brush against his own, temptingly, as I whisper, "Who said I didn't?"

CHAPTER 6
WOLF

This is what I get for giving a girl a knife.

Sabine's lips are achingly close to mine, and with her tight body pinned directly under my hips, my cock is already as hard as that damn silver candlestick. The knife's threat of violence only ignites my powder-keg adrenaline more.

Losing myself in her star-flecked eyes, I slowly take her hand with the knife and guide its point to the side of my neck instead.

In measured words, I instruct her, "Better to stab a man here, if you're in the dark. It's more likely to ensure a fatal wound. Stab the blade in fully to the hilt, then pull downward. Don't just slash the throat—you'll likely cut too shallow."

Her lupine eyes blink calmly, as unfazed as though I've explained how to slice cinnamon cake. *That's my fierce girl,* I think. She doesn't bow an inch for anyone, and I hope she never does.

That damn owl perched on her windowsill makes

sense now. As do the heavily perfumed drapes: to hide her scent. But now that she's on the floor, away from competing odors, all I can smell is her. It's like a hit of opium from the dens that sends users reeling for hours in a rhapsodical state. *She's* my opium. An addiction that I never want to give up as long as her perfect feet walk the earth.

It's been days, and I lied to myself if I thought I could forget about her. I want to bask in her presence like this forever.

"If you're going to kill me," I murmur, not tearing my eyes off hers as a drip of sweat rolls down my temple. "Best get on with it. Because if you aren't, drop that damn knife so I can kiss you."

She swallows a gasp, her pretty eyes widening, before anger bleeds out of her irises. Teeth bared like an animal, she hisses, "That would be one hate-filled kiss."

"Darling, the mental image of a hate-fuck from you is not the deterrent you think it is." My teeth, equally bared, tease the shell of her ear as I confide in a low growl, "We both know you're already gushing for me."

Outrage flashes like heat lightning across her face. She lets go of the knife, but only so that she can deliver a sharp slap to my cheek. I see her hand coming from a mile away and catch it before it lands.

My breath heaves, at war with myself.

I want her. I want her so badly that I'd whip my own flesh until my blood pooled at her feet, reflecting back her perfect face . . .

Wait. What's that on her forehead?

My overwhelming desire to tease her until she's writhing under me vanishes, replaced by a roaring protective instinct. I grip her jaw to hold her head steady so I can investigate the wound better.

A bruise. Near her temple, where her hair mostly hides it.

"Who the fuck hurt you?" I demand.

"Let me go!" She tries to wiggle out of my grasp, and I do let her go, but watch her like a hawk as she pushes herself to a seated position and scoots back against the bed. Her pulse flutters like hummingbird wings in her wrists.

"Gods—can you really see a tiny bruise in the dark?" she asks.

"It isn't tiny. And I don't appreciate you downplaying your wounds. Was it Rian? Berolt?"

"No, no, calm down." She skates a hand down her long throat to rest at her godkiss birthmark, fully exposed by her nightgown's low neckline. Once she catches her breath, she adds, "It was just an accident. Why do you care?"

The question is so ridiculous that I bark a dry laugh. It takes all my restraint not to gather her in my arms and press my lips to that bruise. Why do I care? Because she means more to me than anything ever has. Because I fall asleep with her filling every corner of my mind. Because she's the only chance I have of dragging myself out of the darkness I've dwelt in my entire life. Because just the chance to touch her is like daring to hold a star.

I lick my lips. A faint tang of iron comes off her.

And it hits me.

"The monoceros," I say.

Her hand stills against her breastbone. "You know about that?"

"Yeah. I know about *that*. I'm pissed off about *that*. Rian should never have asked you to tame it—it's too dangerous.

I've spent countless nights watching your bedroom, waiting for enough darkness to be able to climb this tower again and tell you to stop."

Once I got over the shock of seeing a living, breathing, *steaming* monoceros in the abandoned stables beneath Sorsha Hall, my first instinct was to kill Rian. We erupted into a shouting match. I yelled that it would get Sabine killed. He said he and his family were already in too deep—this was how they would take the throne, and Sabine was key.

I had to let it go. I had to pretend my master's bride didn't enthrall me. That I didn't stay awake every night since then, imagining fey fire from a horned horse scorching every inch of her perfect skin.

"I worry about you, little violet," I confess, my voice almost breaking.

My words wear down her anger's edge, and though she's far from offering me anything close to a smile, she sighs.

That's my girl. Able to find patience for even the lowest beasts. Which, in this case, is *me*.

Her fingers absently touch the bruise on her temple. "You don't need to worry about me. I know how to train a horse. I learned from watching my mother. And as for Rian, he and I reached an agreement. He isn't forcing me to work with the beast."

I don't believe for a second that Rian didn't trick her into this arrangement of theirs. "That monster is no simple horse."

"I can handle it, Basten."

I clamp my jaw shut. There's really nothing else I can say. I climbed up her tower tonight to stop her from working with the monoceros, and she's given me her answer. The idea of her working around a monster prickles my every protective instinct, but it awes me, too. Taming a monoceros is a job that, until now, has been reserved only for the gods.

She's going to make it eat from her hand, I know it.

I run a hand over my face. "You shouldn't have kept this from me. I could have helped you."

Her eyebrows lift faintly. "I haven't *seen* you. Besides, I guess I assumed secrets were a given between us."

It's like she stabbed me with that damn blade after all.

I push to my feet, raking back the loose strands of my hair, and hold out a hand to help her up. She's so lightweight—I could lift her like plucking a dandelion.

I tug her to her feet, and there's a moment when our hands are clasped, our bodies close, and my heart claps like a bell, and hers is clanging just the same, and all I want in this world is to crush my lips into hers.

I know she feels it, too.

Her eyes lift to mine, and a spark jumps between us. "What was really on the letter Myst saw you read? I'm not stupid, Basten. Whatever it was changed everything between us."

My jaw tightens. The secret wants to shoot out between my teeth, if nothing more than to ease those worry lines around her mouth.

At my silence, she rests her hands on either side of my face, studying me like an artist would a portrait of one of the Immortals. Seeking out shadows and light. Finding small flaws. Memorizing curves.

"Tell me, Basten," she whispers, and her eyes are so fathomlessly blue, the dark of falling water, that all I can think about is the night we spent beneath the waterfall south of

Duren. The best fucking night of my life. The first time I'd dared to believe I could find happiness.

"I can't, little violet."

A door closes in her eyes, shuttering against the sparks simmering between us.

For a long moment, we're both silent. Then, she looks away.

"At least you didn't make good on that threat to kiss me," she murmurs wryly to hide her hurt.

My heart clamps tight as a fist.

"I know you hate me," I say, cupping her jaw with one hand. "I've earned that. But you're safe with me, Sabine. I won't touch you—won't kiss you—unless you ask."

Though her starlit eyes fill with desire, she presses her lips together firmly as her answer.

The rejection hurts—but it's hardly a surprise.

The ache for her ties me up in knots, the pain of it tearing at both my heart and head, as I pivot toward the window with lead feet. I hope that damn owl doesn't shit on my head while I climb down. That would be just what I fucking need—

Her soft hand falls on my bicep.

"Basten. Wait." Her whisper is faint, but I hear it. Just as I hear the need in her voice. And damn if I'm not blasted with a need ten times stronger.

My breath goes still as I turn back around. Anticipation needles up my skin until my palms are damp with the desire to hold her.

Her pale face tips up to meet my gaze. "It has to be the last time."

The last time? No. There will never be a last time. I've made peace with the fact that I'm betraying a man as close as a brother. I'm never letting Sabine go—she's going to be mine until the end of time, even if she never wears my ring on her finger.

But sure. She can tell herself it's just one more fuck.

Her heartbeat increases as the energy between us shifts. I can scent Maximan through the door; he's currently halfway down the hall, out of earshot, sticking his finger in Serenith's cunt while he thinks everyone is asleep. He's a tough old bastard, but that woman's always been his weakness.

Which means Sabine is all mine.

I step forward with such a commanding presence that a startled gasp tears from her lips.

Leaning one hand on the canopy bed's high frame, I tower over her as I order in a deep voice, "Get on the bed."

Her eyes seem lit from within. "Aren't you going to kiss me first?"

"Oh, little violet. I'm going to kiss you a thousand times tonight, but not first."

I hear the breath catch in her throat. Her fawn-like eyes never break contact as she slowly sinks her plump ass onto the covers. Her blood rushes through her veins like a flash flood in a ravine.

She looks up at me through her lashes as though awaiting orders.

My fist tightens around the bed frame. "Take off your panties."

Her throat bobs as she scoots to the center of the bed, slowly hikes up her nightgown, giving me a flash of creamy skin in the moonlight, and eases the lacy scrap of fabric down over the leather knife holster strapped to her thigh.

I haven't even touched her yet, and I can smell that her

cunt is already soaked.

My gaze falls to the place in question, teasingly covered in her nightgown. "Now, show me how you touch yourself."

Her hand twists in her nightgown's fabric. "I don't do that."

I snort tenderly at her lie. "Darling, everybody does that."

But she spears her bottom lip with her teeth as pink spreads so deliciously up her neck that I want to lick it off like icing. Now, she won't meet my gaze. Suddenly bashful. She doesn't have anything to be embarrassed about—the idea of her touching herself gets me off like nothing else. My little violet is fearless when it comes to taming a monoceros, but blushes in the bedroom.

That's okay. Because I'm going to break down every last thought she holds dear about chastity until her needs are as wicked as mine.

I grip her slender ankles and tug her ass to the end of the bed, so her head is waist-height on me.

I circle my pants button with my middle finger. "Then touch *me*."

Her bottom lip dives between her teeth again as she hesitantly takes over, unsure how the buttons on a man's pants work. But she solves it and then takes out my heavy cock, which strains toward her with a mind of its own.

She forgets to breathe for a second.

"Take it in your mouth," I order.

A worried wrinkle crosses her nose. "I don't know what to do."

"Little violet, if your lips are around my cock, you're doing it right." I guide her by the back of her head toward my aching groin. She wets her lips. Breathes in. And then—

Pure fucking magic.

The feeling of shunting my cock between Sabine's plump lips is nothing short of ecstasy. She takes me so fucking well, like she was born to suck my cock. I swear I'm as hard as I've ever been in my life, so hard that I'm already leaking out the tip.

My hand fists in her silken locks. I heard that Ferra restored her hair's length, but I hadn't seen it myself until tonight. I preferred her chin-length hair, but I'm not about to complain about the braid that I can coil around my wrist as I guide her bobbing head.

I groan at the waves of rising pleasure.

We haven't had sex since her engagement party—will she be ready when my body slams into her?

Will she moan? Pant? Beg for it?

My balls tighten as I reach the cutting edge of how much I can take of her pretty lips milking my cock. If I don't bury myself inside her soon, I'm going to break apart.

Gripping her by her braid, I pull out of her mouth with a ragged moan.

My voice is hoarse as I command, "Now, lay back."

She touches her fingers to her swollen lips with a look like she can't believe what she just did. She sinks back on the pillows as I crawl on top of her like a prowling beast ready to lay claim to its quarry. My muscles are taut. My pulse hammers.

I could rip that nightgown right off her—

"Basten," she gasps with a fire in her eyes, her words fast and reckless. "I want you to hold my wrists down like when we were on the floor."

My Adam's apple jumps in my throat. Is my little wildcat asking for what I think she is? If so, she's braver than I thought between the sheets. Positively wicked. And while what she's asking for is something I've fantasized about plenty of nights, it's not something either of us wants to go into without being crystal fucking clear.

"Like this?" I say, testing, dragging her wrists up above her head and pinning them to the mattress.

She moans in the most delicious way. Her hips wriggle beneath mine like we're sparring again, like she wants to find that tantalizing friction from before. That power struggle.

"Ah," I say. "So that's what you like. You want me to hold you down, Sabine?"

Her big round eyes implore me, telling me she doesn't know exactly what she wants—or at least how to put it into words.

"You have to say it," I murmur.

Eyes locked to mine, she murmurs, "Fuck me like we're fighting."

She has no idea the effect those words have on me. I've had a hard-on practically since the first time I saw her, but it was the night she asked me to teach her to fight that my attraction tipped into obsession. Feeling her squirming body under mine, listening to her pulse speed up in her veins until it was flooding . . .

I lift to my knees as I straddle her, tossing back my hair that's fallen loose from its knot. Her eyes trace my every move as I climb off the bed—off her—and pull open her armoire drawers, rooting around until I find two silk robe ties.

Winding the binds around my palm, I come back to the bed and pin her left wrist to the headboard. She offers me her hand freely, though there's as much fear in her eyes as anticipation as I bind the wrist, then move to the other side to do the same with her other wrist, until her arms are splayed over her head.

On my way back, I snatch up the dagger I gave her from the floor.

"What are you doing?" she breathes.

"What you asked for." I pounce on her, pressing the knife to her nightgown's hem as I slit the fabric right up the center, and then shove the fabric to the side. *At last.* By the gods, how I've dreamed about those breasts.

With her wrists shackled to the bed, she can't stop me from fondling her pert nipples with my mouth.

She moans and arches her back like a cat. Her leg snakes around my hips as she tries to grind herself against me without the use of her hands.

I dig the heel of one hand against her hipbone, pinning down her squirming ass. My cock is tight and demanding as it senses the nearness of her wet heat. My teeth clamp down on her bottom lip as I steal a kiss that turns into both our tongues battering one another.

I groan against her ear, "You have no idea how much I wanted to fuck you each night I bound your wrists in the woods."

"I wanted it, too," she gasps. "I wanted you to fuck me."

This girl. This wicked, perfect girl.

It should be no surprise that both Sabine and I get off on the power play of rough sex, ropes and blades. We both had violent childhoods. It's twisted, but there it is. We desire the dark things that were formative to us because they're a piece of us forever. I was rewarded for violence. She was locked away, beaten.

Yeah. *Seriously twisted.*

But here's the thing. We get to make of our past what we want, and we can reclaim ropes and whips if we so desire.

"Basten," she moans with her head tipped so far back that the column of her throat gleams in the moonlight. "I have to feel you. Now."

The tip of my cock slides against her dripping cunt, teasing the outer folds. A squeal slips from her mouth just loud enough that I worry we'll be overheard. I toss my head toward the door, listening for her guard.

Maximan is still down the hallway, distracted by Serenith, but I don't know for how much longer.

"Keep that pretty mouth shut," I grunt as I roll my hips so my cock's full length teases up and down the outside of her cunt. "Unless you want the whole castle to hear you moan like a whore."

Her hips buck upward, demanding.

One inch. If I just shift one inch, I'll be inside her ...

"I'm going to take you now, little violet. And there's not a fucking thing you can do about it. You're mine."

She whimpers as her eyes dilate in the darkness. Lifting myself on one arm, I slowly push my cock into her tight center. A gasp chokes her throat as her arms strain against the silken ties. I watch as I enter her—I will never not watch that beautiful moment—as a bead of sweat rolls down to my chin.

I don't stop pushing until I'm fully buried to the hilt. Her hips writhe with a mind of their own, searching for friction. I know what my little wildcat wants.

My fingers tear through her scalp as I force a kiss out of her.

She fights against me, rocking her hips, but with my cock buried in her, she isn't going anywhere.

I pull out slowly and drive into her again, reveling in the way her eyes roll back in her head with every thrust. Her bound hands squeeze into balls at the same time as her inner muscles clench.

She moans, "*Basten.*"

She's the only person who calls me by my real name. As though to her, I'm not a predator with a string of kills behind me. When her soft eyes look at me so trustingly, she makes me think there's still a chance I could be something more than a wolf.

"You're doing so good, little violet." My chest wracks with labored breaths as I hold myself back from the darkness that wants to drive into her harder and harder. "You take it so well."

I chase her lips until they're mine, and then I pour everything I feel for her into the kiss. Her mouth wars with me in the sweetest way, like an angry kitten. Her tongue presses the seam of my lips until I sweep mine against hers.

This kiss is holy. It's filthy. It's completely breaking me apart.

I dig my fingers into one of her ass cheeks, squeezing a handful while I pound into her. Her legs wrap around my hips to match my punishing rhythm, asking for even more than I'm giving her.

"Harder," she pants.

I brace one arm against the headboard for a better angle, and adjust her ass until I can slam into her deeper than I've ever gone. She moans in a higher pitch.

"You like when I give it to you there?" I batter my cock on the spot which makes her cry out, and it isn't long before she tips her head back. "Yeah?"

Her lips fall open. I can hear the air gathering in her

lungs a second before her cry tears out of her, and because she can't muffle it with her hands bound, I clamp my palm over her mouth.

She comes into my palm. I catch her scream, warm and damp on my skin.

And as she falls back, spent and ravished with her wrists hanging limp from the rope belts, I speed up my rhythm. Her round, full breasts bounce with every thrust. I can't take my eyes off them. Off her.

She's utter perfection.

My balls tighten, and I ride the edge, reveling in the wicked anticipation. The last time? No. This can't be the last time. Fuck it, I'm ready to damn myself to the underrealm and betray anyone I've ever cared about. The risk is high, but the reward is astronomical. There's no way I can go on, seeing her every day, and never feeling my little violet moaning beneath me again.

With a final groan, I sink as deeply as I can into her. My cock spurts hot ribbons of cum, marking her as mine.

I feel feral. Ready to fight. Ready to do it all over again.

After a few seconds, I wipe the sweat off my forehead as I pull out of her and release her wrists from their ties. I take each of her arms, massaging the joints.

I could stay like this forever—kissing each freckle on her body.

"Lay with me, Basten," she whispers, touching her hand to my chin's rough stubble.

I settle on the bed and gather her in my arms. Her head falls on my chest. I comb my fingers down the length of her long braid, acutely aware of the paradox we've become.

She tried to stay away from me, just as I did from her.

Our love is a dangerous game, a delicate dance of

predator and prey. She loves me, despite the arrows I've let loose on her soul. It's a love both tender and perilous, a deer drawn to a hunter's gaze, unable to resist the pull of an inexplicable connection.

Every stolen moment only deepens the wounds that we know, in the end, will scar us both.

"Basten, do you love me?"

I go rigid from my jaw to my bare toes. Terror. Pure fucking terror, that's what fills me.

I shift my position against the headboard in an attempt to mask my shallow breath. Prize fighters in the arena are easier to face than her right now.

"You're everything to me, Sabine." The words catch in the net of my chest, twisting themselves up. "But love takes selflessness. And I'm the most selfish bastard there is. Look at how I already—"

I can't finish the thought. Can't remind us both of how I already broke her heart and shattered her dreams.

She goes deathly still at my side, and I curse inwardly. *Damn the gods.* I'm not made for this—for emotional talk. It isn't that I don't want to say these things to her, it's that I don't know how.

I grew up bloodying other boys to earn my keep. Amid thieves and card sharps and drunks. A smarter man would promise her the stars in the sky, but I want to be truthful with her. I have only so much to give, and she deserves the world.

She starts to pull away, disappointment dripping off her like beads of sweat, and I panic and pull her back close enough to cup her face in my palms.

Gruffly, I admit, "If I could love anyone, Sabine, it would

be you. It just isn't something I'm capable of. I'm too —broken."

She holds my gaze for a long moment, eyes searching mine for hidden truths, and then she tears away with a sigh. "You're more like them than you think."

The rebuke stings. "Wolves?"

She shakes her head. "The Valveres."

That stings *more*. I know she doesn't mean it as an insult, simply the truth. Something has shifted between us tonight. The times we've had sex before, we've never brought up Rian. By silent agreement, we've always pretended when we're together that there's no ring on her finger, no axe hanging over our heads.

Why?

Because she and I are smarter than to think we have a future.

There's a sad sort of surrender in her eyes, like she knows the path ahead of us is on fire but that we're going to walk right into the flames.

I pull her against my chest, pressing a kiss to the top of her hair.

I won't let her burn.

"I finished my side job." My knuckles flex, still bruised from slamming them into Maks's jaw. "Tomorrow, I'll relieve Maximan as your bodyguard. I'll be at your side every day from now on."

That's my version of a confession of love. Does she know that? Does she understand? It's the best I can offer, though I know it's just crumbs compared to what she deserves.

My voice rumbles as I say, "I'll always protect you, little violet."

CHAPTER 7
SABINE

The line of townspeople waiting to get into Duren's arena winds all the way back to the eastern market, yet Rian's carriage sweeps straight through the gates to stop beneath the columned archway. I peer out the carriage window—up, up, up—at the stadium that soars high enough to obscure the sun. The crowd's roar from the stands is already bone-shaking, and we aren't even inside yet.

Outside, Basten, dressed in his gleaming sentinel armor, opens the door and offers a hand to help me down. "My lady."

He's the perfect unfeeling soldier today. Anyone looking would see only a stoic bodyguard, who might as well be made of wood for as much as he harbors his own secret feelings.

But *I* notice how his rough palm lingers on mine a second too long, and the veil of desire in our brief moment of eye contact before we both look away.

My throat goes dry. *The things we did last night . . .*

My hands tremble, and my folded silk fan slips out of my grasp before I can catch it.

In the same instant, Rian climbs out behind me. The whole ride from Sorsha Hall, he was uncharacteristically silent, lips pursing distractedly, foot jiggling anxiously. But now, he swoops down to pick up my fan, and by the time he hands it back to me, he wears the mask of carefree, indulgent high society again.

"Your fan, my lady."

Weeks ago, I wouldn't have recognized that arrogant smile for the mask it is, hiding private feelings I can only guess at. Crazily, a surge of unexpected guilt rises in my chest. I wear Rian's engagement ring, but it was Basten's name I moaned last night. I've never cared about keeping chastity vows to Rian because our engagement is against my will.

I don't owe him loyalty.

Yet for some reason, lately I can't bring myself to loathe Rian as deeply as I once did. On the journey from Bremcote, he was a devilishly handsome face I'd seen once and a collection of scandalous rumors. Since arriving at Sorsha Hall, though, he's become a person to me.

An arrogant asshole? Yes. A plotting bastard? Sure. But a person just the same.

He hands me my fan, then, with a smirk, his attention drops to my low neckline, and I groan inwardly.

Of course. The one time I slightly start to warm up to him, he proves himself an utter cad.

"Ferra worked wonders with your hair," Rian observes, stroking a curl of my hair between his fingers, but his eyes are still on the exposed upper curves of my breasts.

I tug stiffly on my gown's cap sleeves. Brigit dressed me

in a gauzy white gown with a sinfully plunging neckline and two white silk capes down the back, embroidered with a feather pattern that gives the impression of wings. At Rian's command, my newly restored hair falls in unadorned, loose waves to my ankles.

I tug my hair out of his grasp with a thrum of irritation. "I'd have preferred my hair in a braid. Like this, I'm too reminded of, oh, that time I was forced to ride naked across half of Astagnon."

Rian's puckish smile turns positively devilish. "That's precisely the point, songbird. Today's fights are in your honor. I've opened the arena gratis to all of Duren's citizens so they, too, will be reminded of the extraordinary lengths you underwent to now be on my arm."

He offers me the arm in question.

I skip a look over his shoulder at Basten. His jaw is clenched into a razor's edge that begs me to run my lips across it.

Holy gods—it was a mistake to look at him.

My cheeks immediately warm, my lungs hollowing out as I recall how his talented mouth teased my body into such sinful pleasures.

Never again, I tell myself. *He'll only hurt me more.*

I clasp Rian's arm before my fantasies about his best friend get the better of me.

With Basten as our ever-present shadow, haunting me with memories of last night, Rian guides me into the stands. Duren's arena is famed throughout the seven kingdoms. It holds Astagnon's elite annual horse race, the Feychase, as well as theatrical performances to honor the gods on holidays. But what it's best known for are its fights. Gladiatorial-style matches that reenact the Immortals' mythical battles with costumes and set dressing. In reality, the pomp is just a veneer over pure, bloody spectacle.

But, hey, the Valveres know how to entertain.

The stadium's concentric stands can seat ten thousand people, and today—given its free attendance—every spot is taken, with long lines still stretching out front. Vendors hawk roasted nuts and turkey legs. The roar of so many voices makes the brickwork underfoot vibrate.

We pass through open-air passages beneath the stands that take us by statues of the ten Immortals, then up a marble staircase to the Immortal Box, reserved exclusively for nobility and special guests.

Unlike the arena's lower levels, where the poor scramble over the few seats in the awning's shade, the Immortal Box has a large shade canopy supported by marble columns, with massive curtains hanging on either side of the entrance. A refreshment table offers a mouth-watering assortment of plum cakes, sugared almonds, and dried cherries. The box would comfortably hold a hundred guests, but today, there must be twice that number.

The throngs of elegant lords and ladies in attendance look ready for a ball with their fanciful clothes and golden fey lines painted on their limbs. Lady Solvig, Lord Gideon, Lady Runa, Lord Berolt, and Lady Eleonora are already in attendance, seated on cushioned settees in the shadiest corner while a servant mists the elderly matriarch with scented water.

A striking, silver-haired woman in a flowing tangerine gown gives me a wave across the crowd, and after a second, I jolt with recognition.

It's Ferra. She's altered her appearance with her beauty-sculpting godkiss. Silver hair instead of raven locks. Dark, pointed fae eyebrows. Though she isn't nobility, she must be beloved enough for her godkissed makeovers to have earned herself an invitation to the Immortal Box.

Basten stops at the marble columns, at attention along with the other guards, and I can't help but glance over my shoulder, feeling his loss like a cloud crossed in front of the sun.

I need him, on some level, just as I need air. Even though his betrayal burned me worse than the sun ever could, a part of me knows I'll keep coming back to be scorched again and again. Something happened between us during those weeks in the woods, like two trees grown together that can never be separated now.

Basten's eyes never leave me. Even with my back to him, I know I have every ounce of his attention. He's my bodyguard, sure, but the heat coming off him is positively sinful.

Rian and I have barely taken three paces into the box before a crash of metal from the fighting grounds makes me jump so hard that I instinctively clamp on Rian's arm.

A roar erupts from the crowd, causing the champagne flutes to tremble.

I press a hand to my forehead. "What the devil was that?"

"The first fight," Rian says, eyes sparking with mischievous delight to see me flustered. "Come. Watch. And if you think this is something, just wait until the Everlast trial. It takes servants a week to rake out all the blood-soaked sand afterwards."

He leads me to the box's railing, where I spot one fighter lifting his sword in triumph. Another fighter in silver armor is splayed out in a patch of bloody sand.

Dead.

The crowd chants, *"For the win! For the win!"*

The apple butter pastry I ate for breakfast curdles in my stomach, and all I can think is that I need water before I vomit.

"Was that Magnus Lancaster?" Lady Runa rushes to the railing with her champagne sloshing onto the crowds below. She pouts, "Oh, *fuck*. It *was* Magnus. I had ten silver pieces on him to win."

Magnus Lancaster? The dead fighter? The name is familiar . . .it strikes me that he was one of the show fighters on the night Rian announced our wedding date. At the time, the party crowd worshipped him and his showboating acrobatics.

Now he's dead, and his once-adoring fans mull around the cheese tray, careless to his bloody corpse.

"The Winged Lady finally lands amongst our midst." Lord Berolt approaches me with a long, shameless ogling of my chest in the low-cut gown. *Like father, like son*, I think darkly. Sarcasm oozes from Lord Berolt's voice as he adds, "We've been eagerly awaiting your appearance, my dear."

My lips press into a paper-thin smile. I motion to the dead body being dragged off by arena attendants. "Is this not ample entertainment?"

At my barb, he chuckles deep in his gullet. "There's never enough entertainment. Though today, we're going to give it our all." He slides a cryptic look toward Rian, who clears his throat and tightens his arm around my waist.

A drum roll from the announcer's stage steals our attention as the next fight begins. Rian takes the opportunity to usher me away from his lecherous father. "Come. I want to introduce you to someone."

All eyes shift to me as we pass women in off-the-shoulder gowns and men with pointed silver ear caps. Whispers about "The Winged Lady" trail behind me when they see Brigit's wing-like drapes cascading down my back.

Rian snatches a champagne flute off a servant's tray. "You look like you need this."

"Gods, yes." I snatch it out of his hand and tip back a sip. "Booze might be the only way to get through today."

We stop near the towering lefthand curtain where a tall man with a thick head of dark blond hair cuts a formidable figure as he speaks to a robed priest of the Red Church. Sunlight catches his hair, showing a streak of white at his hairline.

The champagne goes stale in my mouth. *I know this man.*

He was wearing a satin eye mask when I last saw him, but I remember his unusual hair from Popelin's Gambit—he was the man watching me from the bar.

"Grand Cleric Beneveto," Rian says casually, "May I introduce my fiancée, Lady Sabine Darrow of Bremcote."

Before I can stop myself, I spit out a mouthful of champagne. *The Grand Cleric? That's* who this mysterious man is?

I scramble to pretend that my shock was a cough, while a servant runs over with a napkin for the liquid running down my chin.

"Sorry. Wrong pipe." I laugh weakly as I dab my mouth, buying time to recover.

The Grand Cleric's winter-blue eyes drill into me as though they can extract my deepest thoughts. I'd assumed the Grand Cleric was like most powerful men in Astagnon: old, paunchy, and dripping in riches. But he can't be more than thirty-five, and his lithe frame hints more at swordplay training than indulgence in food and wine.

How often have I been told that Rian and the Grand

Cleric despise each other? They both covet Astagnon's throne, and I don't doubt the extreme measures each one would take to acquire it—so why the hell is he here, mingling with Rian over drinks like old friends?

I slide a wary look at Rian, but he keeps a stiff smile on his face.

"Lady Sabine," Grand Cleric Beneveto says with a slight nod. "Word of your sensational ride reached us all the way in Old Coros."

Rian chuckles. "That's hardly surprising. By now, I'd wager the savages who dwell in the Gaetan cliffs have heard of her naked ride."

Both men laugh.

I stare at Rian with blood boiling in my veins. Under the Grand Cleric's orders, priests assaulted me in Charmont. They called me indecent. A *whore*. Rian knows all this. And now he's swapping jokes at my expense with the man.

Basten would slam his fist into the Grand Cleric's nose.

The ground reverberates again as the crowd cheers another death. Drums start up. The drummers might as well be pounding against my temples, given how my head aches.

"Speaking of Old Coros," Rian casually throws out, "How is the honorable King Joruun's health? For weeks, our messengers have been turned away at Hekkelveld Castle's gates with the claim that Joruun isn't taking visitors."

A dangerous current rides just under Rian's conversational tone. I was right, I realize. These men *do* detest one another.

Grand Cleric Beneveto strokes his jaw, which gleams with the golden shadow of a beard despite the fact that priests must be clean-shaven.

"Don't pay any heed to the fearmongers. The king is

ninety years old; naturally, he tires easily and cannot take many visitors. He is well, I assure you—I saw him not but last week."

Rian's sharp eyes cut into the Grand Cleric's like broken glass. "Strange that a sickly old man could make such a startling recovery. A month ago, rumors spread that he was at death's door."

Beneveto slices a biting smile right back. "You doubt our king's fortitude? Why, High Lord Valvere, some would call that treason." He laughs as though jesting, though the dark mirth in his eyes could pierce flesh. "If you ask me, that's one more reason why Astagnon must become a theocracy. It's too risky to place our kingdom's fate in one man's hands. Better to have the broad network of the Red Church shepherding our subjects. The King's Council agrees with me—they've already submitted a petition to change the law. I expect it will go through before winter."

Rian's jaw clenches so hard I'm afraid something will break. Redness stains his cheeks. Fighting to keep his angry surprise under control, he spits with venom, "Is that so? I'm sure it has nothing to do with the coins you're lining the King's Council's pockets with."

The Grand Cleric tips back his drink.

"Excuse me," I say hoarsely, with no patience for political maneuvers. "The champagne. . . my throat . . . I need some water."

My skin crawls with invisible ants as I stumble through the crowd toward the refreshment table, where I slosh water from a pitcher into a glass and guzzle it down.

Ten paces from me, Basten discreetly separates from the other guards, slipping to the far side of the table. He's careful to keep his attention on the stadium below as though scanning the crowd for potential threats.

"You're pale," he says in a low voice, not looking in my direction. "Your hands are shaking."

"I'm—fine. You shouldn't be talking to me in public."

"The Grand Cleric shouldn't be talking to you, either, after what his priests did. Especially not the way he looked at you in that dress when you walked in."

His velvety anger ripples over my skin, making me shiver.

"It isn't your business how men look at me." I try to look anywhere but at him.

His head jerks my way, but he fights the instinct to face me and grips the rail with both hands. "You're right. I guess it isn't. Not with a Valvere engagement ring on your finger."

I can't deny the way my stomach tightens in response. It's *his* fault I'm wearing Rian's ring instead of his. He had every chance to claim me as his woman, but he used me for one cheap night and then dumped me at the door to my enemy's house, knowing full well how much I loathed the idea of marriage to Rian.

His lie is still as fresh in my mind as untouched dew.

In Salensa, I'm going to call you my wife . . .

As the threat of tears burns behind my eyes, I slam down my water glass. It takes every ounce of my strength not to look at him as I hiss, "Not just a Valvere ring. I wear Valvere gowns. Sleep on Valvere sheets. Maybe I was wrong to judge Rian so harshly before meeting him. He gives me everything."

From the corner of my eye, I see a muscle feather in Basten's jaw. He hesitates, the silence pregnant with unspoken words, before he finds the courage to break it. "Everything?"

The timber of his voice carries a raw, exposed quality, like his heart stuttered halfway through getting the words out. My own heart lilts, and I have to stop myself from assuring him that of course I haven't had a Valvere *cock*; my heart still belongs to Basten, even after everything.

But Basten doesn't deserve my soothing words.

I murmur, "That isn't your business, either."

"Isn't it? You were begging *me* to tie you to the bed last night."

Fire sparks between us. Anger. Hurt. Jealousy. Desire. The tension is palpable enough to practically burn up the oxygen between us. Any second, the cloth napkins are going to ignite.

Have we gone mad? We shouldn't be having this conversation here. If someone overhears us, we could both be thrown in the dungeon. Or worse, forced to fight one another in that damned justice trial they call the Everlast.

His fists tighten on the railing until his knuckles turn white. He shifts his head an inch, just enough to catch my gaze. The heat in his dark eyes makes me afraid he's about to drizzle me in the table's pitcher of honey and lick it off in front of everyone.

I fist my hand in my skirt to keep from slapping him, but I can't stop myself from whirling to face him, cheeks burning with indignation. "How dare you—"

But before I can finish the thought, his attention shifts to the arena behind me, and a change comes over his body. His face, suntanned from long days in the forest, pales like leeches have sucked the blood out of him.

His hand on his sword hilt trembles.

Trembles.

I've seen Basten face down four Volkish raiders bare-handed with a smirk on his lips.

Now, he *trembles*?

"Basten?" My voice ghosts, alarmed. "What is it—"

My words die as I follow his sight line down to the arena. At first, I'm not sure what I'm looking at. We're far above the action, and I don't have Basten's heightened vision.

A single fighter crossing the freshly-raked sand. The person is unusually small. In fact, far too small to be a true contender. A little person? My stomach turns at the Valveres' poor taste that they would put a little person in the ring.

But then the fighter's oversized helmet falls off, and when he stumbles after it, there's an innocent clumsiness to his movements.

My breath stops.

This is what made Basten tremble.

Gods in hell—it's a *child*.

Not just any child. Before the boy puts back on his helmet, I spot a curving burn mark on his right cheek.

It's the freezing street boy from outside Popelin's Gambit. The one I sent a cat to keep warm.

"I know that boy," I breathe. "I've seen his burn scar before . . ."

"Not a scar." Basten's jaw locks. "A brand. The letter J. He's one of Jocki's boys."

My head whips around to Basten, eyes tracing the deep

lines in his face because, in public, I don't dare touch him with more than my gaze.

Jocki was the man who raised Basten as a street fighter, who beat and starved him, who made him battle other boys for sport.

No wonder Basten's first reaction was to tremble; how old was he when he was forced into his first fight? This same child's age? Younger?

Even from a distance, it's plain to see that the child is crying as he wipes his eyes.

The poor boy is terrified.

As the drums taper off, the announcer climbs the stairs to the stage and speaks through a cone to amplify his voice. "Ladies and gentlemen, today we recreate the fabled day in young Immortal Woudix's life when he—"

"This cannot be happening." My head reels. "Rian wouldn't put a child into a gladiatorial fight, would he?"

My fiancé's family can be many things—liars, cheats, thieves—but there is no way under Immortal Vale's blue sky that the Valveres would do *this*.

Basten murmurs darkly, "Rian? No."

My lips part with understanding. "Berolt."

Basten's silence is confirmation.

Gears rumble, and a trap door to the arena's basement opens, forming a large rectangular hole about twenty paces from the child fighter. My stomach plummets. What's going to come up? It would be unconscionable to put a child opposite a full-grown fighter.

The stadium's ten thousand-strong crowd ripples with unease, murmurs of discontent spreading like wildfire. I'm not the only one outraged by this crime. Angry shouts ring out as a child's safety hangs in the balance. A glass bottle hurls into the Immortal Box, shattering against the railing.

Basten draws his sword.

"Rian!" I spot my future husband ten paces away and pounce on him, with Basten shadowing me from behind.

My fingers claw into the black silk of Rian's sleeve. "Rian —what the hell is this?"

Rian takes a slow sip of his champagne. "It's the next fight, darling."

He speaks so casually, like telling me the weather. My blood runs cold. Is he truly so heartless? Or is this a bluff? Rian has spent a lifetime masking his true feelings, and I haven't yet learned to read all his tells.

The announcer continues, " . . .in our god's battle with a deadly goldenclaw, represented today by one of the vicious tigers of Kravada!"

There's a rumble as a cage rises from the trap door. A lanky tiger paces within the tight space. The crowd's roar makes the tiger crouch low, ears pinned back, overwhelmed and just as terrified as the boy.

Drool loops out of its jaw—a sign of distress.

Fury drips down the back of my throat until it pools in my gut, turning my insides to molten lead. Another bottle from the angry crowd smashes into the corner of the refreshment table, and Lady Runa shrieks. "They're animals!"

Ferra slams her champagne glass on the table hard enough to tip over and shatter. "*They're* animals? The crowd? I hope the next bottle breaks your fucking nose."

Lady Runa gasps.

The announcer raises his hand. The drums pound faster and faster and faster, and then suddenly stop.

The announcer lets his hand fall.

"Release the tiger!"

"No!" I grip Rian's arm so hard it must leave bruises. As High Lord, he has dominion over everything in the arena. He could put an end to this. "Tell them to stop this, Rian!"

Rian patiently lets me tug on him like I'm a toddler. His head pivots with a cool indifference to meet my gaze. "If only someone *could* stop it."

There's such heavy innuendo in his words. I don't pick up on his meaning right away because the truth of it is all too horrible—but when I do, I let go of his arm like he's fire and I'm dry tinder.

I step back, breath strangled. "You set me up."

Rian's response is to drain his nearly full champagne glass. He tosses it to the ground next to Ferra's shattered glass, where it breaks into pieces, too, as though nothing matters anymore. And in this den of wickedness, maybe it doesn't.

There's an unhinged look in his eye. "What are you going to do, songbird?"

Gods, it all makes sense now. Berolt doubted my demonstration with the mouse. This is a show, but the boy on the sand isn't the performer. *I'm* the one on stage. They want me to use my godkiss to communicate with the tiger. Here, in front of ten thousand people.

Or they'll let the boy die.

I back away slowly, head dragging back in forth as I hunt for adequate words to tell Rian exactly how vile he is. Maybe this was Berolt's idea, but Rian knew. Damn him. *Damn him!*

The tiger rushes out of the cage, ears pinned back, and hisses up at the stands.

I forget Rian. I forget the Grand Cleric—whose job is to

shepherd all of the kingdom's souls, especially children's—and all the powerful elites who do nothing.

"Sabine, wait." Basten murmurs low enough for only me to hear. "They're using you for your power. Give them what they want, and they'll only use you more for worse things."

Basten knows the Valveres almost like his own family, so I don't doubt his warning. But what choice do I have?

"It's a child," I whisper.

I grip the railing and focus every ounce of my mental focus on the fighting arena.

The tiger is about one hundred paces away from the Immortal Box. I've never tried to communicate with an animal at such a range, but there have been times when animals have sensed my need from great distances and come to my aid.

Stop, I say to the tiger. ***Do not harm the boy.***

The tiger doesn't hear me—or if it does, it doesn't listen. I can feel the jumpy threads of its overwhelming fear in the air.

The roar of ten thousand angry voices nearly paralyzes it. It hisses again, panicked.

The boy shakily picks up a spear, and the tiger snaps its attention toward him. I can feel a thread of the animal's relief. Finally, it has a clear target.

Wait! I cry. ***Don't attack!***

The tiger doesn't so much as look my way.

No, no, no . . .

I don't have much time—the tiger is already stalking toward the boy, who raises his measly spear with a slack grip. But what can I do?

Unless, maybe, I'm taking the wrong approach.

I close my eyes. My scattered thoughts fade away as the

invisible connection in my head travels over the boisterous crowd to fall on the tiger's fur-lined ears. Then, I push my reach even further. Further than I've ever gone. Pain splinters across my skull, but I keep pushing until something unlocks like a bolt sliding into place.

Bright sun. Strange sand underfoot. As many people as there are leaves in a jungle.

The tiger's thoughts come to me not as words but as flashes of imagery. Somehow, I'm inside the tiger's mind. I hurt as it hurts. I fear as it fears. I feel its terror crest at the moment when the boy rushes at it with the spear.

The tiger's instincts snap into place like a disjointed bone. I feel its cool wash of certainty as it surrenders to its feral nature. With a snarl that echoes against the arena's awning, the beast bares its three-inch fangs.

The audience falls into a frightened hush. The attendees in the Immortal Box watch, transfixed by the drama unfolding below. I'm dimly aware that Rian is still by my side—the only person out of ten thousand who isn't watching the tiger.

Because he's watching me.

Gods, I hate him.

I hate him more than there are thorns on every rose in the world.

I was so wrong to feel sympathy for him, to feel even a whiff of guilt for betraying him, to feel anything other than outrage . . .

Backing up, I numbly stumble against a chair, and Basten's strong hand on the small of my back catches me.

"Little violet." He whispers low enough for only me to hear, and his hot breath carries the same urgency that I feel rushing through my veins. "You don't have to do this."

"But I do."

I inhale sharply, gripping the railing, my focus snapping back to the tiger charging at the boy with a menacing snarl.

The boy hurls a spear with a battle cry, but it clatters uselessly to the ground.

A tingle spreads up from my fingertips, and I swear I can feel the crunch of sand beneath the tiger's paws.

And I simply say: **Stop.**

Three paces before reaching the boy, the tiger halts, its back arching, ears swiveling. Its massive head cuts a line across ten thousand spectators to hone in on the Immortal Box.

The crowd falls so silent that I hear the awnings billowing in the breeze. Slowly, the cowering boy peeks out from where he's clutching his helmet. One by one, eyes from the audience turn to me as they trace the tiger's line of focus.

Whispers erupt like goosebumps.

"The Winged Lady . . ."

"She's using her power . . ."

". . .standing up to the Valveres . . ."

But I ignore everything except the mental bond with the tiger.

I'm here, I tell the animal. *I'm a friend. You are safe.*

The tiger plunks its rump down and swats a paw over the side of its head like a gnat is buzzing in its ear. But it's my voice in its mind, not an insect. I didn't think it was possible, but my godkiss is connecting to an animal on a deeper level than ever before.

Friend? It repeats cautiously.

I nearly laugh as tears break over my eyes. *Yes! A friend! And that boy? He is a friend, too.*

The tiger swipes its paw over its ears a few more times—it doesn't like the itch of my voice in its head, but it seems to understand my message. For a few tense moments, it remains seated in the sand, facing the Immortal Box.

Facing me.

As it slowly becomes clear that the tiger is going to spare the boy, the crowd's murmurs grow to excited shrieks of disbelief. Chants of "Our Winged Lady!" echo around the stadium, and from the corner of my eye, I see hundreds of hands forming the shape of flapping wings.

At my side, Rian gives a ragged exhale. One could mistake it for relief that the boy is safe, but I know better.

Rian is just glad his trap worked.

"By the gods, songbird," he breathes as his eyes drink me in. "You captivated the tiger. The crowd. You captivate *me*—"

He shuts up when I turn on him with an icicle glare.

I feel myself slipping, slipping, slipping. I'm half tiger now, half girl, and I'm not sure which is more vicious.

Low and dangerous, I hiss, "What was it your father said? Not enough entertainment? I can change that."

Rage blurs my vision, dizzying and intoxicating. I'm losing myself—but I'm gaining something mighty. The Valveres need to learn that every crime they commit will be met with twofold justice. People like them have turned the world at their whims for too long.

I lift my right hand as though it's the tiger's own paw.

A sense of weightlessness buoys me as though I'm floating above myself. Sparks tingle from my palms up through my veins as though I was sleeping but am finally awake.

The breath catches in my throat. Chills grip me. There's

a surge in my brain like goosebumps, and suddenly, I'm looking at the world with someone else's eyes, someone who sees the world in a different light, colors brighter and more vivid than before.

And, somehow, I know what I can do.

I focus my attention on the tiger and say, *I need you to do something for me. Climb up here and claw the face off every Valvere you see.*

The tiger doesn't say no.

It *can't* say no.

Because the tiger and I are one now, and it has no choice but to do as I command.

The audience's cheers turn to screams as the tiger bounds up the announcer's dais, jumps onto the drummers' massive instruments, and climbs into the stands.

CHAPTER 8
WOLF

S creams cascade through the stands like thunder as the panicked crowd fights to escape the tiger.

The drum reverberates from the thud of its paws on its surface, deafening to my godkissed ears. The tiger vaults up the stands in explosive leaps, ignoring the audience's screams.

The beast looks fucking *possessed*.

Golden Sentinels on the lower stands call to the Grand Cleric to climb over the railing. He waves away their offered hands, then smoothly jumps the six feet down on his own.

I seize Sabine's upper arm, shaking her, and hiss, "What did you do, Sabine?"

She doesn't respond. Not even a blink. There's something wrong with her forest-green eyes; they have a distant, burnished look like the patina on a copper kettle.

"Sabine? You have to stop this. It's gone too far!"

Lord Berolt, that fucking bastard, is behind this. If I had to guess, I'd say he wanted the world to witness her power in a spectacle so sensational that word of it would reach their farthest enemies.

And I'll be honest, it feels damn good to see a crowd of ten thousand grovel before this girl with the strength of the summer sun and the heart of the evening moon. But now she's exploded like a constellation, her reach stretching too far across the distance. Stars can't soar like this. Eventually, they fall.

I shake her again, but it's like her mind has left her body.

"Wolf!" Rian suddenly shouts. "To your left!"

The tiger is closing in. Just two levels below.

The whole arena quakes from ten thousand panicked spectators storming toward the exits. My breath quickens. My muscles tense. My senses heighten to the pinnacle of their ability, as instinct takes over to calculate the tiger's trajectory.

The animal bunches its muscles and leaps into the box, clearing the railing with one bound, and I duck out of the way just in time.

It collides with a half dozen chairs, which splinter and crash to the ground, as it snaps its jaws an inch from Lady Runa's elbow. She lets out a scream. A few precious seconds pass while the tiger scrambles to right itself among the broken furniture, giving the Golden Sentinels a chance to hustle the wailing Lady Runa to the exit.

Rian draws his sword. "Get Sabine to safety. I'll handle the tiger."

He spins his sword in a flashy circle to limber up his wrist, then firms his grip as he faces the beast.

I hesitate, but for all his faults, Rian is a master swordsman.

He can take care of himself.

I grip Sabine by the shoulders. Shake her again. Give a few rousing smacks to her cheeks. Nothing jolts her out of her stupor.

And with the tiger so close that I can smell its pungent sweat...

"Fuck. I've got to get you out of here."

Before I can hustle her through the stampede of high-class attendees, Lord Berolt trips right in front of us and crashes to the ground.

The tiger snarls, and I swing my sword into attack position, but its yellow eyes scan past me like I don't exist, only to lock onto Lord Berolt.

A chill rakes down my back as I realize the tiger is only targeting Valveres, not me or the other spectators.

I whip my head to focus on Sabine.

Is she doing this? Not just speaking to it, but controlling it?

I reset my grip on my sword. Sabine will loathe me even more than she already does if I kill the tiger, but what choice do I have?

After all this is over, she'll have to answer to the Valveres. And if the beast draws blood from a single one of them, they'll put her in chains for the rest of her life.

I'm about to strike when Rian puts himself between the tiger and his father. "Don't strike it! Do you know how much this thing is worth? I captured it myself in Kravada; I can capture it again. The beastmaster is already on his way with chains."

He feigns a lunge to the left in an attempt to herd the tiger into the corner of the balcony. Of all the incredulous things I've seen today, this has to be one of the most bone-headed.

"Don't be a fucking dolt!" I snap.

He dances on his feet, sword at the ready, ignoring me.

I stem the argument on my tongue. There's really only one person who can stop this.

"Sabine!" I grab her again. "Snap out of it!"

It's no use. I don't think she's even aware of me. The glazed-over rage in her eyes burns hotter than the sun. Her mouth moves silently as her eyes lock on the animal. Her lips pull back like she's hissing, and behind me, the tiger echoes the movement, hissing . . .

A scream tears my attention to the railing. Ferra Yungblood is dangling over it in a failed escape attempt, one leg on either side, her ridiculous gown caught on a nail.

"Fucking hell," I mutter. If it were anyone else, I'd be tempted to leave them to their fate. Sabine is what matters here. But Ferra is as much a slave to the Valvere family as I am. Her heart is good, even if her head is fixed on scented soaps and silver combs.

I tuck Sabine, still in her strange comatose state, behind the righthand curtain, where she's out of the stampeding crowd's path, and then clamp onto Ferra's wrists.

"Wolf!" she cries, smacking one of her crystal heels against the offending nail. "My dress—it's stuck!"

"Then fucking *rip* it."

"Don't you dare," she warns like I've suggested cutting off a limb. "This is Gaither House tulle."

"It's a dress."

"It's *couture*."

I'm about to curse her couture to the heavens and rip the damn thing off when a familiar figure limps up the stands— the only bastard foolhardy enough to head toward the danger while everyone else is running from it.

"Folke!" I shout.

Folke hoists himself up to the Immortal Box and takes in the scene with a soldier's quick assessment, curiosity sparking in his eyes when he sees Ferra.

"Go," he tells me. "I'll help the lady."

Ferra takes one look at Folke's tattered jacket and goes on the offensive. "I don't give a damn about the shoes, but this dress is worth more to me than sex."

The last thing I hear as I dash back through the crowd is Folke saying, "Madam, I'll save the dress, but we might need to reexamine your bedroom adventures."

Sabine.

I spin back around. The Immortal Box is complete chaos. Half the furniture is overturned, and someone tore down the lefthand curtain. Broken glasses and ceramic trays litter the floor. The overripe smell of smashed fruit and spilled wine coats my throat.

My chest heaves as I cross the box in great strides. When I reach Sabine, still in a daze behind the curtain, I'm hit with a burst of awe. I don't know what power she unlocked, but she looks inhuman, ethereal, like at any moment fey lines are going to burst into light along her skin.

My ears prickle. The roar of the thousands-strong audience is overwhelmingly composed of screams, but beneath it, my heightened hearing picks out another layer. Is that . . .chanting?

"Our Winged Lady!"

"Our Winged Lady!"

All around the stadium, the remaining spectators form wings with their hands. They're cheering Sabine on for turning a tiger against the Valveres. Two men even climb into the box, pumping their fists in the air as they overturn the refreshment table. I can feel a riot coming like a gathering storm, its electric anticipation sparking in the air.

Well, fuck.

Sabine's lips twitch along with whatever messages she's silently sending the tiger. Her fingers paw in the air to direct its movements. She shifts left, and the tiger feigns left, avoiding Rian's swipe with the sword.

This time, I don't try to rationalize with her. The tiger isn't the wild animal I'm worried about here. I deal with dangerous creatures all the time: Bears. Wolves. Stags. There's a time for patient stalking, and there's a time for a predatory show of fucking force.

"You're coming with me." I duck my good shoulder into her middle and hoist her pretty ass into the air with her legs dangling down my front.

She gasps like waking from a dream. Her body quakes strangely. Her heart beats erratically before finally settling.

And then she kicks me in the nose.

"Ow!"

"By the gods!" she shrieks. "Basten, put me down! The tiger . . . It needs me!"

I spit out a line of blood, wincing from the pain, as she squirms her hips on my shoulder. Her angry cries don't sway my stone resolve as I cart her toward the exit. All I think about is putting distance between her and the tiger. I'll carry her on my shoulder across half of Astagnon if it means keeping her safe from her own powers.

"Rian is going to kill it," she cries. "You know he will! He's a fucking—"

In an instant, I drop her to her feet and clamp a hand over her mouth before she publicly slanders her future husband.

Her muffled curses dampen my palm as she rages against me. We're beneath the archway that separates the Immortal Box from the shaded interior breezeway, and dozens of Golden Sentinels and high-class attendees alike are staring at her.

"Quiet," I hiss.

She's just inspired a riot among the peasant class—the elite aren't going to see her as Rian's harmless little pet any longer.

But she's still riding the high of her power, her eyes wide and glassy. When I release her, she tries to run back into the box. "The tiger—"

I snare her around the waist and haul her back. "Rian won't hurt it!"

"You don't know that! Oh gods, I shouldn't have . . . I didn't mean to . . ."

A dawning look of horror crosses her face as she understands that she essentially killed the tiger the moment she ordered it to attack.

Her fingers clamp onto my upper arms as her star-flecked eyes entreat me. "I only wanted it to scare them! The tiger wasn't going to hurt anyone, I swear. But that's already too much, isn't it? They're going to kill it."

She bites her lip so hard I hear the blood throb beneath the skin.

I grip her jaw and forcibly turn her head toward the tiger fight.

"Look—look at the chains! See? The sentinels are trying to corner it. Rian wants to trap it. If *you* tell the tiger to surrender, they'll put it back in its cage. Safe and sound."

Her sweat carries the salty tang of dread. Her little body is trembling with the first warning signs of shock.

"Sabine." I trap her face between my hands, taking control. Locking her gaze to mine, though her eyes keep threatening to roll back in her head. I run my thumb over her cheek, back and forth, as steadily as a rising and falling tide to ground her.

"Stay with me. You have the power to stop this. You can still save the tiger."

Her fingers pull restlessly on my breastplate. She tips her head into my palm like a nuzzling cat, but she's still shaking uncontrollably in response to her flood of power. I slide one hand along her neck, weaving my fingers into the hair at her nape.

She needs to feel safe. Steady. To know that I'd catch her if she fell.

Kiss-close to her lips, I whisper, "Let it go."

"I . . . Basten . . ." She touches her forehead to mine like taking root. She gives a shuddering breath. A shift finally unlocks throughout her body as her muscles release their panicked hold.

"Talk to the tiger, Sabine." I whisper against her lips.

A held breath eases out of her, and I feel the edge of her panic tiptoe back onto safer ground.

"*Stop, friend.*" Her quiet words would be inaudible to anyone but me.

From the corner of my eye, I see the tiger's ears swivel with the look of a lost kitten hearing its mother's mew.

"That's it, little violet." I smooth my hand down to her lower back. "Again."

Her throat bobs in a swallow. She flicks her fingers, directing the tiger, and it lays down like a harmless housecat.

The beastmaster cautiously slides the chain around its

neck with arms that quake like tree branches, but the tiger only yawns, exhausted from all its efforts.

The trainer signals to a team of Golden Sentinels, who secure the chain.

"It's done," Rian announces, sheathing his sword. He drags a hand over his short hair. He, too, heaves a breath as he faces the dozen remaining soldiers in the Immortal Box. "It's done!"

But it isn't.

It isn't at all.

Because the populace is still rioting, overturning vendor carts and hurling anything at hand up at the Immortal Box. There's a crash somewhere below as the crowd pulls down a statue of one of the fae gods. Rian frowns, then gives a low command to the head of the Golden Sentinels.

Soldiers pour down into the stands.

Oblivious to the riot she's started, Sabine buries her face in my chest. "Thank the gods, Basten. I was so afraid that I'd —that I'd—" Her thoughts snuff out with a sob.

I smooth a hand down her hair, wishing I could comb away her guilt as easily as her tangles. "It's all right, little violet. It's over. I've got you."

But my relief immediately tips into something darker.

Slowly, I feel the heat of dozens of sets of eyes— including Rian's, Berolt's, Folke's, and Ferra's—move from the tiger to Sabine.

Or rather, me holding Sabine.

She's tucked against my body with a familiarity that suggests she knows exactly how well we fit together. I had my lips close enough I could have kissed her. I manhandled her, tossed her over my shoulder with a hand on her ass, the way no bodyguard would do to a noblewoman.

Oh, *fuck*.

I release Sabine like she's a live coal and step back, hands raised. The one silver lining is that we're far enough back into the breezeway that most of the thousands of spectators in the stand didn't see, only those dozen or so people still left in the box.

"My lady. I apologize—I was trying only to protect you from the beast."

Her own common sense snaps back into her a second later. "Of—of course. Wolf."

The taste of bitterness is on my tongue, and I can't seem to swallow it down to my stomach without it surging back up again. If people suspect that there's a romance between Sabine and me, rumors will spread like wildfire, and our necks will be in nooses by morning.

The moment is tense, but then Sabine breaks it by staggering over to the tiger. She falls to her knees and hugs it around the neck.

"I'm so sorry. I'm so sorry. I'm so sorry."

It tentatively licks her face.

Rian rolls out his shoulders of any lingering adrenaline, though his keen eyes keep darting back to me questioningly.

Fucking gods, please don't say anything about how I held her

. . .

Someone shouts in the stands, a woman screams, and Rian signals for half the soldiers to peel off to contain the riot.

The weight of all those eyes shifts off me, and my lungs heave with relief.

What did everyone think they saw, anyway? Just a bodyguard protecting his charge. Keeping her safe in an unpredictable situation.

I did what any guard would do.

I can almost wrangle myself to believe that until Folke smacks Ferra on the ass—eliciting an indignant gasp but also a flash of interest in her violet eyes—then sidles over to me and claps a heavy hand on my shoulder.

"Wolf," he murmurs low. "For the second time in as many days: You're a lovesick idiot."

CHAPTER 9

SABINE

After the incident, soldiers lock me in my room with only water and dried mutton. They even lock the window. No one responds when I slam my fists against the door. Breaking the glass won't help—the narrow iron frames around the window panes are essentially the bars of a cage. Through the keyhole, I can see Basten standing guard outside, but Rian posted Maximan, too. Two bodyguards mean there's no way for me to communicate with Basten.

I rest my hand flat against the door, the closest I can get to him. *He* can hear the frightened patter of my heart, the sobs I try to swallow, the nervous way I pick at my nails. I crave him, but I also hate the idea that his godkiss lets him see how broken I am. Ever since we arrived in Duren, I've tried to paint the picture of an uncaring woman. That I'm over him. That nothing he can do will ever form a crack in my resolve.

But he hears everything.

He sees all.

He knows my vulnerabilities sometimes better than even I do.

Well, so be it.

I have years' worth of indignation boiling over inside me to avenge, and I don't care if the perpetrators were Basten or Rian or the Sisters or a drunken father or the whole damn system.

Fuck it. I want to break something. I want Basten to hear something besides my sobs.

Fury seizes me, and I snatch up the heavy silver candlestick. All it takes is one punishing swing, and the window shatters.

Satisfaction bursts in my chest. A broken window might get me nowhere, but the sound of shattering glass is a gratifying chorus to the sharp-edged anger I can't otherwise put a sound to.

I toss the candlestick aside, then slump into the desk chair, shaking, and burst into tears. I rest my head on the desk, squeezing my eyes shut, fisting my hands in my long hair until it's knotted as a fishing net.

My heart feels thin, empty. The memory of the spectacle makes my cheeks run hot. The tiger only lives now by the grace of the gods, and by Rian's inflated ego that made him confident he could catch it alive.

I never want to feel an animal surrender its control to me by force again, and yet there's a terrible part of me—one I'm afraid to admit—that also felt *exhilarated* by forcing it.

Why cry? a little voice says.

Yes, why cry? says another.

I look up, wiping away my tears, to find multiple pairs of soft black eyes blinking at me.

The forest mouse sits on an empty tea saucer. A

nuthatch perches on the teacup's rim. A chipmunk stands on its hindlegs on a stack of books. And a pair of ladybugs have climbed onto my silver hairbrush.

I give a shaky smile. **Hello, friends. It's good to see your faces.**

Girl is sad, the nuthatch says, and the ladybugs take up the chorus.

Sad, they chirp. **Sad. Sad. Sad.**

Smoothing back my hair, I sit up and wipe the tear streaks off my cheeks.

I'm scared, I admit in a whisper. **Today, my godkiss did something new—**

But I halt my words, not wanting to explain to the little creatures that I compelled an animal, for fear that they might look at me differently. It would break my heart if they feared I might do the same to them.

It's nothing. I stroke the chipmunk's white stripe. **Thank you, friends.**

The ladybugs meander back toward the window, the nuthatch flits up to perch on my dresser, and the chipmunk naps in the teacup. The forest mouse stays with me, curling up in the nest of my hair on the floor.

When I finally dry the last of my tears, my bleary-eyed gaze falls on the stack of books the chipmunk was sitting on.

It's the ones I picked out from the library with Brigit. I'd hoped to find information on the monoceros to help with training, but maybe they can guide me now, too.

I run my finger down the tattered spines until I land on *The Gift of the Godkiss*. It's an encyclopedia of documented godkissed powers from between the Second Return of the Fae and now. I flip past descriptions of fire-wielders and cloud-movers, scryers and potions experts.

Finally, I find an entry about speaking to animals:

/Dolphin-speaker/ Sailors reported that in the Cratian Islands, a twelve-year-old godkissed boy was rumored to have the power to speak to dolphins and understand their language in return. Though the king of the Cratian Islands hoped the boy's power would lead to greater fishing yields, it was found that while the dolphins could hear him, they ignored any request for help.

There are no other mentions of people communicating with animals, certainly nothing about the ability to take over their minds.

I thumb through a few more books, then pause on the threadbare copy of *The Last Return of the Fae*. It's the oldest of the books by far. The handwritten print is so faded it's nearly illegible, and there's more text on the spine I can't make out. This is the book that reminded me of my mother's cherished personal copy of the Book of the Immortals.

A trail of pain burns through my chest, so jagged and stark that it robs my breath.

I miss you, Mama.

If only she were here to counsel me. As a girl, I was always getting myself into scrapes, and she would inevitably be there to gather me in her arms with patient nods and wise words.

I remember a time when she was saddling Myst for a fox hunt, and I begged to be allowed to go with her on one of the farm horses. I couldn't have been older than four. Barely tall enough to reach a horse's belly.

You haven't yet mastered riding, Sabine, she said.

I don't need to learn, I objected, stamping my foot. *I can talk to the horse. Tell it what to do.*

She knelt to my level with a patient smile, stroking my hair that was already halfway down my back. *There is more to communication than talking, my heart. Words only go ear-deep. To truly understand one another, we must reach someone in their heart.*

I looked longingly at the stable. *I don't understand what that has to do with a fox hunt.*

She laughed. *You can talk to a horse, but you cannot make it listen. Look at your father and me. He tells me to do things all the time; how often do I listen?*

I gave a sly smile. *Never.*

Exactly, my heart. It takes more than your godkiss to communicate with a horse. You build trust with time. You speak with your arms and your legs. Most of all, you listen not just with your godkiss but with your heart.

Now, I run my nails over my godkiss birthmark, gazing into space. Is that what happened in the arena? Did I reach the tiger on a deeper level than words?

Rubbing my face, I sigh and open the book, finally finding a legible section halfway down the page:

FIRST TO RISE, LAST TO SLEEP. Immortal Vale was the last of the fae to enter slumber. He was preceded by Immortal Meric, whose cruel judgment upon humans thrust the seven kingdoms into such punishing cold that famine reined. Tens of thousands died. This is the way of the fae.

May they never rise again.

—Age of Frost Year 22

. . .

A strange chill makes my toes curl in my slippers, as though Meric himself is blowing a cursed cold upon my bedroom floor.

The Age of Frost is the ancient form of telling time before the modern calendar. Some quick calculations reveal that the Age of Frost Year 22 was nine hundred forty years ago.

I sit back in the chair, staring at a spot on the wall, as goosebumps erupt along my forearms.

From what the Sisters told me, the oldest book in existence is a three-hundred-year-old copy of the Book of the Immortals owned by King Joruun, which is why everything we *think* we know about the two previous Returns of the Fae is unreliable, seven-hundred-year-old conjecture at best.

But if I did the math correctly, that means *this* book was written only sixty years after the end of the Second Return of the Fae. When memories were still fresh. When humans who had lived through the Second Return were *still alive.*

My mouth goes dry to think that I'm holding something nearly one thousand years old, that might reveal the truth about the fae by people who actually saw them. Rian must know how valuable this book is, right? Why wasn't it under lock and key?

Instead, it was on the floor, meaning someone had it out to read. But who?

With unsteady fingers, I comb through the book for more legible passages.

. . .when the world was but a canvas upon which the gods painted their whims, the deities ruled with an iron fist. Vale the Warrior, with his mighty fae axe, reveled in the chaos of battle. He

demanded blood-soaked tributes from mortal realms, leaving behind desolation and grief.

Iyre the Maiden, proclaimed to be the embodiment of virtue, was a deceiving siren of falsehood. She tricked young men and maidens into compromising positions, only to condemn their loss of innocence and lock them into abyssal prisons with a red key. Were it not for Solene the Wilderwoman's tree roots that broke apart the captives' stone walls, many would suffer there still.

Artain the Archer, God of the Hunt, found pleasure in the suffering of both predator and prey. His arrows sought not only the flesh of beasts but also the hearts of lovers. In his twisted game, mortal bonds were shattered as he aimed his arrows at the most vulnerable moments of passion, turning joy into heartache.

"Fuck." The whisper rides across my tongue before I can rein it in.

The modern-day version of the Book of the Immortals portrays the fae gods as mischievous and licentious, sure. *Nowhere* does it say that they were tyrants bent on enslaving humanity to serve their capricious whims.

I flip to the final page and read:

Thus concludes this first volume, recounting how the fae were awoken and the horrors of their Second Return; the second volume shall detail how the ten fae were, at long last, defeated and put back into slumber.

. . .

I examine the spine again. Yes—that flaking paint could be "Volume I." So where in the gods' names is Volume II? Anyone who possessed the knowledge of how to put the gods back to sleep would hold the fate of our world in their hands.

I rest my palm on the book's cover, then jerk it back when I realize my palms are sweating. I cast a quick look at my bedroom door. Basten must be able to smell the sweat. Hear my staggering breaths.

Okay? The little mouse asks, nosing at my hand.

I slam the book closed, heart rapping a dangerous melody along my ribs.

I'm okay, I answer, though the fear sliding down my throat tells a different story. My tongue darts out to wet my lips as I scan the room. *I need a hiding place for this book. Somewhere the maids won't find.*

Follow me! The mouse scales down the desk leg and crosses the carpet. It digs its little paws at the wooden baseboard that hides the carpet's seam. The carpet pulls up, giving me just enough room to slip the book under. It leaves a slight lump, but in an old castle like this, it isn't unusual to have warped floorboards.

Thank you, friend! I stroke my index finger down its head, and its whiskers lift in joy.

A sudden knock at the door makes me jump. The mouse darts like an arrow under the bed.

Basten, I think on instinct. *His senses told him about what I found. The book.*

But when the key turns in the lock, it isn't Basten's rugged face that appears.

It's the only person I currently hate more.

"You." I jab a finger at Rian, narrowing my red-rimmed eyes.

Suddenly, the revelation about the Second Return of the Fae is shoved back into the corner of my brain as anger burns like a lit match down my spine. What good is it to worry about the next return of the fae, when I have a cruel tyrant in the here and now?

I add, "You *bastard*."

Rian casually strokes the edge of his jaw. "Haven't cooled off yet, I take it?"

"You're a festering dung pile not even slugs would devour. You tricked me. The whole spectacle was designed to force me to use my godkiss!"

He replies calmly, "And you did. Brilliantly. You should hear what's being said about you in Duren. Hell, they've even heard in Old Coros by now, I imagine. It was a stroke of luck that the Grand Cleric was there to witness your performance before he departed."

My eyes narrow. "The Grand Cleric? *That's* why you invited him?"

His face splits in a smile as his prying eyes swallow me up in nothing but my robe and slippers.

"That mockery of a priest has the King's Council in his pocket. He's rubbed elbows with them for decades, whoring and gambling together. His grandfather was King Joruun's top advisor for nearly fifty years. Now, he's keeping old Joruun locked away so no one can verify his condition."

"So? You can prove a blood tie when a bloodtaster tests your blood—the Grand Cleric can't."

"That is why he's lining up the pieces for Astagnon to become a theocracy, completely sidestepping the requirement of a blood relation. And with the gods as witnesses, his efforts are working. They've always hated me in Old Coros. Looked down upon the Valvere family for being from the provinces. Making our fortune from the vices. None of them have ever wanted me to take the throne." Rian pauses. "The Grand Cleric is playing a dirty game. So I have to play dirty, too."

My chest heaves beneath the silk gown. "You risked a child's life for this game of yours!"

He reaches out to stroke a strand of hair off my face, but I jerk backward before he makes contact. After a tense second, his hand falls.

"The child was never in danger, Sabine."

"That's a lie!"

His eyes flash. "For once in my life, I'm not lying. The spectacle was at my father's insistence. He demanded to see your godkiss under pressure. I had no choice but to go along with it; I assure you that I had archers at the ready with sedative-tipped arrows in case the tiger attacked the boy. After the spectacle, I bought the boy from the fightmaster and gave him a job in the stables. He'll never have to bloody himself for food again."

My gaze dances over Rian's face, trying to read the truth in the green pools of his eyes, the quirk of his brows, the tilt of his head. My ears roar with warnings not to believe a word he says, though I can't find a tic that would indicate a lie.

"We're allies, songbird." His eyelids sink to half-mast. "I swore it to you."

Something about his words rings true, yet I still don't dare trust them.

Clenching my jaw, I draw the blade from the holster

strapped to my thigh on impulse and press it against his neck.

His eyes widen in genuine shock. "By the gods," he murmurs, "you *are* full of surprises."

"How can I trust the Lord of Liars?" I say through a clenched jaw, a sincere question. Rian has earned a disreputable reputation, so only a fool would believe his promises. And yet, a part of me wants—needs—to know how to trust him.

For better or worse, we're bound together.

Suddenly, his left hand darts up to intercept the blade—in a second, he's redirected it away from his neck. With a swift twist, he seizes the blade and pins my wrists behind my back.

"Hey!" I struggle in vain. "Let me go!"

He takes his time studying the blade's carved wooden hilt. "Who gave you this little piece, songbird? The last I saw this particular knife, a different noblewoman was holding it against my neck after her husband's gambling debts forced them into the pauper's house. I can only surmise they pawned it."

I growl low in my throat, struggling against his grip.

Rian combs one hand down my long neck, circling my jugular. His hot breath caresses my skin as he murmurs, "Was it Brigit? Ferra?" Then, after a pause, "Or was it Wolf?"

When I don't answer, his low voice hardens. "Apologies. I mean *Basten*. I had forgotten how well acquainted you two were until he had his hands all over you at the arena, and everyone heard you moan his real name."

My throat bobs with a swallow as I calculate my next words carefully. Over my shoulder, I hiss, "If I'm not mistaken, a bodyguard's job is to guard my body. Are you implying he was supposed to do that without touching me?"

I wonder if Rian can feel how my heart is lurching. Thank the gods he doesn't have Basten's godkiss, or else he'd smell the lie on me.

He leans close, lips brushing my ear. "Did you fuck him on the journey to Duren?"

My heart trips over itself. "Of course not!"

"A kiss, then? You can tell me. One kiss is easily forgiven. Maybe you were trying to seduce him to escape. Or those cold nights in the wilderness drove you both to a mistake."

"Nothing happened between me and Bas—me and Wolf. I hate the man, haven't you noticed? I'd sooner spit on him than kiss him. Now let me go—"

Before I finish, he releases me. I stumble away a few steps, breathing hard, clutching one of the bedposts like a barrier between us.

He says, "You want to know if you can trust the Lord of Liars? Hold a knife to his neck and then see if he gives it back."

He tosses my blade on the bed with as little care as if it's a woman's comb.

I lift my chin, heartbeat galloping, thoughts tangled in knots that only pull tighter the more I try to tease them apart. "So that's it? I'm supposed to believe we're still allies after what you did? Go on helping you train a war machine?"

After the day that my mother forbade me from going on the fox hunt, I started to see the world differently. I understood that some creatures were worth listening to—mice, birds, horses, cats—and some that weren't. Namely, *my father*.

So, even though I recall my mother's exact steps when training her horses, I have no reason to obey Rian.

His eyebrows dip down. "Look at it this way. Would you rather the monoceros be in *your* care or in mine?"

My stomach clenches against my will. I look away.

After a weighted pause, I murmur, "Are you so determined to make me hate you?"

His answer is swift. "I'm determined that when you fall in love with me, you'll know exactly who you love."

That knot in my mind only tightens further until I'm nearly hopeless of ever unraveling the truth.

"I am not your enemy, Sabine. All I ask is that you let me prove that."

I eye him sidelong. "As allies?"

"As allies. As fiancés. As everything a man and woman can be to one another." Rian holds out his hand, waiting.

Indecision laces through me. He's trapped me again. There's no winning here, that is clear. There is only playing the game. The monoceros and I are both players, and if we want to survive, we have to bow to the gamemaster.

But I am my mother's daughter. She bowed to no one— especially not tyrants.

"Fine," I say tensely, taking his hand.

But Rian is mistaken if he thinks I don't intend to win this game. There was one more lesson I took away from my mother on the day of the fox hunt: Words are cheap, and so are lies.

CHAPTER 10
WOLF

When I trudge home to the game warden's residence long after the spectacle, aching and exhausted, I freeze as I reach for the knob. My door is open.

My senses flame to life like a lantern. It's been a long day of standing guard outside Sabine's room, then processing criminals from the riot, and all I want is to fall into bed and sleep for ages. And now I have to deal with an intruder?

Even from twenty paces, I can see that there are no scratches around the lock that would suggest forced entry. Whoever broke in must have had a key.

As far as I knew, *I* had the only key, which is currently clanking on the key ring hanging from my rucksack.

I sniff the air.

Saddle leather and sandalwood incense.

A jagged inhale cuts down into my lungs. What the fuck is Rian doing here?

I harden my jangling nerves as the hinges groan beneath my hand and open the door the rest of the way to find him sitting on one of the wooden chairs in front of the hearth with my half-finished bottle of whiskey dangling from one hand.

He raises the bottle in greeting. "This stuff of yours is terrible. Remind me to give you a bottle of barrel-aged Spezian single malt for Midtane."

I dart a quick, assessing scan around my cottage for anything I might have left out that Rian shouldn't see. The table is covered with maps and open books to track my route up to the Volkish border wall. The kitchen larder is as meager as ever. The bed is unmade. Relief slowly unwinds the knots pulling at my neck.

What did I expect him to find? Sabine, naked in my bed?

Still cautious, I drop my rucksack on the floor and drag over the second chair. I hold out my hand for the bottle, give it a deep drink, then wipe my mouth. "It does the job."

The corner of his mouth curls, but the smile doesn't quite reach his eyes. After a tense silence, he says, "We need to talk about what happened at the arena."

He looks uncomfortable in the simple wooden chair. And no wonder. This is his first time in the game warden's residence. Before, I lived in the army barracks, and in the evenings, we'd sit in his fine leather club chairs with plush carpet underfoot, not these rickety wooden things.

I clear a sticky clump in my throat. "Sabine's godkiss is remarkable, but she doesn't understand the full extent of it. Her magic overtook her. She couldn't control her actions."

"I'm not talking about the tiger." He swipes back the bottle and waves it dismissively in the air. "If I dwelled on all the times a woman's tried to kill me, I'd have no time for rounds of Hazard."

A log pops in the fire. I skate the hearth a nervous look.

There's no way any scraps of Lord Charlin's letter remain in there, but the ashes still make me jumpy.

Rian suddenly slams the bottle onto the floor. "I mean how you held her like a plucked damn wildflower."

The words rattle across my bones. He must have heard me call her "little violet." I'd hoped that in the chaos, everyone would forget how she and I had clung to one another like swallows in a hurricane.

I have to tread carefully now. By the scent of his breath, Rian isn't so drunk yet that his own senses are lacking.

"I'm her bodyguard." I dismiss it with a snort as I kick my feet up on the hearth. "She's safe, isn't she?"

He slides me a look stonier than the chimney bricks. For a long moment, the fire crackles between us, throwing out heat that makes sweat break out on my brow. "People are saying it looked intimate."

I scoff, raking back my hair. "She was possessed by her magic. I was trying to snap her out of it. Fucking gods, this is what I get for doing my job? Come on, Rian. You know she hates me. In fact, I think she hates me even more than she hates *you*."

"Hmm." He pushes to his feet and takes his time strolling around the cottage's small space, poking through the meager pantry, then absently sifting through the maps on the table. The knots in my chest start to loosen when he snaps his gaze back to me and says, "*Tamarac.*"

It's our old boyhood word for complete honesty with one another. When we used that term, it was the only time I ever knew the Lord of Liars was being truthful—and that he expected truth from me in return.

"*Tamarac,*" I repeat cautiously, afraid of his next words.

"She told me about the kiss."

Ice crystalizes in my veins so that I'm not even sure I can move—my heart has frozen, and with it, every breath in my body. "What?"

"Sabine told me you kissed her on the journey from Bremcote. She admitted it. Quite readily, in fact."

All at once, the ice in my veins snaps, and shards of molten blood sprint through my body instead. My heart squeezes like a fist against my lungs.

Sabine told him?

I have no right to feel betrayed after everything I did to her, but still, I do. Maybe she does hate me so much that she wants me to rot in the dungeon. Hell, I'd deserve it.

And yet, something about it doesn't feel right. Sabine could have confessed our affair to Rian at any point before now, and she didn't.

She hates me, but she loves me, too. I know it from the way her pulse springs to life when I'm close, like flowers stretching open to the morning sun. The only way she would tell Rian about our affair was if he threatened her. And the one thing I can't have is for Sabine to be in danger.

I saunter over to join him at the map table, buying time while my mind claws around for answers.

Finally, I confess, "Look. It was a stupid mistake. I was drunk off ale at an inn. She immediately rejected me, for what it's worth." I drag a hand down my face, hoping it hides my tells. "Anyway, I have a girl at the Velvet Vixen."

The gears in his mind churn, calculating any lies. He says slowly, "I didn't know you had a girl. What's her name?"

My throat closes up like a fist. "Carlotte. Spreads her legs easy and doesn't complain that I kill animals for a living. *That's* the type I like."

It's a plausible lie. Everyone at the Velvet Vixen would

confirm I'm a client of Carlotte's, and Carlotte herself would play along for the right price.

I make a mental note to send her some coin first thing in the morning.

The wind rattles the panes and snakes down the chimney to make the fire flicker. I cram my hands in my pockets so Rian can't see how hard I'm clenching them. Somewhere outside, an owl hoots.

Rian takes another long swig from the whiskey and then extends it to me as a peace offering.

His half-smile curves in a boyish way. "I understand. Sabine is a beautiful woman, and you *are* a horny bastard. Just don't let it happen again, or you'll find yourself one of the sixteen contestants in the Everlast."

I huff out a nervous laugh as I take the bottle. "No worries there. *You're* stuck with her quick-tempered ass, and I don't envy you."

He laughs, too, but it doesn't fully ease the tension. There's still a dark gleam in his eyes. His pulse is unnaturally steady—as though he's about to cheat someone at a game of Basel.

He rests his palms flat on the map, clearing his throat as though the topic of me kissing his intended is done.

But something tells me it's far from done.

"This is the route you're taking north?"

I nod, still on high alert, but I have no choice but to play along.

Tracing my line along my charted course, I say, "I'll hike up by Runhaven village where the goldenclaw abducted the godkissed girl. Then, I'll continue to the wall's westernmost checkpoint, and follow the wall to checkpoint at Havre Peak. That's a twenty-five-mile stretch of the border. Given the dense growth, it should take about four days."

Rian flips through the underlined copy of the Book of the Immortals with middling interest until he stops on an illustration of a goldenclaw.

The beast is twice the size of any normal bear. Its fur is fine, spun-gold filaments edged as sharp as needles. Five scythe-like claws cap each appendage and can be used as either hooks or blades. There's no way of knowing how accurate the drawing is, however, since the last goldenclaw went to sleep a thousand years ago. And this book can't be more than fifty years old.

"I'm coming with you," Rian says with a casual scratch on his chin.

My body frosts over with a numbing chill like he's just announced we're going to war. My hands fist deep in my pockets, my fingers flexing against my palms like I might find the right words to say if I just dig enough.

"There's—there's no need for that, my lord. I can handle whatever danger lurks at the wall. In any case, you're needed here. That ass of a Grand Cleric, Beneveto, is lying through his teeth about Joruun's health. The king could die at any moment, and if the King's Council declares Astagnon a theocracy..."

Rian slams the book closed, making me flinch. A thin smile hardens his lips. "Exactly. That's my point. If I'm to be king of Astagnon, I should know what dangers our kingdom faces, shouldn't I?" He slaps me hard on the shoulder. "Besides, it'll be an adventure, like old times."

The playfulness of his tone doesn't extend to his eyes.

A paranoid part of me can't help but worry that this is about Sabine and our confessed kiss. If only I knew exactly what details he'd wrung out of her—if only I could talk to her to get our stories straight, but Rian insisted Maximan guard her, too, for "extra security."

What if she told him about the full affair? That I was going to run away with her and betray my duties? How I climbed the tower to bed her as recently as a few days ago?

If Rian knows about the whole affair, then deep in the remote Blackened Forest would be the perfect place for murder.

It takes effort to swallow around the lump in my throat. I manage a rasping, "As you wish, my lord."

He takes out his Golath dime, flipping it over his knuckles in an effortless roll, little finger to thumb, little finger to thumb, then tosses the coin in the air and stashes it back in his pocket.

He swipes up the sloshing whiskey bottle.

"To what lies north."

He takes a deep sip, then passes me the bottle. His flinty eyes bore straight into my innermost sanctum.

I throw back a drink of the liquid fire. "To what lies north. Whatever it may be."

Let's hope, I think as the alcohol burns down my throat, *that it isn't my death.*

I spend all night hoping Rian will change his mind, but sure enough, the next day, when I show up at the Valvere stables at the ass crack of dawn, he's there with his horse's saddle-bags already packed.

"Sleep in?" he asks wryly.

"Ah, fuck off. It's practically still nighttime."

Rian wears loose-fitting riding clothes with a simple sentinel captain's jacket. His usual swipe of blue eyeliner is gone. He looks younger like this. It could almost be ten years ago, the two of us setting off on a wayward adventure. He's twenty-eight to my twenty-six now, but it feels like lifetimes since we were those puckish boys.

Rian gives a wink that almost feels like old times.

The soft crunch of straw underfoot steals my attention. A second later, the smell of violets tickles my nose.

Sabine enters the stable with Maximan trailing behind her, one hand resting on his sword hilt, and I swear my fucking heart stalls.

She wears an oversized wool sweater around her dress for the early morning chill. Her hair is down and loose. For a second, she looks as bare-faced and innocent as our days together in the forest, and my body aches with longing all the way to my teeth.

"Lady Sabine." There's a vein of surprise beneath Rian's smooth tone. "When I told you I was leaving, I didn't expect you to wake early to see me off."

"Nonsense," she says evenly. "I said I would give you a chance to prove your sincerity. I keep my promises."

Rian's horse stamps, and Rian strokes its long neck. In the second his attention is diverted, Sabine's eyes dart to me briefly—but I catch it.

She continues, "You're going to a border with a cursed land. No one has been there for centuries. There are ancient beasts in the woods. Of course, I came to say goodbye—" She pauses for a beat too long. "—Rian."

My heart tightens with hope that her words are meant for me, not him.

I busy myself saddling my horse, Dare, to stay out of

their way, but every inch of my body is attuned to her. Without meaning to, I keep track of her steady pulse, her soft breaths. There's a trace of mint tea on her lips, and I want so badly to taste it.

Rian takes her hand to brush a kiss against her knuckles. "Don't you have some parting words for Wolf, too?"

There's an edge to his voice. The air goes so still I can feel every horse's heart pumping away in their chests.

Don't say anything, Sabine, I urge her. *He's baiting you. Baiting us.*

"For Wolf?" She shoots me a glare beneath her long lashes. "Why, of course. Wolf, I hope you're eaten by a gold-enclaw, long and painfully, and left for the crows."

Rian's mouth curves ever so slightly.

The next stall over belongs to Myst. The mare hangs her head over the stall gate, munching on hay while watching the three of us like we're actors in a new stage production about star-crossed lovers.

I gently shove her snout away.

She snorts in objection, briefly disappears, then returns with a fresh mouthful while she continues to watch the show.

Rian warns Sabine, "Remember, you aren't to work with the monoceros while I'm gone. It's too dangerous on your own."

"Relax, my lord. I won't." She rests her hands around Rian's neck.

Like this, she's facing me over his shoulder. Our eyes meet. Desire slams into me like one of Dare's grumpy kicks. It takes effort not to reach out to her physically.

I focus instead on tightening Dare's girth strap, letting

my loose hair curtain my face, with the hope that Rian will forget I'm even here.

"Can't I give my fiancé a kiss before he leaves?" she murmurs.

My eyes briefly close, the ache almost unbearable. And I'll keep them closed, because the last thing I want is to see her lips on his.

"That depends," Rian says wryly, "if you're wearing poisoned lipstick."

But his tone is jesting—Rian is too arrogant to think any woman wouldn't want to kiss him. Sure enough, I hear the rustle as he slides a hand behind Sabine's waist. I groan inwardly, cursing my godkiss.

My eyes might be closed, but my other senses paint a crystal-clear picture of their embrace. The rasp of his lips on hers. The shift in the air as she tips back her head. The flutter of her heartbeat—

Calm down, Wolf, I tell myself.

Her heartbeat has a lighter thump, which means she's afraid, not aroused, and I'm so fucking relieved that I could curse.

She's doing this whole act to protect us both from Rian's suspicions.

My clever little violet.

Rian and I mount, and Sabine lifts a hand in farewell as we urge our horses into a canter. As soon as we plunge deep into the morning fog, I try to put her out of my mind, but it's as useless as chasing shadows under a new moon.

The city is quiet this early. In the market, the fishmonger and bread carts are out, but everything else is still sleepily stumbling to its feet.

We shouldn't need to stop for supplies during the trek; I

packed provisions for four days, as well as the maps and as many weapons as I could stuff into the saddlebags. There's no telling what we'll face at the border wall. Volkish raiders? Starleons and their plague dust? A goldenclaw twice the size of a regular bear?

And the greatest danger might be my companion . . .

Rian and I talk little until we're outside the city walls and over the crest into the Darmarnach Valley. The mountain peaks rise above the valley fog like they're suspended in the clouds. The road gets rockier here, and the horses slow to a walk.

"Fucking breakfast sausage," Rian says, pressing a hand against his stomach. "I ate too fucking much."

"You know," I point out, "when you're king, you'll have to watch the filthy things that come out of your mouth."

He snorts. "Fuck that."

We share a wicked grin that feels only slightly forced. The thorny brambles that constrict my chest ease, and I wonder if my worries are overblown. Rian and I have fought over women before; though granted, not his fiancée.

Still, all he knows about is a kiss. What is one lapse of judgment against nearly twenty years of trust?

In the afternoon, the trail takes us deep into the mountains, where it ends at a ramshackle village, and we have to blaze our own path from there. That night, we make camp at the outskirts of the Blackened Forest, then push on the next day through dense foliage and difficult terrain until, finally—

The border wall is in sight.

The horses come to a sudden halt, unwilling to continue.

Rising thirty feet high, the wall's formidable structure seems to scrape the clouds. Nearly five hundred years of history are etched into its weathered stones. Slick moss hugs every stone, and entire trees have taken root in its deepest crevices, their contorted roots trailing vine-like into worn-away pockets of collected rainwater.

A heavy mist clings to the wall, but its color is too bluish to be fog, and it crackles every few seconds with protective energy wards.

We dismount under the wall's oppressive hush.

It's cold in the wall's shadow, like a deep cave where the sun never touches.

A strange, sharp cry of a bird pierces the evening from the Volkish side of the wall, and a rash of chills crops up my forearms.

As a precaution, I tug the kerchief knotted around my neck to cover my mouth and nose. The ancient wards are supposed to prevent birds from flying over, but that plague wing starleon in Blackwater had to have gotten here somehow.

Rian tosses a stone as far as he can over the wall. It sails twenty feet high before plinking against the bricks, not high enough to scale it.

"Stand back and see how it's done." I throw next, and my rock clears the top of the wall—but hits a gathering mist that plinks it right back at me.

I observe, "Looks like the old wards still hold. So, the raiders didn't climb over the wall. They got into Astagnon some other way."

The wind tumbles the leaves around us in a quaking dance that makes me jumpy, like we're being watched.

"We'll make camp here." Rian kicks aside twigs for a makeshift fire ring. "In the morning, we'll head east along the wall. Should be able to reach the Havre Peak checkpoint before nightfall."

"Not if the foliage is as dense as this." I point to the knotted brambles hugging the wall that would even hobble a dog. "We'll be lucky to hike five miles tomorrow, especially staying close enough to the wall to check for breaches."

Rian groans as he tosses sticks into a kindling pile. "Tomorrow is for tomorrow's problems, Wolf. Now dig out the good whiskey, let's get a fire going to warm my balls, and once we're good and drunk, tell me every filthy detail about how a whore at the Velvet Vixen tamed Duren's notorious Lone Wolf."

For a second, it feels like old times. This was us as wayward teens, thinking we were indestructible as the gods. That we could drain a bottle of whiskey between the two of us and still be ready for sparring drills in the morning.

A part of me misses those times with a pain equal to the old injury in my shoulder.

But those times are gone.

Because we aren't boys anymore, and for all his playful grins, one of us might not make it out of this forest alive.

CHAPTER 11

SABINE

On the first night after Basten and Rian left for the border, I sat through the worst supper of my life. Rian's presence at supper is usually a dull thorn; his absence, somehow, was an even sharper one. The food looked delectable—succulent roasted boar, buttery rosemary vegetables, almond cake—and it might have even tasted as such, but the bile rising up my gullet made everything feel like sand against my tongue.

Old Lady Eleonora was drunk enough to be mean but not so sloshed as to nod off and leave us in peace. She spit insults at Lady Runa's thickening waist until Runa swiped a wine bottle and stormed off. Lady Solvig and Lord Gideon spent the entire meal slandering the poor for failing to pay the recently raised tax rate. But worst of all, naturally, was Lord Berolt. Every bite my future father-in-law took, eyes glued to my neckline, he licked his lips.

So, on the following evening, I feign an upset stomach to escape to Myst's stable. Maximan shadows me, of course, but he gives me the small blessing of standing guard outside, where I can almost forget he's there.

The barn's quiet is heavenly. From the kitchen, Brigit sneaks out a tray of cheese and wine for us, and apples for Myst. Against Brigit's protests, I force her to join me for the meal. We even have a stowaway: my little forest mouse pokes her nose out of Brigit's apron pocket and hones in on the cheese.

We kick back our heels on the soft, fresh hay pile in Myst's kingly stall and nibble and sip and giggle the evening away until my head spins delightfully.

A maid. A horse. A mouse.

It might not look like much of a family, but to me, it's as close as I've come since my mother died. I have Charlin's blood, sure, but there's no love between us. And the convent? "Sisters" was a misnomer if I've ever heard one. Those women treated me worse than a thieving stranger.

After downing just half a glass of wine, Brigit falls asleep in the hay, muttering in her sleep about the shepherd boy who's caught her eye. The mouse curls up in Brigit's pocket to sleep, too.

Myst's jaw stretches in a contented yawn, her belly full of apples.

Lazily picking straw out of my hair, I gaze up at the terra cotta tile ceiling, letting my wine-addled thoughts unfurl.

Nighthoof? I ask tentatively.

Myst swivels her ears at me. *Are you drunk?*

I'm not drunk! I wag my finger at her, though it wobbles a little, belying my point. *I'm trying to guess the monoceros's name. What about Madoc?*

She snorts.

Strikker?

A stamp of her hoof.

Bane?

Her head tosses dismissively. ***You will know when you know.***

I sigh as I sink back into the hay. Could she *be* any less help? I've run through so many name possibilities: Storm. Shadowfall. Darkken. Brim. None of them *feel* right, but how would I know?

And what if I say the wrong name? Will the monoceros burn me alive with fey fire?

I puff air to blow the hair out of my eyes, then reach for the wine bottle, only to find it's empty. Brigit and the mouse snore softly in unison. The night is still, unbroken by Duren's city noises. My thoughts sway like reeds in a current, drifting across the city wall to the borderlands.

What is Basten doing now? I imagine him roasting freshly caught game over a fire, his senses at ease with the calm of the woods. Chitters of chipmunks. Smells earthy and mild, just how he likes it.

Rian is probably splayed out across the fire, reclining on a fur coverlet while Basten does all the heavy lifting, regaling Basten or anything with ears about his schemes to become king.

They're like sun and moon, the two of them. Basten, as guardian of the night, moves with the grace of moonlight on fallen leaves. Whereas Rian is bright as high noon, his ambition casting a long shadow all the way to Hekkelveld Castle. And then there's me. Like the earth hanging somewhere in between their worlds. We're as linked as celestial bodies.

My eyes sink closed as my mind drifts further. The straw is warm and yielding beneath me. My fingers find a stray piece, twirling it languidly.

Basten. Rian. Would one be the same without the other?

Would *I* be the same?

"Lady Sabine." An amused female voice interrupts my daydreaming. "Hiding out, are you? Shouldn't you be at supper?"

I jolt upright, straw flying everywhere.

Ferra Yungblood smiles down at me over the stall gate with a teasing curl to her gold-lined lips.

"Ferra! I was just resting—" As I struggle to stand, my boot kicks over the empty wine bottle, which clatters to the floor, rousing the mouse temporarily.

Huh? The mouse says. ***What? Zzzz . . . .***

Ferra chuckles. "You needn't make up excuses for me." She drapes her elbows over the stall door. "If *you* get to escape that torture session they call supper, then I do, too. But sprawling in hay? With your maid and a field mouse? You're to be the High Lady of Duren!" She folds her silk-clad arms over her chest, tutting teasingly, then darts a mischievous look toward the door. "Can you escape your bodyguard?"

My nose wrinkles warily. "Why?"

She unlatches the stall door and taps her elegant, impractically crystal high-heeled shoe on the floor. "Because I'm taking you out, that's why."

I blow another errant strand of hair out of my face. "Out . . .where?"

She blinks her lavender eyes with disdain at my meager supper. "My lady, you're free of the High Lord for the night. You should be doing much more than wallowing in straw with cheese."

Popping a bite in my mouth, I protest, "But it's *Brie*."

She snorts before leaning in conspiratorially. "There are far tastier sins."

Tipsy, I swallow down the bite, unsure what to make of Ferra's tone. For a girl who slept on moldy straw for twelve years, a full belly and a quiet night with Myst *is* a sinful delight.

Ferra claps her hand as if it's decided. "If you're to be the Lady of Duren, it's high time you get to know the real city under your command. I mean, it's only *practical*."

I give her a doubting look. "Rian would allow that?"

"Pssh." She flicks a dismissive hand. "Rian is twenty miles deep into the Blackened Forest. You aren't a prisoner here—the Valveres go out on the town all the time. You're allowed your own fun."

Something tells me the Valveres would strongly disagree, but it's true that they've never expressly forbidden me from leaving Sorsha Hall. Under a bodyguard's care, I'm free to walk to the Valvere stables to visit Myst, even to ride her around the hedge maze or the army barracks outside the walls.

I try to sober up as I think about how to give Maximan the slip. Eyeing the long row of stalls, then Brigit and the mouse, a sly grin slides over my face.

"Leave Maximan to me," I say, standing up.

She claps in delight, then turns me by the shoulders one way then another, frowning down at my gown. "We'll have to hide your dress—those embroidered wings will give you away, and we can't very well explore if the whole town is flocking to see the Winged Lady. A cloak should do the trick. As for your hair . . ."

"I can braid it to hide the length," I volunteer, already separating the strands with nimble fingers. "At the convent,

I wore it up to do farm chores . . .see?" I secure the simple hairstyle with a pin.

Ferra tugs on one fae-capped ear as though she couldn't possibly have heard correctly. "Did you say 'farm chores,' my lady?"

I count off on my fingers casually. "Mucking the goat barn. Weeding the raspberry patch. Pressing apples for cider —and I wasn't allowed a sip!"

"Dear gods." Ferra's horror isn't feigned, but it quickly gives way to a wicked smile. "Well, you'll try cider tonight, or Immortal Popelin isn't the God of Pleasure."

All it takes to distract Maximan is quietly unlatching the stalls, politely asking the horses to stampede out the rear entrance, and then having Brigit scream about a fire while the mouse kicks up dust to look like smoke.

Ferra and I? We just waltz out amidst the mayhem.

Easy.

At night, Duren transforms from a dusty market town to an enchanted realm. Painted paper lanterns bob in the breeze on ropes spanning the streets. Their lights dance on townspeople below spilling out of shops and stopping to greet friends.

Amidst the labyrinthine alleyways, shadows play hide-and-seek with the children and dogs that scamper home. The smell of woodsmoke and night-blooming jasmine fill the air. Music flows out of taverns on every street corner.

As I marvel at the scrumptious smells coming from a roasted hazelnut cart, Ferra laughs. "Is this your first night out in Duren, my lady?"

"Rian took me to Popelin's Gambit once," I say distractedly, craning my neck to peer down an alley at a fortuneteller in full fae regalia.

"Popelin's Gambit? Pssh. Then you haven't been out in the *real* Duren."

I bury a frown. Granted, I realize I've been sequestered most of my life, but I thought my night out with Rian was suitably disrespectful. The whores were high-class but still shoved their tits in men's faces. The sweet reek of opium clung to the walls. And the gods know how Rian held me in his lap, whispering filthy things in my ear . . .

I pull my cloak's hood higher to cover my warming cheeks.

Ferra's lavender eyes light up at a wooden sign swinging from a tavern. A fresh red ribbon forms a bow on the door handle.

She croons, "Ohh! Perfect. In here." Before I can object, she herds me through the doorway into a crowded tavern.

At first glance, the only scandalous thing about the pub is the way "Imortal Tavern" is misspelled on the sign. It doesn't appear much different from the taverns that Basten and I stopped at for meals on the road from Bremcote, with wooden tables and benches, a fire crackling in the hearth, and a rosy-cheeked barkeep with hair pulled into a messy knot.

As Ferra smooshes next to me onto a bench near a small, empty stage—the last two open seats in the place—the only thing that strikes me as odd is that the vast majority of patrons are female.

Most wear simple homespun dresses colored with vegetable dye, though there are a few cloaked women, like us, who I suspect are wealthier courtesans.

Laughter and chatter fill the cozy common room, along with the sound of earthenware glasses clinking, and a single guitar player crammed in the corner.

"Hey! Two ciders!" Ferra shouts to a circling barmaid laden down with empty glasses, and flashes a silver coin to ensure she has the girl's attention.

Peeking out from my cloak's hood, I ask, "Why was there a red ribbon on the door?"

Ferra's eyes twinkle. "It means the tavern is hosting a dramatics tonight. That's why there are so many female patrons."

"A dramatics? Is that like a play?"

A wicked crinkle plays at her lips. "Something like that. Wait and see—it should start soon. Oh! Thank you." She accepts two flagons of cider from the barmaid and shoves one in my hands. "Down the hay chute, farmgirl."

My head is still floating from the earlier wine, but I can't see any reason not to partake. Don't I deserve this? All those years of mashing apples so the Sisters could get drunk, and not a drop for me?

The cider is sweet and effervescent and entirely too drinkable. Before I know it, half the flagon is gone.

I sway, more than a little tipsy, but who do I have to behave for?

Grinning, I clink my cup against Ferra's.

It isn't long before a man steps onto the stage. A hush, punctuated by drunken giggles, falls over the crowd.

He's a young, muscular figure with a preening attractiveness, adorned in heavy fae makeup. His costume, consisting of leather pants and a bow over his bare chest, unmistakably portrays him as Immortal Artain, God of the Hunt.

I guzzle more cider, wiping my chin as I eye his well-honed muscles. It's becoming very clear why this all-female audience is all titters.

"Ladies!" the actor exclaims, hands sweeping out theatrically. "Tonight, we present reenactments from the Book of the Immortals for your, ah, *educational* pleasure. Brace yourselves first for the tale of the Night Hunt!"

Excited squeals pop up around us, along with nervous laughter from more demure audience members.

My face pales. Everyone knows the Night Hunt story. It's the tale of Immortal Artain as he tracks a doe from dawn to dusk until the first star emerges, at which time the doe transforms into Immortal Solene, Goddess of Nature. After a little coy resistance, she's all too ready to let him catch her and, suffice it to say, he ends up piercing her with something that *isn't* an arrow.

I whisper to Ferra, "Of all the stories in the Book of the Immortals, they chose this one for public display?"

She pats my knee. "My lady, the scandal is the *point*."

I hiccup, blink, then grin.

The actor playing Artain steps aside for a scantily-clad actress to take his place. Her heavy makeup and wig make it impossible to tell if she's young or old, pretty or plain. Two antlers rise from her head, attached to a ribbon tied around her chin. Brown and white paint dotting her cheeks gives her the look of a fawn. When she scampers from painted tree to painted tree, her gauzy dress's high slits flash bare thighs.

Artain leaps back on stage, drawing his flimsy prop bow. "Ho, there! Yield to me, woodland creature, or prepare to feel my *tip!*"

The audience snickers louder.

The actress gasps and freezes before the drawn bow. "Spare me, kind archer, for I am a mere fawn searching for a warm den for the night."

Artain strides over to her, lowering his bow as he grips her thigh, tugging it around his waist so her slitted skirt parts.

"A fawn?" the actor bellows. "You do not fool me, my fae sister. Now, transform into your true self!"

Thankfully, the ancient fae speak of one another as "brother" and "sister" in the metaphorical sense; otherwise, this scandalous scene would be *truly* torrid.

The actress squeals as he tears off her antler headband and tosses it aside. Two more actors jump up with a bed sheet, waving it like a mist as the actress sneaks off stage.

"Show yourself, Solene, Goddess of Nature!" Artain commands.

The assistants drop the sheet, but the actress has crawled behind the tavern's bar. Artain stands tall, shading his eyes as he scans the crowd of gathered women.

"Alas, where are you in your maiden form, fair Solene? Is that you there, in the periwinkle gown?" He points his arrow toward a portly woman in the front row, who squeals as she clamps her hands over her mouth.

"Is that you, you tricky fawn?" His arrow whirls to point at a thin girl with a harelip, who blushes.

Women in the audience thrust their hands in the air, waving enthusiastically.

"Here, Artain!"

"It's me, Solene!"

"Come stick me with your *arrow*!"

My eyes are fixed on the performer, but my thoughts drift, unbidden, to Basten. The other hunter who haunts me.

Mouth dry, I down another sip of cider, but it's starting to cloy in my belly. I can almost feel Basten's broad hand, as bare as the actor's, gripping my thigh. The rasp of his lips on my cheek. The thunder of my heartbeat when he chased me through the woods . . .

Suddenly, I feel an unexpected tug at my arm. One of the assistants, grinning widely, begins to tug me toward the stage.

"Here, Artain!" the assistant calls. "I found her! Solene is here!"

Disoriented, I swivel around toward Ferra, reaching a hand toward her like a lifeline.

"What? Wait!" I breathe. "I don't know—"

Ferra snatches the flagon out of my hand and nudges me toward the stage with one graceful, crystal shoe. "Enjoy yourself, my lady!"

As the crowd erupts in bawdy whistles, the half-naked actor playing Artain grins devilishly at me, slowly pointing his arrow straight at my heart. Thrust forward by the assistant, I stumble on stage, pulse thrashing between my ears. The combination of alcohol and the heady crowd makes my head roar. Laughter and cheers from the audience echo in my ears, but they sound distant, muffled.

"I've got you now, Goddess. Yield to me!"

Artain pulls me close with a bulging bicep until I'm straddling his leg like the scantily clad actress before me. It's all I can do with every eye in the establishment on me not to blubber like a landed fish.

The actor finally nudges me in the ribs until I remember the line I'm supposed to say. Like everyone here, I know the story by heart after hearing it in countless bedtime stories.

"I . . .I do not yield," I stammer, trying to keep pace with the play.

The audience lets loose a collective gasp at my—well, Solene's—defiance, though they've all heard these words a million times.

The actor playing Artain replies, "Twice, I say, yield!"

"Twice," I echo in a stumbling voice. "I—I do not yield."

Ferra leans forward, munching roasted almonds, big eyes twinkling in amusement.

The assistants thrust a stool on stage, and Artain guides me backward until I sink onto it. He then straddles my knee, his groin about three inches from my face, as he slowly begins to peel off his flimsy belt.

"Then, fae sister, if I cannot dominate you as a hunter, I shall seduce you as a man."

My cheeks burn so red I think they must light up the whole tavern. A sheen of sweat breaks out on my brow as the actor gyrates his hips in my face, bumping his leather trousers against my chin.

Holy gods.

He whips off his belt, tossing it into the audience, where two women scrabble to catch it.

The man begins to roll his hips close to my chest, and from the whoops and calls that echo in the tavern, the women are loving this. Ferra whistles loudly between her two fingers.

I draw my cloak's hood further over my hair, mortified, wishing I could vanish into it.

Goosebumps crop up on my arms. My legs clamp together. My traitorous lower half tingles even though my upper half knows this is a ridiculous spectacle. But as the handsome actor traces his finger up my throat, tilting my chin so my eyes meet his heavily fae-lined ones, my heart still falters.

The actor suddenly grabs my waist, swings me around, and then plunks me back down in his lap facing away from him. My eyes widen as I feel the massive bulge that everyone else saw, too. He wraps a hand around my throat from behind, pantomiming kissing my jaw.

The echo of the crowd and the effects of alcohol deafen me. Dizzy, I close my eyes. Surrendering to the play. Like this, I could almost imagine I'm with Basten. That it's his hand encircling my throat. His chiseled thighs under my hips. Suddenly, I'm back in my bedroom, wrists bound to the bedposts with silken ties, Basten's talented face between my legs . . .

My breath comes faster as I adjust my hips on the actor's lap. His hands worship places he shouldn't touch—my ribs, my thighs, my throat.

"Thrice, now, I ask you," he projects loudly for the audience. "Do you yield?"

My lips part. I know the line I'm supposed to say. I can even hear the closest women in the audience whisper it under their breaths.

"Once. Twice. Thrice. And forevermore, I yield."

But the words catch behind my teeth. This is all too much. I squirm on the stool. Embarrassed, yes. Titilated, yes. But there's something deeper rumbling in my bones, pushing at my skin like it's trying to break free. In the back of my head, strange slips of half-forgotten dreams flicker and vanish. Artain. The woods. The deer. In my addled state, the fae tale and my time with Basten blend together until this all feels unnervingly familiar.

Suddenly, I'm on my feet, stumbling down from the

stage. My legs are slack. My lips tremble. Cries from the audience chase me, but I might as well belong to another world.

I shove the tavern door, gasping for air as the cool night hits me like a splash of cold water.

A second later, Ferra tipsily barrels into the street on her crystal heels. "My lady!"

I lean back against the brick wall, guzzling deep breaths. "I'm fine. I . . .just needed air."

For a second, I'm not sure if I'm going to break into tears, my blood still burning from that strange, out-of-body sensation.

But then Ferra blurts out, "Well, no wonder you needed air; he practically had his massive cock down your throat!"

Her lips twitch, and I think of the gyrating hips in my face, and before I know it, we both collapse back against the wall in a fit of laughter.

"At least one part of him was impressive," I point out.

"It certainly wasn't his acting." Ferra leans against me, snickering. After we wipe the tears from our eyes, she tugs my hand. "Come on. You need another drink after that performance."

I laugh as I press my hand against my stomach. "Any more alcohol, and I'll turn into a pickle."

A drunk passes us, swaying as he sings an old fae ballad. Under most circumstances, I'd feel ashamed to stumble about tipsily in public, but everyone else on the Sin Streets is just as shameless. The air is a mix of thick opium smoke, dueling music from buskers, and the titter of prostitutes cajoling any man with coins jingling in his pocket. Not to mention the moans from behind curtained windows of whorehouses.

"Now, spill." Ferra's voice drops as she thrusts her arm through mine. "How does Rian's *arrow* compare to fair Artain's back there?"

I balk, mortified. "How would *I* know?"

"You intend to tell me you haven't rolled in the sheets with the man every Durish woman desires?"

"I'm not Durish," I point out.

She blasts me with a sly look. "Then maybe you can tell me all about Wolf Bowborn's, ahem, shaft?"

Breath struggles in my throat. "Ferra!"

"Oh, don't give me that. I was in the Immortal Box during the spectacle. I saw him throw you over his shoulder like he'd done it more than once."

Panic rises like a tide to drown my already watery thoughts. Basten and I would be hung if the affair was found out. Not to mention, it would end: The breathless need. The quiet touches. The looks from across a room that say I'm all he thinks about.

But it has *to end—Basten will never love me like Artain loved Solene.*

Ferra suddenly stops dead in her crystal shoes as a strange, garbled sound comes from her throat. Her attention is aimed at a street-level window. The gaudy lace curtain marks it as another brothel, but unlike the others, this curtain is cracked open.

Inside, a man with short grey hair has a woman bent over a bed, fucking her from behind, his bare ass cheeks squeezing with each thrust. The sight alone is a shock, but the moment I see what the prostitute is wearing, I under-stand why Ferra paled at this particular prostitute: The girl wears a cheap set of feathered wings and a blond wig of woven flax long enough to brush the ground.

Wings? Long hair?

It's supposed to be me.

A crackle roars between my ears as I stumble, catching myself on a wooden crate. I don't think this moment can get any worse until the man slaps the whore's ass, tilting his head just enough so his profile comes into view.

My stomach drops.

Save me, any of the ten gods who might be listening . . .

The man in that brothel is my future father-in-law.

Lord Berolt Valvere.

Fucking a whore dressed up to look like *me*.

Ferra and I stare at the cracked curtain, speechless, as a group of off-duty soldiers curses us for blocking the sidewalk.

My stomach cramps—the wine threatening to come back up—and a strange noise crawls up my throat. Ferra suddenly seizes me by the arm and drags me toward the upbeat music of the nearest gambling den.

"Oh! Um, look!" Her voice is high, forced. "I, uh, love this place. I come here *all* the time. It's the—" She has to check the name on the sign. "Serpent and Scepter!"

We thrust inside the bustling warmth of a gambling den, where clinking coins and glistening candles dazzle my eyes but are not nearly enough of a distraction. All I can see when I blink is that revolting scene of Lord Berolt slapping that winged woman's ass until it was red.

"Here!" Ferra swipes a glass of champagne from a mustachioed man who's too drunk to notice. She forces it into my hands.

I guzzle the champagne. Anything to drown out that image. But then, my stomach forcefully objects. At the beginning of the night, drinking felt defiant, but now, it brings only sour notes of regret.

I double over, taking deep breaths as Ferra rubs my back.

I hate this city. I hate this family. I hate—

A woman's chirping voice rings out in front of me. "Sabby? Is that *you*?"

I jolt upright. My childhood nickname? No one has used that for years. A cheerful figure with walnut brown skin bounces in front of me, chattering away faster than my spinning head can make sense of.

I stutter, "S—*Suri*?"

Lady Suri Darrow beams at me. What is my father's wife doing here? It's hard to believe she's technically my stepmother since she's only two years older than me. In the short time we spent together after I was released from the convent, we always felt more like instant friends than forced family.

Suri clutches my hands as she bounces up and down on her toes. "It *is* you, Sabine! Oh, I've missed you more than the daffodils in spring!"

I brace myself against a gaming table as my legs threaten to give out. My stomach complains again, more vociferously. "Suri? W-what are you doing here?"

"We arrived earlier in the week to visit you and Lord Rian! We've come to Sorsha Hall repeatedly, but the guards said we had to wait until Lord Rian returned from his trip, so we've been biding our time in town. It's so much more exciting here in Duren than in Bremcote!"

I squint, still not even sure Suri isn't some drunken hallucination. "Wait. *We*?"

"Your father is here, too, of course."

She points behind me.

Frowning, I spin around and come face to face with my father at a Basel table. Dwindling pile of coins at his side. Scowl on his face. Red cheeks from too much gin.

His watery eyes lift to meet me, filled with nothing but hatred for his daughter.

And suddenly, I'm ten years old again, about to be shipped off to a convent, my mother's body still fresh in the grave.

Before I know it, bile shoots up my throat, and I lurch forward, emptying the night's contents all over my father's losing hand of cards.

CHAPTER 12
WOLF

On the third day of our trek, I'm proven right. The forest's undergrowth is a complete bitch.

Bayberry briars smother the steep slope that runs south of the wall, like nature has cast out nets to ensnare us. Roots catch my horse's hooves with every step. Thorns as sharp as Golath blades shred my clothes and carve up the skin beneath. Within hours, every inch of our exposed skin is hatched with red welts—and the horses, too.

We dismount, pasturing the horses as close to the wall as we can, and continue on foot.

Though a preternatural chill clings to the wall's southern shadow, trekking through the brush is a chore, and sweat soon pastes my shirt to my chest.

Every hundred paces, one of us throws a rock over the wall to make sure the mist-like protective wards still hold. The rocks clear the top but hit crackles of bluish energy and are cast right back down to us. We make a contest out of it, and Rian gets pissed when twice as many of my throws clear the wall's top as his.

By the time dusk falls, we're both exhausted. We've seen no sign of breaches. The wall is old but structurally sound. No rope ladders hang over the edge. In fact, there's no indication at all of how the raiders have been getting across.

We're both irritable and snappy until we make camp and get a spit-roasted rabbit sizzling over the fire. I unhook the spit from the iron loop that holds the rabbit over the coals, sensing by its smell that it's finished. We pluck greasy chunks of meat from the stick with our bare fingers like we're carefree boys once more. Once we finally have some meat in our bellies, trading the bottle of whiskey back and forth, the day's strain finally falls away.

Kicking out my feet, I jest, "By my count, it's your turn to entertain tonight with tales of your sexual conquests. So, who's been wetting your cock these days?"

Though I keep my tone light, I know I'm treading dangerous territory. This is as close as I can get to asking about his intimacy with Sabine without raising suspicion against me.

He takes his time licking the grease off a bone. "Who says my cock is getting wet at all?"

I snort. "You? In fifteen years, I haven't known you to go seven hours without a fuck."

"I'm telling the truth," he insists. "I haven't slept with anyone since signing Sabine's engagement contract. I'm doing it right this time, Wolf. I vowed to be a respectable husband."

I give Rian a sideways glance, skepticism practically dripping from my gaze. Respectable? Rian? It's like saying a fox in the henhouse is just admiring the decor. But I'll be damned; my intuition's sharper than a knife, and it's telling me he's not lying this time.

"*Tamarac*?" I ask.

"*Tamarac*," he vows.

As I mull over this, stripping the rabbit down to bare bones, something doesn't sit right in my chest. Not just about Rian, but our dinner. Guilt? Over killing a rabbit? A man needs to eat—it's simply nature. Even Sabine, who's as gentle as a spring fucking breeze, eats meat. But ever since knowing her, my perspective on the world has shifted. A rabbit used to be a meal on legs. And now? It's a life. A soul. Folke would say that makes me soft, but there's nothing weak about the way Sabine finds worth in even the smallest mouse's life.

In fact, it might be the toughest damn thing I've ever seen.

An insect trills high in a tree, breaking my thoughts. I toss a small pebble toward the roasting spit's iron loop but miss.

I ask again, a little harder this time, with a forced grin. "So Sabine won't fuck you until there's a ring on her finger, eh?"

I shouldn't push it; if I keep testing the waters, I'm going to pass the point of being able to swim back to shore.

"Why? Are you wondering which one of us she finds the better kisser? Let me put it this way: You got a tipsy peck. I've had my tongue down her throat and my hand between her thighs."

A flare of jealousy burns up my throat until I bite my cheek so hard blood fills my mouth. I pretend to find the whiskey bottle fascinating to keep my emotions in check.

Casually, Rian reclines back, stretching out his boots

toward the fire. He tries throwing a pebble toward the iron loop and makes it this time.

"You know how Sabine intends to tame the monoceros, right?" His velvety, dark voice cuts through the smoke. "She doesn't jump on its back the first day. She gives it space. She offers it a feast after it's been starved. She moves it to a spacious stable after it's been imprisoned. It's about taking her time. Letting it get accustomed to her."

He picks up a whole handful of pebbles. Watching Rian slowly throw them at the iron loop one by one, my stomach knots with dread.

His eyes are pools of calculated ambition as he continues, "I'm going to tame Sabine Darrow the same way. Serve her a banquet at every meal. House her in a palace. She would deny that such luxuries matter to her, but I guarantee you, after what she's been through, her trauma makes her primed for even the slightest comfort. So, I'm letting her take her time to fall in love with me. Mark my words: by summer's end, she'll have the monoceros eating out of her hand, and I'll have her begging for my cock."

My fingers thrust deep into the fallen leaf cover, needing grounding to quell my anger.

He thinks he can tame her? Break her? *He doesn't know my little violet.*

I throw another pebble through the iron loop, angrily this time.

Rian throws another one, putting too much force behind it, and it sails far to the left.

"You used to have better aim," I quip, only half in jest.

"Well, I don't spend every day targeting chipmunks. I have real work." His smile is bladed as he stares into the fire.

The tension burns between us with the flames' same intensity.

He knows I kissed her.

But that's all—just a kiss.

He turns his calculating smile on me, and the firelight paints half his face in orange, half in shadow. "I bet you're rusty at a few things, too, Wolf. Come on. Spar with me. Like old times."

I snort. "Rian, for fuck's sake."

"Afraid I'll trounce you?" he goads me. There's something darker than boyish mischief in his eyes. Fuck, it's black as night, that look. It calls to the competitor in me, the boy who survived by his fists, who came to crave a bloodthirsty crowd's cheers.

He unfastens his leather breastplate, drops it on the ground, and then tugs his shirt over his head. His bare chest gleams in the twilight. Years ago, when we sparred daily, I knew Rian's body nearly as well as my own. But now he's leaner, hardened. Ridges of pure muscle have replaced any youthful plump. I have thirty pounds of muscle on him, but I know better than to underestimate his ability.

One by one, I curl my fingers into a fist as though testing out the movement. "You? Trounce *me*?"

Oh, hell no.

I tug my own shirt over my head. I roll my neck, then slap my pecks to wake up my adrenaline. Sparring right now is a bad idea, but fuck it. This tension with Rian has been building even before my return from Bremcote.

It's been building for years.

We kick aside leaves to make a clearing, then face each other. The last glow of daylight disappears beyond the border wall, which looms over us like the world's edge. An owl hoots from somewhere on the Volkish side.

Eyes locked, we circle each other. It doesn't matter that it's been years since we sparred—in an instant, it feels like no time at all has passed. My body shifts into the familiar stance like sliding on a well-worn pair of boots.

Rian moves first, lunging with a right hook. But I already tracked how he was holding his weight on his back left foot, and I duck the swing easily before countering with a jab to his ribs. He blocks the strike with a sweep of his arm as he shifts his weight to keep his balance.

We break apart, circling again.

"You'll have to be faster than that," I say with a playful smirk, though there's an edge to it. "Maybe I should wear a blindfold. Make it easier on you."

"Or I could just poke your godkissed eyes out." He gives a wicked laugh that doesn't feel like teasing.

This time, I lunge first, but he dodges. It was only a test strike, anyway. To see if his body gives away the same tells it did years ago.

While I'm watching his right hand—his dominant one—he suddenly throws an uppercut with his left, and the punch clips my chin before I can spin away.

Fuck! Where did he learn that move?

My mouth fills with blood, and my heightened taste buds burst with the iron-rich tang, underlayered by Rian's salty sweat.

I spit a line of blood into the dirt and wipe my lip, chest heaving more than I'd like.

Rian wipes sweat off his brow, too. He spits, "You gave Sabine the knife, didn't you?"

Strands of my hair have worked loose, and I rake them

back out of my eyes. A smart man would deny it, but I'm sick of all the lies.

I growl, "Someone had to keep her safe."

His eyes narrow. "What's that supposed to mean?"

We keep circling each other, shifting our weight in anticipation of one another's blow. "It means you dropped her into a den of vipers. The way your father looks at her . . ."

I bite off my words before I say something that's going to spike my anger to an uncontrollable level. Lord Berolt's fascination with godkissed people, paired with his lust toward beautiful young women, are a powder-keg combination in Sabine.

I murmur darkly, "Let's not forget the brilliant idea of having her cozy up to a lethal beast."

"Sabine can handle herself with the monoceros."

"I know she can! That woman is a force of nature. But you're riding her like a thoroughbred in a race that's too fast, too soon."

Rian shakes his head slowly. "Wow. You *really* want to fuck her, don't you?"

I see red at his words. I can't help it. Suddenly I'm a feral beast ramming my full weight into his solar plexus. His lungs deflate like a punctured sail as I tackle him. Our damp arena of mud and rotting leaves fill my nostrils with a primordial scent that stokes a wild edge in me.

We roll and struggle, sweat-slick muscles tangled, each trying to gain the upper hand. Sticks and rocks dig into my back as Rian momentarily wrestles me into a takedown, but I dig a foot into solid ground and use the momentum to shove my lower half up, taking him with me. But before I can pin him, he throws an elbow into my jaw.

I curse and spit out even more blood, falling back to the far perimeter of our ring.

The thick of night has fallen. Our wrestling has taken us far from the campfire's glow. But with my sight, I can see every hair on Rian's skin as if he were standing in plain daylight. It gives me the advantage, and I dodge his next swing with ease.

He growls in frustration, then lunges again with renewed vigor, trapping my neck in a lock and trying to wrestle me back down to the forest floor. As we continue to grapple, bare chests heaving against one another, all pretense of an innocent sparring match is gone.

There's menace in his eyes. Blood on my tongue. We both want Sabine, and now the words have been spoken.

I was right—this backwoods forest would be the perfect place for murder.

Did he bring me here to kill me?

A cold whisper rolls over the ground, chilling my ankles with forbidden thoughts. Maybe it's not *my* murder destined for these woods. What if his plan to win her over actually works? Sabine doesn't care about finery, but she might be drawn to his ambition.

If I want Sabine for myself, he's in the way . . .

Despite the night's chill, our bodies are hot and sweat-slick. When we come back together, I get him in a bear hug and wrestle him to the dirt, pinning his left leg with my knee as I throw my weight against his chest to keep him down. He struggles with explosive strength, but I have his hips restrained. He can't overturn me if he can't thrust upward.

"That all you got?" I breathe hot against his face. Taunting. Threatening. We're teetering on the razor's edge between roughhousing like boys and genuine, blood-boiling hatred. There's still a chance this can end with both of us walking away. A few bruises, a busted lip—nothing we haven't done to each other a hundred times.

His eyelids narrow to slits. Our tussling has rolled us even further from our campsite into brambles near the wall's base. The ancient stones smell of mossy dampness. The wards' mist shimmers over us like we've been swallowed by sparking clouds. There's so much ancient energy in the air; a deep foreboding thrum of power sends my teeth buzzing.

Rian gets one arm free and slams a punch toward my temple, but I block it with my forearm.

"You think you can be king with a weak punch like that?" I mock.

"My punch would be a hell of a lot stronger if you hadn't left my side," he spits at me. "You were supposed to always keep me sharp. *Tamarac*, remember? When I'm on the throne in Old Coros, you should be one step to my right. Not hunting fucking rabbits."

There's venom in his words, but it masks an undercurrent of pain. *Oh.* So this is what it's really about. He bent every rule to set me free from his family, and how did I return the favor? I went ahead and fell for his damn woman.

Well, I have venom in my throat, too. No one is the hero here. We're a viper and a wolf, and we always have been.

"So I can keep doing your dirty work while your kingly hands stay clean?" I yell.

"I wanted you at my side as a brother!" His shout sends a speck of spit flying onto my bare chest. His stacked muscles strain beneath my own as I struggle to keep him pinned.

Rian has brothers by blood, sure, but there's about as

much warmth there as in a blizzard. Kendan and Lore couldn't hack it under Lord Berolt's iron fist. It was either leave Duren, or someone would have ended up on the wrong end of a sword. Rian loathes his father just as much as his brothers do, but he has a knack for playing the long game with the old tyrant.

So I'm the only half-decent family Rian has, a brother not by blood but something stronger.

"My hands are just as dirty as yours, Wolf," he says in a dangerously low voice.

The wind rustles the trees overhead, raining a shower of pine needles. If the wards' mist were simply fog, it would blow away, but it remains perfectly immobile.

I can end this.

One apology, and we'll go back to the way it always was. Brothers once more. I've always been more of a sibling to him than Kendan and Lore ever have been. After all, they fled and left him alone.

Instead, a maelstrom builds in my core.

"Basten." My voice is thick. "My fucking name is *Basten*."

As adrenaline shoots through my veins, I catch him in a vicious headlock. It's time to end this, all right, but I'll be fucked if I'm going to apologize. Out here, there are no rules. No law. The strongest man wins, simple as that.

Rian tries to toss his hips up to throw me off. He gags for air against the chokehold I have him in. I dig him harder into the ground, our heads knocking together.

He manages to get a breath, then grips my head with fingers like claws, tugs me close, and screams with his full lungs in my right ear.

Fuck!

Pain stabs into my brain as I fall back, scratching at my

ear like there's a wasp buried deep inside. With my hearing, his scream was like a thunderclap against my eardrum. My right ear rings, deafened and disoriented. It throws off my balance, and Rian hauls himself to his feet and slams me backward.

"Fuck you!" I bark.

I scramble to all fours, shaking my head to try to get the ear-ringing to stop, as he smashes into me with a full body slam. We spin backward, rolling over one another further from our campsite. Briars slash our arms, spilling the acid tang of blood into the crackling mist.

We roll, and roll, and roll, continuing to grapple in the gristly mud—

—Until the mud is gone.

Everything is gone.

We're falling.

After a fevered second of weightlessness, we crash down in a tangle of bare-chested joints and elbows. Dirt clods rain down on us, tree roots swipe at us like skeletal fingers. My back slams into solid ground hard enough to kick the air from my lungs.

I'm not sure how much time passes before a groan finally eeks out of my lips.

Rian echoes my pain from a few feet away with a curse.

As we crawl to hands and feet, both struggling to pull air into our dirt-clotted lungs, I feel the tension crack. The last of my iron-fisted adrenaline was knocked out of me in the fall. The mud dulled his razor's edge fury.

Wincing, Rian sits up. It's pitch black in whatever hole we fell into, but my heightened sight tracks a line of blood flowing down his cheek. He coughs out a spray of dirt and squints up at the faintly lit circle of night overhead. We must have fallen fifteen feet.

"What the fuck is this hole?" He gives an abrasive cough. "A tomb? Did we find one of the Immortal's fucking resting places?"

In the dark, he can't see what I see: the fact that this is much more than a hole.

"No," I say darkly, eyes pinned to a passageway so freshly dug that I can still see shovel marks. "It's a tunnel."

CHAPTER 13
SABINE

Groaning, I flop back against my bed pillows and clutch my roiling stomach. "I am never drinking again."

Suri, perched on the right side of my bed, nods sympathetically, staying true to her role as my stepmother. Brigit, on my left, dabs my forehead with a cool rosewater compress while the forest mouse perches on her shoulder.

Ferra, on the other hand, smirks as she admires the jewelry box's treasures on my desk. "Give it until next weekend," she says over her shoulder, as she holds up to the light a set of emerald earrings Rian gifted me. "You'll beg me to take you out again."

Looking at my three friends, I'm struck by how much their personalities remind me of animals. It's no surprise that Brigit—quiet, hardworking, introspective—has become fast friends with the mouse. Suri, in contrast, is like a playful rabbit. Always excited to see her loved ones, content with a sunny day and a full belly. Ferra would be the butterfly of the group: Outwardly stunning in presentation, with a hidden depth overshadowed by her beauty.

"No. Never again." I forcefully shake my head but have to stop when the movement makes my head spin. "I'm actually *grateful* those stingy old Sisters kept me from the cider for all those years."

"These. Aren't. Emeralds!" Ferra suddenly announces as though she's just discovered the tomb of one of the Immortals. "They're taragite!"

Suri, Brigit, and I stare at her blankly, the word meaning nothing to our ears. She sighs at our lack of fashion knowledge before tucking the earrings back in their case, then moving on to a velvet necklace rack, where a diamond-and-gold necklace hangs from one end, with the nuthatch perched on the other.

Briefly, my cloudy mood lifts. In a million years, I never dreamed that I'd find friends in the gilded halls of Sorsha Hall. When Basten brought me here, I'd expected only more cruelty. A black-hearted fiancé. Boring political dinners. To be nothing more than an adornment, like the earrings.

Instead, between my human friends and my animal ones, I'm drowning in riches of companionship. Hell, even Rian is tolerable when separated from his family.

A warmth spreads up from my toes, wiggling under the sheets.

Despite my aching head, I grip Suri's hand.

"I'm so happy you came to Duren."

Her grin stretches, guileless and true. "We missed you, Sabby."

A shadow of my stormcloud mood momentarily returns. "You mean *you* missed me. My father couldn't care less. In twelve years, he didn't visit me once at the Convent of Immortal Iyre."

The nuthatch flits over to land on the bed covers, interested in the bowl of roasted pumpkin seeds Suri brought me to ease my stomach. Suri busies herself stroking the little bird's tail feathers, not meeting my eyes.

She finally admits, "Well, it's true that Charlin wished to have an audience with Lord Rian. Something about a letter he sent with the guard who escorted you. A debt Charlin claims Lord Rian owes him that he intends to collect."

Ah, I think. *My father's after money. That makes more sense—*

But then my brain, still muddled from the hangover, catches up with the rest of her words.

A letter? Sent with Basten?

There was no letter . . .

A tingle begins in my toes and creeps up the back of my legs until I can barely sit still, shifting beneath the covers like they're on fire. Basten said nothing about any letter from my father, I'm certain of it.

And yet, Myst saw him reading from a piece of paper in the waterfall cave while I slept. It's branded into my memory like a thorn, because after Basten read that document, he changed his mind about running away together.

What Myst saw me reading? he said. *It was the list of Lord Rian's rules for this ride. No great mystery, I assure you. It reminded me of my duty, that's all.*

My chest suddenly feels too tight. I rub my knuckles against my breastbone, needing the bite of pain to keep me from spiraling someplace darker.

"Sabine?" Suri asks, cocking her head just like the nuthatch in her palm.

I force a smile, tucking away the numbing tingle rapidly creeping up my neck, demanding I find out what that piece of paper said. But how? Basten is dozens of miles away—I can hardly throttle him for an answer.

"Well," I force a cheerful tone to mask my nerves, "Regardless of my father's motives, I'm delighted to see *you*. I hope you've been spending your time in Bremcote sleeping with some dashing young stable boy instead of rubbing my father's gouty feet."

Suri's lips part in a horrified gasp. "I would never! Not the stable boy, at least—" Abruptly, her hand clamps over her mouth, eyes widening in mortification. "I mean, no one! I wouldn't sleep with any other man. I'm the Lady of Bremcote!"

A sly grin slides across Ferra's face as she saunters over and plucks a pumpkin seed from the bowl. "Too late, my lady. You've given yourself away. Who's warming your sheets, then? A footman? The butcher's delivery boy?"

"No one!" Suri insists, her eyes big and round. She straightens her dress, taking a moment to calm herself before her voice drops to a conspiratory hush. "Not even Charlin, if I'm being honest. He starts drinking at breakfast. By mid-afternoon, he's too drunk to fuck."

Ferra licks the salt off her fingers. "And you expect us to believe a pretty young thing like yourself just goes *celibate*?"

Suri's lips press together under my and Ferra's scrutiny. Even Brigit slips her curious looks while folding my handkerchiefs.

Finally, Suri blurts out, "Oh, fine! The gardener and I have become friendly, but I swear that's all! He's from Kravada, like me. I barely know anything about my birth kingdom. He's been telling me stories about it."

From what I know of Suri's background, she came to Astagnon as a barely-weaned baby, orphaned or separated from her parents as a result of the Kravadan Civil War that displaced tens of thousands. Most headed south to the kingdoms of Clarana and Spezia, whose warm climates were closer to the deserts they were used to. Some, however, found their way into Astagnon. Suri was brought over the border under King Joruun's decree to shelter orphans, then adopted along with six other children by a wealthy noble family in Old Coros.

Ferra flounces down on the bed. "You most certainly need to fuck this gardener of yours."

Suri clasps her hands over her face, then slowly peeks above her fingers with a glimmer of mischief. All four of us burst into laughs.

A knock at the door quiets our giggles.

"That would be my delivery." Ferra jumps up to get the door, and to my surprise, it's Basten's old friend from his soldiering days. Folke—I remember him from the spectacle. Up close, his rugged features are charismatic, if not exactly handsome. His dark brown hair is peppered with gray, but the contrast has appeal.

Ferra lowers her voice. "Did you bring it?"

Folke leans against the doorframe, a half-smile on his face. "Not easy to obtain, but for a pretty lady like you, I could find the gods themselves."

Ferra huffs, perhaps protesting a bit too much. She snatches a parcel from his hands and dismisses him.

"There was mention of a favor." He reveals straight, pearly teeth. "In the form of a kiss—"

"Later." Ferra toes him backward with her crystal shoe and closes the door in his still-grinning face.

When she turns back to us, she paints on an innocent smile as if she wasn't just flirting with a known scalawag.

"This is for you, Lady Sabine." She hands me the mysterious bundle. "Brigit, could you fetch us a kettle of hot water?"

Brigit jumps up. "I'll be right back."

When she returns, Ferra unwraps a noxious-smelling cluster of orange mushrooms. Suri discreetly waves her hand beneath her nose.

"Wicken mushrooms," Ferra explains, delicately dropping them in a cup and filling it with boiling water. "Very hard to locate, but if you have a connection, they'll cure a hangover in a snap." She wrinkles her nose as she peers at the murky liquid, then thrusts the cup into my hands. "Drink up."

Though Ferra's urging got me into this mess in the first place, I dutifully hold my nose and gag down the tea. Thankfully, it tastes better than it smells, with an earthen-clay aftertaste.

She motions to the other women as I pass the cup back to her. "Time for us to be off, ladies. That'll knock out our dear Winged Lady. When you wake, Sabine, you'll feel fresh as a honey cake straight out of the oven."

"I'd settle for a three-day-old cake," I say, already yawning. "Thank you. All of you. I mean it."

Eyes already heavy, the last thing I see are the ten Immortals overhead, gazing down at me with knowing fire in their painted eyes.

~

As the tea's effects spreads, I slip in and out of sleep like an ocean tide, and in my more lucid moments, think about my father's letter. Why would Basten lie about it? What secret could it possibly contain that made him go from packing his bags to run away together, to thrusting me into his best friend's arms?

The instant he returns, I'll confront him. He'll regret giving me the knife when it's pressed against his hips, ready to sever his favorite appendage unless he's finally honest. After all this time, I'll know why he chose cruelty over love.

But what if he doesn't return?

Uneasiness weaves between my ribcage as I toss and turn, caught in half-sleep, fearing what he might uncover in the borderlands. Goldenclaws? Starleons? Volkish raiders?

As I roll to my side, my heart tightens with a brief hope that the letter's contents somehow forced Basten to lie to me. That he never would have pushed me away otherwise, and if that piece of paper didn't exist, he and I would be warming our toes in the sand while the Panopis Sea lapped at our ankles.

But as I flop back over, fisting my hand in my pillow, my stomach clenches. There's nothing that could compel Basten to abandon our plans. My life has no great secrets— I'm the daughter of a provincial landowner, and if not for a particular godkiss that Rian happened to need, no one powerful would look twice at me.

Even if, by some miracle, the letter absolved Basten of his betrayal, there would still be his cruelty to consider. His lies.

How could I ever forgive someone who hurt me as he did?

Deep sleep finally overtakes me. Thanks to Ferra's

mushrooms, I dream more fantastical dreams than ever before. I'm back on stage in the tavern, only the Night Hunt is happening in real life. I feel horns attached to my head—not fastened by a ribbon, but growing from my skull. Fawn-colored fur sprouts up on my arms. Artain's skin glows with golden fae lines as he cups the curve of my jaw and purrs low, *And now do you yield?*

CHAPTER 14
WOLF

In twenty-six years, I've never experienced pure darkness. I can see as well as a bobcat on a moonless night. When there is little or no light, the world takes on a faded hue, as if the Immortals stripped the land of color in punishment for our sins.

So, in the tunnel, my eyes easily pick out dangling tree roots clustered like cobwebs to the earthen ceiling. Pick-axe scars in the chunks of exposed bedrock. The blueish mist of the protective wards blanketing the frigid ground.

Rian, though? *Rian is fucked.*

"It's black as tar," he complains, raking dirt clods out of his hair. "I can't see my nose in front of my face."

"Take my word for it," I murmur. "Still ugly."

He makes an unpleasant sound in his throat as he pats the air, trying to find the tunnel's wall. His boots splash in puddles of groundwater seeping from above, dripping unseen in the distance. He grimaces when his hand connects to the damp, fungus-ridden dirt, but he continues to feel along until he reaches smooth stone. "What's this? It feels like there's mortar."

He's perceptive for someone who can't see. Gazing at the desaturated colors around me, I observe that most of the tunnel is dug out of soil or bedrock, but a portion is buttressed by primitive granite columns that match the stones used in the wall above.

I run the pad of my thumb over a faded inscription in one stone that looks like one of Immortal Vale's fae axe emblems—but it could be anything, even a scratch. "These are subterranean supports for the wall. Whoever dug out this tunnel in the last few years must have known there was ancient construction work that would make a tunnel possible."

"The raiders, you think?"

I pace deeper into the tunnel to inspect some shovel marks, leaning close to smell as if there might still be a trace of the diggers' presence—but there is only the musty taste of dust and trace minerals from the rocks overhead.

"The Volkish army, more likely," I say. "The digging marks here don't look like any standard shovel. It's more like deep scratch marks. Giant ones, from a tool with a metal claw."

Subtle, almost whisper-like sounds of the dirt shifting and breathing, as if alive, echo down the tunnel. There are rustles of unseen insects and vermin all around us. Thank the gods Rian can't hear them—he hates spiders.

"What about the wards?" Rian asks. "Do they hold down here?"

The soldiers who built this wall five hundred years ago weren't fools. They knew it was just as likely their enemies would tunnel under the wall as try to scale over it, so they extended the godkissed protective wards a hundred feet below ground.

I turn to focus on the swirling mists, which are harder to pick up with my night vision. Glimmers float lazily on the cloudy blue mist, chasing each other like fireflies.

"The wards hold. I don't see— Wait."

Twenty feet deeper, the mist acts strangely. It splashes against the sides of the tunnel, the glimmers crackling with an energy burst that feels wrong.

Almost...*broken.*

I head toward the strange mist, and Rian follows the sound of my footsteps. Two more column supports rise on either side, indicating that we must be directly beneath the border wall. Instead of forming a dense barrier as the wards should, the mist seems torn apart, revealing an eerie gap.

A foul odor, reminiscent of long-decayed flesh, causes my stomach to churn.

I recognize that smell.

I extend my hand to halt Rian just before he steps on a corpse chained to the wall.

"Wolf, what the hell?"

"There's a body."

Rian shrieks like a spider's crossed his face. "You said a fucking *body?*"

"The body is desiccated," I explain. "Probably been here two, three years. By the clothing, I'd say it's a Volkish priest. Wool robe died dark blue."

"Priests didn't dig this tunnel," Rian observes. "Not with their soft hands."

I nod in agreement. Poking through the cadaver's tattered robe, I grimace. Though the man is long dead, the smells are still pungent. His leathery flesh is mostly decayed, but my sharp eyesight picks up a faint mark at the base of his neck.

I wipe my hands on my pants like he's contagious. "He's godkissed. Probably a wardcaster, and my guess from the way he's positioned is that they killed him and hung the body here to break the ward."

Rian hunches against the cold. "Charming people, the Volkish. If we cut him down, will it mend the ward?"

"One way to find out." I hack off the corpse at the wrists and drag him twenty feet down the tunnel—but the broken crackling mist remains. "That didn't work."

"Naturally," Rian mutters. "That would be too easy." He faces the direction we came, then the opposite one. The owl hoots again from the Volkish side. "Well, let's see where the tunnel leads."

We slowly pick our way toward the tunnel's far end, Rian's steps growing more sure as the moonlight increases. Finally, fresh air splashes down into the tunnel. A rustic wooden ladder is propped against the wall—leading to Volkany.

For some reason, my feet don't want to move. The smells are strange here. The nearby pine trees smell metallic. The soil is smoky. There's a tang of blood in the air.

Rian, however, doesn't share my caution and reaches for one of the ladder rungs.

I snap my hand out to grab him by the closest thing— the waistband of his pants—and jerk him back. The force of it wedges his undergarments into his ass crack.

He cries out with a hiss of pain, rubbing at his backside. "You bastard, that fucking hurt! My ass cheeks are not a horse to rein in!"

I point to the thin metal wire he didn't see at the

ladder's base. "A trip wire. I just saved your life, *you* bastard. Step back."

I herd him away from the ladder, inspect the trap, and then use the tip of my boot to spring the wire. With a rush of air, a spring-loaded spear hurtles out of a gap in the dirt, slamming into the exact spot where Rian's spine had been.

Rian's face pales. "Well. Fuck me."

Ten minutes ago, Rian and I were at each other's necks. I'm still nursing a headache courtesy of his ear-splitting shout. My bad shoulder's aching up like a bitch in heat. It was a coin toss if he would kill me for coveting Sabine, or if I would end him to have her to myself.

But hey, I guess discovering the entrance to a forbidden kingdom has a way of putting rivalries on hold.

As if thinking the same, Rian's eyes meet mine in the moonlight filtering down between tree roots. A familiar, tense air of rivalry lingers, the kind that's always one match strike away from a bonfire, but now there's a hint of restraint.

He runs a hand over a developing bruise on his jaw. "Back at Sorsha Hall, we'll settle that sparring match, eh? Loser licks the other's boots."

Our issues haven't vanished into thin air, of course. We were a hair's breadth from throttling one another. But, I nod. What fucking choice do I have?

Once we've swept for more traps, Rian ascends the ladder. Gripping the primitive rungs behind him, I emerge into moon-drenched air, heavy with strange scents and whispers. It sparks a memory—a tale from the Book of the Immortals that one of Jocki's boys used to tell. A human shepherdess, unknowingly stepping through a portal in a neglected shed, finds herself in Immortal Popelin's fae realm. Enchanted by its magic, sensuality, and Popelin's own beguiling dance, she loses track of time. When she finally returns, years have flown by; her sheep are but bones, and Popelin's mocking laughter haunts her from afar.

As my head clears the tunnel, I half expect to stumble into such a cursed fae realm. But my fears ease when I see it's merely a forest, as real as any other.

It's wilder than on the Astagnonian side, though. Evergreens tower twice as high as those we left behind. Overgrown vines weave like a basket over dead shrubs. My pulse speeds with a warning, and my hand goes to the hunting knife at my side.

But fuck if my throat doesn't tighten with awe, too.

No Astagnonian has set foot in this kingdom for five hundred years. Rian and I are entering a realm that's opposite our world. A place of legends and nightmares.

Rian scans the dark forest with a squint. To him, it must not look significantly different.

But to me?

Fuck, this place is strange.

Silvery-green pines sway with clattering needles that give off the taste of poison. An aspen's branches grow in an unnaturally geometric pattern.

My senses crackle, going haywire. For a second, I smell the pines' dark green color. I hear the smell of smoke in the air. It leaves my mind reeling almost as much as when Rian shouted in my ear.

"There's magic here." Rian spins in a slow circle. "I think it's spreading to me—Wolf, I can see in the dark! That purple flower, I see every detail!"

"That's not *you*." I bite back the urge to call him an idiot. A vine of delicate purple buds glows in the shadows with a phosphorescent luminosity. "The flower is emitting its own light somehow. Look—that beetle is doing it, too."

A vibrant green light emerges from a forest scarab's shell. I've heard tales of sailors speaking of strange glowing lights in the Panopis Sea, a sort of natural light emission from algae, but I've never heard of anything quite like this.

Rian's disappointment that the gods haven't suddenly blessed him gives way to interest as he picks withered vines off an old statue by the tunnel's entrance.

"Immortal Iyre." He frees the life-sized statue from the tangles, then steps back to admire her. The statue is weather-worn and as ancient as the wall itself, if not older. A demure cloak covers her hair, and her praying hands hold the worn shape of a key. "They must worship her in this part of Volkany."

A spectral white shape suddenly bounds past us, a blur of motion pinwheeling through the trees. It's the size of a small dog yet moves with a graceful, weightless agility, defying the physics of any earthly creature.

Rian draws his sword. "What the fuck was that?"

My hunting knife is already in hand. "Hell if I know."

We chase after the bounding white creature, which moves with a preternatural grace through thick underbrush that leaves us cursing and picking thorns out of our clothes. My lungs are straining within minutes, but the creature shows no sign of slowing. It leads us away from the border wall, up a rocky precipice where gnarled junipers cling to shallow pockets of soil in the stone, then it scrambles down a scree slope to another outcropping—where it disappears straight over the edge.

Rian comes to a scrambling stop, holding out his arms for balance. Coasting down the loose scree toward him,

uselessly grasping at shale pieces, all I can think is, *oh, fuck . .*
.

A second before I slam into him, which would knock us both off the precipice, I dig my foot into a ridge and catapult myself to the left, where I can latch onto a juniper trunk.

"Ow," Rian complains as he collapses back on solid ground.

I only groan in response. My back is shredded from the sharp shale. The taste of my own blood fills the air.

After a moment, I cautiously lean over the cliff's edge, scanning the valley's contours below. There is no sign of the creature, as if it gently floated away.

"What was it?" Rian distractedly attempts to comb his hair back into place because, of course, his first priority is his looks. "Because I'll tell you what *I* saw. *I* saw a—"

"Cloudfox," I cut him off.

He grunts in agreement, and for a second, neither of us speaks. For centuries, rumors have spread that far more magic thrives on the Volkish side of the border than the Astagnonian one. Maks claimed it was true. And after seeing the starleon in Blackwater, maybe I shouldn't be surprised.

But fuck, it's a *cloudfox.*

A legend.

A fae beast from a forgotten age.

Hell, no one even knew if they were real or myth . . .

And Rian and I just chased one off a cliff.

It's almost spooky, the way reverence gathers behind my ribs like flickering moth wings. I feel like a boy again, listening to tales while curled up in my cell. I bite the inside of my cheek, needing the grounding pain.

I expected to find danger over the border . . . not wonder.

Rian murmurs, "Just wait until I tell—"

"*Quiet.*" I cut him off with a jab, whipping my head toward the valley, ear cocked. Not more than half a mile away, I hear the presence of people. The steady pounding of a hammer. A clatter of cast iron. Someone plucking at a lute.

My heart shoots into my throat, and I grab Rian's shoulder, motioning for him to stay silent and follow me. We double back around the precipice and through a small copse of windswept trees until we come out at an outcropping facing the eastern valley.

I sniff the air, picking up on roasting meat and the scent of campfires. There's a whiff of human and animal sweat, too. Lines of smoke rise toward the sky.

A village? An outpost?

"Come on. We need a closer look," I say.

It takes us a good hour to hike through the dense foliage until we reach a closer outcropping—this time, close enough for even Rian to see that a military encampment occupies the entire valley. Along both sides of a stream, hundreds of canvas tents rise. The encampment is divided into four distinct factions, each marked by a different tent color and emblem.

North of the stream, the tents are a burnt orange with an arrow symbol—the archer division, I assume. Just east are indigo tents with a starburst pattern. South of the stream, another faction has red tents with an axe symbol. The last faction's tents are brown and marked with a stag. Judging by the smell of polished leather, it must be the cavalry.

From the smells and jovial music, it's dinner time. Soldiers in various states of armor mill about, their voices rising to my ears in laughter, chatter, and arguments, but I can't understand their Volkish words.

My pulse thumps so loud in my ears that it's hard to

hear anything in the valley. Still, it's clear: this is no mere village.

This is an *entire fucking army* scarcely a mile from the border wall.

Rian's tongue darts out to lick his lips, his eyes lit from within. "There must be, what, a thousand soldiers?"

"More." I silently work out the calculations. "Four factions, thirty-five tents per encampment, looks like about ten soldiers per tent. That would be, let's see, one thousand four hundred troops. Not including any officers in those central tents. Plus, there must be horses somewhere we can't see, which means there could be more soldiers elsewhere, too."

Rian mutters a curse.

The air feels tense, alive. A breeze brings the smell of gin, the clatter of tin plates, exclamations from someone's dice game. As innocent as the sounds are, I'm all too aware of the massive threat before us.

"Are those emblems on the tents?" Rian asks, straining to see.

"The red ones are axes. Purple ones starburst. Orange are arrows. Brown are stags."

"The emblems of the Immortals." His hand snakes up to his hair, twisting at a curl like he can tame it back into place, but there's no finding control in this situation. "Yet none of those are Iyre's symbol, whose statue we saw."

"I don't think their army divisions have anything to do with that old statue. I think their legions have patron gods. Calvary for Solene, archers for Artain, infantry for Vale."

"And Thracia's starburst?"

I focus again on the indigo tents, where even my exceptional sight can't quite pick up on individual people's faces, but the air feels different there, that same haywire crackle that I felt when we crossed the tunnel's midpoint. "Thracia is the patron of mystics. So, I'd wager it's a godkissed faction. A mage army."

Rian grips my forearm with an iron hold, fingers unknowingly digging into a still-oozing gash from my slide down the mountain.

"A mage *army*? Fourteen hundred soldiers in all? Wolf, Old Coros is lucky if it has a dozen godkissed soldiers in its ranks. And this is just one encampment, hundreds of miles from the Volkish capital. There could be thousands more soldiers throughout the kingdom."

My fist tightens, in part against the pain in my arm.

He continues, "This is so much bigger than anyone thinks. Their army . . . their magic . . . Old King Joruun has no fucking idea what he's up against, I can promise you that."

I settle back onto my heels, feeling numb. "I don't think anyone did."

After a second, he says quietly, "That's not true. You did. You took those goldenclaw rumors seriously. You wanted to investigate—I should have listened to you."

I flinch out of my stupor. There's a strange, bitter triumph in hearing those words from him, a vindication for all those sleepless nights, the endless tracking, the hours bent over maps.

Yet, any triumph feels hollow.

I never wanted to be right. I never asked to be the only one who heard the silent warnings near the border. All my life, I've been a lone wolf who preferred the peace of the forest, and now I find myself at the heart of a storm I can't ignore.

"We should head back to Duren." I tighten the laces on

my boots. "Change out our horses for fresh ones, ride straight to Old Coros to speak with the king. Tell him to send his best spies here—"

"Spies?" Rian spits. "Fuck that. *We're* here. Now. Who are better spies than us?"

I curse as he draws his sword and starts down the mountainside toward the encampment. It kills me to admit that he might have a point—and that this pampered third-born son might have more balls than me.

"Wait, gods damn it."

He's already on the outskirts of the mage tents when I catch up to him, hissing that we should be more cautious. He merely sniffs the air, grimaces at the smell of human waste, and picks his way toward a section of bushes designated as latrines and a washing area. There, draped over branches, are a few capes and helmets. He swipes up a pair, tossing me a helmet.

"Are we seriously doing this?" I ask low.

He winks.

My heart pounds as Rian, disguised, plunges into the row of indigo tents with the confidence that earned him the Lord of Liars nickname. The air is thick with that strange crackle. We pass tents that smell heavily of sorrel and borage, and inside, I glimpse healers bent over bandaged soldiers, their uniforms open at the neck to display their godkissed birthmarks.

At the end of the row of tents, Rian turns sharply. Everything passes in a blur; all these new sights and smells overwhelm my senses. A voice in my head reminds me that we'll be butchered if we're caught.

Hell, I might just kill Rian myself for his foolhardiness.

I take everything in with furtive glances from my

helmet's slit. We pass a female godkissed waterwielder who draws moisture from the air to fill barrels, which soldiers dip their tin cups into. A godkissed blacksmith bending metal bars with his own iron-red fists. With some exceptions, most of the soldiers have the white-blond hair and fair eyes characteristic of the Volkish. It's jarring to think of how seamlessly Sabine would fit into their midsts with her coloration.

Rian turns the corner and smacks straight into a hulk of a man who mutters something confrontational in Volkish. My blood freezes over. One word of Astagnonian, and we'll be roasted on those giant spits.

Thinking fast, Rian flicks his hand dismissively at the man as if he doesn't have time for him and darts to the left, striding toward the forest. I follow, not daring to look back over my shoulder but listening for pursuing footsteps.

We come out of the forest in front of a tent set far from the others. From all indications, it's unguarded. Quiet. Probably kitchen supplies, set away from the other tents to draw off wild animals.

"We've seen enough," I mutter. "We should head back to the horses."

He quietly scoffs, "Pussy."

"What did you call me?" I puff up my chest, because even with the threat of a fourteen-hundred-strong Volkish army, Rian Valvere does *not* call me a pussy.

A sly smile tilts up his mouth. "You heard me."

I narrow my eyes, then throw open the unguarded tent flap and pull us both inside. "Fine. You want to spy? We'll spy."

CHAPTER 15
SABINE

When I wake, I feel disoriented, out of breath like I've bound across an entire valley. The scent of a phantom forest lingers in the air. I glance at the empty cup of mushroom tea on the bedside table, then let out a long puff of air.

Slowly, I press my hands to my cheeks, my chest, my stomach. Ferra wasn't lying about those mushrooms—my head and stomach feel better, but that's more than I can say for my heart.

Tossing and turning, I dreamed of Basten. That scowl-faced ruffian belongs nowhere in my head, certainly not my dreams. He was in the mythical forest painted on my ceiling, with the sentient vines and sharp-needled trees. The fluffy white cloudfox painted above my toes ran past him, and I tried to call out in my sleep not to follow it—it only led to danger.

But he didn't hear my cries.

The nuthatch lands on the teacup's rim, cocking his head.

Awake now? he asks. *Feel better?*

I nod, swinging my feet out of bed as I shake the last of the dream away. *Yes, friend. Can you find out where the Valvere family members are now?*

He takes wing out the window and, in a few seconds, circles back in and lands on my bedpost. *Not in castle. Gone to town.*

Well, that's one silver lining. If Lord Berolt, Lady Eleonora, and the other relatives were stalking the hallways, I'd chain myself to the bed—it's the lesser of two evils, really.

An idea occurs to me, and I glance sidelong at the raised lump in my carpet. I've almost never had the castle to myself. My heart speeds into a daring rhythm. Dropping to my knees, I wriggle the ancient copy of *The Last Return of the Fae* free from its hiding spot.

If there's ever a time to search for the missing second volume, it's now.

Maximan follows me to the library, but I act as though I'm simply hunting for an entertaining book to keep me occupied during Rian's absence, and he dutifully stands guard outside the door.

Inside, alone, I take a moment to marvel once more at the towering shelves, feeling a tingle of magic as I trace the map table's wooden frame.

Surrounded by these ancient books, I'm enveloped in a world where knowledge whispers from every corner, secrets linger in the air, and stories unroll like endless fae tapestries.

I start by dropping to hands and knees and searching under every table, but if the second volume was ever here, the servants long ago tidied it up. Next, I rifle through stacks of paperwork left behind by Berolt along with a bowl of ashes from his herb pipe. *Nothing.* I do a quick pass of the shelves, squinting between large volumes for any smaller books someone might have slipped between them, but that turns up a loss, too.

Finally, I spy an ornate wooden box high on a shelf. I climb one of the library ladders and take it down, then sort through what appears to be correspondences between Berolt and Lore and Kendan—Rian's estranged older brothers.

In the back of my head, I hear the door's well-oiled hinges sigh open, but I'm so engrossed in the letters that it takes a second before the sound registers.

A gruff voice says, "Your mother wasted her time teaching you to read."

I whirl around, cramming the letters in the box. "Father? You startled me!"

Charlin Darrow stands beside Maximan, who gives him a loathsome look as if he just crawled out of a swamp.

"Lady Sabine," Maximan says. "You have a guest, but I can escort him out—"

"No. Let him stay." There's nothing my father can do to me now to hurt me more than he already has.

Maximan rests a hand on his sword hilt. "I'll be just out here, should you need me."

Once it's the two of us, my father scrutinizes me with the same detached coldness he reserves for a lame goat destined for slaughter. His lumbering footsteps echo through the library as he moves to the closest desk, each step laden with contempt for the books lining the shelves.

Fishing into his jacket pocket, he retrieves his flask, thick fingers fumbling with the lid. He peers into its mouth with a grimace as if searching for answers at the bottom.

"I'm surprised you still call me father, girl." He throws back a long drink of gin.

By the gods, I think. *Does he have to be so dramatic? I'm only getting married.* I'll be a Valvere instead of a Darrow, but that hardly negates our relationship.

I return the rest of the letters to the box. "Why wouldn't I?"

He gives a slurring laugh that turns into a cough. "After the letter I sent your High Lord? The man must have balls of iron to continue with the wedding." He takes another swig, not bothering to wipe his mouth of gin dribbling onto his unkempt beard. He murmurs to himself, "You must have bewitched him. Just like your mother. Witches, both of you."

As I close the box of correspondence, my hands go perfectly still. I'm afraid even to breathe.

All I can think is: *The letter?*

I shift from foot to foot, thinking fast. My father thinks I already know the letter's contents. How can I keep him talking? He's mind-numbingly drunk, as usual. If I play my cards right, then I can get him to reveal what it said.

I walk casually toward the map table and trace a finger along the winding blue line of the Innis River.

I force my voice steady, even casual. "Yes, about that letter. Fortunately for me, my future husband doesn't share your sentiments about female literacy. Lord Rian let me read what you wrote. I'd like to know your thoughts on its contents." I aim for a tone of indifference as though I'm more interested in the map.

Behind me, I hear a clink and slurp as he drinks again from his flask. Then, he slurs, "Your mother was eight months pregnant when Bremcote's head priest sent for me. She had knocked on the church door, desperate but too proud to beg for scraps. I'm no fool, mind you. All it took was one look to know that a woman with her beauty and bearing was no peasant as she claimed; her lockbox of belongings and fine horse proved it."

The air solidifies in my throat like a block of ice. Slowly, drip by drip, frigid shards slice into my chest.

Eight. Months. *Pregnant?*

That would mean . . .

"I assumed she was a married woman fleeing a heavy-handed husband," my father continues in a slurring ramble, oblivious to my blooming distress. "Or a lord's daughter ruined by rape. I'm no fool, no fool indeed. I saw my opportunity—a woman so fine would never marry a minor country lord unless she were desperate. She made me promise that when you were born, I would swear that you were my own blood. We had to sack all the servants and hire new ones from three towns over who hadn't seen her pregnant at our wedding."

My hands shake so badly that I squeeze the edges of the map table, lean over it, and briefly close my eyes.

Charlin Darrow . . . isn't my father.

Is this the secret that Basten learned? Was he so cruel to me because he discovered I'm not noble by blood?

Impossible. Basten can be many things, but not an elitist.

It makes no sense.

That ice in my core has my whole body shaking now, and it's a sick reminder that my body has never belonged to me. It's always belonged to the men who owned me and the women who beat me.

My old mantra surges back like a thunderclap: *They can have my body, but my mind is my own.*

The words give me the strength to trace my finger up the

map to the border between Astagnon and Volkany, following Basten's footsteps.

"And . . .my real father?" I ask. My voice shakes, my heart stumbles, but Charlin is too drunk to notice.

"A royal *whore*," my father murmurs to himself as though he didn't even hear my question. "That's what Isabeau wrote in that book of hers. Twenty-two years of lies. About everything. Her godkiss. Her fucking face. The fact that she whored herself to that mad king Rachillon!"

On the map, my hand freezes at the border wall checkpoint at Havre Peak.

Fucking gods.

I replay Charlin's words back through my head slowly because I don't trust my panicked mind not to miss something. My pulse raps painfully against my temples. My heart flutters back and forth like a trapped titmouse, wearing itself out.

He's saying that my mother was a concubine to King Rachillon of Volkany. A *godkissed* concubine. The king must have gotten her pregnant, so she stole Myst and ran away across the border.

Which means I'm not a lord's daughter. I'm not a peasant either.

I'm a . . .

I lean on the map, gathering all my strength to keep from crying out so that Charlin won't know that this news shifts my world.

I'm not who I thought I was. If the information got out that I'm Rachillon's daughter, I'd likely be imprisoned as a traitor.

Still, a tiny part of me questions if this news could be welcome. After all, what has Astagnon ever done for me? It's a kingdom where girls are locked away, beaten, and then sold as brides. Maybe I don't *want* to be from this corrupt place. In Volkany, I could find a loving father. A just realm where girls can be free. A home that would embrace me not for my powers, but simply for who I am.

Yet a cruel voice deep in my mind only laughs at that thought.

You know that's a farce—Volkany is cursed for a reason.

Seething, I say quietly, "It's a wonder all of Astagnon doesn't know this already, given how loose your lips are when you're drunk."

He chuckles. "I know how to keep a secret when money is involved. If your fine High Lord doesn't want the world to know, he needs to *pay* me. Charlin Darrow is no fool, no fool indeed . . ." His extortion rambles continue, deaf to my ears.

Through watery eyes, my gaze falls on the map of Volkany. The capital city clings like a bat in the night to the shadows of the Darmarnach Mountains.

The words penned there send spider-steps down my spine:

Norhelm.

Drahallen Castle.

Tangled thoughts batter the inside of my skull with punishing strikes. This has to be why Basten lied to me.

Rian has always been the right match for you, Basten said. *He has an army that can protect you if there is ever danger.*

At the time, furious and heartbroken, I couldn't fathom what danger Basten possibly meant unless it was at the hands of the very same future husband he was delivering me to.

Now, I understand everything. Basten read in that damn letter that I was the daughter of the enemy king. The same king who had just sent four raiders to find me and abduct me back to Volkany. He knew that more would be coming—maybe even an entire army.

My mind suddenly locks, a door slamming closed against a battering storm as though to protect the few survivors within. A bolt of cold rips down to my tailbone. I double over, swallowing a cry.

The pain cuts too deep: Lies from my father, from Basten, even from my mother. In fact, the only person to give me straight answers in this twisted drama is the Lord of Liars himself.

What fucking irony.

I'm a lost feather in the ocean. Drowning, falling. The watery depths pull me into a spiral as I drift down, down, down toward the murky bottom—when I was always meant to fly.

Bracing myself on the map table to keep from collapsing, I dig deep to let my anger loosen against my ribs, bouying my strength. Because right now, anger is the only thing keeping me afloat.

"Charlin?" Locking my jaw, I turn to face him. "You *are* a fool. You are a fool for never seeing who my mother truly was. You were a fool for casting me off. You were a fool, too, for thinking Lord Rian would pay you one copper demi to keep you quiet."

I take powerful strides across the library until I can look him in his beady eyes—dark eyes that are nothing like my fair ones. "The only good thing to come out of my marriage will be that when Lord Rian is crowned, and I am queen, I will strip you of your title, your land, and every last coin you own until it's *you* begging at a church door."

CHAPTER 16
WOLF

The kitchen supply tent on the outskirts of the Volkish army encampment is pitch-black inside, and the last thing it smells like is vegetables. Musty and oddly metallic, the scent reminds me more of the pelts hanging to cure at the gamemaster's cottage.

"Stay here," I bark at Rian, low and warning. That ass has gotten us in enough trouble. "I'll find a lantern."

My night vision hones in on heavy coils of chains, barrels, and tack from the cavalry division. I dig around a few crates: Plums packed in straw. Bags of unshelled black walnuts. Charred, leftover bones from the soldiers' dinners.

Well, that's fucking strange.

Finally, on a table covered with rounded blades attached to leather straps—a weapon I've never seen before and can't fathom how it would work—I find a rusty oil lamp next to some marked-up maps and a worn Volkish copy of the Book of the Immortals.

I strike my flint rod, get a spark, and adjust the lamp's flame.

First thing I do is hold the light closer to the mysterious weapon for a closer look. "Rian. What do you think this is for?"

The weapon clatters as I pick up its leather harness, which is worn in places like a horse's bridle. Sniffing, I frown. The scent is definitely animal, not human. But sure as hell not any animal scent I know.

Closest thing I can pin it to would be a—

Rian examines the weapon, equally baffled, then looks closer at one of the maps. I recognize it instantly. It's a map of Astagnon's Red Church locations.

"Those are our immortal temples." I rub my chin, confused. "Why would Volkany attack those?"

"They wouldn't." There's a strange, dark look in Rian's eye. "The Red Church has no formal political affiliation. They only bow to the gods themselves. I wouldn't put it past the Grand Cleric to work with Rachillon to ensure he takes over our throne. This map demonstrates how far-reaching his power is in Astagnon."

I snatch the map, frowning, struggling to believe it. "You think the Grand Cleric sent this? How could he possibly be in communication with Rachillon?"

"I have no fucking idea. The tunnel? A godkissed communicator?" He thumbs through more maps, pulling out one of Volkany. About a dozen points are circled in red ink. At first glance, I can't figure out any connection between the locations. Most are in forests or fields. Some in small towns. One is here, in this riverbend across the border.

There's Volkish writing on the bottom of the map, along with a symbol that looks like a paw print.

"A map of outposts like this one?" I ask.

Rian shakes his head. "Most of these placements would

have no strategic value. And look—" His lips move as he reads the foreign script. "—*galdenclawe*. It's the same word in Astagnonian."

My stomach draws in with a sharp ache.

Rian's eyes light up as he slams the map down. "This is a map of goldenclaw resting places. Their *tombs*, Wolf. That bastard Rachillon isn't full of shit—his godkiss really can raise the fae. He must have abducted enough godkissed wayfinders to locate the beasts' tombs. That's why the army is here, to raise a goldenclaw!"

I snatch the map as my heart slams like a battering ram. "Wait—so Rachillon is *here*?"

"Here or on his way."

Everything is happening too fast. My senses are still out of wack—I swear I can smell the iron tang of a fae beast. Mind scrambling, I drag my nails through my hair. The rumors are true? Holy fucking hell. If so, this changes everything.

What does this mean for the gods themselves?

Has he found them?

Awoken them?

No, I assure myself before my heart smashes out of my chest. *It can't be. If gods were walking the earth, we would fucking know.*

As Rian moves around the table, he steps on a tarpaulin covering the floor. But his foot gives way—the tarpaulin isn't just lying on the ground; it's covering a pit.

He immediately crashes down into it.

A cloud of straw and dust rises in the air. Ten feet down, Rian scrambles with the tangled tarpaulin, fighting against the ropes that had lashed it down. There's a thud as his head connects with hard earth.

"*Ow.*"

Something rustles at the far end of the pit.

Instantly, my body petrifies. Below, Rian has gone even more still, so that he looks like the statue of Iyre in the woods—if it was about to piss itself.

Across the pit, twelve feet away, a goldenclaw rouses, its fur bristling as it shakes off its slumber. Bones litter the bottom of the pit, and now everything makes sense.

A metallic taste coats the back of my tongue. All I can do is stare as the creature's scent—the same scent from the harness weapon—splashes over me like cold water. Its golden fur catches the lantern's light, sparkling like a prism to cast shimmering lights on the tent ceiling. A halter loops around its snout, and a leather harness is fastened around its torso. Iron hooks are welded into the chest harness as though ready to attach to a saddle.

For a moment, I'm so shocked to see a goldenclaw in the flesh that I forget to be scared. It's more beautiful and terrible than the cloudfox. The only thing that rivals its fae strangeness is the monoceros chained in Rian's basement.

"Wolf?" Rian speaks in slow, measured words through a clamped jaw. "Get. Me. The. Fuck. Out. Of. This. Pit. *Now.*"

Reason slams back into me, shaking me from my stupor.

I need one of those chains *now*—

As I scramble to grab a chain, the bear emits an earth-shaking growl. That's all the warning we get before it hurls itself at Rian. With quick instinct, Rian drops into a roll just as the bear slams into the side of the pit, shaking the earth hard enough that the lantern loses its balance and falls in.

Glass shatters.

The light goes out.

The world becomes grayscale again, all color drained, as my night vision focuses.

"Wolf!" Rian bellows, voice ringing with panic. The air vibrates as he slides out his sword, aiming blindly.

He can't see.

But the golden claw can, if it's anything like regular bears. *It's going to tear him into pieces.*

Muscles tensing, I forget about the chain. There isn't time. The bear is circling the pit, preparing to take Rian unaware from the side while his sword is aimed forward.

Fuck!

Before I can make a decision, my body does for me. Drawing my knife, I jump into the pit, putting myself between Rian and the goldenclaw. It draws up fast on me, baring its teeth.

I slash the knife against its snout.

Roaring, it tosses its head, and instead of blood, a golden-tinged fluid drips out of the gash.

"Wolf?" Rian shouts. "Take my sword—kill it!"

"We can't!" I shout back over my shoulder. "If the soldiers find a dead goldenclaw, they'll know we were here. We can't risk this army attacking Astagnon before we're ready."

"Well, we aren't going to fucking feed it plums!"

I think fast, calculating our options. If I can cut away one of the tarpaulin's ropes and attach it to the tent's main support post, there's a chance we could use it as a pulley to get one of us out.

But first—

Another growl comes from the pitch black. Before I can react, the goldenclaw swipes his left paw at my skull. I dodge the worst of the blow, but the tip of his claw catches my right cheek. Warm blood spills onto my jaw.

Brandishing my knife, I retreat until I can grab Rian's shoulder, and we stand back-to-back with our blades aimed outward for whatever direction the bear might attack first.

"Do what I say," I bark.

Behind me, I feel his head jolt in a nod.

The bear lowers into a battle stance that looks more like a trained war animal than a wild beast, then charges.

"Ninety degrees to your left, two paces forward, swing low!" I shout.

We break apart, and as the bear charges between us, we both spin on it with our blades and slash—we make contact, but our blades only glint off its shaggy metallic fur.

Dammit, the thing is made of *actual* gold. It has built-in armor.

Great.

"Three steps backward!" I shout to Rian. "Back to the wall, sword at high guard!"

He follows my lead just as the bear retaliates, swiping a paw toward Rian. If I didn't know better, I'd say the bear was intentionally targeting Rian, as though he can sense Rian is the weaker of the two of us, without sight in the dark.

"It's targeting you!" I call. "You have to distract it to give me time to cut a rope from the tarpaulin."

"Distract it with what, a minstrel's song and dance?" Rian cries.

"Just follow my call. Bear's on your right. Take three steps forward, then downward thrust!"

Rian dances forward with a soldier's practiced obedience, swiping his sword downward as the bear shifts just enough so the blade glances off its studded harness with a shower of sparks.

"It's doubling back now." I glance between Rian and the rope I'm sawing through. "Preparing to charge. It tends to swipe with its left paw. So run left, make it have to pursue you."

Rian feels along the wall with one hand while circling backward, spinning his sword in a wide arc.

I hack through the rope until, finally, the last cord breaks free. Jumping to my feet, I wrap a discarded bone around the rope's end and toss it so it sails around the thick timber tent post. There's no way for me to tie it down to secure it—the rope dangles from both sides.

This means one of us will have to hold it for the other.

I shout, "Three steps to your right, one back. Feel for the rope. I'll hold the other end—climb out!"

Rian doesn't argue as he stabs his sword as high as he can into the pit wall, then uses it as a stair step, along with the rope, to hoist himself up.

Like this, with both hands on the rope, I'm a trussed pig just begging for the slaughter. My muscles burn as I strain to hold the rope against Rian's cantilevered weight.

Sweat rolls into my eyes, blurring my vision. I grit my teeth. *Gods damn it.* I can't let go of the rope or Rian will fall. Still, even with blurry vision, it's clear as fucking day when the goldenclaw sees his chance and charges me.

It closes in fast. *Eight feet.* I can't draw my knife with my hands on the rope. *Six feet.* Fuck, I can't run without letting go. *Four feet*—

Rian pulls himself up the final stretch and reaches back to free his sword.

"Clear!" he shouts.

I drop the rope like it's a live snake and dive out of the way a second before the bear slams into me, head angled low for ramming. A crashing thud rips through the tent as it collides with the pit's wall.

I'm splayed out on my stomach, tangled in the tarpaulin bindings, the breath punched out of me.

A groan rolls up my throat.

Thank gods for my training, which has my hand instinctively reaching for my knife.

Rian paces at the top of the pit, breath ragged, hair wild, uselessly searching the dark for me. The rope rests at his feet. All he has to do is pick it up, haul me out.

For a terrible second, fear throttles me.

He could leave me here.

Rian has resented me for years: I escaped his family's business. I had the freedom not to be a Valvere. On top of it all, now he knows I want Sabine.

The truth is, I'm a liability.

The key to his future as king rests upon Sabine's godkissed ability to speak to the monoceros. If he were to see me as an obstacle in his scheme for the throne, I don't doubt that he'd kill me. With me trapped in the pit, he could call it a simple "accident," and his hands would remain clean.

It wouldn't be the first time a Valvere faced this choice. When I was still a boy fighting for Jocki, one of Lord Berolt's business associates was "accidentally" shoved into a fighting ring with savage dogs. As the man pleaded for help, Lord Berolt only watched as the dogs mauled him to death.

The memory tightens its grip on me.

Just how much is Rian like his father?

But as soon as that fear intrudes on my mind, Rian grabs

the rope and tosses the end back into the pit. "Hurry, you ass! For fuck's sake, why couldn't you have been godkissed with speed?"

An exhale of relief exits my body.

The stunned goldenclaw recovers, pushing to its feet, clots of dirt raining down from its metallic fur.

I grip the rope and, hand over hand, climb as fast as Rian can pull me out. As soon as I clear the rim, he clasps my forearm, and I clasp his, and he throws his whole weight into pulling me out the rest of the way.

We collapse together in a messy heap of sweat-soaked, filthy, blood-crusted limbs.

"*Now* let's get the fuck back to Duren," Rian says.

The return journey to the tunnel is a blur. Blood drips down my back and arm. Strange bird calls chase after us. We scale the scree; we tear back through the forest of poison-tipped pines; we run like frightened rabbits.

I never asked for this war, but now I'm at the forefront.

And I'm not alone, either. This discovery means King Joruun's seven decades of peace are about to end. Publicly, the king is called the Benevolent Boar for his steadfast reign, like the stalwart wild animal. Behind his back, though? More like the Benevolent *Bore*. At ninety and frail, the Benevolent Bore is no kind of king to lead us into battle.

Not against saddled goldenclaws. Mage armies. A king who will sacrifice his own priests to break a ward by turning him into a fucking doorstop.

Oh yeah—a ruthless king who also happens to be Sabine's father.

As I follow Rian, limping through the pain, I can't help but curse him for being so reckless as to get us nearly killed. At the same time, the idea crops up in my head that maybe

Astagnon *needs* someone reckless at the helm. A leader who is daring and unconventional, as ruthless as Mad King Rachillon himself. A king who wouldn't hesitate to plunge straight into the enemy's camp.

Fuck. I never thought I'd say this, but maybe Rian *should* be king.

We don't bother with the ladder, simply hurtling ourselves into the tunnel entrance and splashing down in the frigid mud. As we hobble through the passage, a clattering tangle of straps and blades falls out of Rian's shirt.

He doubles back to swipe it up, and I recognize the gleam of the five-bladed goldenclaw gauntlet.

Damn the man—there I go thinking Rian might be redeemable after he saved my life, but the Lord of Liars can't help but steal something on the way out, can he? Even though he damn well knows that when the Volkish soldiers realize it's missing, it will raise suspicions.

"What?" There's a defensive note to his voice, though I voiced nothing. "I had to take it. Proof is crucial, my friend. Without it, who'd believe our story?"

His eyes glint with mischief, bright like the polished sides of his Golath dime, as we climb out the Astagnonian side and head for our horses.

CHAPTER 17
SABINE

Days of mid-summer showers turn Duren's streets to mud. I keep myself distracted by helping Brigit with the laundry, and taking care of the castle's animals. Brigit and I have our arms elbow-deep in sudsy water as we fight a grumpy, water-logged cat, when the door rattles with a knock.

"Would you get that?" I ask her, as I have a better chance of keeping the cat from tearing out of my copper tub and staining the priceless rug with dirty paw prints.

Brigit dries her hands on her apron as she goes to the door. The cat scowls up at me, *Unhand me, witch! This is torture!*

You were the one who fell into Cook's honey barrel*, I point out. *You're lucky I got to you before she took the butcher knife to your neck.*

The cat grumbles, lids lowered over eyes that still spark hatred at me as if I've somehow conspired against him with the pantry's wobbly shelves.

"Lady Sabine." Maximan's insistent voice makes me drop the soap. "You're required. It's urgent."

His helmet is off, graying hair mussed, sweat streaking his face along with—

"Is that *blood*?" I ask, wiping my hands on my borrowed apron.

"It's the—" His guarded gaze shifts to Brigit. "*Potatoes.* Hurry."

Potatoes. Our code word for the monoceros. Immediately, I'm tugging off the apron and pressing it into Brigit's hands.

You haven't finished cleaning off the honey! the cat pouts, but his complaints fall on deaf ears as Maximan jerks his head for me to follow him down the hall.

His strides are swift, almost a run. I have to jog to keep up. My pulse speeds with my steps, worried because I've never seen Maximan ruffled like this, not even when I set the tiger loose on a stadium of ten thousand spectators.

"The builders finished the monoceros's stable last night," he explains in low, quiet words. "We tried to move the creature to the new location. We used iron chains and spears. Moved it long after sunset so it couldn't harness the sun . . . It killed a few men regardless."

Gods in hell.

My throat closes up, and I have to remind myself to breathe as we jog down Sorsha Hall's front steps. "I don't know what I can do. He won't listen to me. The only thing he might even consider heeding is one of his own kind—"

My boots skid on the cobblestone path toward the city gates as I pinwheel my arms to spin me back toward the Valvere stables.

"We need Myst!"

By the time we bridle Myst and get her to the Golden

Sentinel training grounds, my whole body is shaking like a twig. I'm afraid of the monoceros hurting more people, but I also know there's a line where even Rian would agree he's too dangerous to keep alive.

As we make our way to the old barracks, Myst eyes me sidelong. *You didn't come for our ride yesterday. Or the day before. Did I do something wrong?*

I speed my steps, chewing on the inside of my cheek. Since learning the truth about my mother, my mind has turned like a fitful sleeper. Reexamining twelve-year-old memories. Juggling what it means to be a daughter to the Mad King of Volkany.

Finally, I admit: *I didn't know what to say to you. You lied to me about my mother. You were with her when she came to Bremcote. You told me she hailed from the northern forest.*

Myst and I have rarely argued, but I can't deny it's gnawed at me that I had to learn the truth from Charlin Darrow instead of my best friend.

Myst eyes me sidelong, blinking calmly. *That was no lie. She was from the north. She was from a forest.*

From the Volkish side of the border! My internal voice explodes in my skull. *You left that key piece of information out!*

She tosses her head—the horse equivalent of a shrug—and I grit my teeth against a boiling wave of frustration. Damn horses and their over-literal take on the world.

Still, maybe I'm being unfair to expect more from her. It isn't as though horses can grasp the concept of political borders.

Sensing my hurt, Myst nudges my shoulder as we wait for the soldiers to roll back the gate to let us into the compound. *In this place you call Volkany, I lived in a stable even grander than the one now. There were many more like you, who could do magic. I was being trained to pull a black carriage. One night, Isabeau snuck in. She was a stranger to me. She saddled me. Bid me to gallop.*

And you just went with her? I ask.

She gave me an apple.

I shake my head. It's hard to stay mad at my sweet girl— and I know she didn't hurt me on purpose. With a tweak of her snout, I tease, *You and your apples. You'd let the devil ride you if he gave you an apple.*

But my anger melts away as we pass three bodies laid out by the barracks, covered in white sheets splotched with blood.

Maximan signals to two pale soldiers who look like they've seen a ghost. They unbolt the monoceros's stable and roll back the reinforced door.

My stomach shrinks like a dried leaf as I step inside, leading Myst by her halter. The space is vast and dark, with a strange pregnant silence like waiting for a storm to break. The previous soldiers' barracks have been cleared out to make a riding ring filled with sand and a row of stalls converted from officers' quarters. Overhead, thick timbers support shingles forged from iron, cutting off all sunlight. The only break is a small trapdoor in the roof's center, closed and locked for now.

As Rian promised, everything is stone, sand, and iron.

Nothing that can burn.

Suddenly, a vicious, unnatural scream pierces the air. The monoceros comes charging out of the shadows, kicking up its heels. Froth foams at its mouth. An iron chain flies loose from its bridle. Its hooves tear up the sand into dust devils.

Maximan draws his sword even though we're protected by the riding ring's sturdy metal railing between us and the beast.

My heart shoots up to lodge in my throat. Soldiers aim iron-tipped arrows at the ready. Blood pools in the sand, left over from one of the monoceros's victims.

I summon my inner voice to command him to stop, when—

What do you think you're doing? Myst scolds in a prim, stern voice.

The raging monoceros skids to a halt like a snuffed candle. Eyes wide enough to see the outer rims, he stares at Myst like he's never seen another horse. For all I know, he hasn't.

Myst stamps her hoof in disapproval. *Look at you. Making a mess. Causing a ruckus. Over what, a new stable all to yourself? Fresh alfalfa? How terrible for you.*

The monoceros's head jerks up, ears swiveled forward, head slightly back and aghast. Myst is six hands shorter than him and half his weight. She has no deadly horn. No hooves of iron.

And yet he instantly seems to respect her.

Slowly, the soldiers lower their bows. Their attention volleys between the two horses of such different statures, astounded by the magic occurring before their eyes.

Maximan murmurs in an awe-filled hush, "I'll order the builders to make up a stall for Myst next to the monster's. She's the only thing that has tamed it. When Rian returns, he'll understand."

I curl my fingers protectively around Myst's halter rope.

"You don't know if it's safe to put them together. He could have ill intent."

Maximan's lips part, and he fumbles with his words before stammering, "I . . .uh . . .don't think the beast's intentions toward her are of a violent nature." He clears his throat, nodding toward the monoceros.

Confused, it takes me a minute to spot the animal's stiff, ah, *attention* between his rear legs. I groan up toward the iron ceiling at the same time that Myst tosses her mane, batting her long lashes.

I think to myself, *All males are the same, melting like a candle before a pretty female.*

I spend the remainder of that day supervising Myst and the monoceros, listening to their mind-numbing chatter about hay preferences, the mysteries of human behavior, and how they both dream at night about carrots. It's only when I'm confident the monoceros isn't going to maltreat my sweet girl that I agree to leave Myst in one of the stalls.

The bells toll ten at night when I finally tromp back into Sorsha Hall, stomach ringing its own hunger bells. The instant Maximan and I step into the grand foyer, however, the air feels charged—as if we've just walked onto a stage mid-scene.

Harried servants dart back and forth, carrying platters of provisions to the ballroom. Someone's muddy footprints cover the foyer's Clarana rugs. A maid on all fours scrubs the prints with a scouring brush and soap bucket.

Maximan stops Serenith, her arms laden with firewood, before she climbs the stairs. "What happened?"

"The High Lord has returned," Serenith replies in a hush, nodding toward the ballroom before hurrying to finish her preparations for his room upstairs.

A bolt of fear slides between my ribs. Rian is back, but what about Basten? Why didn't Serenith say his name? *Easy, Sabine.* I have to remind myself that Basten is a servant here —no one thinks of his safety but me.

My exhaustion vanishes as Maximan and I hurry to the ballroom, the air somehow too warm and too cold at the same time, as if a season's change is upon us. A shiver coils through me with the premonition that none of us are prepared for whatever comes next.

I race into the ballroom and catch myself on a chair back, my heart continuing to stampede straight ahead of my body. The Valvere family members are gathered around the High Lord's table, along with the uniformed captains of the Golden Sentinels divisions and a few of Duren's wealthiest merchants.

In the center of the small crowd, Rian's deep voice, sharp and exuberant, cuts through the murmuring hum. Everyone is tightly crowded around a few objects on the table, and I have to stand on tip-toe, craning my neck, to try to see anything.

It isn't until Lady Eleonora plops down in a chair that I get a solid look at Rian. His sentinel captain's jacket is streaked with mud. His perfectly tamed hair now dangles unkempt around his temples. There's a strange, almost blue-flame light in his eyes as he claps one of the captains on the shoulder.

I teeter on my toes, searching the faces in the crowd.

Where's Basten?

As I push forward between Lord Berolt and Lord Gideon,

my heart strangely tensing, I finally slip to the front and see an unrolled map held down by candlesticks.

" . . .a tunnel," Rian is saying with a hint of hushed wonder. "They broke the ward somehow. We think it had to do with a sacrificed godkissed wardcaster and some sort of ritual. Rachillon is ruthless, I tell you."

"A king with no care for his own subjects?" Lady Eleonora deadpans as she motions for a servant to refill her glass of wine, then waves him back with a glare when he didn't fill it to the brim. "What a groundbreaking concept. Truly unheard of in our times."

Despite her sarcasm, Rian taps the map and continues, "The encampment was here." He indicates a location in the forest about two miles north of the border. "Fourteen hundred troops. At least a quarter of them godkissed. The finest weaponry anyone has seen since the days of King Byrne."

"Did you overhear attack plans?" one of the captains asked.

Rian rubs a hand over his stubled chin. "Rachillon isn't fool enough to attack our lands any time soon. It was only a coincidence that the Volkish army was near the border. They were in that specific site because of what they uncovered." He lets the silence unspool for dramatic effect. "The rumors about Rachillon's godkiss are true. Wolf and I saw its effects with our own eyes. He found and raised a goldenclaw from its tomb. It's only a matter of time before he moves on from the fae beasts to the gods themselves."

There's an instant commotion as the small crowd breaks into urgent arguments over what this means. People shout that it can't be true. Others call for an immediate trip to Old

Coros to report it to King Joruun. One elderly lord begins to pray.

Rian pounds on the table to quiet everyone. Eyes shifting toward the doorway to my back, he says, "Tell them, Wolf."

Lightning strikes down my spine as I turn slowly, breathless, to see the figure who's just entered with heavy boot falls.

Thank the gods.

Basten is here. Safe. He's even filthier than Rian; dirt clodded in his tangled raven hair, streaks of blood on his arm, and a bloody gash on his right cheek. Still, my heart-strings pull so tightly that it's all I can do not to run across the ballroom and throw myself into his arms.

Basten's eyes slide to mine, wavering with something I can't read. His lips part. He swallows hard before returning his attention to Rian as if nothing happened.

"My lord," he says in that deep, rumbling voice that makes my bones tingle. "Apologies for my delay—we discovered a wound on one of the horses when I returned them to the stable."

"Is this true?" Lord Berolt demands as all eyes hone in on Basten. "You found a goldenclaw's tomb?"

Basten hesitates, dragging his dirt-caked fingers through his tangled hair. He nods. "Yes. The goldenclaw, too."

Rian grabs a frightening-looking weapon made of leather straps and curving blades from the table. "The Volkish cavalry mounts goldenclaws, not horses, as war beasts. We believe they train them to battle with these gauntlets harnessed to one paw. I brought one back to silence those who would claim my words are lies."

He tosses the gauntlet back on the table, where it clatters onto a tray of fruit and cheese, sending grapes rolling.

The crowd leans in amid soft gasps.

Rian braces his arms on either side of the map, dropping his voice in warning. "Grand Cleric Beneveto wants the Red Church to rule Astagnon, but he bears no loyalty to our kingdom, only to his gods. Not only do I doubt his loyalty, but his priests are no match for an army such as we infiltrated. Astagnon will need the Valvere Golden Sentinels."

As assenting murmurs grow, Rian stands at full height, lording over the table. "The Midtane celebration approaches; we'll invite the heads of all the powerful houses. Magistrates. Guild leaders. I'll present them with this goldenclaw gauntlet. It will convince them I'm the only one strong enough to stand against Rachillon. That we must remain a monarchy. With their backing, I'll go around the King's Council. Straight to King Joruun and force his decision to name me successor."

As everyone examines the goldenclaw gauntlet, I quietly slip away from the crowd. I find a servant's door disguised as part of the ballroom paneling, then push through it.

Once inside the narrow hallway, I press my palm against the door and whisper, "*I need to talk to you.*"

Though Basten is halfway across the ballroom, far out of normal hearing range, it isn't long before the door silently swings open. He steps through, face as unpredictable as a stormcloud.

Tangles of dark hair fall over his burning eyes as he quietly says, "Sabine. It's dangerous to meet like this. Rian is right on the other side of this door, and he's as suspicious as a scent hound that the two of us are sleeping together." He brushes his fingers softly over my cheek as though he can't help himself. "You must do everything in your power to convince him that—"

Before he can finish, I fist my hands in his dirty shirt and shove his back up against the tight wall, thrusting myself to tiptoe.

He smells of the forest: campfire and pine.

It gives me pause.

My chest heaves, and in the tight passageway, we're close enough that my breasts graze his shirt. His muscles relax against my hold. With a mind of their own, my nipples harden from the friction. His eyes fall to my lips, and he briefly snags his own bottom lip with his teeth to capture a low moan.

I twist my hands harder in his shirt, forcing myself to focus. *I'm here because of anger, not love.*

"You knew," I hiss.

His eyes flash in surprise as they fire up to meet mine. "What are you talking about?"

"The letter, Basten!" I hiss as I pound my fists against the hard planes of his chest. "I'm talking about the letter!"

Silence beats along with our discordant hearts, and a myriad of emotions cross his face like a shifting spring storm. Is he going to pretend not to know about it?

Something finally settles in his eyes, a kind of soft surrender, and his throat bobs in a hard swallow. "How did you—"

"You had no right to keep that information from me!" I coil my fists tighter in his shirt. My knee knocks against his thigh, and he opens his stance, instinctively drawing me closer despite the fact I'm pummeling him.

"Sabine—" His voice tears like a broken seam.

But I'm too peppered up to listen to any half-hearted

apologies. "Charlin Darrow isn't my father, Basten! It's a mad enemy king with an army of *goldenclaws*! That isn't even the part that hurts most—that letter described my mother, too. Do you have any idea what I would give to know the truth about the woman who birthed me? The only woman who loved me?" My eyes fix like dagger points on him, my curled lips kiss-close as I demand, "You stole that from me. Give it back."

His bottom lips graze mine, rough like sandpaper, as he quietly says, "I burned it."

The blood drains from my face, pooling somewhere down around my knees. I step back, letting my hands fall at my sides.

On impulse, I deliver a sharp slap to his already bruised cheek. The wound reopens, and a line of scarlet blood rolls down his stubble.

"Fuck you, Basten Bowborn."

My heart is sprinting marathons around my ribcage. Basten leans back, resting his head against the wall, hooded eyes trailing over my curves. I have to fight my body's urge to lean in that missing inch and keep the distance close between us.

My skin feels suddenly too bare, antsy, like I need to run my hands over my arms. My insides don't know if they're about to explode or melt into liquid cream.

A drip of blood hovers at the base of his jaw, about to drip onto the swell of his chest. Before I can stop myself, I smooth my thumb over his stubble to catch it, and some crazy impulse makes me pop my thumb in my mouth to lick it off.

The air stutters out of his lungs. He grips my wrist with an iron hold, towering over me, and pulls my thumb out of my mouth to run his tongue over the pad himself. Not releasing my wrist, he backs me up the short distance to the passageway's opposite wall, mirroring how I had him trapped before.

Slowly, he braces his powerful arms against the wall to bring his emotions in check.

"If you'd seen what I have seen," he growls, "you'd understand. What was I supposed to do, little violet? I had just murdered four raiders to save you. I'd eagerly kill four hundred more. But I'm just one man. I can't fight off an army. Especially not the one that King Rachillon commands."

A hot wave of frustration splashes against my skin.

Briefly, I glance at the door. How long have we been gone? When will someone notice?

"You could have—have told me." A sob breaks my words, but I refuse to give into tears. "We could have made the decision together."

"Yeah, *right.*" His voice is rigid, like a shield against his own heart. "You'd never marry Rian if you thought you had a choice. I had to force you into his arms by any means necessary." He lowers his head to mine. "You speak of truth? So be it. I'll tell you the truth. The truth is that it's killed me every passing hour to see you at his side instead of mine. Every night, I lay awake in a cold, empty bed, cursing my foolish heart for pushing you away."

I stare baldly at him, frozen breath frosting my lips. After weeks of trying to wring the truth from him, now that I have it, I'm like a dog who finally caught a squirrel.

I have no clue what to do with it.

He dips his head to the crook of my neck, breathing in my scent like it's air and he's been drowning. "I meant every word I said in that waterfall cave. I was ready to burn down the world for you. Turn my back on the man who's been like a brother to me. Whatever you do, never doubt what we felt for each other was real."

His lips skim over the pulse point in my neck, sending stars shooting down to my toes. I melt back against the wall, nothing but a throbbing bundle of nerves as he continues, "It's more real than any fucking thing I've felt in twenty-six years of life."

His hand cups the curve of my shoulder like a crystal chalice, sliding down the length of my arm until his hand forms a shell around my own. He interlaces our fingers, then brings my palm to his lips.

My lungs heave so hard I can barely get the words out, whispered against the bruise on his cheek. "You hurt me more than anyone ever could."

"I know."

My fingers move in an exploratory circle around the cut on his cheek, as though they can't make up their mind whether they want to tend to his wound or else dig in my nails to make it hurt more.

"I don't hate you, Basten. Gods, but I wish I could."

Heat prickles along my spine as he slowly pulls me closer, pressing my palm flat against his chest.

An inch—that's all it would take to seal a kiss.

My legs tremble beneath me like two quaking saplings. My breath grates, my thoughts churn between wicked desire and wanting to shield myself from any more pain.

"Oh, little violet." His nickname for me rumbles through his throat as if he savors it. His lips press to my forehead and stay there a beat too long. "I wanted to tell you everything—"

A shout from the ballroom tears his lips off me. "*Valvere! Where are you, Lord of Liars?*"

Beligerent, masculine, drunk.

I know that voice.

"Charlin," I gasp. "He's how I found out about the letter. He came to Duren to confront Rian."

Basten presses his finger to his lips for me to be silent, then guides me by the small of my back to the servants' door. Ear cocked to listen, he waits a few seconds.

"Go now—they're all turned the other way. I'll wait a minute, then join you." The flat of his strong, wide palm presses me forward.

I slip through the door as unnoticeably as I can, skirting the room until I'm just another face in the crowd, craning my neck and nodding like I've been there the whole time.

Charlin storms up to the High Lord's table, swaying slightly. I don't need godkissed senses to smell the gin on his breath. His entrance is enough of a commotion to render the crowd silent.

Suri darts behind him, clutching a wooden lockbox to her chest like she doesn't know what to do with it, her courteous smiles doing a poor job of hiding her jangling nerves.

"Tomorrow, Charlin," she hisses through her smile. "Let's come back tomorrow. You aren't *yourself* at the moment."

He hiccups, waving her away meanly, then jabs his finger toward Lord Rian. "You! I've been waiting three days for you to return. On top of the months of waiting for your response to my letter. Thought you could just ignore me and I'd go away, eh? Sitting on the powderkeg of information I have? Ho, ho, I'm no fool." He slams his fist on the table, accidentally hitting a china plate, which rings. "You owe me an answer to my proposal."

Guards step forward to arrest him for his insolence, but Rian holds up a hand. There's a mix of amusement with his bafflement, and he's still riding the high of his discovery at the border.

"Wait. Let him speak. Old man, I haven't the faintest fucking clue what you're talking about. I believe I agreed to a proposal to your daughter, not *you*."

Everyone laughs, and Charlin's cheeks burn beet red.

From the corner of my eye, I see Basten slip out from the servants' door and join in among the soldiers, one hand casually on his sword. A tense look passes between us.

We both know what information Charlin Darrow has; if he tells Rian about the letter, it will come out that Basten never delivered it. The suspicions Rian has about our affair will be confirmed.

Charlin *can't* be allowed to talk.

Charlin grabs the lockbox from Suri's hands, dropping it on the table, where it makes the forks clatter. He smacks his hand on it dramatically. "I have the proof of my claims right here. Unless you want every town crier in this wicked city to proclaim at dawn that you are knowingly marrying our enemy king's daughter—"

Time seems to stop. *No, no, no.* Everything is happening too fast, and I don't know how to stop it. Basten shoves through the other guards toward Charlin with anger sparking in his eyes.

"Excuse me, what the fuck?" Rian says.

"Sure, pretend you don't know that Sabine is the daughter of that mad king Rachillon—"

Before Charlin utters another word, Basten clamps a

hand over his mouth, silencing him. He yells, "Shall I throw this liar in the dungeon, my lord?"

But it's too late. The crowd is already buzzing. Whispers about my fair hair, blue eyes, and unusual magic abound.

"You'd better explain what the fuck you just accused my bride of," Rian says to Charlin. "And if I hear one more lie when your mouth is free, I'll cut your lips off."

In the chaos, Lady Eleonora calmly drags the lockbox over to her seat, sloshing back wine as she tries to figure out the latch. "He claims there's proof, so let's see this proof."

My thoughts tumble like rocks in an avalanche. Twisting, plunging, spinning. There is no point in denying Charlin's claim if the content of that box—whatever it is—will prove it.

"It's true!" I blurt out, shoving my way to the High Lord's table. My chest heaves as I grip the back of a dinner chair.

All eyes turn to me, but the only ones that matter are Basten's. He watches me closely, trusting I know what I'm doing.

I lick my lips as sweat breaks out on my brow. "It's true," I repeat, quieter, lifting my eyes to Rian's. "I only learned the truth myself while you were away. This man isn't my biological father. My mother was a royal concubine to King Rachillon and kept it secret until her death. Charlin Darrow seeks to extort you to keep the information secret."

Lord Berolt immediately turns to the guards. "Seal the door. No one in or out without my permission. Servants included."

My heart pulses between my ears. There are, what, twenty people in the room? The Valveres. A few guards.

Servants. Merchants. Few enough that this secret can still be contained.

Lady Eleonora looks disgusted, eyeing me like I'm a smudge on her wine glass, and Lady Runa openly balks. I hear her no-so-subtle complaint to Lady Solvig that it isn't fair *I'm* a princess—of an enemy nation or not.

Rian, however, remains quiet. His card-player face reveals nothing. The only hint I have to his thinking is when his gaze falls to the goldenclaw gauntlet on top of the map of Volkany, and a twinkle of scheming fires in his eyes.

"You are the mad king's daughter?" His voice is flat, unreadable.

I try to swallow with a bone-dry throat. "We can keep the information secret. No one outside of this room needs ever to know."

His eyes dart from person to person, fixing with disdain on Charlin, then settling back on me. "And this man, Charlin Darrow? You have no loyalty to him? No love?"

I ball my fists on the table. "I have more love for a slug."

Rian nods, picking up the bear gauntlet, slowly making his way around the table. His index finger traces the sharp blade meant to fit over a bear's claw. He hooks it over his own finger as he stops in front of Charlin.

"Grandmother?" he asks over his shoulder.

Lady Eleonora lifts out of the lockbox a golden disc decorated with glittering gemstones—a royal calling coin. A collective hush falls over the crowd.

Lady Eleonora inspects the disc and nods. "It's authentic."

Charlin gives muffled, insistent cries, but Basten holds his mouth tighter than an animal trap.

Rian flexes his fingers in the gauntlet's blades, testing

out the hinged mechanics, and then uses the one hooked to his thumb to slice Charlin Darrow's throat in one quick, clean slash.

Blood spurts out in a crimson spray, splattering Rian and me. Basten releases his prisoner, who slumps to the floor. Charlin uselessly grasps at his neck as he sputters for breath. The crowd steps away from the blood, speechless.

Finally, after a torturous few minutes, Charlin stops moving.

"Charlin!" Suri screams, falling to her knees in the puddle of growing blood.

Rian turns to me, gently running one of the blades down my cheek. "I'd have killed him even if he was your real father, but the fact that you bear no love for him makes it cleaner. I'd hate to disappoint my bride by murdering her father."

He pulls off the gauntlet and tosses it back onto the map, where lines of blood stain the illustration of Drahallen Castle.

"No one extorts a Valvere," he says measuredly to Charlin Darrow's corpse before grabbing a silk napkin and striding away to clean up the blood on his perfect face.

I'm shaking. Warm blood soaks into the soles of my silk slippers. It feels as though my mind hovers somewhere outside of my body, looking down on the violent aftermath as Suri collapses beside her husband with a wail that nearly shatters every stained glass window.

As Rian's footsteps echo down the hallway, Lady Eleonora takes her goblet, slurps a sip of wine, and quips to Suri with disdain, "Oh, don't pretend you didn't wish to be a widow."

CHAPTER 18
WOLF

The days leading up to Midtane are a blur. When I'm not on Sabine's bodyguard duty, I'm in the Golden Sentinels' camp, running training drills under Captain Fernsby's relentless command. Since returning from the border, Rian has had every able-bodied man in Duren brushing up on their sword skills.

Meanwhile, the servants run themselves ragged preparing for the grandest Midtane celebration in decades. Most years, it's a simple affair. A white tent raised in Tolver Wood. A fiddler. Fruit platters. Everyone getting drunk in white tunics and splashing in the hot springs, half-naked like bitches in heat. This year? Rian is spending a king's ransom to impress the heads of Astagnon's most powerful houses. He'll buy their support with fine wine. Blackmail or bribe if he must. Or, simply put the fear of war in them with talk of waking gods.

During all of it, Sabine spends long hours in the monoceros stable with Myst and the creature. If not there, then she's pouring over ancient books in the Valvere library, mumbling to herself the rare names she finds amid the pages. Fuck if I know why, but I trust she has her reasons.

She barely acknowledges me unless it's to loudly complain about how I smell like sweaty barracks. I'm no idiot. I told her to do everything in her power to throw Rian off his suspicions, and she's doing it brilliantly. Frankly, a little too well. Anyone watching would think she loathes me more than the plague.

I'll take her insults, though. I'd bear the worst pox just to bask in the fringes of her light. Finally, there are no more secrets between us. I harbor no illusions of gaining her forgiveness, but at least I don't have to keep pretending as though she meant nothing to me. Not when every moment without her is like an echo I'll forever be chasing.

Because she *still* can't be mine.

Technically, the truth about her parentage doesn't change anything. She's still engaged to Rian. She still needs his army. The threat from King Rachillon hasn't decreased—if anything, it's swelled tenfold. We have no more chance of being together now than we ever did.

And yet, everything has changed.

Because Sabine doesn't hate me—she only hates what I did. Worlds lie in that small difference. It's the thin, fragile thread in a tapestry that holds together the possibility of redemption for my cursed soul.

On the morning of Midtane, I'm up early to help harness the carriage horses. The courtyard is a whirlwind of servants loading provisions, stacks of white tunics, and freshly laundered towels.

When Sabine and Rian climb into the High Lord's carriage, I try my best to blend in with the general chaos. The last thing I want is to be noticed—in fact, I'd rather Rian forget about me entirely.

Including the sparring match we left unfinished in the woods.

It's a languid journey of four miles to Tolver Wood. The second carriage, carrying Lady Solvig, Lord Gideon, and Lady Runa, sways as they sing ribald songs within, already drunk on ceremonial wine.

The third carriage, holding Lord Berolt and Lady Eleonora, is silent to everyone else's ears. Only I can hear their conspiring whispers, though they're shrewd enough to muffle their voices with scarves pressed to their lips.

When we arrive at the fairgrounds, a dozen carriages are already hitched at the tree line, the horses lazily swishing their tails in a roped-off pasture. White canvas tent points rise over the treetops like a ship's sails.

Wildflowers are woven around tent poles to form living archways, and colorful paper lanterns painted with scenes from the Book of the Immortals hang from the tented ceiling. On each of the buffet tables, carved ice sculptures of Immortal Solene in various suggestive poses drip water onto refreshment platters. Prepubescent girls in flower crowns perform a dance to the summer sun, accompanied by a full orchestra of flutists.

Dozens of men and women laugh around low tables overflowing with glazed figs, strawberries with clotted cream, and delicate pastry shells filled with herbed goat cheese. They wear sackcloth tunics that are simple rectangles with an embroidered neckline, fasted around the waist with a twine belt. The tunics leave little to the imagination.

Hems fall to mid-thigh on both men and women. Flashes of side boobs and flopping balls abound.

Sentinel armor might be uncomfortable as thorns in my ass, but I've never been so thankful for my chainmail.

Despite the peasant guise, the women's intricate braids, threaded through with expensive flowers, and the men's soft skin mark them as Astagnon's wealthiest residents. Magistrates. Guild masters. A gaggle of lords I don't give a fuck about, half of whom brought their mistresses instead of wives. Lady Suri is absent, which is no surprise—she's suffering through her month of mourning.

Notably, the wealthy merchants who were present during Charlin's death are also not in attendance. I don't recognize many of the servants or soldiers from that day, either.

Are they all six feet underground? Silenced to keep Sabine's secret? There was a time when Rian would have had *me* hold the blade. Now, I have no idea what gears turn in his brain, or who does his dirty work.

The only familiar faces I'm happy to see are Folke and Ferra, currently engaged in a battle with one another, dripping with sexual tension, over the last mushroom pastry.

I stroll into the main tent, scoping out the grounds. Tradition dictates that attendees bring a modest offering to the gods: a handful of berries, a honeycomb, a pewter thimble. The Valvere's Midtane altar, however, drips with riches. Crystal figurines. Rare peacock feathers. Bottles of port from the Spezian hill country. And so many tottering piles of golden coins that they spill onto the grass.

The grandest treasure of all, though?

The Valvere family's own offering: the goldenclaw

gauntlet, polished and oiled and laid out on a faux bear's paw carved of mahogany.

The air is electric with murmurs about the gauntlet. Everywhere, conversations are animated with the Volkish army's threat and the necessity to bolster Rian's forces in the impending conflict.

A blur of puffy white darts past me, and I grip my sword hilt, flashing back to the Volkish woods, before realizing it's one of Lady Eleonora's terriers dressed as a cloudfox.

"Too fucking soon," I mutter under my breath.

My pulse is just settling when I see Sabine step out of the dressing tent. *Oh, fuck.* Her presence is a punch to the gut, an ache that I crave and curse at the same time. I nearly lose my footing, stumbling like a youth with his first sip of ale.

In the barely-there tunic, her exposed thighs are the color of sunlit cream. She's free of makeup or jewelry, as bare-faced as the first time I saw her standing in her father's courtyard. Where is the Volkish in her features? Does she resemble the mad king? Would she feel more at home there? Because here, she stands out like a goddess. Her bare feet tease the grass, which bends as if even the plants yearn to caress her. Her hair is coiled in an immortal braid dotted with hundreds of tiny purple flower buds.

I groan. *They're violets.*

Of course, they would be fucking violets.

Every man's head turns to stare at her whether their wives are at their side or not. She stands out like the sole star in the night sky.

I swipe a hand over my chin—Gods be damned, I'm drooling.

As the hours pass, I linger in the main tent's shadow,

content to merely stand vigil over her. She's a breath's distance away, yet miles from reach. She tries to sip her wine slowly, but Rian tips the base upward. She laughs as she playfully pushes him away. When she straightens, a bloodred drip rolls down her chin.

Rian catches it with his thumb, lingering a second longer than he needs to.

The sight of another man's hand on her sends a jolt of jealousy burning behind my ribs, and it's all I can do to remain like a statue. Beneath my armor, I'm a river of want running deep. Obsessing over the curve of her lips. The way her hair catches the sun like it was made to shine only for her.

Gods, this woman is perfection.

Once everyone is good and drunk, and more than a few couples have disappeared behind the tents to rut like animals, the priest lifts his prayer stick.

"On this the longest day of the year, we profess our gratitude to the Goddess of Nature for her plentiful bounty that has kept us mortals fed and clothed for one thousand years. We have drunk her berry wine. Hunted her woodland game. Built homes from her trees. Now, let us bathe in her blessed waters, and demonstrate our devotion through revelry worthy of the gods!"

A lute player leads the procession toward the sound of babbling water. The attendees form a line, belting half-slurred fae ballads, bare feet tripping over their own toes. It's a gods damned parade of idiots.

I trail behind with the other guards to take my place at the streambank, tucked back in the treeline with the servants who wait with towels and wine refills.

The stream is picturesque, I'll give it that. At first glance,

I'd think it was a painting in Sorsha Hall. Steam rises like a fine mist over the glen. Springy ferns hug stone-lined shores, shaded by willows dangling their leaves in the breeze. Naturally hot water flows from one shallow pool down a series of cascades to another, then another. Each pool is flanked by blooming azaleas, creating the impression of intimate, private spaces.

The revelers break off into groups, moaning in ecstasy as they sink into the steaming water. Their wet tunics cling like paint to their skin, leaving nothing to the imagination. Every curve, every rise, every nipple is clear as day.

"My darling." Rian sinks waist-deep in the water and offers Sabine his hand. "Grace me with your presence? Let's outshine the Goddess of Nature with our own legendary revelry."

As she dips one elegant foot into the water, she quips, "Shouldn't you be charming some wealthy baroness who can help buy your way to the throne, instead of the woman who already wears your ring? After all, this is one big game, isn't it? With you and the Grand Cleric as players?"

Rian's mouth pulls in a wry half-grin. "The Grand Cleric and his pasty priests can scheme all they want in Old Coros. They think only the capital has power? They have no idea how much strength we have here in the provinces. Even here. In this pool with me."

He takes her hand, pressing his lips to her knuckles.

As Rian helps her into the water, her foot slips. I lurch forward sharply, every instinct ready to catch her. But Rian is already waiting with strong arms. She gasps, catching herself against his chest, then laughs as she shyly gazes at him through her lashes.

"Easy, songbird," he teases quietly.

My heart punches against my chest, a relentless drum sounding the punishing rhythm of want, need, want, need.

This is fucking torture.

There's a tension in my shoulders that won't ease. I sniff the air. There's wine on Sabine's breath. More damningly, there's also a telling musk between her legs.

What the fuck?

My protective instinct roars like a beast.

It's the wine, I have to remind myself. Fortified from an ancient recipe in the Book of the Immortals with ginseng and maca root, it leaves drinkers as horny as the fae.

The rest of the attendees waste no time pairing up—or tripling up—and soon half the glade is heavy with the sound of moans and lapping water as bodies connect. In the pool highest on the hill, Lord Berolt pushes a poor girl's head beneath the water to service his cock. Lady Eleonora sits opposite the pair, reclined against towels laid over the rocks, oblivious as she sings Popelin's Ballad with her head lolling to one side.

But every sense the gods blessed me with is pinned on Sabine.

As steam rises from the hot spring, her laughter, light and teasing, pierces through the veiled air, striking my ears like an arrow point. There she is, half-submerged in the water's warm embrace, her breasts nearly bare beneath the wet fabric, her cheeks flushed from steam—or is it Rian's touch that color them?

I shift my stance, my duty chaining me to the treeline like an anchor. As I watch Rian's fingers graze the water at Sabine's waist, my hand clenches reflexively at my side. I feel the rough texture of my own skin, aching for the softness of hers.

Rian settles on a rock, his back to me, and tugs Sabine down on his lap. As the water pools around her curves, she wraps her hands around Rian's neck and her eyes lift—directly to mine.

For a fleeting moment, the world narrows to our electric gaze.

"You know," Rian purrs in her ear, shamelessly caressing her wet tunic around her waist. "Today was our original wedding date."

"You think I would forget?" There's a barely-there slur to her honeyed voice that has me shifting, tension coiling like a spring.

"My father had hoped to unveil the monoceros here, with these gilded gooses as witnesses to its destructive power. Fortunately for you, Wolf and I found that golden-claw's gauntlet. Not as impressive as a living fae creature tamed by a beautiful woman, but sufficient."

She strokes her finger down the short hair at his nape. "And, what? You want me to thank you by riding your cock in *honor* of the Immortals?"

"A kiss will suffice," he murmurs.

Her eyes lock to mine, a flush spreading down her neck. Is that a mark of hesitation? Of regret? I sense her indecision in the falter of her pulse, but I can't read her tumbling thoughts.

"Fair." The word leaves her lips like a prayer, and only I can detect the tremor of reluctance in her vocal cords. She swallows, never breaking my gaze as she whispers in Rian's ear, "A kiss would be fair. After all, you spared me the pain of having to call Charlin Darrow my father one more time."

Rian adjusts his hips, his hands sliding lower on her waist. "I murder your father, and you thank me? Gods, songbird, you're positively feral. How would you thank someone who killed *me*, I wonder?"

At his jest, her lips curl. "Oh, please. I stopped wanting you dead when I saw that you'd placed perches around my room for my animal friends."

"Hmm?" Rian's head tilts in slight confusion before straightening. "Oh. Right."

Sabine's eyes narrow as they flash between me and Rian. Then, a moment of understanding eases her features: All along, it wasn't Rian who saw what her heart wanted most. It was me. Whispering in his ear. Telling him what thoughtful things to do for her, letting him take credit.

Her eyes soften, then the irises blow up as she licks her wine-stained lips. Her heartbeat strikes doubly fast. The air is thick with the scent of minerals and lust, and I feel like I'm about to burst out of my armor.

You did this to yourself, Basten, I remind myself. *You told her to do everything in her power to throw Rian off the scent of our affair. What the fuck else did you expect her to do?*

With her arms still propped around his neck, she murmurs into his ear.

"Do you know what I want, Rian?" Facing him, she presses the rim of her nail lightly against her bottom lip. "I want you to kiss me here."

A surge of silent rage grips my throat. My jaw tightens, a small slip to show the storm raging beneath my stoic exterior.

Is this a game to her?

"Darling, I live to oblige." Rian cups the back of her skull with two hands and claims her lips in a kiss that teases as much as it obliges. His tongue brushes her top lip, asking for entrance, but Sabine pulls back—eyes on me—and touches the soft line of her left jaw. "Then here."

Rian chuckles, game for whatever she wants to play. "Consider me your slave." His hot mouth traces from the back of her jaw to her chin.

With slow, deliberate moves, Sabine tilts up her neck and rests a finger on the hallow at her throat's base. "Then here."

As Rian pounces a kiss on the spot, my thoughts slide into place like a lock. *That little wildcat.* This is a game I've played before, too. Our night together at the Manywaters Inn, these were each of the places I vowed I would kiss her.

Later, at the waterfall, I made good on those promises.

Lips.

Jaw.

Base of the neck.

Next, her birthmark . . .

"Then, here." Her eyes spark against mine as she drags her finger to her godkissed birthmark, barely covered by the wet fabric pasted to her chest.

As Rian kisses her upper chest, I stare in baldfaced lust, a man undone by the simple acts of a woman and his rival unfurling before him in a veil of steam.

The spitfire malice she's hurled at me with those blue eyes is absent now. There's only a mirror of my own forbidden need in those cobalt depths. She's soothing Rian's suspicions, kissing him while conveying in secret code that every word is meant for me.

Fuck. My eyes are hungry traitors, devouring every detail. My balls ache and tighten. Next in our game? It was her pert little nipple. If Rian so much as breathes against that bud, the beast in me is going to go fucking wild . . .

"My High Lord." A sentinel strides toward the stream with urgency, knuckles white on his sword hilt as he averts his eyes from his master's nearly-naked woman. "My apologies, but there's an issue."

Rian shoots the soldier a look that could cut Golath steel. "Can't it fucking wait?"

The sentinel lowers his head to speak in Rian's ear. I cock my head so I don't miss a word.

"It's one of the servants, my lord. Part of the extra help we borrowed from Madame Anfrei." The soldier points behind him, where two sentinels stand guard over a dark-haired servant with a patch over one eye. "He slipped in disguised as a porter, but he is actually a priest. He serves Grand Cleric Beneveto."

Rian's face darkens like a night storm. He growls loudly, "That man is a spy?"

"I'm not a spy!" The one-eyed man's voice rises, mild-mannered but unwavering. "I came on my own, disguised to protect myself from the Red Church's retaliation. I wish to tell you, High Lord Valvere, the truth of what is happening in Hekkelveld Castle. I cannot in good consciousness allow the Grand Cleric to manipulate me further into abusing my godkiss, all in the name of the Immortals."

Rian's eyes narrow to such thin slits that a needle couldn't pass through them. He says curiously, "This has to do with the Grand Cleric?"

The one-eyed priest nods.

Rian signals to the soldiers. "Take the priest to the auxiliary tent behind the carriages. Out of earshot of the attendees."

I bristle, because how many times have I heard that code for imminent torture?

Distractedly, Rian glances at me as he moves Sabine off his lap. "Wolf. Take Lady Sabine back to the fairgrounds. She's yours now to protect."

He hurriedly climbs out of the water into a waiting robe, combing his hair back reflectively. As he and the soldiers stride away toward the auxiliary tent, my eyes fall on Sabine.

Mine now?

Fuck the Grand Cleric. Fuck whatever gossip that priest has to spill. The only thing I care about in this world is the woman whose lustful look up at me is a blade that twists in my chest, fraying the edges of my resolve.

She asked me once if I loved her. I thought I was too damaged even to know the meaning of the word. But now, with this light-filled ache in my chest, the way my heart beats only for her, the fierce need to protect her, I realize what a fucking idiot I've been.

Quietly, I say so low it vibrates against my teeth, "Yes, you are."

A servant waits with a robe as Sabine exits the hot springs, but I snatch the cloth out of his hands and hold it open for her myself—there's no way I'm letting another man clothe her.

As she steps onto the soft grass, her tunic clings to her curves like a second skin, water forming rivulets down her perfect legs. I'm not sure which is throbbing harder—my heart or my cock.

"Thank you," she says quietly as I ease the fabric over her arms, letting my hands rest a second too long on her shoulders. I can't help it—I feel a primal urge for this woman. I'd slaughter the ten Immortals themselves if I could just remain this close for another breath.

But servants are watching. I step back, averting my gaze.

The clouds are growing dark overhead, but rain holds off for now. She follows me quietly on the path, her footsteps like the gentle patter of raindrops, the steam rising off her skin begging to be licked off. My body doesn't give a fuck that she belongs to another man. My balls ache. My cock strains, heavy with need. Every surge of blood through my veins urges me to end this torture.

She stumbles on a root and reflexively grips my hand. In that single touch, a charge shoots through my system, and any moral qualms are decimated.

What can I say? *I'm no saint.*

The moment we're free of watching eyes, I tug her off the path to a weeping willow. The swaying branches caress us as I guide her back against the trunk and grip her jaw between both hands.

"You didn't have to fuck him with your mouth," I murmur, lips parched for her.

She pins me with a challenging stare, tipping up her lips until they nearly brush mine. "I wanted to kiss *you*, you idiot."

"Then do."

I finally steal the kiss I've needed like air. Our lips come together like meeting oceans, colliding and crashing until I'm not sure where I end and she begins. I press my weight against her, pinning her to the willow trunk, letting her feel exactly how much I crave her.

A small moan escapes her throat, and I nearly die of pleasure.

"Basten . . ." she pants.

But I swallow her words, the need to touch her all-consuming, driving me into a primal state. I force my tongue between her teeth and slide the tip along the roof of her mouth, which earns me another moan.

A sharp laugh from the hot springs cuts through the trees, jolting me back to reality. I break the kiss, resting my forehead on hers, unsure if I will ever breathe normally again.

"Not here," I murmur. "It's too close to the others."

She gives a stuttering nod, her pupils blown with matching need, and slips her small hand in mine. *Like she trusts me.* My groin tightens with every step, sensing that release might be near. We come out of the path at the fairgrounds, which is a ghost town. The buffet tables are a mess of half-eaten plums, spilled wine, and overturned nut bowls picked at by birds. Extra robes are draped carelessly onto tree branches. Half the wildflower vines hang loose, torn down by drunken revelers.

I tilt my head, listening. Every guest and servant is at the hot springs, and Rian is far away at the auxiliary tent.

"Here." I pull Sabine into the main tent, which is as much a mess as everything else—save for the altar to Solene. My eyes latch onto it. With lounging pillows and low tables around us, it's the only thing high enough to kiss her against.

So, fuck it.

I sweep my armored arm over the altar, knocking coins, crystal figures, and expensive incense to the ground.

"Basten," she hisses. "Have you lost your mind? The servants will see. They'll suspect something."

"Everything is already a mess."

"It's the holy altar!"

I drop a crystal duck figurine on the ground. "I give absolutely zero fucks."

Her eyebrows raise: First in shock, then rolling into desire. I know this woman—she has no love for the gods, either. I tug roughly on her twine belt to free it, then peel the wet tunic up over her head as she lifts her arms. I toss the tunic, soggy and still steaming, to the ground.

Yes. Finally. Fuck.

I take a step back, allowing myself time to look over her. It's been months since I've seen Sabine as naked and natural as on the journey from Bremcote. Her hair is piled high in an immortal crown, not hiding a speck of the perfection before me. She's filled out since arriving in Sorsha Hall; her breasts are heavier, begging to be squeezed. The triangle of soft hair at her legs' apex glistens with need.

She tilts one knee out as though in invitation.

Moving like a hurricane, I grip her by the waist to sit her pretty ass on the altar. The scent of her sweet arousal in my nose goes straight to my brain, driving me feral. I press one palm against her belly, moving slowly up between her breasts like a shadow, then wrap my fingers around the long column of her neck.

With my other hand, I pull free the pins that hold her hair high. The locks cascade down, braid sliding partway loose, until she's as natural as a doe.

"You let Rian play our game from the inn," I chastise in a low voice, eyes hooded as I gently flex my fingers around her throat. "Lips. Jaw. Throat. Birthmark. Lucky for him that he didn't make it to the last one—he'd be a dead man."

She arches her back like a cat, already begging for my lips. And who am I to deny her? I take one nipple in my teeth, teasing and nibbling until her hips writhe on the holy altar, sending more coins clattering to the ground.

"Basten . . . Oh, fuck . . ."

I manage to tear myself away, holding back from the demanding need that's urging me to take her right here, now. I grip her braid, working the sections loose from her shoulders to her hips; then drop to my knees to unwind the braid to the ground.

Kneeling before her, I take one perfect foot in my hand, kissing the curving arch. She flinches, gushing more arousal from between her legs. Slowly, I kiss my way up her bare leg until I can nestle my face in her hot core, breathing in the scent of her need.

My whole body trembles, taut as an archer's bow.

Her hips buck toward my face, demanding. More coins slide to the ground with metallic clatters. She's become so greedy about sex. So shameless. And I fucking love it—so, I reward her with a teasing flick of my tongue on her cunt's hot, tight button.

But that's all my little violet gets for now.

As I return to my feet, she whimpers, "Don't stop."

I shake my head slowly. I take her jaw in my hand, guiding her to look at me, reveling in the telling breathlessness in her lungs.

The air grows heavy with the scent of the coming storm. The clouds darken overhead, the wind whips at the tent's sides.

"Ask me again, Sabine," I say quietly.

She whispers, "Ask you what?"

My voice rakes like boots over gravel as I reply, "What you asked when I climbed the tower to your room. Ask me if I love you."

CHAPTER 19
SABINE

Ask me if I love you.

Shock hits me like a swollen wave, leaving me gasping for air. The world tilts on its axis—what is he trying to say?

The shadows of the tent seem to lean in, eager to hear the words that will surely break me one way or another. This is it—the final, terrible rift between us. My heart thrashes like a snared rabbit beneath my ribs. Frantic. Terrified. My heart isn't shielded with golden armor like his.

A drip of frigid water from the altar's ice sculpture drips on my shoulder, searing me with a sudden chill that charges as much as it shocks.

Why is he asking me this? Why now? His godkissed ears *heard* the terrible rip through my heart the first time I asked him this question. He tasted my bitter pain. He saw with his preternatural sight how my chest hollowed out with devastation.

My lips tremble, but I refuse to give him—or the gods—

the satisfaction of looking away. So, pinning him with the full burn of my gaze, I repeat, "Basten, do you love me?"

His shoulders ease as he lets out a held breath. His thumb skates along the soft ridge of my jaw as his eyes fall briefly to my lips.

"Little violet," he says, "when my heart was cold, you warmed it. When my soul was sick, you healed me. When I thought loneliness was my lot, you were at my side." As his thumb blazes across my bottom lip, his throat jumps in a hard swallow. "Do I love you? With the gods as my witness, you are the only thing in this life I have *ever* loved. I was broken before meeting you—hell, I still am. But you breathed life into an ember I thought was forever extinguished. I loved you the night you asked me that question. I loved you in the waterfall cave. I loved you when I killed the raiders who dared to touch you. I think I've always loved you, Sabine Darrow—I just didn't know it. Because I didn't know what love was before you."

Listening to him, my heart and lungs are at war with one another, pulsing together in fits and starts. The wind billows the sides of the tent, snapping with a distant roll of thunder, robbing me of every last thought.

Words? Gone. All I am is a blank puddle, as lifeless as the ice sculpture.

Because I'm still afraid. Afraid this is all another game. An illusion. A cruel dream puffed into my sleeping ear by Thracia, Goddess of Night.

Another drip of ice water lands on my arm, reminding me to breathe. "Do you mean it? Tomorrow, you won't change your mind?"

He cups my face, his eyes fathomless as a winter sea. "I love you today, and I will love you every day since. Even if death separated us and I was sent to the underrealm, I would battle my way past Immortal Woudix himself to return to you."

My heart tumbles into a freefall, afraid of ever landing.

His lips ghost against mine as he murmurs, "I thought love was for fools. If that is so, then I never want to have a single wise thought again. Because, little violet," he finishes, and the pulsing shadows around us hold their breath, "I am irrevocably, undeniably, inescapably in love with you."

He meets me with a claiming kiss that is both gentle and charged at the same time.

I tip my head back. Brace myself against my arms. Briefly, my eyes sink closed as our lips press together, breaths mingling. Because I need to steep my soul in this moment. Let it saturate into my mind until I can really, truly believe it is real.

When I'm ready, I open my eyes.

Basten's blaze with intensity, his body coiled and ready to spring, while a slight tremor in his hands betrays an underlying vulnerability. I ease my legs open a few inches, knocking over a wine bottle that falls to the floor and shatters.

"Basten?" I say, voice hoarse. "Fuck me on this altar."

The softness in his eyes glasses over at the same time that his lips draw back in a primal smile. He doesn't need to be told twice. He grips me by the back of my neck, drawing a gasp from my lips as he leans me backward over the altar.

"Darling, you have no idea how much I wanted to hear that."

His gentleness gives way to the animal in him—the one who knows how to make me moan. He attacks my neck with his lips, biting as much as kissing, like a wolf claiming its mate. A wave of desire rushes to my core, flooding my swollen pussy until I can feel my desire staining the altar cloth. On impulse, I shove off a set of silver spoons, reveling in the sacrilege.

Gods, this is wicked. Fucking on a fae altar.

"Tell me that you meant what you said that night," he commands as he roughly cups my breast, tormenting the swollen nipple with his thumb.

"That I love you?" I say breathily.

"I want to hear it again."

"I love you."

He takes the nipple in his mouth, rolling his tongue and sucking until I feel like I'm about to shatter. Then, he wipes his mouth and stares at my lips instead. "This is far too much pleasure than a bastard like me deserves—but I'll earn your love. I promise you that, princess."

He moves in for another kiss, but I press a hand to his chest, suddenly overtaken with a deep-set fear. "Does it change things? That I'm Volkish? A princess?"

He snorts. "I don't care if you're Volkish or Astagnonian. A peasant or a princess. Godkissed or plain. Don't you understand yet, little violet? There are men who want you for your power—but I just want *you*."

The first patter of raindrops hit the tent, sending the paper lanterns quaking, the shadows dancing over us like capricious gods. Lightning stabs the sky, flashing electric light on our faces.

I gasp at the crack of air lighting up the afternoon sky. "It's beautiful."

"It is." Basten isn't looking at the storm, though—he's looking at me. A fluttery sensation fans me like bellows until my nerves blaze.

"You came here on Rian's hand," he says wickedly, sliding his left hand between my legs, "but now you're going to come on mine."

I gasp at the rough touch of his thumb on the slick seam between my legs.

"Fuck, little violet, you're wet as morning dew."

My eyelids fall to half-mast as his hand rubs up and down my opening, teasing me with the slightest pressure.

Glancing at the tent flap rolling in the wind, I whisper, "What if we're caught?"

His voice is sandpaper as he says, "There is nowhere under Vale's blue sky that I give the slightest fuck about anything other than worshipping your perfect body right now."

He picks up a candied violet petal from a plate of pastries, holding it out expectantly until I obediently take it between my teeth. The petal dissolves on my tongue, its subtle floral essence mingling with the sweet crunch of crystallized sugar. He watches me with a burning intensity as I swallow and then slowly lick the sugar crystals off my lips. "*Mm.*"

A ravished breath tears from his lips. "Fuck."

He urges my legs further apart, his hand still teasing my soaked opening. As one thumb presses against my clit, he picks up the massive peacock feather with his other hand—eyes never leaving mine—and commands, "Lie back. Be a good girl. I'm going to make you fucking moan."

The tent seems to spin as he shoves off more precious offerings, pushing me backward until I'm gazing up at the ice sculpture to my left, a flickering candelabra to my right. A drip of wax lands on my belly, and I writhe—but the pain doesn't hurt as I thought it would. It only excites me.

Without warning, Basten hoists himself onto the end of the altar by my feet. A bolt of precious silk crashes to the ground along with an illuminated copy of the Book of the Immortals.

Slowly, he crawls over the sacred offerings until his hips straddle mine. Gazing down at me, he drags the peacock feather against my nipples.

I buck, back arching, at the torturously soft tickle. He drags the feather down my belly to my quivering cunt, teasing the tight, hot bud.

"By the gods, Basten!" My foot jerks, knocking more coins to the floor.

Another drip of hot wax falls on my thigh, contrasting so exquisitely with the ice water pooling at the base of my neck, until I can't imagine my body undergoing a single more sensation without shattering.

"I can't take any more!"

"Take it, little violet. Take everything I give you. You might be a princess and I a filthy pagan, but when we're fucking, I'm your god."

Basten picks up the pitcher of honeyed cream, then slowly dribbles the liquid over my swollen cunt.

"Late at night," he purrs, "you're going to remember this. You're going to close your eyes and touch yourself all the places I am now, wanting it to be real again, impatient for the next time it is."

I whimper even before he drops to all fours, mouth to my cunt. With long strokes of his tongue, he laps at the cream between my legs. A sudden flush of sexual throbbing grips my lower half. Shudders of pleasure fill me with the urge to bear down, and I curl my fingers around the edges of the altar.

He licks at every part of my pussy, long and punishing like he can banish any trace of another man. My thighs, shaking, try to close up, but he wrenches them apart and feasts again on the honeyed cream. His fingers squeeze at my ass like ripe fruit, his thumb coming around from behind to press into my molten core.

I cling to the table for holy mercy, but the melting ice sculpture keeps flooding my back with frigid water that has me writhing.

He takes my clit in his mouth, sucking and flicking his tongue like he's feasting on sweet cakes, and I feel myself building to a crescendo.

"I'm close—"

He looks up devilishly and says, "Not yet, little violet. Come, and you'll earn yourself a punishment." He wets a finger with my own dampness and then holds it over the candle flame, pressing into the hot wax. "Be a good girl, and I'll take care of you. If not . . ." He tilts the candle to drip wax along the base of my belly, and I cry out with my head tipped back, but then the pain shifts into a different kind of ache. My writhing hips knock over a bottle of port, which pops open and stains the altar cloth with its scarlet liquid.

"So eager, wicked girl? You want me to fuck you here like a pagan?"

"Yes."

He pushes to his knees, unbuckling his leather breastplate. Impatiently, I pull at the straps around his waist, anxious to have him out of the rest of his armor.

He unbuttons his pants with torturously slow movements, gazing down at me between his legs. "Fuck, little violet. I want to pray to you. I want to worship you. I want to sing songs in your honor until a thousand years pass, and people tell stories of this night." Finally, he frees his cock—his hard, throbbing length like a sword hilt—and positions himself at my entrance. "How do you want it?"

"Hard, Basten. Hard and *now*."

He drives into me with one long thrust that has my hips rising up to meet him. For a second, we stay like that, caught in the candlelight's burn and the ice water's scorch. Finally, my lungs heave, as though this is what I've been searching for across ages. My body rewards me with a flush of warmth that curls my toes.

Sweat drips off Basten's brow as he pulls out, then plunges in again with hard, slick thrusts.

"That's it. Such a naughty little goddess, aren't you?"

His thrusts are pure heaven, channeling streams of delight straight to my depths. My hand snakes down to one nipple, pinching the already aching tip.

Basten grabs both my wrists, pinning them over my head in the shackle of his hand. I gasp with a rush of desire. A knowing smile curls his lips—he knows what I like.

"You don't touch yourself. Do you hear me, little violet? You come when *I* tell you to."

I can barely hear him through the pulse thundering in my ears, but a part of me is cognizant enough to nod.

"Good girl." He leans low as he thrusts again, his cock reaching impossibly deep in my core. "I'm the one who deserves to be punished, but you'll let my sinner's hands all over you, won't you?"

My nerves are blinking. I feel feverish, possessed. Basten grips the altar cloth, re-angling himself, and then drives into me even harder. Stars bloom at the edges of my vision. I'm so close—it feels like the rain outside is driving down on me; that one more thundercrack will send me over the edge.

"Come for me," he says, dropping his free hand to press his thumb against my clit.

I ride the edge of the coming storm. I want to break the altar with our fucking. For the gods to weep with our sacrilege. As I cry out from the climax, I hope it pierces the gods' pointed ears.

"That's it," he says. "That's how much I love you."

My body shakes, thighs quaking, as the wave of my orgasm floods me with warmth against the ice water at my back.

Basten doesn't release my wrists as he slides his other hand under my ass to pull me closer as he speeds toward his own finish.

"I worship you like a goddess."

He drives deeper.

"Crave you like a whore."

I'm floating, riding the aftershocks, still tingling with renewed pleasure whenever he pumps into me.

His balls tighten against my ass, his own release imminent. "I love you like a—"

Suddenly, light floods the tent as one of the flaps is lifted. At first, I think it's the wind, until I feel Basten freeze.

Dimly, I realize there are faces watching us. The gods?

No—*oh, fuck, no.*

Rian Valvere, Berolt Valvere, the magistrate from Wezzen, and a half dozen servants and soldiers who had begun to take down the tent stare at us, equally frozen.

My eyes latch onto Basten's in silent horror. This is it—everything we feared. My heart scrambles like a trapped bird. Basten braces his arms around me as though he can shelter me from the coming storm.

For a second, we stay like that, clasped together, as my

future husband stares at us with red bleeding into his cheeks.

"Fuck it." Basten growls low in my ear. "Fuck *them*. It's you and me against the world now, Sabine."

He thrusts inside me one final time, coming with such force that hot cum leaks out around his cock onto the altar cloth.

I gape at his brazenness, but that's nothing compared to the expression on Rian's face—stunned not only that Basten dared to fuck his bride but, when caught, had the balls to *finish*.

CHAPTER 20
WOLF

I *just fucked the High Lord's woman—in front of him.*
This is bad. Bad doesn't begin to cover it. This is hitting rock bottom, then having the gods toss me a shovel and tell me to dig deeper. I've done an impressive job of fucking up my life, actually.

Bravo, Wolf, bravo.

As Rian's nearest two Golden Sentinels reach for their swords, my cock is still sheathed deep inside Sabine, my naked ass shining like the moon. I just had to goad Rian with that final thrust, didn't I? Well, what can you expect from an animal that's been pushed to the brink?

Rian turned me back into a killer when he ordered me to torture Maks. He threw a beautiful morsel in my lap and told me not to feast.

So, yeah. *Rock fucking bottom.*

Time seems to slow. My body tenses as a final tremor runs through me from heart to heels. My eyes sink closed as I try to hold onto the last slips of this spell-bindingly perfect moment of having Sabine's sweet body under me, before—

Two sword blades flash.

Time seems to restart, but in strange, stuttering fits. My senses are going haywire like when I crossed the Volkish border. Sabine lifts to her elbows in slow motion, the wine making her reflexes more sluggish than mine. She takes in the soldiers. Her future husband. Hell, even her future father-in-law, that old letcher.

She's as still as a statue except for a single breath that catches in her throat.

When I pull out of her and do up my pants, her gaze springs to mine like a triggered trap. Her blue eyes well up with all the pain in the world, and she presses a soft palm against my cheek. "Oh, Basten."

I groan deep enough to rattle every bone in my body, her whispered word a balm to the bristling parts of my nature. I can die happy now, having heard my name spoken like that on her tender lips.

My voice, heavy with regret, breaks. "Sabine—"

Two Golden Sentinels cut me off when they haul me off the altar with as much delicacy as raging bulls. They drag me through the rain to shove me into the mud at Lord Rian's feet.

One of the soldiers slams his boot into my back, digging in his heel until the bones of my spine crack. Inside me, something menacing rumbles, teetering on the edge of restraint.

Keep it together, Wolf.

But then, I watch a third sentinel pull Sabine down from the altar with just as much force. Crying out, she struggles against him, trips, and slams to her hands and knees. A shard of a broken wine bottle cuts into her right calf, blood pouring out in a crimson rivulet.

The growl within me escalates to a roar at the scent of her spilled blood.

With an inhuman cry, I shove myself up, throwing out my arms to knock the two sentinels backward onto their asses. One of them drops his sword, but the other holds fast to his and swipes it toward my feet while he's still splayed out on the ground.

I dodge the blade easily—saw it coming a mile away—and grab a heavy gilded box from the altar to hurtle into his golden helmet. It slams into the nosepiece with a satisfying crunch of bone.

The second sentinel gets to his feet, but I slam a foot down on his fallen blade before he can reach it. He responds with a punch to my gut. I grunt, bracing myself against the pain, then slam a fist into his throat—one of the only unprotected places on Golden Sentinel armor.

Choking, the man staggers back, clutching his throat with both hands.

The third sentinel—the walking dead man who caused Sabine to bleed—draws his sword and lunges at me. I duck —it's almost too easy—and throw my shoulder into his ribcage, slamming him back against the altar so hard that it tips over. The ice sculpture, candelabra, a kingdom's worth of riches—all of it crashes to the ground.

Another roll of thunder claps, echoing the fall of the broken altar.

Out of the corner of my eye, I see Wezzen's magistrate wringing his fat little hands, calling in the direction of the forest for more soldiers. But Rian? Lord Berolt? Those two vipers might as well be carved from stone, their years of concealing emotions making them as unreadable as brick walls beneath the falling rain.

A cruelty bristles within me.

I want Rian to experience pain like I've felt.

The first sentinel lunges at me with a downward cut. It's so by the book; he must be a new recruit, still wet behind the ears. He might be well-trained, but he sure as hell doesn't know how we fight in the streets.

I step back to grab his wrist, forcing his hand up over my head, then spin him around, disengage the blade, turn it, and stab him in the chest with his own sword. At the same time, the second sentinel rushes me bare-handed, and I pull out the first one's sword and neatly swipe it across his throat.

Both of them fall to the ground, dead.

Still, Rian doesn't react.

The clouds overhead darken. The rain increases. With a grunt, I kick over the closest candelabra onto the ruins of the altar, letting it burn the precious treasures from across the kingdom. *How about your finery now?* I want to shout. As the flames eat through the altar cloth, sweat pours off my brow.

I double over, bracing myself on my knees with two dead sentinels at my feet.

The remaining sentinel moves to attack stance, but Rian lifts his hand.

"Stop. That's enough."

The sentinel hesitates, throwing glances at Rian, daring to question his call.

My chest heaves. My muscles are primed. I could rip this man's head off with my bare hands—but already, more sentinels are headed our way from the direction of the hot springs.

"I said that's enough!"

Rian's raised voice makes the sentinel finally lower his sword.

My back is to Sabine, but with my senses on high alert, she might as well be standing an arm's length in front of me. She's covered herself with one of the extra robes, though it reeks of spilled wine and blood. She's favoring her right leg, leaning on one of the tent posts for support. The earthy smell of my seed on her thighs gives me a sick satisfaction, even now. Even in the middle of a fight.

Her heartbeat is strong—strong enough to give me courage.

Rian shoves one of the servants toward her. "Don't just stand there, tend to your mistress's wound! Can't you see she's fucking bleeding?"

The young man stumbles toward Sabine, shrugging out of his own white sash to wind around her calf.

"My lord—" the sentinel starts, but Rian silences him effectively by drawing his own sword, then slashing the man's throat from ear to ear with one clean slice.

The sentinel falls to the ground with the other two.

Sabine lets out a cry. "*Rian!*"

"He caused you pain." For the first time, Rian fully takes her in, letting his gaze rove over her with a mixture of possessiveness and tightly bridled fury. "You didn't think I'd hesitate to kill one of my own men if they hurt you?"

She presses a hand to her mouth.

The other sentinels reach us. Breathing hard, I glance over my shoulder at one of the cadaver's swords lying two paces away in the dirt.

Sabine catches my eye, shaking her head hard.

Though my instinct is to kill anyone within reach, her

presence pacifies me, as though I'm as much in her thrall as the raging tiger was at the spectacle.

Two sentinels rush up to flank me—Maximan and a youth. I don't fight as Maximan, that mean old brute, twists my arms behind my back and the other holds his sword at the ready. Well, fuck. It's the dungeon for me for sure. If not straight to the gallows. I'm surprised Rian doesn't run me through with his own sword.

As for what retribution Rian will enact against Sabine—

"It was me," I shout, drawing every eye, breathing hard against the strain of Maximan pinning my arms behind my back. "I forced myself on Lady Sabine. It wasn't her choice."

The tent goes silent except for distant thunder and the patter of rain. It plinks against my face, catching in my eyelashes.

Rian cocks his head, lips pursed, eyes narrowing.

"That's a lie!" Sabine hobbles forward, pushing away the servant trying to bind her bleeding calf. "He did nothing of the sort, he—"

"Shut your mouth," Rian orders before she says something to incriminate herself. Then he snaps his fingers at Maximan. "Maximan—shut her up *now*."

Maximan releases me and ensnares Sabine in his meaty arms instead, cupping his thick palm over her rosebud mouth. Her eyes bulge as she struggles against him, muffled cries falling on deaf ears.

My heart slams like a blacksmith's hammer. Anyone with two eyes could plainly see that I was not forcing Sabine, but this is the only way I can think to yoke myself with the blame and spare her.

The sky opens now, rain falling in sheets.

Rian slowly approaches me, ignoring both the rain and

Sabine kicking and flailing against Maximan. His eyes briefly shift over my shoulder to the broken altar that we desecrated with our sex.

"Wolf Bowborn," Rian says measuredly, though I can see the fury crackling at the edges of his eyes. "I'll give you one fucking word. *One*. Do you swear you took this woman against her will?"

"Yes."

It comes swiftly on my tongue. Immediate. Confident. To protect Sabine, I'd confess to every crime in the last thousand years.

A muscle feathers in Rian's jaw. Maybe it's the sweat and rain in my eyes, but I could swear my godkissed sight picks up a minuscule crinkle of regret in the twitch of his mouth.

He spins around, striding off toward the carriages.

"Take Lady Sabine to Sorsha Hall. She isn't to leave her room. And throw Wolf Bowborn in the dungeon with the rest of the criminals."

Two days pass. Or is it three? The dungeon guards, Rian's personal welcoming committee, treat me to a thorough beating, leaving me so dazed that finding a shit bucket to vomit in is like winning a game of blind man's bluff.

I've had no food. Only rancid water to drink. Bathing? What's that? Caked-on blood and filth cover me like a second skin. The cell's darkness doesn't bother me, but it's cold as hell. If the guards don't kill me, then starvation or a bite from a diseased rat will.

Still, I don't regret a single choice. Sabine knows now

that I love her—that I've always loved her. And I pray that she knows I always will.

The guards' game of Basel goes quiet when someone's clipped footfalls echo down the dungeon's hallway. I can smell sandalwood and saddle leather long before he turns the corner.

Rian stops at my cell, grimacing at the filthy pile of bruised rags before him—*me*.

"You are the most treacherous, snake-tongued, gutter-born cur I have ever met. A festering boil on the face of Duren, unworthy of the sentinel clothes you wear. I would kill you, except then I'd have no spineless fools left to work out my rage upon."

Wincing from the pain coursing through my bruised bones, I hobble to the iron bars, giving an ironic tilt of my head. "Lord Rian. To what do I owe the honor?"

Rian drags his head back and forth, mussing his hair with frantic fingers. "Why, Wolf?"

I open my mouth, but before I can speak, he raises a finger like a dagger.

"*Tamarac.*"

I hesitate. Tamarac means strict honesty—but does my word even carry any weight anymore?

"Tamarac," I echo with the ghost of a nod. I draw a breath into my aching lungs, warring with myself. What good are lies, now, anyway? When the worst has already happened?

Quietly, I say, "It's been going on since the ride from Bremcote. I took her virginity in a cave behind a waterfall. I promised her that I'd run away with her—but I changed my mind when I learned of her parentage. She was safer with you."

The confession unlocks a tightness in my chest, an itch that has bothered me ever since I first set eyes on Sabine Darrow, and I knew that my bond with Rian would never be the same.

His lips form a line as flat as parchment. For a second, I read more hurt than anger. "Do you love her?"

I'm already a dead man, so why not seal my fate? "More than I thought humanly possible."

He pinches the bridge of his nose, lets out a long breath, and asks, "Even behind bars, you profess your love? Do you *want* me to cut you down right here? Do you crave death that much?"

I grip the bars with both hands. "If there was ever an ounce of love for one another in our dark hearts, Rian, then I beg you to spare her. Lay the blame on me."

Rian holds my gaze—memories flash in my mind's eye of years spent as each other's sole confidants—then lets out an expletive as he paces before my cell in tight steps.

Finally, he slams the flat of his hand against the bars, making me flinch.

"You *idiot*. If you and Sabine had committed this sin privately, there could be a private cost to pay. Your tongue cut out, and a post at the Kravadan military base a thousand fucking miles from here. But you had to fuck her in front of witnesses, didn't you? The loose-lipped servants. My father. Wezzen's magistrate, who has already blabbed his fat mouth all over Duren. Oh, yes. Your affair is the talk of the town. Do my subjects feel sympathy for me, the jilted High Lord? *Oh no.* It's you and Sabine they're rooting for. Star-crossed *fucking* lovers."

I close my eyes briefly, hands tightening around the bars

until my knuckles blanch. "Hang me, then. Draw and quarter me. Just spare Sabine."

"Oh, *gods*." Rian groans up toward the dripping ceiling. "Don't fucking turn into a hero on me now, Wolf Bowborn. It's as improbable as fish for Sunday lunch." He rakes his hair back so hard I hear the scrape of his nails cutting into his scalp.

He paces back and forth. Once his pulse finally steadies in his veins, he returns to the bars and looks me straight in the eye.

"I can't count how many times you've saved my life. Even just days ago in the goldenclaw pit. We've been like brothers for almost twenty years. Because of that—*only* because of that—I'll spare you the gallows. But I don't think you'll find my other offer any more palatable."

Dread rises in my gullet. I know all too well the offer that prisoners are made when they're thrown in the dungeon around this time of year. Especially strong men in their prime. *Especially* if they're godkissed.

But I wait for him to say it.

"The Everlast," he spits. "It starts in a couple of weeks. Not much time to train, but then again, you've always been good at improvisation."

The Everlast.

Duren's supposed "justice trial" where prisoners beat each other to death. It's all thanks to Immortal Meric, God of Judgment, who was known for locking thieves in a labyrinth filled with deadly goldenclaws. Because who needs a fair trial when the fae would much rather see spurting blood?

"Well?" Rian prompts.

"Do I have a choice?"

"Win, and all will be forgiven." There's a blade to Rian's words. All forgiven? Not a chance in hell. If I win the Everlast, I might not go through life with iron chains, but Rian will never forgive me for this.

He starts to leave, but I blurt out, "Wait. What do you intend to do about Sabine's origin?"

It's been gnawing at me. That cunning glint in his eye when he heard King Rachillon was her father. The whole reason I avoided telling him the truth was for fear of how he might use the information.

Without turning, Rian says over his shoulder, "That's none of your fucking business. Anyway, everything hinges on my trip to Old Coros. I leave Saturday morning. You remember the Grand Cleric's spy who interrupted us at Midtane? He had some very incriminating information to spill about his holy overlord."

A spider of warning climbs up my spine. "What information?"

Rian pauses, then says as casually as describing the weather, "The priest is godkissed with the ability to temporarily bring the dead back to life. It only lasts a few weeks. The Grand Cleric has been making use of his talent on the primary resident of Hekkelveld Castle. Again. And again. And again. For nearly three months now."

A chill slithers around my ankles in the already frigid cell. Rian's suggestion is hardly subtle, but it's so far-fetched that my brain has to leap to grasp it. A deathraiser? Duren had a deathraiser pass through once: a tiny, ten-year-old girl who was so terrified of the lurching corpses that her parents bade her reanimate that she drowned herself in Silver Lake.

The way those corpses moved was ungodly. Their eyes were glassy as old marbles. And the smell—the rot of old blood forced through desiccating veins made me want to hurl myself in Silver Lake, too.

Now, I'm to believe that King Joruun is one of those walking corpses? Kept "alive" to keep the rule of Astagnon from falling into anyone's hands but the Grand Cleric?

Rian casually combs back his hair. "I might not be able to prove the Grand Cleric is in communication with King Rachillon, but I can fucking prove this. Not even the King's Council will be able to keep it quiet. I'm going to expose the Grand Cleric and secure the succession for myself. When I return, there will be the grandest fucking ball of all time to celebrate. Mark my words: Sabine will be queen before the first snow falls this winter, seated by my side in Hekkelveld Castle, wearing a gilded crown."

My muscles go slack, my breath rickety, like I'm just one step away from turning into old dead Joruun myself.

Rian takes another step, then stops. When he turns, he picks distractedly at the crumbling mortar between two stones as though warring with himself. "I'll return to Duren before the Everlast begins. And Wolf?"

"Yes, my lord?"

His eyes find mine one more time, wavering slightly. For once, there's a glimpse of the boy I knew, who sheltered me from his father's wrath, who let me sleep in his bed by his side when the soldier barracks froze over, who damned himself so I could escape his family.

"*Win.*"

CHAPTER 21
SABINE

Once more, I'm locked in my room like a caged tiger. Pacing. Claustrophobic. Am I any different than an animal? Just one more creature Rian can use for his aims? It's small comfort that Rian didn't kill the tiger after the arena show—not because he valued its life, only because of how much it had cost him.

And I've cost him ten times more.

As time passes, Brigit shares what gossip she can: Basten is in the dungeon. Rian has been ordering servants to pack his trunks in preparation for a trip to Old Coros, but no one knows the purpose of the trip or how long he'll be gone. Suri is still sequestered in a mourning berth in Duren's east side. Fortunately, I'm spared the monthlong grieving period: it's only for family, and in a twist of irony, I wasn't actually related to Charlin.

But wasn't I? Didn't twenty-two years of believing it make it true?

Serenith asked me about funeral arrangements the day after he died. Since Charlin's treason negated his status as a lord, tradition dictated that he be buried without ceremony in the pauper's mass grave.

However, Serenith continued, *Lord Rian will permit a small, private funeral if you so desire.*

All I desire, I said, *is a bottle of Bad Badger's Gin.*

That night, I'd sat alone in my bedroom and raised a glass of the noxious liquor to Charlin Darrow. "*Out of our hearts, into Woudix's hands.*"

Rian's coming absence will leave a rare opportunity, and Brigit, Ferra, and I whisper plans and possibilities like a pack of starving coyotes whenever we can.

Guards lock my windows, but nature always finds a way in. Spiders slip through the cracks. The nuthatch comes down the chimney. The mouse navigates her way through the walls.

They prove to be even better informants than my human friends.

According to the mouse: **The family calls you an unfaithful woman.**

And the nuthatch: **There is discontent in the streets. The townspeople wish you freed. They paint paper lanterns of you and the huntsman. They hold dramatics of you in taverns.**

And the spiders: **Tck-tck-tck, sssSssss, Tck-TCK-tck . . .**

There was a time in my childhood when I feared spiders. My first few weeks in the Convent of Immortal Iyre, bruised and alone, they were unlike the other animals who offered me comfort. Spiders came only at night, crawling in packs over the thatched ceiling like a liquid shadow hovering overhead. Hundreds of black eyes. Watching. Blinking. Waiting for *something*. Sometimes, they would inch closer, trying to crawl on me before I could slap them away.

In general, insects don't have much capacity for complex language, but spiders only emit an ominous hum: all of their tiny thoughts colliding like a child smashing piano keys at random.

Then, one night after Matron White had rapped my knuckles bloody with a prayer stick, I'd fallen into a deep slumber. When I woke, spiders covered my hands, crooning their awful sounds. I panicked until a gecko on the wall said: **Be not afraid.**

I waited. Perfectly still. When the spiders retreated, my bloody knuckles were licked clean, spider silk bandaging the wounds, their venom a powerful antiseptic.

All along, they'd been trying to help me. The reason I couldn't speak to them as I could other animals was because I didn't understand that spiders don't speak—they *sing*.

Tck-tck-tck, sssSsssss, Tck-TCK-tck . . .

It means something like "danger in the air."

Anyway, it's no surprise that while the Valvere family is busy slandering me as a whore to all the bejeweled ears of high society, the commonfolk of Duren are idolizing Basten and me, captivated by the tragic story of the lord's forced bride who fell in love with her bodyguard. The Winged Lady and the Lone Wolf, they're calling us. Rian may think little of his subjects, but I know the people of this town are powerful.

Someone coming! The mouse ducks under my pillow a second before a key turns in my lock.

"Lady Sabine?" Maximan holds open my door. For once, his stern face is a comfort, because at least *he* doesn't look at me like I'm a whore. "Lord Rian wishes to see you in his chambers."

My heart falls all the way to my toes.

I tap my fingers for the mouse to crawl onto my shoulder, but Maximan grunts a firm, "No animals."

On the long walk down Sorsha Hall's winding halls, my stomach twists in knots. Rian doesn't have a quick temper—I'd prefer if he did, so that we could have one explosive argument and then move on. No, Rian is the kind to patiently stew over wrongs for a lifetime.

"High Lord Valvere?" Maximan says, stopping at a doorway. "She's here."

When Maximan motions for me to enter, I hesitate before stepping through. I've never been in Rian's personal chamber. It's twice the size of my tower bedroom, with a massive mahogany bed to one side, and around the corner, a fireplace with leather chairs and a table carved with a map of Astagnon, the map's details now covered by open books and correspondences pinned down by daggers.

Rian, braced over the table, slams closed the book he was reading and stabs me with an unreadable look.

"Leave us, Maximan."

The door closes behind me, making me flinch. A log pops in the fire, sending my heart jumping.

Rian walks around the table with slow, deliberate steps until he towers over me, eyeing me like a wayward hunting dog who strayed off its course.

"Do you love him?" His voice has a rare hoarseness to it.

I try to swallow, but my throat is a drought. Finally, I hedge, "I—I don't know what love is, my lord. I thought I loved Adan, the raider who abducted me, too."

Rian slowly shakes his head back and forth, disappointed in my obvious lie. He leans back against the map table, eyes dragging down me like a blade, sharp and calculating.

"Well, love? Aren't you going to beg me for his life? Trade a fuck for his freedom?" He casually tilts out one knee, giving access to his hips. He looks at me expectantly.

My body jerks as though another log has popped in the fire, though the flames are quiet now. Out of the corner of my eye, that dark-wood bed looms. Is that what Rian wants? One pre-marital tumble in the sheets and Basten is spared?

As my heartbeat kicks up, I take a shaky step forward, my hands going to his belt as slowly as if moving through cold honey. My fingers shake so badly that I can barely undo the brass buckle. My pulse hammers between my ears, incessant and painful. Rian only watches me steadily like an opponent across the Basel table.

Taking a deep breath, I press my hands to the flat of his chest, standing up on tiptoe to kiss him—hesitating at the last second.

His arm comes around my waist, pulling me the rest of the way into the kiss.

Our lips meet, hard and clashing, and my body goes stiff. Rian's kiss is punishing and angry, his lips hungry thieves. I feel like I can't breathe. Like someone else is in my body, reaching again for his belt with shaking hands—

Suddenly, he shoves me away. I fall back against one of the chairs, breathing hard, the heat from the fireplace staining my cheeks.

His face contorts as he spits, "You think all I want is your cunt? You don't even begin to understand, do you? I want you to cherish *my* life enough to beg on your knees for it. As you would his."

I fall back into the chair, blinking hard.

A test. It was a test—and I failed.

"Please," I whisper. "I know there is love for Basten

somewhere in your heart, Rian. You know as well as I do that he didn't force me. If he deserved the dungeon, then so do I."

Rian sneers, "Don't dig your own grave, Sabine. You dishonor a good man by throwing his sacrifice in his face." He grabs my jaw with one hand, squishing my cheeks as he forces me to look at him. "I told you once what happens to cheaters. I gave Basten the option to fight in the Everlast. He's been fighting his whole life, so he actually stands a chance of coming out alive. You? You'd be slaughtered in seconds. No mouse can stop a battle axe."

The Everlast? A tiny flicker of hope finds a crack in the fear walling up my heart. The dungeon is a death sentence, and the Everlast would be, too, for ninety-nine percent of criminals. But with his godkiss and his training, who could be a better fighter than Basten?

"Everyone in Duren is stabbing their grandmother in the back for a ticket to the fight," Rian purrs an inch from my smooshed face. "To see the lovesick huntsman who insulted the *reviled* High Lord fight for a chance at redemption. Your crime is good for one thing at least: ticket sales."

There is no humor in his biting joke.

He finally releases my jaw, turning to stare moodily at the fireplace. There was a second, however, when I swear I saw true pain in his eyes. Rian's heart is black, sure, but he still *has* one. He's dealt me cruel hands, but then again, I've dealt them right back. Basten and I hurt him deeper than anyone could—and I almost feel sorry for him. I've been lonely, but I've always had my animal friends.

Who has Rian had? *Lord Berolt?*

"Rian—" I say softly, wanting to drop our masks once and for all.

"I'm leaving for Old Coros tomorrow." He's as cold as December, and any hope I had of reaching him vanishes. "Which means this evening will be the last monoceros training session until I return. You wish to save your lover? Then I suggest you tame that monster, because the only thing that will distract me from wanting to slide a knife across Wolf Bowborn's throat is a weapon as powerful as the beasts your Volkish father is waking."

The first stars make their debut as Maximan escorts me to the stable in the Golden Sentinel training grounds, where Rian is already waiting on the far side of the steel guard rail. The monoceros races circles around the riding ring, kicking and bucking and snorting steam—while a poor Golden Sentinel is carried off in a stretcher, moaning for his mother.

"You should have waited for me." I barely glance at Rian as I pull my skirt off over my knees, revealing the trousers that Brigit found for me in the laundry. "It isn't safe to let someone else open his stall door."

Ignoring the wounded man's wails, Rian takes in my clothes with a slight cock of his eyebrow. "Trousers?"

"You demanded I mount the monoceros even though he's far from ready. Did you expect me to ride in a ballgown?"

Turning back to the monoceros, he murmurs under his breath, "Well, I can't complain about the view from behind."

I roll my eyes. I have no doubt that Rian loathes me after my crime—but he still can't help remarking on my ass.

Myst trots over, all sunshine and haybales as she drapes her head over the railing for a forehead scratch.

She warns, *The fire stallion is especially grumpy today. There was a bee in his hay. It stung the roof of his mouth.*

Fantastic, I deadpan. *Because Rian is demanding progress* now.

Myst's eyes roll to the side in doubt for my chances. *Um . . .good luck?*

My heart wallops as I enter the riding ring, but I force my breath to remain steady—a horse can sense fear, and the last thing I want is for the monoceros to think he has the upper hand.

Besides, I have a special card up my sleeve. Since the last time I trained him, I've combed through nearly a hundred books from the library and picked out rare fae names to suit a thousand-year-old creature.

Holding my hands in a soothing gesture, I carefully approach the bucking fae horse. The guards have retracted the ceiling's skylight, and moonlight falls on his horn. It gleams like a sword's blade—but only sunlight can summon its deadly fey fire.

A burst of steam shoots out of his nostrils.

Easy, I say, edging closer. I'll say this about men's trousers—they're a hell of a lot easier to move in. *I'm a friend, remember? I read you stories. I bring you apples. Plus, Myst likes me. That must count for something.*

He tosses his head up, black eyes sparking.

I do! Myst vouches for me. *I adore her. And if you'd stop your whining, you would, too!*

He stops bucking, though he eyes me warily, his muscles tensed to bolt at any second as I approach. Carefully, I inch closer until I can rest a hand on his long neck. His muscles spasm, not used to being touched, but he doesn't move away.

Dear gods. This is actual progress.

I clear my throat, glancing back at Rian, who leans on the guard rail, his brow low and stern as he watches. Hesitantly, I steel my nerves and say testingly: **Ferno?**

A burst of molten steam fires out of the monoceros's nostrils, scalding the left side of my face.

Letting out a cry, I shield my head with my arm.

Well, I guess *that's* not his name.

Taking a deep breath, I try again: **Nighe?**

He lets out a blood-curdling screech toward the ceiling. I step back, heart thrashing against my ribs. Looking over my shoulder, I see Rian's face fall into an even deeper scowl.

Calas! I shout in my head, matching the beast's roar.

He rears, tossing his razor-sharp mane, muscles rippling in the moonlight. As he bolts away from me, his rear hoof catches me in the left forearm, and I'm thrown backward into the sand. My back slams hard, jolting the breath from my lungs.

My vision blurs. My ears ring like a bell. There's a stab of pain in my forearm that skates all the way up my side until even my molars ache.

Tears break across my eyes. The bitterness of defeat bites at me. Today *has* to work. If I don't find a way to earn the creature's trust, Basten might rot in the dungeon or die in the arena. I might wear a crown I don't desire. All while my true father razes my homeland to the ground.

Tears flow harder now, and I pull my knees into a ball.

I don't know if I can do this.

Myst charges over, nudging my shoulder with her muzzle. **Sabine? Why cry? Can you get up?**

Clenching my jaw against the pain in my arm, I push to a sitting position with her help. After a few breaths, my vision refocuses, but the ringing in my ears persists. Myst noses her muzzle under my right arm, helping me to my feet, and lets me lean on her as I hobble over to the guard rail where Rian chews a hole in his cheek.

"Well?" Rian demands.

I wipe away my tears, pretending they're sweat. "I tried to name him. He didn't like my suggestions."

"Try again, then."

Myst might not understand Rian's words, but she's perceptive as hell to a person's tone. *You need more time*, she insists. *These things cannot be rushed. Your arm—*

It's fine, I snap without meaning to, cradling my aching arm to my chest.

"My lord," Maximan says quietly, "Perhaps you're pushing Lady Sabine too hard."

By the gods—that must have been a serious fall if even dour old Maximan is advocating for my safety.

Rian doesn't answer, but his gaze challenges mine with a silent question.

"No—I can do it." My toes curl in my boots, trying to distract my brain from the pain in my arm. "I want to try again. Not a name this time. I'll—I'll mount him directly. Tame him by force."

A hush falls over the soldiers. Maximan's mouth firms into a disapproving line. I know what they're all thinking: *She's just a girl. Nothing compared to a fae beast. She can't do it.*

Rian seems to war within himself, but then slightly dips his chin. "Do it, then."

Fear tightens its fist around my throat as I face the arena, questioning myself. There's a chance I could forcibly control the monoceros with my godkiss, but I swore after the tiger I'd never possess another animal against its will.

And if I cross that line, what will I become?

No—there has to be another way.

Myst chases down the monoceros, using all her energy to keep up with his wild gallop, scolding him with nips on his neck. I know what she's doing: trying to wear down his energy to give me an advantage. After a few laps, it works: the monoceros falls into a fast but steady gallop as she circles along beside him.

A memory rises from my mind's depths: *I've seen this before.*

Once, when my father was out of town, my mother invited a performing troupe to our stables to show her new riding techniques. There was a pint-sized girl who couldn't have been older than twelve, dressed in a cheap Immortal Alyssantha costume, who rode bareback on a bay gelding with Myst alongside. With graceful confidence, the performer climbed to her knees as the horse ran in a smooth canter, then stood on its back, arms outstretched for balance. Next, she stepped one foot onto Myst's back, balancing on both horses at once.

I'd never seen anything like it—and the girl wasn't even godkissed.

There is no way that the monoceros would let me saddle and mount from the ground, but maybe I can vault as the girl did.

A burst of energy fills me as I climb the rungs of the guard rail, struggling with my hurt arm, and balance on the thick steel post. The soldiers murmur behind me, low and concerned, but I ignore everything except the approaching pair of horses. I track their speed. Bend at the knees. Let them do one more lap just to be sure—

Stay steady, I tell Myst.

When she comes around, I leap from the post onto her back, swinging one leg over her side and clutching onto her mane with my right hand. As her hooves slam into the sand, not missing a beat, my heart matches in time.

Holy hell, I did it.

But my legs go numb and my heart stalls as I swing my left leg behind me, preparing to push to my knees. Luckily, I know Myst's gait almost as well as my own. I can trust my brave girl not to slow or speed.

Carefully, I get to all fours on her back, then push on unsteady legs to a stand. The wind rushes through my hair. The riding ring passes in a blur. It feels like *flying*. I'm vaguely aware of the exclamations of surprise from the soldiers, but I don't dare spare them a glance. I can feel Rian's eyes on me, all burning intensity. Quickly, I learn to relax my legs so I can bounce along with Myst's canter as if I'm a boat riding ocean waves.

It's as exhilarating as it is terrifying.

Right arm outstretched, left still clutched to my chest, I ride Myst twice more around the ring to steady my stance and give the monoceros more time to work out its energy. I throw assessing looks at his back—Myst is keeping his pace steady, nipping him when he tries to speed back into a gallop or drop to a trot.

I'm going to mount you now, I say to him.

The hell you are. He snorts steam—but it's thinner now; he's getting worn out.

As we circle back around, I spy Rian out of the corner of my eye. Every soldier leans over the railing, utterly speechless as they watch, and now, Rian is no different.

The hell I AM, I say.

Breath held, I raise my left ankle, supporting my weight

on only the ball of the foot. Sensing my shift, the monoceros tries to speed up, but Myst gives him a sharp kick to keep him in line.

Now.

I throw my weight to the left, setting my foot on his back. He's nearly twice the size of Myst—his back as wide and sturdy as a millstone. For a brief, electrifying second, I'm straddling them. One foot on either horse. The monoceros snorts a burst of angry steam, but he keeps cantering in a steady circle.

Am I really doing this?

As though daring to tread among the clouds, I shift my full weight to my left leg, ignoring the aching throb in my arm, and slide my right foot to the monoceros's back. My knee buckles—I nearly fall—but then catch my balance and quickly drop down to a seated position with either leg hugging his massive frame.

Thank the gods for trousers.

The impossible becomes reality—I'm astride the monoceros, heart racing with disbelief. Myst keeps a steady rhythm to our right, though I can hear her labored breathing. The monoceros keeps his head low, bursts of angry steam continuing to bellow. I curl my right hand in the base of his mane but immediately pull back when the strands slice my palm—I should have worn gloves.

Still, there's a brief, beautiful moment when I'm riding him like Immortal Thracia herself in the Ride of Sun and Moon story. With a bolt of confidence, I think: *I can do this. It really is possible.* For the first time, I see a way forward. A strange buzz starts in my chest, a whisper that somehow I've done this before, a deep connection to the beast that makes the birthmark on my breastbone throb like a second heartbeat.

The whisper takes on a strange sound, like a forgotten dream. A word. No, a name. T—?

I can't have been on the monoceros for three seconds before he skids to a sudden stop, bucking his powerful hips, tipping me straight over his head in a spiraling arc until my back slams into the sand.

The HELL you are, he snorts.

Despite the pain blooming through my body, I give a dazed smile up at the stars winking through the skylight above.

I did it. For a moment, I rode.

I'm dimly aware of soldiers thundering into the riding ring, herding the monoceros back into his stall with iron-tipped spears, and Maximan's rushed footsteps as he drops to his knees at my side.

"Gods be damned," he mutters, tenderly feeling my left forearm. "She has a broken arm—fetch the healer!"

The last thing I remember before blacking out is Rian's face looming over mine, utterly expressionless as he says, "You see, songbird? You only needed the right motivation."

CHAPTER 22
WOLF

Brick walls. Iron bars.

Here I am in yet another cell, chained to a past I thought I'd broken free of long ago. Back then, I fought for my supper. This time, for a pardon. I can almost hear the rumble of the crowd's bloodthirsty cheers in the stands overhead, echoing in my skull.

My knuckles flex, remembering the old dance.

I'll say this for the fighters' barracks beneath Duren's arena: it's still a prison, but the food is galaxies better than the dungeon's.

For the last week, along with the other prospective fighters, I've been fattened on beef stew and buttered bread. Tended to by the godkissed healer that the Valveres employ. Treated like a prize hog before slaughter. And no, it isn't lost on me that this is exactly what we did to Maks to get him in good enough shape to torture and kill him.

There are sixteen fighters in all. All of us are "criminals," though that term is used loosely to get adequate contenders for a good Everlast spectacle. There are twin teenage farm boys built like oxen whose uncle owes taxes, not them. A whole crew of sailors accused of piracy. A Golden Sentinel captain who sold stolen army explosives in the Sin Streets. A prostitute who strangled an abusive client. An elderly blacksmith with fists like anvils, even at his age. And—bad news for all of us—two other godkissed fighters, a man and a woman.

The man is a Spezian with godkissed strength. Intimidating enough on his own, but he also has steel plates covering his biceps, forearms, chest, and back that are literally bolted to his bones. How the fuck that's possible, I have no idea.

Still, it's the woman who worries me more. A thief who's been locked away in one dungeon or another for years. Best I can tell, her godkiss lets her control wind, including anything it can harness, like soil or water. Her birthmark has been cut out, and years-old scars run down her neck, limbs, and face in a gruesome mimicry of the gods' fey lines.

She doesn't speak. No one knows how she came to be in such a mutilated state. There's only speculation passed among our individual cells like coins changing hands.

But the thing I haven't told anyone is, *I* remember her.

I was sixteen years old. Looking for Rian, who was late to our sparring session. I opened the wrong door in Sorsha Hall's east wing, ignoring the strange smells that my senses picked up on, not realizing it was Lord Berolt's experiment chamber.

There she was. Unconscious on a table. In a thousand years, I won't forget seeing her eyes, open but unseeing. She didn't have those scars yet, but her godkissed mark was already excised.

Which makes me reason that I do, after all, already know how that Spezian got his fucked-up grafted armor.

If we prisoners aren't eating, then we're training. Push-ups. Squats. Jumping Jacks. Isolated from one another by bars so we can't spar, I can only guess what fighting skills the others have. I don't want to give away my own skills, but I have to train. I'm rusty as fuck.

Every night when I sleep on my dirt bed, the old fighter in me, the monster, the shadow that I was, hangs over me. It's clawing its way back. For a brief moment, I thought I had made my way out of the gutter, reaching for the light. For *her*. Because loving Sabine is the only holy rite that could purify a bastard like me.

Especially when I have to deal with the likes of—

"Up and at 'em, Wolf," a hoarse voice rasps, his throat permanently damaged from an incident five years ago, when I stumbled upon him in an opium den and tried to strangle him before sentinels pulled me away.

Jocki—older, wrinkled, still tough as fucking leather—grins with his crooked teeth that so haunted me as a boy.

"Time to tour the arena. Prepare for the Everlast. Just like old times, eh, boy?"

So be it, I think to myself. *Let's fucking dance, then, one last time.*

"The Everlast begins in one week. Four in the afternoon. Which means the sun will be there, in the southeast." Jocki points his folded sunshade over the now-empty seats. "One more week to figure out how you're going to be the only one standing."

All sixteen of us stand in the center of Duren's arena, surrounded by three dozen heavily armed Golden Sentinels, as a team of servants rakes the sand at the far end. Though we're technically here to assess our battleground, we all know we're really here to size up one another.

"This year's theme is the Pit of Secos." Jocki points his sunshade at the large trapdoor half-buried in the sand. "The infamous battle between Immortal Vale and Immortal Woudix. If you don't know it, I suggest brushing up on your fae tales with haste." He hocks and spits in the sand. "That trapdoor will be open. Set with spikes—you don't want to fall in, got it? Sixteen weapons will be scattered around the arena. A variety of axes for those of you dressed as Vale, scythes for the ones in Woudix costumes."

One of the farm boys' hands shoots in the air. "Do we have to use the weapon that corresponds to our costume?"

"No, you idiot. Don't overthink the theatrics. Use whatever's closest and sharpest." Jocki pinches the bridge of his nose before continuing. "Sixteen fighters enter. You slash. You push each other into the pit. Only one wins. Trumpets. A fucking parade. Any more dumb questions?"

At our silence, he opens his sunshade and saunters off to the water station set up at the perimeter. "You have one hour."

We break apart in uneasy groups, eyeing one another as we test the sand's traction, figure out how to keep the sun in our opponents' eyes. The pirate crew huddles up, whispering among themselves, while the old blacksmith begins pacing out the length between the pit and the wall.

The other two godkissed fighters stand back in the shade, wordlessly, watching the rest of us.

I set off to circle the arena, kicking at the sand to find

any buried rocks or bottles thrown from the crowd that could be helpful during the Everlast, when one of the servants bumps his rake into my hip.

"Hey!" I snap. "Watch it."

To my surprise, Folke winks at me from beneath his cap's wide brim. "Oh, a *thousand* pardons, good *sir*."

"What the fuck are you doing here?" I hiss quietly.

"Haven't you noticed that pretty wench at the water station? Or do you only have eyes for one woman now, eh?"

I pivot sharply toward the uniformed servant at the water station.

"*Ferra*?" I gag with surprise. "How the hell did you get her out of a ballgown?"

"Oh, I've gotten her out of many dresses, my friend." Folke flashes his rogue's grin. "Your pretty Winged Lady asked her to get information on you, so naturally, she came to me. I paid off a few of the arena's servants so we could make sure you still have all your limbs."

Fear lands hard and heavy in my gut. "How is Sabine?"

"Well. She's well. Erm—there was a rumor of a broken arm, but the healer fixed her."

My vision sparks with red at the edges. "Rian hurt her? I'll *kill* him." My fists tighten.

"Easy, big guy. She wouldn't tell Ferra how it happened, but she insisted it wasn't Rian. What you need to know is that tomorrow night, you have to get put in the prisoners' barrack's last cell. That small one off to a corner."

My eyelids narrow. "Why? What are you scheming, Folke?"

"It wasn't my idea. It was your Winged Lady's."

"*What* is Sabine planning?"

The godkissed female fighter, twenty paces away, seems

o catch onto the fact that I'm talking to a servant, and a sudden gust of wind—moving in a zigzag pattern—slaps a spray of sand in my face. She lifts an eyebrow in a challenge.

Coughing, I pretend to go back to looking for rocks.

Glancing over my shoulder to make sure no one is tracking us, I hiss to Folke, "Whatever Sabine has planned, it's too dangerous. Tell her to call it off."

"Sorry, friend. Wheels are already in motion." As Folke shuffles off with his rake, he calls over his shoulder a reminder, "Tomorrow night. Last cell, around the corner."

All that day and the next, I'm a strangled knot of nerves. Ice floods my veins to think of Sabine taking any risk, and it kills me that there's absolutely nothing I can do to stop her. She should be keeping her head low, staying on Rian's good side.

But I know my little wildcat—she keeps her head down for no one. And gods help me, I adore her for it.

Dinner is a rare treat—half a roasted chicken and an entire bottle of wine each—and it leaves the fighters in reasonably good spirits as we file back in from our second day assessing the arena. I elbow my way to the front of the line to race to the last cell, but the sentinel captain beats me to it.

I have to trade him my bottle of wine to get the cell; he agrees, but his eyes glint with curiosity.

I pace as I throw glances at the cell's high window until dusk bleeds into night. Then, when I've practically worn a track in the stone floor, I smell the telltale scent of clove perfume, which can only mean one thing.

Dragging a hand down my face, I mutter a curse under my breath. "Oh, fuck, little violet. What did you do?"

The titter of feminine laughter drifts in, and soon, the other prisoners hear it, too. They move to their cell doors, craning their necks.

"A treat for you tonight, boys!" Jocki rasps. "A morale booster in the days leading up to the Everlast! You can thank me by giving us a good show before your deaths, eh?"

My cell is half-hidden around the corner, with only a portion of the bars open to the hallway. I grip them tightly, staring intently at the hall, waiting for the owner of the footsteps I already recognize.

Madame Anfrei of the Velvet Vixen sweeps in with her jeweled shawl clanking and silk fan fluttering. "My dashing warriors! Ooh, so much testosterone dripping off these halls, I could come with one deep breath!"

Revulsion would climb up my gullet if I weren't so focused on the hallway behind her.

"Ladies, come!" Madame Anfrei snaps her fingers, and a parade of whores follows her into the hall. Fourteen of them —one for every man, even the farm boys. I guess the two female fighters are out of luck. None of my business, but that hardly seems fair.

My godkissed eyes search the low light frantically, methodically.

And finally—she's there.

Coming around the corner, so doused with clove oil that I had to recognize her by her footsteps instead of her scent. She's dressed in the Winged Lady costume that the whore named Mathilde usually wears. Cheap blond wig, flouncy chicken-feather wings. A dress that reveals every inch of her thighs. There is so much makeup caked onto her that if I didn't know her face by heart, I'd think her a stranger.

Hidden in plain fucking sight.

The captain reaches between his bars, beckoning to Sabine, but Madame Anfrei smoothly shoves her down the hall in my direction instead. "You, Mathilde. Last cell there —in the corner."

She grabs a buxom, curly-haired whore instead and pushes her in front of the captain. After two bottles of wine, he's all too happy to swipe at whatever breasts are in front of him.

Jocki unlocks our cells one by one, giving me an extra leer. "Cheer up, Wolf, my boy. No hard feelings, see? Look at what I do for my boys. And you tried to say once that I wasn't like a father to you."

I want to think that my real father—whatever gutter rat he was—would have more class than to encourage his son to wet his dick at a whorehouse. But I have to be honest: he was probably someone exactly like Jocki.

The moment Sabine approaches my cell, however, any thought of Jocki or the bastard who got my mother pregnant vanishes.

Because *my fucking gods.*

After weeks in this hell hole, smelling nothing but the reek of unwashed bodies, hearing nothing but Jocki's hoarse laughter, Sabine Darrow is a vision.

Keeping her face averted from Jocki as though coy, she slips into my tiny cell. Jocki slams the door closed, giving me one more wink, followed by a jackal laugh.

My eyes sink closed because, for one moment, I want to let my senses wash over her like a breeze through the willows.

Then, I trap her against the wall in the cage of my hands.

"Sabine," I growl low. "What the hell were you thinking?"

She blinks her long, kohl-darkened eyelashes at me, and all the anger melts out of me like winter runoff. I'm left as a barren wasteland, begging for a touch of spring sunshine.

"You think I'd just let you die?" she whispers.

"Who said anything about dying?" My voice is quiet, too transfixed by her beauty to think of anything else—such as my own life. "You don't think I can win?"

"Probably, if things were fair. But I'm not leaving anything to chance. You have enemies, Basten. If Rian doesn't want you dead, then Lord Berolt definitely does. That gamemaster seems to have it out for you, too, based on what I heard him whispering to Madame Anfrei while we were waiting to enter. How easy would it be for any of them to rig the fight?"

My thoughts lurch to a halt, because I've never had anyone be concerned for my life before. My chest softens in a foreign way, and there's a gods damn sting in my eyes. For fuck's sake, what is this woman doing to me?

Here I thought I was content with a bow on my back and an ale in hand—but then Sabine came along and showed me that I'd been living in a cave, not knowing sunlight was just a step away.

"Where's Rian?" I ask.

"He left four days ago for Old Coros. He said he'd return in time for the Everlast."

"And your guard?"

"Maximan is currently outside my bedroom door, listening to my clattering plates while "I" eat dinner. Brigit and I traded clothes. She's wearing my house gown now, stomping around and sighing to throw Maximan off. Ferra used her godkiss to disguise my face so I could sneak out the servants' passages."

"Gods be damned, little violet. With those wiles, you missed your calling as a hunter."

A hint of a grin curls her lips.

The moans and thrusts of the other male fighters taking advantage of Jocki's *gifts* flood down the hallway. Though we're mostly hidden from sight, I glance over my shoulder and see the sentinel captain still eyeing me curiously while his whore is on her knees in front of him.

Sabine grabs my hand, placing it on her right breast. She presses up to tiptoe to whisper in my ear, "Touch me, Basten. Or they'll be suspicious."

By the fucking gods.

Slowly, I knead my hand over Sabine's pillowy breast beneath her paper-thin dress, and my mouth goes dry as the Kravadan desert. She leans back against the wall, offering me her neck.

Moving like I'm underwater, I drag my lips against her throat, whispering as I pretend to kiss.

"The Everlast is for me to worry about. Your only job is to keep this perfect throat safe until I win and can watch over you again."

She parts her legs, silently inviting me closer. As she snakes her arms around my neck, she buries her lips in my hair and whispers, "You think Rian would ever allow you to guard me again? If you survive, he'll ship you off to the provinces."

I grip her jaw, placing a hot kiss on her cheek as I murmur, "Then we'll run away, just like we always said. I'll take you to Salensa. Throw you over my shoulder, drop you in the sea, make love to you in the surf."

A whimper escapes her mouth that has nothing to do with our playacting. "Oh, Basten."

I'm not sure entirely where our charade ends and where the real lovemaking begins, but I grip around her narrow waist, guiding her back against the shadows of the cell, as far from prying eyes as I can. We have to pretend as though she's my whore for the night, but that doesn't mean I want to share a glimpse of her with anyone else.

"Let me help you," she says breathily.

"How?"

"Tell me about your opponents. Their weaknesses. We still have a few days before the fight—I can come up with something." She slowly winds her right leg around my hips, her sweet cunt flush as it grinds against my rigid cock beneath my pants, and I can barely remember what my name is.

It takes effort to swallow. "Most aren't a threat. There are some good fighters—some even trained—but I can beat them. It's the godkissed two I'm worried about."

Her head jerks back so that her eyes can latch onto mine. "There are other godkissed fighters?"

I drop my head to kiss the tops of her breasts, slowly sliding off one dress strap. "A male blessed with strength and a female who controls wind. They've been . . .enhanced."

She digs her nails against my scalp until it's almost painful. "More than being godkissed? What do you mean?"

"You've heard the rumors that Berolt experiments on godkissed people?"

Her hands freeze before continuing. "Yes."

"Well, I've *seen* it. He's tinkered on those two. Mutilated them into ultimate fighters. And in the process, probably driven them mad." My lips hover a half-inch above her birthmark. "I—I don't know if I can best them."

She grips my shoulders hard, shaking me. "You won't die in the arena, Basten Bowborn. Do you hear me?"

I lower my head, ashamed to look her in the eyes.

She jerks my chin up, pressing her soft palms against either side of my face, forcing me to look at her. "We're godkissed, too—never forget it. I'll be in the stands. I'll make sure of it. Rian can't keep me from the fight. The public demands it. They're singing ballads about us in the streets—we're a fae tale come to life to them. Duren's famous star-crossed lovers."

My palm finds the small of her back, but the closeness I crave feels forever out of reach. "They'll never let you close to the tigers."

"Stupid man," she chides affectionately, stroking her thumb down my cheekbone. "Men always think of the big, showy animals." She leans in until our lips are kiss-close. "Trust me, Basten. I'm more powerful than you think."

"Then you truly must be a goddess, because I think you're fucking incredible."

I capture her lips with a kiss that has nothing to do with playacting. For weeks now, I've been plunged back into one dank pit or another like the ones I spent years fighting to crawl out of. I'd rather be tortured than return to that dark past. The only thing that can bring me back from the edge of despair is her.

She wraps her leg tighter around mine, rolling her hips. Moans and the smack of flesh coming together echo down the hallway, the tart smell of sex saturating the air.

Sabine coils a strand of my hair around her finger.

"I'm supposed to be your whore," she reminds me breathily, swallowing me with her siren's gaze. "Shouldn't we make it convincing?"

This woman is going to be the death of me—and I'll happily succumb. I grip her chin's point, sliding my tongue over her parted lips. She tastes like lavender, floral and so delicately sweet. She weaves her fingers in the hair at my nape, holding on like she would a stallion as I use my other hand to grip her ass and hoist her legs around my hips.

Her flimsy dress rides up over thighs as smooth as butter. The brick wall would scrape her back and destroy Mathilde's costume, so I press her against the bars instead. She arches her back to roll her breasts against my chest. Holding her with one hand, I grip the bars behind her head with the other hand to hold myself back from riding this wave of pleasure into the fucking sky.

I snare her lips in a heated kiss, melding my mouth to hers. Our hungry lips devour one another until I don't know if a trace of breath is left in my lungs. She tugs on her hem as if her dress is too restrictive. Her velvet kisses leave moist prints along the tendons of my neck.

Her pulse flares. Her pupils are huge. I press her back against my cell bars, pouring every ounce of love I have for her into the kiss until her body shivers, her breath reduced to shallow pants.

Then, I break the kiss. Touch my forehead to hers. Let my eyes sink closed against the ugliness of the barrack cells and flood my senses only with her.

She nuzzles my neck. "Basten? You don't want to—"

Hoarsely, I say, "Not here. Not like this. Let everyone believe I fucked Madame Anfrei's whore in this dank cell.

Tonight, though, I only want to look at you. To brand your face into my memory until, with my dying breath, it's the last thing I see."

She presses my cheeks again between her hands, a wrinkle between her brow. "That dying breath had better not be for many, many years, Basten Bowborn."

I revel in the feel of her weight in my hands, the way our bodies fit together like sea and shore. "Whenever I die—in five days' time or in fifty years—it won't be the end for us. I'll find you in the next lifetime. I'll always find you, even if death separates us."

She captures my lips again, softly this time. *A promise.*

I rest my head on the crook of her neck, breathing in her floral scent beneath the layers of painted-on clove oil. "The next time I make love to you, little violet, it will be as a free man, and it will be *my* ring on your finger. I don't know how, but I swear this to you."

She holds me tightly around the shoulders, the only shelter from the storm I've ever known, protecting me from the ravenous shadows of the coming battle.

"One more week," she whispers. "I'll try to come back again before—"

"Don't," I say, staring into those beautiful eyes one final time. "It's too dangerous. The next time I see you will be in the arena."

She touches my cheek. "I'll wear a violet pinned to my dress to signal that my animals and I have your back."

We embrace until the last possible minute, holding one another like figures lost in fae time, until Madame Anfrei tells her it's time to go.

CHAPTER 23
SABINE

That night, I don't sleep for a second. How could I possibly? I'm afraid of dreaming about Basten in the arena, his blood puddling in the sand, the light dimming from his sensuous brown eyes.

My skin still sings with his touch from earlier, though his palms were so much rougher than before. Calloused. Dirty. At first glance, he hardly looked like the same quiet huntsman who led me through Mag Na Tir forest. With his muscles ripped and primed, his hair filthy, he looked like a beast ready to tear the world apart.

A part of me liked it. Seeing him like that. Unyielding and vicious. A part of me knows that's what it will take for him to stay alive.

Lying in bed, I think through all the possible ways I can give him an advantage in the arena. Hawks swooping down to pluck out Basten's opponents' eyes would be too obvious. I can't smuggle in anything larger than a mouse. As I toss and turn, I go over each animal I could use as well as the risks.

If I'm caught helping him, it would mean trouble for both Basten and me.

But to save his life, I'll risk anything.

It's five more days until the Everlast.

Then four.

The whole castle is tense as a drum. Everywhere I go, I have curious eyes on me. Everyone wants to know how the star-crossed story of the Winged Lady and the Lone Wolf will end.

The only bright spot is when Suri is released from her month of mourning. I wait anxiously for her in the library, along with Brigit and Ferra, pacing through the multi-hued light filtering in from the stained-glass windows.

A knock sounds at the door, causing all our heads to whip around.

"Sabine!" Suri bursts past Maximan, guarding the other side of the door, her brown face splitting into a dazzling grin as she pounces on me with a hug as warm as a dumpling. She squeezes a squeak out of me. "Oh, I missed you!"

Maximan eases his grip on his sword when he realizes the latest addition to our gaggle of women is no threat—except, perhaps, to his patience. He leaves us to our peace.

"We feared you'd become a ghost in the mourning berths," Ferra quips.

Suri groans. "It was close."

I gently stroke the ends of the black mourning ribbon knotted around her waist. "How are you?"

She touches the black sash wistfully, taking her time before saying, "It wasn't my choice to marry Charlin. My parents saw only his ability to provide financially for me when they had so many other hungry mouths at home. He was drunk from dawn to dusk. Rude to the servants. Gods know he was hardly a prize, yet there were good times." She sighs. "But how are *you*? I know your feelings about Charlin were complicated. But the Everlast is only four days away . . ."

Her eyes glisten with sympathy.

Before I can answer, the door opens again, this time for Captain Fernsby. The three of us women—and the mouse, tucked into Brigit's pocket—fall silent as the captain strides up to the table. He wears a soldier's usual mask of indifference, but his jaw has a strange tic that no amount of training can hide.

A warning bell chimes in my chest.

"My lady." He stares ahead at the bookcase instead of me. "High Lord Rian sent a messenger to inform us that he'll return tomorrow. He commands that everyone within Sorsha Hall pin a black ribbon to their chest—"

"A black ribbon?" Suri tugs on her own black sash. "Has someone else died?"

Captain Fernsby's hesitation is so slight that a marksman could miss it. In a formal voice, he announces, "King Joruun, the Benevolent Boar, ruler of Astagnon for seven decades, has passed away. Out of our hearts, into Woudix's hands."

Suri gasps, pressing her hand to her lips. The news is so shocking that it even draws Maximan from the door over to our library table.

"Out of our hearts, into Woudix's hands," Brigit murmurs.

"Out of our hearts, into Woudix's hands," Suri and I repeat, and Maximan quietly speaks the same refrain.

Ferra picks up the teapot to refill our drinks. "He *was* ninety-one years old," she drawls. "His death is about as shocking as an oven being hot."

Maximan growls like a guard dog, and Ferra tuts as she sets back down the pot. She deadpans, "I meant to say, of course, 'Out of our hearts, into Woudix's hands.'"

Maximan's pinched brow eases.

"He was found burned alive," Captain Fernsby continues, lowering his voice. "It is believed that in the throes of pneumonia, he attempted to climb out of bed and fell into his fireplace. They are calling it a mercy in Old Coros. To end his long-suffering illness."

Suri sets down her tea so fast the cup rattles. "He was accidentally *burned alive*?"

King Joruun was as much a stranger to me as the gods themselves, so I cannot find the will to pretend at tears, but this news whips my pulse into a frenzy that I can barely quell with hands clasped under the table.

Captain Fernsby's lips work like he's holding a bee in his mouth, warring between his soldier's duty and his desire to gossip. "As the king never formally declared a successor, the King's Council has named High Lord Valvere as Astagnon's next monarch, according to tradition, as the closest blood relation." The captain bows his head to me. "Lady Sabine, I swear my sword and soul to you, our future queen."

Ferra, Suri, and even that old grouch Maximan stare at me like I've sprouted an extra ear. A strange buzz stirs in my belly.

Queen. A title that falls heavily on my ears.

"Something doesn't feel right about this," I murmur,

staring into the middle ground, piecing together the time-line. "Rian leaves for Old Coros with no reasons given, and then just days later, the king dies and Rian is named successor, when the Grand Cleric already had control of Astagnon all but lined up for himself?"

Before any of us can answer, the door is flung open again.

Lady Runa Valvere shoves Maximan out of the way as she throws herself against the table in front of Ferra. "Ferra, did you hear? I'm to be cousin to a king! Rian is on his way back! He's ordered a ball in three days' time to celebrate the news. Now, timing is tight, so we're going to need at least one full day for you to work on my throat. These jowls belong on a hippopotamus—"

"Three days?" I blurt out. "That's the evening before the Everlast!"

Lady Runa only smiles dreamily. "I know. Can you believe it? A ball, then a show. I'll need *two* dresses. I'll have to hire extra seamstresses . . ."

Hand snaking up the column of her throat, Suri interjects, "The king is dead and Rian wants to hold a *ball* to celebrate?"

Lady Runa snaps defensively, "We're all to wear black ribbons on our ballgowns to mourn his Highness's passing."

My blood runs cold. The last I heard of the situation, the Grand Cleric had very nearly succeeded in his bid to turn Astagnon into a theocracy. Rian was the disliked underdog from the provinces despite his blood tie.

So what card did Rian have up his sleeve to turn the tables in his favor?

~

For the next three days, while the castle throws itself into preparations for the Succession Ball, I am bathed, shampooed, buffed, lotioned, and primped by a fleet of servants who fall over themselves to garner favor with Astagnon's future queen. The castle seamstresses stretch measuring ribbons along every possible angle on my body. The perfume merchant drenches my pulse points in dozens of scents until he declares, "Jasmine!" Brigit shapes my fingernails into perfect almonds, then Ferra uses her godkiss to give them a gold-dusted sheen. I have shoe fittings, corset tightenings, and a stern etiquette lesson from Serenith.

True to Lady Runa's word, everyone from the castle's goose girl to old Lady Eleonora Valvere wears a black ribbon for King Joruun's passing—but the ribbons are so small that they could barely wrap around my little finger.

What will we toast his ninety-year legacy with, thimbles of wine?

Rian returns, though I don't see so much as a flicker of his shadow—which suits me, as the last time I saw him, I ended up with a broken bone. According to the forest mouse's report, he and Lord Berolt haven't left his chamber since he got back.

It leaves me uneasy, wondering what they're scheming.

On the day of the ball, Ferra staggers into my room under the weight of a large, flat wooden box. "Behold, the gown of gowns!"

Ferra and Suri watch the maids strip me bare with detached amusement while sipping their tea. They're already dressed and ready. Suri wears a charming dandelion-yellow gown, its bodice gleaming with golden filigree as sunny as her disposition. Despite Suri's radiance, it's Ferra's gown—as usual—that steals the show. She wears a corseted top with a plunging off-the-shoulder neckline. Russet and gold brocade are artfully cut back to reveal tantalizing glimpses of a cream-colored silk underdress the exact color of her skin, giving her the appearance of flashing scandalously bare curves.

When the maids lift my gown from the wooden box, the sound of slinking metal draws gasps of admiration. I catch my breath to see the gown under the chandelier's glow. "Fabric" seems a misnomer here. The dress, devoid of silk, cotton, or brocade, is crafted entirely from metal. Its skirt is a cascade of delicate gold chainmail, while the scant bodice is forged from the same golden iron as sentinel armor.

"High Lord Rian brought the gown back from Old Coros," Serenith utters in a rare show of awe. "They say he had the former queen's godkissed tailor make it especially for you. It's a copy of Immortal Alyssantha's gown from the Akbasi illustrated edition of the Book of the Immortals."

Maids drape the metal dress onto my perfumed skin. I'm breathless as they spin me around to secure all the gilded buckles, then fasten a complicated necklace around my neck and arms.

Finally, Brigit tilts the standing mirror for me to see my reflection.

Everyone is silent—me, most of all.

Slowly, I skim my palms down the gown's outline, almost afraid to touch it. This is no flouncy silk gown for a timid princess. Drawing on Duren's fashion trend of chainmail and faux armor, the metallic skirts are secured by a thick gilded belt that rests low on my hips.

The bodice, which daringly only covers my breasts, leaves my shoulder, ribcage, and navel exposed. Two golden cuffs—miniature sentinel arm guards—circle my wrists.

Yet, above all, the necklace commands attention: an intricate network of jewel-encrusted chains draping my neck and shoulders, anchoring a clear crystal the size of my palm over my birthmark. Within the crystal, tiny obsidian specks scatter light. The stone seems to tell tales of olden days, of queens that came before me.

Anyone looking would see a queen ready for warfare: commanding, resolute, unbreakable. And yet, the dress is deceptive. The delicate-looking chainmail is, in actuality, impossibly heavy. The cuffs squeeze too tightly. The necklace, locked at the back, is more of a harness. I tug at it uncomfortably, but it doesn't budge.

Everywhere, I am marked as a Valvere soldier. Stripped of my wings.

Rian's message is clear: *I am his, in chains.*

It took the maids longer than expected to dress me. By the time we leave my bedroom, the ball has already begun. The heavy gown threatens to bow me over as Ferra and Suri escort me to the ballroom, supporting my weight on the stairs. The sound of music spilling down the hall is overshadowed by drunken laughter and clinking glasses.

When we step in, the room is a dizzying contrast of light and dark, soft and hard. A new iron chandelier, cast in the shape of a king's crown, shines glittering candlelight over the revelers. Enormous billowing golden curtains hang at the windows—the Valvere color. Couples dance in sinfully tight embraces. Loud wagers are placed on who will pass out from wine first. The magistrate from Wezzen wears a champagne bucket on his head as a jaunty hat.

Clearly, no one has wasted a moment falling head-first into debauchery.

How fae of them.

"Step quickly." Serenith prods me in my bare midriff. "The High Lord is about to give his speech, and he wants you at his side."

The crowd parts as Serenith swats away revelers, who gawk at me in my uniquely feminine take on sentinel armor.

"Friends! Future subjects to the Astagnonian crowd!" Rian's voice rings out from somewhere ahead, and Serenith tugs me even faster. "A few words to grieve our fallen monarch. The late King Joruun, may Immortal Woudix shepherd his soul, ushered in nearly a century of peace for Astagnon. We salute his memory. Out of our hearts, into Woudix's hands."

"Out of our hearts, into Woudix's hands," the crowd repeats in chorus.

Rian gives an exaggerated sigh, looking upward to the heavens. "And yet on this, the evening before the Everlast, I am reminded that there is a shadow side to the good king's achievements. Peace means that for one hundred years, the Astagnonian army has been untested. Insufficiently trained. Dwindled in numbers. Our royal soldiers spend more time building roads than training for battle. And that, friends, has left our kingdom as open to attack as tomorrow's fighters in the arena."

Murmurs of agreement ripple among the attendees.

He continues, "Long have I warned our kingdom's leaders of this vulnerability, even to the point of building up my own private Golden Sentinel army, and yet there were those who still wished to stand in my way. Who wanted Astagnon weak. Protected by prayer, not swords." A dark smile curls his sensuous lips. "None of them stand in my way any longer."

A chill prickles over my exposed skin despite the warmth from so many nearby bodies.

He motions to the door. All heads turn. The entire ballroom seems to hold in a collective breath.

Grand Cleric Beneveto enters.

He's the last person anyone expected to see. He wears an elegant charcoal suit with fae-knot trim, yet despite his party attire, his face has no mirth. His hair is uncombed. Deep lines mark his face. He stalks into the ballroom with all the enthusiasm of a thief sent to the gallows.

Loud murmurs ripple through the crowd.

Facing Rian, the Grand Cleric glowers as he says through a clenched jaw, "We have reached an agreement in Old Coros. The King's Council, the Red Church, and the army generals agree. What Astagnon needs now is unity. Tradition must be upheld. We shall remain a monarchy, and King Joruun's closest blood relation shall sit on the throne."

Given the Grand Cleric's spitfire glare at Rian, this clearly wasn't his choice.

Somehow, he lost the game.

A chill sinks further into my marrow. How the hell did Rian convince the Grand Cleric to side with him? What could he have possibly offered him that's greater than the throne? I would think that he tortured him, but I don't see any evidence of broken bones.

"I am honored, Grand Cleric Beneveto, to accept your support." Rian's voice drips with delighted condescension. Then, his eyes snap to mine in the crowd. "And at my side, ruling from Hekkelveld Castle, shall be your beloved future queen, Lady Sabine Darrow!"

The instant my name leaves his lips, the crowd parts, and Serenith prods me forward. Passing directly beneath the crown-shaped chandelier's light, I'm a glittering spectacle. A shiny jewel on display.

The crowd is silent, stunned by the dazzling gown of a warrior queen. No one seems to see that beneath it all, I'm a *girl in chains*.

I lift my eyes to Rian's dark, unreadable irises. He killed Charlin Darrow in cold blood. How many people in this room suspect that he murdered King Joruun, too, to expedite his own rise?

Little friend, I call to the mouse, who rode down in Brigit's apron pocket. *Do me a favor? Drop a fruit tart on his head?*

But there's no answer from the mouse. Brigit must be down in the kitchens. And yet, something feels peculiar. It's too quiet beneath the party's din. I don't hear *any* animal voices. And there are always at least a few flies throughout the castle complaining of the cold.

The crowd leans toward me almost as one multi-headed beast, banishing all other concerns except for the man sauntering toward me across the ballroom.

"You have known her as the Winged Lady." Rian's voice cuts like a knife through butter. "Astagnon's future queen, however, is no mere forest creature. She is a fighter! And she shall fight at my side for all of Astagnon!"

Gasps give way to broken retellings of the tiger fight, though the story has swelled into legend now. I could swear that I overhear someone say that they saw me riding the tiger's back with a sword in hand.

Gods spare me from gossip's grip.

Rian extends his hand to me. "Dance with me." It isn't a

request. He pulls me close, whispering in my ear, brushing his fingers over my gown's militaristic belt. "What do you think of the gown? I thought it was time you had a new image."

Was this his plan all along? To shift the public's narrative of me as an outsider, rebelling against the Valveres, to fighting alongside them?

I begrudgingly take his hand, bracing myself more for a battle than a dance.

As the music starts, Rian leads me in sweeping steps with a firm hand on my lower back, holding me closer than convention dictates. But what does he care for decorum? The entire point of this party is to celebrate his victory in true Valvere style: licentious, scandalous, oh-so-*fae*.

I respond to the challenge in his dark eyes with the last thing he expects: grace instead of resistance. Matching him step for step, my movements fluid, never breaking eye contact. He wants to twist me into something hard in the eyes of his people. A soldier, not a bird. A Valvere, not a butterfly.

But I refuse to let anyone forge me into something I'm not.

As the dance escalates, the feeling of hundreds of eyes weighs me down as much as the golden chainmail. The attendees whisper into each other's fae-capped ears, discussing what their lord's ascension will mean for them. As we pass each subject, they bow to us, kohl-lined lashes lowered.

"A true fighter," one murmurs.

"A warrior queen," another says.

They are all too happy to embrace Rian's new image of me, and yet at the music's climax, when Rian spins me outwards, I have a brief glimpse of the servants standing at the room's outer edges.

They quietly make the Winged Lady symbol with their hands—one fleeting flap of their fingers and then it's gone, like a ghost at the corner of my eye—before Rian reels me back in.

It gives me the strength I didn't know I needed.

Curving my arm around Rian's shoulder, I say low in his ear, "Tell me what happened in Old Coros. How did you beat the Grand Cleric at his game?"

Rian's hand slides to my lower back, palm hardening against my gilded belt. His face might as well be carved of ice, except that not an ounce of emotion drips off.

"All you need to know is that I ensured you will have everything any woman in the seven kingdoms could ever desire. A crown. A throne. A stable full of well-bred horses. A team of ladies maids. As much fine cuisine as ten stomachs could hold."

The litany of treasures falls like dust upon my ears. Those aren't what any woman would want—they certainly aren't what *I* want. I've never cared about ladies-in-waiting or ornate carriages. For a woman starved for twelve years in a bleak convent, simple beef stew and a warm hearth to call my own are my dreamed-upon riches.

A candle wax drip falls on my bare shoulder, and I flinch.

Gathering my nerves, I say quietly as he swings me around, "I'll go willingly to Old Coros with you. I'll be your queen. Whatever you like—but grant me one favor first."

His smooth, freshly-shaven cheek slides against mine. "Ask it, then."

Behind his back, my hand tightens into a fist. "Do not make me attend the Everlast tomorrow."

I pour supplication into the request, letting my voice break at the end.

His body goes rigid against mine. An audible rush of air fills his lungs as he fights to tame his irritation that I would dare ask anything that has to do with Basten.

But a second after his mask slips, he throws it back up.

"Were it up to me, songbird, I would spare you watching your lover's death. But I'm afraid the crowd demands it. You and Wolf have given them a story—and it would be cruel to rob the people of the ending."

I sniffle. "Rian. If you have any mercy—"

"I don't, songbird."

The music ends. Wiping at my eyes, I pull sharply away from him and disappear into the crowd as though tormented with grief. It's a challenge to hide the smile pulling at my lips.

No better way to ensure I get what I want than to ask for the opposite.

For the rest of the ball, I keep my eyes on the candles, willing the wax to run out. Stomach too roiling to eat. Losing track of the wine I down until my bladder strains.

It's an effort to heft the dress's weight to the latrines down the hallway, and only once I figure out how to gather up all the slinking sheets of chainmail, I finally get relief.

" . . .*saw the council's notice with my own eyes . . .*" A male voice comes from the next wooden partition over, and I clamp my mouth, realizing I'm not alone in the latrines. "*It read 'Lord Valvere' clear as day.*"

"*Bah, an oversight,*" another man answers, his voice significantly more slurred. "*High Lord. Lord. The difference is merely a technicality.*"

"*The King's Council does not make oversights. The*

misleading title was intentional, and Lord Rian is too arrogant to listen. It isn't his title on the succession documents—it's his father's!"

My metallic bodice suddenly feels so restricting that I can hardly breathe. I don't have Basten's sharpened hearing, but the voices in the next partition, drunk and careless, are unmistakable.

The voices continue:

"You shared your concerns with Lord Rian?"

"Yes, and he confronted Lord Berolt. The former High Lord is the closest blood relation to Joruun, not Rian. Berolt insists it was just a formality, and the crown will go to Rian as planned."

"And Lady Sabine?"

The first man laughs darkly. *"If I were Berolt, I'd take that ripe peach as my own queen."*

The partition's hinges squeak as the men leave, but even after it's safe, I still hardly dare to breathe.

Berolt's title is on the succession document? Is this why he hasn't pushed harder for my marriage to Rian? Could he possibly intend to steal the crown from his son?

Even . . . steal his son's bride?

Lurching out of the latrines, I wipe a damp, perfumed cloth over my face. My limbs quake like pudding as I pass the row of guards in the hallway.

Back in the ballroom, I try to seek out Ferra and Suri to tell them this information, but Suri is dancing with a count from Salensa, and Ferra is showing off her gown's slitted pockets to the other courtesans.

"I'll have a dance with Astagnon's future queen," a deep voice rasps.

My stomach shrinks.

Before I can react, Lord Berolt traps my hand in his and

drags me among the other dancers, his advanced age making him no slower than the drunken couples around us.

My heart crashes all the way to the dungeon as I tug helplessly against his hold. "L—lord Berolt . . ."

He pulls me into his arms, one hand clutching mine and his other a vice around my waist. For a second, I'm temporarily rendered speechless. His stature is closer to Basten's than Rian's. He's taller and broader than his son. His stilted steps have none of Rian's smooth grace.

"Don't think you can use your godkiss to save that huntsman at the Everlast." Berolt's hot breath burrows into my ear. "I have a way to muzzle your talents, girl."

His thumb slides down my neck to rest on the crystal necklace covering my birthmark. "This stone is embedded with shards of solarium filed off the monoceros's horn. Eight men died to get it. Last winter, I made a discovery in my laboratory: solarium has a means of blocking godkissed magic."

My blood curdles in anger. Now, I understand why I can't hear the mouse's voice or any other animals': My godkiss is walled up like a fortress behind the harness-like necklace.

I've been *collared*.

I curl my fingers around the crystal, trying to rip it off, but the necklace is designed to lock in a way I can't get it off.

"That isn't all," Berolt continues, holding me tighter. "Should you decide to retaliate against me at a time when your powers are unblocked, know that I've ordered all dangerous beasts in Duren to be locked away. The smaller beasts, you're thinking? The ones I can't cage? Those won't affect me, either. I take antivenom regularly. No insect or snake can bring me down." His fingers dig into the bare swell of my waist. "Do you understand now, girl, who is truly in command?"

With that final, damning whisper, I lose any doubt that what I overheard in the latrines is true.

Now, with panic clawing at my chest, I realize Basten isn't just fighting for his own victory tomorrow; he's fighting for us both. I can't face this storm without him. Yet, in one fell swoop, all my carefully laid plans fall apart.

With my godkissed blocked, I can't call to any animals.

Tomorrow, Basten faces the arena's roar utterly alone.

CHAPTER 24
WOLF

"**F**ae of the Immortal Court," I announce to the silence of my cell. "Listen well, you blade-eared bastards. I was content going twenty-six years believing you'd never wake again. Hell, I hoped you wouldn't. But here I am, on my knees, to beg like a pauper. Not for me—I'll take my fate as it comes. But for the girl who holds my heart alongside her own. If I die today, protect her. Or so help me, I'll crawl back from the under-realm, carve those pointed ears off your pretty skulls, and mount them above my mantel. *Amen*."

The last place I want to be is on my knees, in the dank fighters' barracks beneath Duren's arena, but here I am. Overhead, the ceiling quakes from ten thousand spectators filling the stands. Dust rains down as they stomp in unison, calling for the Everlast to begin.

The town's been salivating for this bloody trial for weeks. And who am I to deny them? Locked here in the dark, I've become a beast again. An entertainer who trades in blood sport. It's me against fifteen other prisoners who have committed the same crime as me—being in the wrong damn place at the wrong damn time—and only one of us will make it out.

Are you still listening, fae? Because I swear this: I'll do whatever vile, unforgivable, heartless act it takes for that victor to be me.

I won't leave Sabine in the viper's den alone.

"Fighters!" Jocki steps into our barracks, jingling his keyring to get our attention. "Last chance to piss, drink, or make amends to whichever patron god you're about to meet."

His pupils are huge, his cheeks bloodshot. High as a fucking star. Twenty years ago, he used to dose hashish religiously before every match. I see nothing's changed.

"We have a full stadium for your trial!" His tongue snakes out to wet his twitchy lips. "They've even let in overflow seating—the lower levels are standing room only. So, don't fucking die too quickly out there, got it? Draw out the show so they get their money's worth. We don't want another riot on our hands."

The prostitute spits in his face between her cell bars. "Fuck you. Why don't *you* give them a good show?"

Jocki is so stoned that I don't even think he notices the spittle on his cheek as he unlocks her door and hands her a bundle of black clothes. "Fighters, put on the costume you're given. Here—Woudix for you, darling."

The prostitute examines the heavy black cloak, black trousers with steel skulls for knee guards, and a metal breastplate forged from iron bars shaped to look like a ribcage. She holds up a black eyepatch last. "What the hell is this?"

"Never seen an illustration of Woudix?" Jocki thrusts

another black Woudix costume at the godkissed woman in the opposite cell, who I've nicknamed the Wind Witch for, well, obvious reasons.

"An eye patch?" the Wind Witch seethes. "We'll be half-blind on the battlegrounds! And this breastplate is a farce—a blade can pass right through the gaps between the metal ribs!" She thrusts a scarred finger toward the guard behind Jocki, who is passing out bundles of the other costume. "I want that one. The Vale costume."

The guard hands one of the Vale costumes to the giant godkissed man—who I think of, fondly, as the Spezian Anvil. The Vale costume is composed of a sturdy helmet flanked with steel horns, a chainmail doublet with a thick fur collar, and two wooden shields to go over the chest and back as armor.

"That isn't fair!" one of the pirates shouts, who's just been handed a Woudix costume. "Half of us are hobbled by an eye patch, and the other half get full armor?"

"Take it up with the fates," Jocki yells, stumbling.

The other prisoners continue arguing as they begrudgingly dress and then, one by one, are herded out by the stadium guards. Finally, Jocki reaches the last cell. Mine. Grinning through his uneven teeth, he passes me the remaining costume.

To my utter shock, it's a Vale.

Now that it's just the two of us left, he lowers his voice to a suspiciously paternal tone. "Saved one of the good costumes for you, my boy. See what I do for you? How I take care of my boys?"

He reeks of hashish and piss so badly that I have to cup my hand over my nose. "What, is the helmet lined with broken glass? Did you take out half the shields' nails?"

An offended look washes over his face. "Now why would I do that? You're like a son to me."

Yeah, right. As I tug on the Vale costume, I'm sure to check for poison patches sewn into the fur cape.

Eyeing Jocki warily, I step out of my cell and am about to head down the hall when his face twists into a cackle.

He slams the metal cell door against my right hand, closing my knuckles between the bars with enough force that bones snap with sharp bursts of pain.

"Fuck!" I yell, pain shooting all the way to my elbow. My right hand is mangled. Blood oozes from torn skin. The distorted knuckles are clearly broken.

Jocki claps me hard on the back as he laughs cruelly. "Fate be with you, boy."

An arrow of rage shoots through me, threatening to burst out of my chest. The ache in my hand makes my vision blur. But pain isn't the problem—how the hell am I supposed to fight with only one hand?

Fucking Jocki!

Soldiers return for me, and I realize I'm screwed. As much as I want to smash Jocki's uneven teeth up into his brain with my good hand, if I kill him, I won't live long enough to make it to the arena floor.

And Sabine? She'll have to face the monsters alone.

As they lead me up a flight of stairs, I tug one of the costume's leather gloves over my broken knuckles, biting back a scream—but I have to hide this weakness from my opponents. If they know I have a broken hand, they'll only target me more.

We pass through a tunnel and come out at the arched fighter's entrance. The other prisoners wait here, gazing out at the crowd. The prostitute, the Wind Witch, the twins, and four of the pirates wear Woudix costumes. The Spezian Anvil, the army captain, the blacksmith, four pirates, and I are dressed as Vale.

Beyond, the arena's raked sand ripples like the dunes of a manicured desert. Thousands of bodies fill the amphitheater seating, stomping to the drum beats and throwing paper curls into the air.

The audience is mainly made up of the Durish masses. Lords and ladies relax in the Immortal Box. Even hundreds of priests of the Red Church are scattered throughout the stadium, wearing crimson robes and full-face mourning masks for King Joruun.

What the fuck are *they* doing here?

Among the crowd's cheers, I pick out the most common call: *Lone Wolf! Lone Wolf! Lone Wolf!*

Oh, fucking *great.* My star-crossed lovers saga with Sabine has made me a celebrity, which only paints another target on my back.

The other prisoners throw me assessing glances. I just try not to fucking cry from the pain in my right hand.

Once Jocki has checked our costumes, he gives the guards the thumbs-up. We're paraded out onto the arena in a single-file line, shielding our eyes against the bright sun after so long spent underground.

The throngs go wild, jumping to their feet. The air vibrates with palpable excitement, thick with the scent of sweat and fervor. Even the stadium's very bricks seem hungry to taste our blood.

Eight axes and eight scythes of various sizes and styles are spread randomly through the arena—I clock each of them as I testingly flex my broken hand, judging which ones I can best wield with only my left hand.

In the center of the arena, the trapdoor hangs open like a gaping maw. It's only when the soldiers herd us around its perimeter that I glimpse the sharpened stakes inside.

"Good people of Duren!" The arena's buffoonish announcer shouts through his amplifying cone. "Before all else, raise your voices in celebration of High Lord Rian Valvere and the Winged Lady herself, Sabine Darrow—soon to be the future sovereigns of Astagnon! May their reign be victorious!"

"May their reign be victorious!" the crowd answers, throwing more paper curls.

I tune out the crowd's fawning as I feverishly scan the faces in the Immortal Box. *There*. I finally spot Sabine. She's seated to Rian's right on a pair of gilded thrones as if they've already been crowned king and queen.

Sabine wears a striking gown reminiscent of ancient warriors: a forged gold-steel bodice atop a sheet of burgundy satin that swaths her body in draping folds that give a suggestion of having just tumbled out of a king's bed.

My heart steadies at the sight of her. Fuck, for just this look at her beauty, it's almost worth dying.

But then, I realize there's no flower pinned to her gown. She said, *I'll wear a violet pinned to my dress to signal that my animals and I have your back.*

Fuck—something is wrong.

She tries to act calm, but even from this distance, I can see how her lips tremble. She brushes her fingers in a casual gesture over an ornate piece of crystal jewelry that covers her godkissed birthmark. She tugs on it subtly, as though trying to adjust it, but with enough intention that I know she's trying to tell me something.

Rian rests his hand possessively over hers, and she lets her other hand fall.

The announcer continues, "Today, the sands of our grand arena bear witness to a trial ordained by the God of Judgement himself, Immortal Meric. Prepare for the holy Everlast! Sixteen criminals shall battle to determine who is worthy of forgiveness. Only one shall emerge, but who shall it be? The beautiful prostitute who took justice into her own hands? The good-natured twin farm boys? The elderly blacksmith, renowned for his craftsmanship?"

The throngs of spectators yell, "*The Lone Wolf! The Lone Wolf!*"

The announcer is ready for this answer. "Ah, yes, or will it be the tragic hero of the latest tale told over pints of ale: Wolf Bowborn, the Lone Wolf?"

Everyone goes wild, and I feel the heat of ten thousand eyes on me. My Vale helmet warms until sweat drips down my temples. Still, there's only one gaze I care about. Those forest green eyes that could lash my heart a thousand times and still have me begging for more.

The announcer lifts his hands. "Oh, but fair citizens of Duren, your hero is a sinner! This man betrayed our High Lord by coveting his promised bride. Our High Lord is merciful; he has forgiven his beloved Lady Sabine, soon-to-be queen of Astagnon. But will he find it in his heart to forgive the huntsman who has been at his side since adolescence? How many of you could forgive such a transgression?"

The hum in the stands rises and falls as if my fate is the latest hot wager. The Spezian Anvil and the Wind Witch move a step closer to me. Yep—I'm their first target. Fucking great.

The pirates whisper low amongst themselves, glancing among us.

The announcer continues, "Today's spectacle is inspired by the tale of the Pit of Secos, where the King of Fae, Immortal Vale, quarreled with Immortal Woudix over the soul of Vale's latest human lover. When a jealous human rival killed her, sending her to Woudix's underrealm, Vale challenged Woudix to a battle for her return. Because fae cannot be killed, it was decided that whoever pushed the other into the Pit of Secos, a hole in which time vanishes for one hundred years, would win."

I roll my eyes at the pageantry of it all.

Can't we get on with killing one another?

"And indeed," the announcer goes on, "fae magic lives on in the stadium today! Not only do we have three godkissed fighters, but Lady Sabine graces us with her godkissed presence. Ah—I have heard your concerns! The last time she was in these stands, her godkissed ability commanded a tiger. This time, to keep us safe, our former High Lord, Berolt Valvere, has devised a means to block her abilities. No tigers! No wolves! No swarms of locusts! Like all of our sixteen brave sinners, the Lone Wolf is on his own. Will this battle be his end, or shall it etch the legend of the Winged Lady and the Lone Wolf deeper into the annals of our history? Only time shall tell as we turn our eyes to the arena, where destiny awaits!"

Wait, what the *fuck*? Berolt blocked Sabine's godkiss? Is this why she didn't wear a violet?

It's that damn necklace covering her birthmark, I'm sure of it. Rage ripples beneath my muscles to think of Berolt laying one wrinkled finger on her perfect skin. If he dared to tinker on her like one of his vile experiments, I will fucking climb these stands and ram a scythe down his throat . . .

"Let the Everlast judgment begin!"

My pulse is still so fired up about Sabine that I barely hear the pounding drums that signal the fight's start. Immediately, half the fighters sprint for the choicest weapons. The twin farm boys each grab heavy double-sided axes and stand back-to-back, ready to defend each other. The pirates forego weapons entirely in favor of an immediate coordinated assault on the weakest fighters: the prostitute and the old blacksmith.

I barely have time to step toward a single-sided axe before the Spezian Anvil slams his iron-plated fist smack toward my chest.

Luckily, his enhancements slow him down, and I'm able to duck a second before he would have sent me flying straight into the pit.

With a roar, he circles around and comes at the Wind Witch instead, who dodges the full impact of his iron fist, but gets clipped in her shoulder and thrown back on the sand, near a scythe. She grabs it and breaks off the handle over her knee.

The Spezian Anvil squares up immediately and turns back to me.

"Yeah, I get it, big guy," I mutter, moving into a defensive stance. "Take out the other godkissed fighters first while you're still fresh."

He swings both arms at me like a crushing vice, but I throw myself into a roll, pain shooting through my right hand when it connects with the sand, and then grab the only weapon in reach with my left—an axe so small it could barely cut grass.

He circles back on the prostrate Wind Witch, trying to fight us both simultaneously.

Which is his first mistake.

Sand rises ankle-deep throughout the arena as the Wind Witch lifts her hands, beckoning the wind. Wind sweeps down from the stadium like a maelstrom, picking up sand until it clouds around our heads so thickly that I can't see a foot in front of my face.

On the one hand, thank you, Wind Witch. The sandstorm means the Spezian Anvil can't track me. But my godkissed senses? The ones that give me such an advantage? Useless now. I can't see more than a foot in any direction. The wind deafens my hearing and strips away all scents.

A scythe blade suddenly cuts through the sand—I barely duck in time—and hear the cry of a pirate somewhere to my right.

The sandstorm dies down—visibility improves, as does my hearing—though sand still cakes my eyes and nostrils. Squinting, I make out a dead pirate near the fighters' entrance with the broken scythe blade embedded in his chest.

The fucking Wind Witch made the scythe *fly* to stab him. Well, note to self: Flying weapons are possible.

The Wind Witch shoves to her feet, breathing hard, taxed from the energy it took to summon the sandstorm. The crowd boos her—they didn't like her sandstorm blocking the carnage from sight.

A scream comes from the pit, stealing my attention. I look just in time to see a pirate fall in during a misstep while battling the twins.

I don't have time for plans; the Spezian Anvil lumbers

toward me while the remaining six pirates launch an assault on the Wind Witch while she's weakened.

My right hand aches—I'm screwed if I can't punch—and all I have is the minuscule axe. The Spezian Anvil is also dressed as Vale, but has shed the costume's bulky wooden armor; I guess his own reinforced skin is armor enough.

As he raises his fist to swing toward my head, I crouch in a defensive stance. Before his fist connects, however, the old blacksmith jumps him from behind with a scythe in hand. There's a squeal of metal as the curved blade scrapes against the Spezian's iron-plated skin.

What the hell does the old man think he's going to accomplish? For fuck's sake, he should have gone for the hulk's heels instead.

The Spezian throws an elbow backward toward the blacksmith, hurtling him toward the pit, but the old man catches himself before rolling in.

I'm about to take the opportunity to dart between the army captain and the prostitute to collect a heavier axe near the northern stands.

But the blacksmith whispers low and urgently as the Spezian Anvil stalks toward him, "Lone Wolf—if what they say about your hearing is true, listen! The Spezian's armor is iron alloy, impenetrable by blades. But the pins bolting it to his bones are tin. A weak metal, easily broken!"

It hits me like a slap in the face what the old blacksmith was trying to do—not pierce the Spezian Anvil's metal plating, but break off the pins. Without his armor, the Spezian is still godkissed-strong but not undefeatable.

The Spezian Anvil drops to one knee by the old blacksmith and brings down an iron fist toward his chest, but the old man rolls to his left, revealing a scythe blade hidden under him in the sand.

With a shout, he slams the blade against a bolt on the Spezian's back, popping it free like a cork. The edge of the Spezian's back armor pulls away from his shoulder—showing raw, mutilated flesh beneath that weeps lines of blood.

By the gods—the Spezian's skin is *nonexistent* beneath the armor.

"Hold on, old man!" I sprint across the sand, dodging a pirate's axe circling toward my head. The blacksmith manages to wrench free another bolt on the Spezian's back armor before the giant flings him to the ground.

I raise my small axe, ready to strike, when the Spezian wraps his meaty hands around the blacksmith's neck.

"No!" I shout.

The blacksmith's cloudy eyes meet mine a second before the Spezian wrenches the blacksmith's head off in one swift twist and throws it into the pit.

Gasps from the audience fall like snow around us as I crash into the Spezian's back.

I dig my axe's blade under a bolt on his right bicep armor and pop it free—now, only one bolt remains on the arm piece.

He shoves to his feet, lifting me up on his back like I weigh nothing. Clinging on with my aching right arm, I wrap my legs around his waist and wrench free the last bolt on his right bicep armor. Freed, the piece falls to the sand, exposing his right upper arm.

Blood flows down his fingers.

Out of the corner of my eye, I'm vaguely aware of the other fighters' positions. The twins have killed another pirate, and the rest of the pirate team has retreated to attack the two female fighters instead.

On the other end of the arena, the army captain takes on the twins. He's a clever bastard, well-trained in tactical strategy. He knows he can't defeat them together, so he hurls an axe from ten feet away straight between them, forcing them apart. In the few seconds that they aren't guarding each other's backs, he rushes the closest one with the helmet of his Vale costume and shoves the metal horns into the boy's chest.

As soon as one brother falls, the other screams and lunges at the captain, but the captain rips an iron rib off the fallen brother's Woudix costume and stabs the other brother in the neck.

I bring down the axe again on the last bolt holding on the Spezian's back armor. He curses in his language and shoves me away with explosive strength, just as the bolt pops free. My right side slams into the sand, pain shooting from my busted hand all the way to my jaw.

My vision blurs from the pain—*fuck*.

Dimly, I perceive the Wind Witch summon a gust that cleanly knocks one of the pirates into the pit. The crowd moans as his screams linger far too long—he must not have landed on a spike with a killing fall and now has to bleed out.

The Spezian, back and one arm exposed now and seeping rivers of blood, staggers away from the fight as his blood puddles onto the sand.

I do a quick calculation of who remains:

The Spezian. The Wind Witch. The army captain. The prostitute. And four pirates.

I spare a moment to check on Sabine in the stands. I

haven't forgotten for a second that she's most at stake here. Even if I'm the one with blades coming at me, countless dangers face her, too. I can't let Berolt take her into his laboratory. I have to survive if only to keep her miles from that room.

I guess that means it's time to go on the damn offense.

I hone in on the prostitute, who is wrestling with one of the younger pirates, trying to push him into the pit. She's clawing and biting, but he's still got thirty pounds of muscle on her.

In a few swift strides, I close the gap between us, rip the pirate off her, grip him by the nape and rear pants band of his Woudix costume, and hurl him head-first into the pit.

His scream ends in a squelch.

I have only a sigh of warning to duck out of the way as an axe flies toward my head. Right behind it, the army captain lunges at me, throwing a punch into my side between my costume's wooden shield armor. I double over, the wind knocked out of me. He rips off one of his own Vale shields and slams its hard edge into my right knuckles.

Blinding pain rips through me. *Fuuuuck.* With my glove on, there's no way he could know about my broken knuckles —unless Jocki told him.

As if I needed another reason to end Jocki once this is over.

The crowd boos, and calls of "Lone Wolf!" start up again. Dammit if there isn't something motivating about hearing my name on ten thousand lips. Gathering my strength, I spring up to tackle the army captain around his waist.

"Shouldn't have taken your armor off." Grinning, I rip off my helmet and stab the horns into his unprotected chest.

Thanks for the idea, bastard.

Footsteps race up behind me, and in the next instant, the prostitute shoves me from behind. But I heard her feet in the sand from a mile away and brace myself against her weight. As I spin around to grab her, a sudden gust of wind swirls around us. The prostitute's long Woudix cape wraps around her neck. It pulls taut, and she gags. Her eyes bug out as she tears uselessly at the cloth.

I step back, snatching up one of the pirate's fallen scythes.

The wind pulls the cloth tighter until the prostitute's pretty face turns beet red, and she collapses in the sand.

Dead.

I lift the scythe toward the Wind Witch, but she raises a protective hand over her head. "Wait, Lone Wolf! A truce. You and I, we end that Spezian bastard. Then, it's you against me."

A truce? *Lady, I don't make truces*, I want to say. But she has a point—only we three godkissed fighters and three pirates are left. The pirates will be easy, but the Spezian Anvil is a match for both of us, even with only half his armor.

I rest my scythe against my side and offer her my good hand to help her up. She glances at my right hand curiously, clutched tightly against my side.

"I guess my secret is out of the bag," I murmur, holding up my busted hand. "Not much use as a fighter without my favored fist."

"Keep your right side to my back—I'll cover you."

I raise an eyebrow and nod.

On the far side of the pit, the three remaining pirates have finally turned against one another. One loses his balance and tumbles into the pit. While the remaining two scrabble over a double-sided axe, the Wind Witch and I face the Spezian.

"The bolts on his skin armor are vulnerable," I murmur quietly. "We get it all off, we don't even have to cut him down. He'll bleed out. He's halfway there already."

Her mouth forms a grin line. "So, let's watch him bleed."

I nod, and on the count of three, we rush him from either side. I favor my left side, using my costume's front shield as a battering ram to smash into his exposed right shoulder.

He manages to shove me off with incredible strength, knocking my ass onto the sand, but it gives the Wind Witch cover to rip off one of her costume's rib-shaped metal pieces and slam it between his chest armor and skin. She heaves her weight against it, prying the armor away from his skin as a bolt snaps.

Fuck—why didn't I think of that? Way easier than breaking the bolts off one by one.

I'm on my feet in a second, throwing a punch with my left hand into the raw, oozing flesh of the giant's back. He roars, dropping to one knee, and shoots out a hand that clips the Wind Witch in her chin, grounding her.

She rolls into a ball, writhing in pain.

Someone's screams echo in the distance—another pirate down.

I rip out the flat metal piece the Wind Witch used and cram it in the seam between his pectorals and the iron plating. His massive fist slams into my thigh, reverberating all the way to the bone, but I hold like hell to the metal rib, set my left foot against his shoulder, and use my weight to cantilever backward.

With a rip of metal, his front chest armor pries away.

His cry is loud enough to temporarily silence the whole

stadium. For a few seconds, it's quiet enough for me to hear hawks circle overhead, their wings rustling against the wind.

A thick pool of blood forms under his knees. His eyes glaze over. He mutters a prayer in Spezian before slamming face forward into the sand.

The stadium shakes with the crowd's sudden roar of excitement.

Panting, I push myself to my feet. The Wind Witch is still moaning, trying to get herself to all fours. I pick up a fallen axe that belonged to one of the twins, step over the Wind Witch, and approach the final pirate.

He's bleeding from his right ear. His Woudix cloak is gone, half the metal rib armor pieces broken off. The eyepatch dangles around his neck.

He swings a scythe, but I easily block it with my costume's back shield, letting the curved blade embed itself in the wood, then torque in the other direction to rip the weapon out of his hands. He lifts his arms plaintively, but I shake my head.

"Only one of us is getting out of here—and I have someone who needs me."

The axe is too heavy to wield with just my left hand, so instead, I square a kick against his chest and send him pinwheeling his arms as he falls backward into the pit, where he lands on a spike with a sickening thud.

Now, it's only me and the Wind Witch.

Shading my eyes, I search out Sabine in the crowd. She's on her feet, leaning anxiously over the edge of the railing, with Rian at her side. To his credit, he looks genuinely concerned. Which is rich, given that *he* put me here.

Sabine drags a hand down her throat, fingers plucking anxiously at her locked-on necklace.

"I said that I'd fight a thousand men for you, little violet," I murmur under my breath. "Fifteen is only the beginning."

Sand begins to fly around my knees even before I turn. A few more gusts, and sand billows around my entire body, blinding and deafening at once.

This time, though, I'm prepared for the Wind Witch's powers. I rip a Woudix cloak off a fallen twin and wrap it around my nose and mouth, leaving only a small gap for my eyes.

I can't use my godkissed senses, but at least I can breathe.

From somewhere deep inside the sandstorm, a scythe blade shoots out, carried by the wind, but I was expecting this. I've seen the Wind Witch fight now—I know her tactics.

An axe suddenly flies toward me on another gust, but this one I catch with quick reflexes. I know from her previous sandstorm that she can't keep it going long, so I just need to tire her out.

I feel around the arena ground until I find more Woudix cloaks from the fallen prostitute and a pirate, then toss them into the swirling wind as decoys. The Wind Witch's weapons fly on the wind to strike down the woolen garments.

I drop to my stomach, hugging the ground, letting the decoys do my work for me. It isn't long before the wind dies down. She's losing steam. But this time, instead of dropping the whole storm at once, she keeps the wind circling around the two of us to form a wall.

"Only one of us, Lone Wolf!" She coughs up blood as she points toward the stands. "But them? They don't get to watch."

I nod.

I grab a fallen Vale helmet, ready to rush her, but with a cry, she gathers the last of her energy and summons a wind that sweeps me off my feet.

I fly twenty feet into the air, clawing at nothing. For a terrible second, I hover there—

And then she drops me.

I freefall, scrambling, but there's nothing to hold onto. My back slams into the sand with enough force to knock the air from my lungs.

The Wind Witch is waiting with a scythe raised over-head. This is it. It happens too fast for me to roll out of the way. Any second, that blade is going to come down on my neck.

Sabine—I'm so fucking sorry. I tried.

As the Wind Witch prepares to lower the scythe, her eyes suddenly widen enough to see the full whites. Flecks of pinkish foam form at the corners of her mouth. Her body tremors, causing the scythe to slide out of her hand and fall uselessly to the ground.

In a flash, I roll to the side, prepared to fight. Ribs aching. Lungs still starved. But the Wind Witch doesn't attack.

She grips her heart, crashes to her knees, then face-plants in the sand.

For a second, I don't move, muscles still tensed in case this is a trick.

The swirling sand thins—the wall hiding us from the crowd will collapse at any second.

I scramble over to feel her pulse. It's fading . . .fading . .

.gone. Her lips are blue. Her eyes are as glassy as a frozen lake.

A tiny spider—so small only my eyes could catch it—crawls out from under her Woudix costume and tunnels into the sand. It's an arrowwood spider. One bite is deadly.

Understanding slams into me.

Sabine. She did this. She saved my life. Fuck if I know how, with Berolt blocking her godkiss. But I'm as sure as I've ever been in my life.

As the wind continues to die, I think fast. I have to protect Sabine. The Valveres can't know that she did this. So, I bring down the axe in the center of the Wind Witch's ribs so no one will know that she didn't die by my blade.

The sandstorm finally stops, clearing the view to reveal me as the last fighter standing, and ten thousand spectators jump to their feet, calling my name until it pounds sense-lessly against my ears.

"Behold, your victor!" the announcer cries through his cone. "Duren's Lone Wolf is absolved for his sins!"

As I stare up at the deafening crowd, my hand aches. Ribs, too. My lungs grate. My senses flicker on and off like a firefly, overwhelmed by the deafening noise. Dimly, I watch as more hawks circle overhead. Or are they vultures? By the gods, there must be *hundreds*.

What, are they drawn by all the blood?

Golden Sentinels march into the arena to surround me in a wide circle. The trap door's gears whir until it rises up to hide the carnage below. Already, stadium servants haul away the dead fighters, while more rush in with rakes to comb over the bloody sand.

Rian forgoes the aisle: unable to restrain his emotion, he vaults directly over the Immortal Box railing, pushing through the gasping throngs, only to repeat the feat with the lower barrier, dropping down into the sand.

He comes striding across the arena floor with powerful steps, his face perfectly inexpressive, and for a second, I'm certain he's about to draw a knife to finish the job the fifteen other fighters failed.

He stops two paces in front of me.

My mouth goes dry. I'm unarmed—this could be it.

"Wolf Bowborn, you tough bastard." He suddenly throws his arms around the blood-stained tatters of my costume, embracing me hard enough to thrust the air from my already aching lungs. "I knew you'd win!"

My jaw hinges open, speechless. I've lost a fuck load of blood. I have bruises in places I didn't even know could bruise.

Rian cups a hand around the back of my neck and says in my ear, voice brimming with excitement, "All is forgiven. Your sins washed away in blood. Brothers once more, yes? But, Wolf?" His voice cracks. "Don't break my heart again."

He squeezes my shoulder. I feel myself nod, dazed, but maybe it's just the jolt.

The main entrance opens, and Sabine comes anxiously striding out, flanked by soldiers. Her eyes are wide as silver coins. She seems as breathless as me, as though she's been in her own battle.

My eyes drink in every inch of her, desperate to discover if Berolt harmed her, but from what I can see—and that dress shows *a lot*—she's as perfect as dawn.

She stops short of embracing me, swallowing down a lump. Her eyes volley nervously between Rian and me.

In a formal voice I almost never hear from her, she announces, "Wolf Bowborn. I salute your victory."

My jaw clenches as I nod, struggling to match her tone. "My lady. I cannot hope for your forgiveness."

"And yet, you have it." Her words are stilted, formal, as though we're reading from a script.

Rian faces the crowd and, lifting Sabine's hand in his right and my hand in his left, shouts, "All is forgiven!"

Tears stream down spectator's faces. Children hug their parents' legs, and teenage girls fling tulip blossoms to the arena floor.

The announcer catches one of the flowers and presses it to his heart as he raises his cone. "Betrayal. Disgrace. Death. And in the end, forgiveness. What a conclusion to the tale of the Winged Lady and the Lone Wolf! An ending befitting the fae themselves! Our shamed huntsman caught himself the greatest quarry of all: a pardon from the future king and queen!"

My stomach lurches. Pain hits me in waves. Sabine glances over her shoulder at me, her gaze as fleeting and delicate as a moth. If only the populace knew the real story.

I didn't win absolution—*she* killed for me.

"Bow before me, Wolf Bowborn." Rian draws his sword. "And be reinstated among the Golden Sentinels."

I lurch down to one knee, but a shadow falls over me as I bow my head. The air takes on a strange smell. Old iron. The sulfur of pestilence. Something tart, like black cherries. The temperature cools drastically—are my senses going berserk again?

However, this time, Sabine also hugs her arms like she's cold.

As the shadow spreads over the arena, the spectators' enthusiasm rolls into shouts of confusion.

"What are those? Hawks?" Rian frowns skyward.

Thousands of birds—enough to block out half the sky—swarm as thick as storm clouds.

A boulder sinks into the pit of my stomach.

"Not hawks," I murmur, honing my vision on the birds' outline. "Starleons."

Better known as plaguewings.

Screams ring out in the stadium. Dust rains down from the birds' wings when they tremble their feathers: a shimmering multi-colored powder that would be beautiful if it wasn't deadly.

Standing in front of the fighters' entrance, Jocki is one of the first to be doused with the dust. He swipes at his face as though attacked by gnats, screaming. In seconds, blood pours out of his eyes and nose. He collapses face-first into the sand. Dead.

Holy fuck.

I'm just sorry I couldn't kill him myself.

More screams cut at my ears. People are dropping throughout the stadium. Crying blood. Crashing into one another in a panic to flee. The high-class spectators in the Immortal Box aren't spared; Lady Solvig collapses against the railing, blood drizzling from her ears as she screams, then tips head-first over the side.

There's a crack as her skull shatters.

This is a goddamn bloodbath. But an itch scrapes at the back of my neck. Not a single priest of the Red Church has fallen. They all stand upright, unafraid. Is it their mourning masks? Protecting them from the plague dust?

As I watch, they begin to rip off their heavy crimson robes to reveal cutlasses hanging from their belts and white-blond hair beneath their hoods.

Those aren't priests.

They're gods damned Volkish raiders.

The aghast announcer lifts his cone to call for calm, but the plague dust falls on him, and he withers like a crushed tulip. His cone falls onto one of the drums, sending out an echo like thunder.

It all happens in seconds as the wave of plague dust sweeps toward us.

Rian draws his sword. "Fuck! What is this?"

"Volkany. It's Volkany." I kick the sword out of his hand, grab him and Sabine into an embrace on either side of me, then sweep a Woudix cloak over our three heads just as the rain of plague dust reaches us.

CHAPTER 25

SABINE

Basten wraps his left hand around my waist, drawing me close beneath the suffocating cloak as the three of us blindly make our way toward the fighters' entrance. To hell with decorum—it's a starleon attack. No one will judge him for touching me now. Rian throws his right arm around me from the other side.

The two of them—my bookends.

One my sword.

One my shield.

Once the sand turns to bricks under our feet, Basten finally tosses the cloak free, and the three of us gasp air. Sheltered under the brick archway, we're safe from the falling plague dust. Several soldiers in the arena follow Basten's lead and cover their faces with Woudix cloaks or Vale shields scavenged from the Everlast, but already, a spate of dead soldiers litter the blood-pooled sand.

In the stands, much of the public has taken shelter or covered their faces, but a startling number of dead are slumped on the seats.

Masked raiders methodically strike down the survivors, making their way toward the arena floor.

Toward *us*.

"Plague dust is only deadly if breathed while in the air," Rian shouts to those of us gathered. "Once it touches down, it's harmless. It only affects people, not animals. So, if anyone can get down to the tiger cages, now would be a good fucking time to release them."

But none of the soldiers move—because doing so would mean going back out in the plague dust.

"Suri." My throat is so dry that the name barely comes out. "And Ferra. They're in the Immortal Box. And Brigit was somewhere in the stands—"

"I'm sure Folke got them to safety." Basten locks eyes to mine. His left hand twitches, almost reaching out, but he glances at Rian and holds himself back. "Are you unharmed?"

"The plague dust didn't touch me."

"I didn't mean—" He stops himself. His gaze falls to the crystal necklace covering my godkissed birthmark. He glances again at Rian, who is speaking urgently with half a dozen soldiers, ordering them to search the stands for raiders.

Basten moves closer and says quietly, "What did Lord Berolt do to you?"

The dark look in his eyes makes me shiver—it's the same look he had before slaughtering a whole team of Volkish raiders.

"Nothing." I, too, have to hold myself back from touching him as I want to. "It's only this collar. It blocks my powers."

"But then how . . ." he mouths, " . . . *the spider?*"

I pluck at my tight bodice but, forged from golden iron, it can't be adjusted like a silk gown. I whisper, "Spiders don't talk, they sing. The spiders' song has nothing to do with my godkiss. It's simply the language of nature. When Berolt blocked my powers, I was still able to sing to them—one responded."

Basten says no more, but I can read his gratitude in his wavering eyes.

Rian suddenly grabs my wrist, pulling me toward a pair of soldiers. "You two. Take Lady Sabine to safety before those gods damned raiders reach us. Get her into a covered carriage and back to Sorsha Hall. I want twenty guards posted at her door."

"No, wait!" I wrench my wrist out of Rian's grasp, heart thrashing against my ribs. My fingers claw at Lord Berolt's collar covering my godkiss. "Rian, I can help. Let me try to control the starleons as I did the tiger."

"Sabine, that nearly killed you," he argues.

"Hundreds of people are dying now!"

This damn collar—it's designed to fasten and lock in the back, where I can't reach it. As I tug at the golden chains, Basten unholsters a knife from a nearby fallen soldier and uses the hilt to wrench apart the locked buckle.

It snaps free.

"Get it off!" I cry. Basten helps me shed the collar like it's poison, stuffing the clinking jewelry into his pocket.

Finally free of it, I run to the edge of the archway. The starleons overhead still flutter their feathers, dropping their toxic dust.

In the stands, dozens of Golden Sentinels with cloths tied around their noses and mouths battle against the masked raiders. Overhead, the birds circle like a cyclone, far too synchronized a pattern to be natural.

Someone trained the starleons for this.

I suck in a few breaths, trying to concentrate. I focus my attention on the flock and firmly command, **Leave these skies.**

The birds' voices hurl back at me like stones plinking into the puddles of my mind, but none of their words make sense.

Not what you . . .

. . .on the wind . . .

gray, gray, gray

. . .DAUGHTER . . .

The last one jolts me so strongly that I stumble, catching myself against the archway's brick wall. A strange hum in the air makes my knees tremble. When I feel dampness beneath my nose, my fingers come away with blood.

"Sabine?" Basten is at my side in an instant.

"The birds," I start. "There's—there's something wrong. It's as if they hear me, but something is in the way."

Determined, I face the skies again. I possessed the tiger: some deep, buried part of me knew how to do it, and I still have that part within me.

Bracing my feet, I pour all my will into shouting one word: **Leave!**

The flock of starleons emits deafening caws, unceasing in their swirling pattern, ignoring my command.

Opening my stance, I try something else: **Who commands you?**

The answers assault my mind like hail:

him

he

346

the one
the king

Nausea grips me hard enough to make me fold over. I lean against the brick wall, the bite of pain from its rough surface keeping me grounded.

"Rachillon." I dig my hand against my burning godkiss birthmark. "It's Rachillon. He commands them."

Rian and Basten exchange a look lined with dread.

"They train goldenclaws," Rian mumbles under his breath. "Why not starleons?"

Sweat breaks out across my brow. I feel dizzy, unmoored. A Volkish raider jumps down into the arena sand, and Rian draws his sword even though there are dozens of Golden Sentinels between us.

"Go." Rian urges me toward the exit. "Sabine, for the love of—"

VAL-VER-E

The sound crashes between my ears like a thunderclap, and I clamp my hands on either side of my scalp.

I shove my way between Rian and Basten to look at the sky, where the birds have shifted their formation. As the birds overlap and space themselves out, the terrifying shape of a visage takes form against the clouds.

The soldiers beneath the archway gape up at the face made of winged creatures. I watch in slow-boil dread as the sky becomes a canvas for the sinister face of the Mad King, wrought from shadows and feathers. His eyes are dark pools of gathered birds. His mouth shifts with their beating wings.

I can't help but tremble as King Rachillon's silent stare crawls beneath my skin. This is no benevolent ruler; this is a harbinger of darkness, his message woven through with threats, and I stand rooted, unable to look away from the terrifying spectacle.

From my *father's* face.

The flock shifts slightly, and the grotesque mouth moves.

VAL-VER-E, a dark voice rumbles again through my mind. The birds are speaking to me collectively, and yet something else speaks through *them*.

DOES OUR DEAL PLEASE YOU NOW, VALVERE?

My fingernails dig into Rian's arm hard enough to draw blood. "Rachillon is talking to you. Communicating through my godkiss with the birds."

Rian's face is pale, yet his eyes burn with courage. "And his message?"

"He said something about a deal?"

Rian's face immediately shutters. He rests a hand on his sword hilt as a muscle jumps in his jaw. "Deal? What does he mean?"

The voice roars back into my head, so demanding it steals my breath.

HEARKEN, KINGDOM OF THE SOUTHERN SHORE. THE CHOSEN AWAKEN. THE TAPESTRY WEAVES ANEW. THE OLD BONDS FORGE AGAIN. VOLKANY'S ALLEGIANCE HOLDS TO AGE-OLD PACTS, A TORRENT OF POWER UNMATCHED. BEHOLD, PEOPLE OF ASTAGNON: THE ECHO OF YOUR DEFIANCE IS BUT A FLEETING SHADOW AGAINST THE INEXORABLE TIDE. AS THE VEIL THINS, HEED THE CALL. WILL YOU STAND AS A SAPLING IN THE TEMPEST'S PATH, OR YIELD TO THE INEVITABLE DAWN?

I grip the archway to keep from reeling as I stumble out a rough translation of the cryptic warnings.

"He—he warns the people of Astagnon of coming strife. The waking gods. He says that the gods will side with Volkany as part of an ancient pact, and Astagnon must swear fealty or face their wrath—"

The voice shifts from the booming force into a sudden, sinister whisper between my ears.

I found you, daughter. I always find you. You'll be with me soon.

My knees threaten to give out. Swords clatter as sentinels clash with Volkish raiders in the stands. Plague dust still rains down from the sky.

Everything around me is dying.

"Me." My voice is hoarse, barely audible. "He's talking about me now. That he—he found me. I think the raiders are here for me."

"Dammit, Rian!" Basten's curse rips through the air. "Did I not predict this? He's coming for her, just as I said. He's relentless when it comes to her!"

Rian's mask slips an inch, revealing a moment of uncertainty. But his shield is immediately thrown back up. "Sabine is to be my queen—I'll be damned if I let Volkany take her."

He draws his sword.

"What the hell are you going to do, cut down the plague?" Basten roars.

"I'll start with a few dozen raiders," Rian quips.

My breath catches, a vice gripping around my chest as my father's words echo in my mind. Each syllable is a hammer to my sanity. No human has the power to speak through starleons like Rachillon did—unless the gods themselves offer aid.

So, is it true? Are the gods already awake? Helping him?

A soldier comes limping in from the arena, caked in sweat and blood. When he tugs the protective cloth down over his chin, I recognize Folke. His graying hair is dusted with sand. A bad scrape mars his left temple.

"Lord Rian. Wolf." He's breathing hard. "There are too many raiders. We outnumbered them at first, but plaguewings took down too many of our troops. We must retreat."

"Retreat?" Rian seethes. "Do I look like I know the meaning of the word?"

Frantic, I let my hand fall on Folke's arm and ask urgently, "Did you see Suri and Ferra in the box?"

He nods as he coughs into his shirt sleeve. "Maximan got them into a closet, I believe—they're safe for now but trapped there."

My thoughts spiral, fear for my friends intertwining with my own personal, dark worries. I'm overwhelmed with the urge to act—but how? The feeling of helplessness is suffocating, a relentless weight that threatens to drown me.

"Your orders, my lord?" Folke asks Rian. A half-dozen soldiers remain with us in the fighters' entrance. If I had to guess, I'd say there are maybe three dozen surviving soldiers throughout the entire arena. It feels utterly hopeless, a single brick to hold back a raging tide.

Can I let it end like this? Captured, snatched away into a cursed realm while my loved ones lie fallen or ravaged by disease?

Once, when my father's raiders sought me, I summoned the bees, and they heeded my call, a living shield against his will.

But what now? What force in nature can I beckon? Bees, tigers, hawks, wolves—none can quell this storm.

But then, from the depths of despair, a flickering ember of hope whispers.

Sabine! I'm coming!

My flicker of hope catches and spreads like wildfire. The vice around my chest loosens, the panic receding. As I stagger toward the arena, a familiar figure stampedes across the sand from the direction of the broken-open gates.

It's Myst. My beautiful mare. My brave girl. Like a comet's white tail, she tears through the plague dust that falls around her as harmlessly as dandelion seeds. Mud streaks her legs, and one hoof is chipped—she must have kicked down her stall door, sensing my need.

A pace behind her, the monoceros tears across the arena with all the force of a night storm made flesh, sparks trailing in his wake.

I look overhead—the sun is just breaking through the clouds.

"Basten!" I throw out my hand, and he takes it. Trusting me. Supporting me. "I need to stand on your shoulders. Quickly."

"Little violet, you could stomp on my heart if you wish."

He forms a stirrup with his hands, and I kick off my high-heeled slippers and step barefoot into his hold. I rest my other foot on his bent thigh, then scale up to his shoulders. Supporting myself with the wall, I lift to my feet, balancing on his broad shoulders.

He clamps his hands over my feet to steady me, looking up with intense focus, as if he would sooner die than drop me.

"When I say the word—" I rip a piece of silk off my gown and fasten it into a mask around my nose and mouth, "—catapult me into the air."

I adjust my feet to rest in his sturdy palms, though he winces when my heel digs into his right hand. I flick him a worried look, but he only grimaces and answers, "At your command."

Rian, Folke, and the soldiers watch in shock as Myst and the monoceros stampede across the arena toward us. Even the Volkish raiders battling in the sand pause, unable to tear their eyes off the awe-inspiring sight of the horned fae horse of lore. They might have starleons and goldenclaws in Volkany, but Lord Rian Valvere has a *monoceros*.

A being even rarer than the gods themselves.

"On my call!" I shout to Basten as Myst thunders toward me. "Now!"

He hurls me smoothly toward Myst. His right hand—normally his stronger hand—feels strangely unsteady beneath my heel, and only when I rest my full weight against it do I realize it's broken.

But it's too late. I leap toward Myst. My fingers curl into the base of her mane as my right leg swings around her back, calves sliding around her smooth sides to clamp on.

"Wooo!" I shout through my muffled mask, triumphant to be astride my faithful mare. No one could ever tell her advanced age by how swift her stride is; unfaltering and steady as the Innis River.

We circle the arena with the monoceros by our side, the Volkish raiders so dumbfounded that they temporarily forget they're supposed to be slaughtering our soldiers.

You've done this before, Sabine, I tell myself. *You can do it again.*

I hoist myself onto Myst's back, crouching as I cling to her mane. My hair whips around me, the heavy braid threatening to come undone. I throw glances at the monoceros's back. His muscles ripple like floodwaters. His ethereal and terrible beauty is hypnotic. For a second, I feel trapped in an eddy of time: as though a pocket of another world has opened up, giving me a rare glimpse at a time before time.

The cryptic, ancient voice deep in my soul whispers to me again.

T—

The starleons break apart overhead, stealing my attention just when I almost had the voice's mysterious message. King Rachillon's face hovering in the sky is shattered back into nothing but birds, though plague dust still rains down.

My calves tense.

If I'm going to do this, it has to be now.

With a cry, I vault off Myst and land squarely on the monoceros. His back is broad, stretching my hips, but I curl my ankles around his sides and dig in my heels.

"Go!" I urge him.

Given free rein, he bolts even faster. Myst falls away behind us as his powerful strides eat up the arena. The world beyond is a blur. Sweat foams on his neck and shoulders, but he doesn't tire. The sharp wires of his mane cut into my palm, but I ignore the pain, focusing only on the breathtaking ride.

I don't know when it happens exactly, but we hit a rhythm. A beautiful moment when his movements and mine are perfectly in sync like two dancers lost to the music. A surge of adrenaline courses through me. His power is palpable, a wild energy that demands respect. Awe washes over me as the wind whips my hair.

It's more than mere exhilaration; it's a connection that touches some forgotten place within myself.

The voice whispers anew: *Tòrr.*

Tòrr, I repeat in my mind's voice, a sacred incantation.

The monoceros instantly responds. His pace speeds, his hooves moving like wings over the sand as he skirts the far end of the arena and doubles back. A shiver runs through me, a promise of some ancient magic I can only begin to explore at the edges.

But the name burns through me with the certainty of a morning star.

Tòrr! I shout. *I name you Tòrr!*

The monoceros's muscles ripple beneath me as though he's been reborn. I, too, feel changed. In this moment, mounting a fae beast only the gods have dared to ride, I feel like I'm treading among the greatest mysteries of the galaxy. As though I am Immortal Solene herself. Goddess of Nature. Connected to magic on a level mankind can never know.

But I know it now. Somehow, I *feel* it.

A shift comes over us; for the first time, Tòrr does not fight my instruction. When I guide him left, he instantly veers. When I urge him on, he picks up his pace. He and I are one in a way I have only ever felt when riding Myst.

With a tremor of awe, I realize that I have a weapon at my command with no rival throughout the seven kingdoms.

I sit back, shifting my hips, and Tòrr comes to an immediate halt. His lungs heave beneath my thighs. Steam shoots from his nostrils. Foamy sweat beads along his thick neck; and yet I sense he has only used a fraction of his power.

The arena is a battlefield. Dead bodies slump on the stands and hang over railings. Fallen soldiers bleed out in the sand. This is a tragedy that will be written about for ages —and it's far from finished.

The Volkish raiders have the upper hand, having trapped the last stronghold of our soldiers at the fighters' entrance.

Rian and Wolf fight alongside the soldiers, but they don't have the numbers to win.

By any historian's account, this battle is all but won in Volkany's favor.

Still, if any raiders think they are stealing me away to Drahallen Castle, they underestimate a woman's will.

Tòrr, I say, ready to issue a command, but pause.

I swore to myself that I would not possess another animal. That I would never rob any living creature of its will. Plenty of men might laugh at me for that—but they don't understand that true power comes not from force, but trust.

Instead, I ask him, **Please burn every last one of our enemies to ash.**

A burst of steam clouds from his snout. He lowers his head so that his horn catches the ribbon of sunlight breaking through the clouds, and I feel the flood of adrenaline in his own veins. For one thousand years, he has been kept from sunlight, the source of his power.

Until today.

Finally, little fae, he says, *a command I like.*

As sunlight winks off the solarium in his spiraling horn, a prism of fey light erupts over the arena in a blinding, awe-inspiring flash that would bring even the gods to their knees.

CHAPTER 26
WOLF

As swords clash throughout the arena, battle sounds and smells roar in an avalanche over my senses. The metallic tang of blood. The sharp cries of combat. I pivot as a raider raises his sword. My sword meets the steel, sparks flying from the clash. I parry another strike, the force reverberating up my arm, and counter with a swift thrust that finds its mark. Another raider lunges from behind me, but I hear him coming and duck, then drive my blade into his back.

I can't help but feel the exhilarating rush of danger, the thrill of the hunt.

But that's not what matters.

Only she does.

I swivel around to the arena, and time seems to stop.

Sabine charges across the sand astride the monoceros in a scene that could be a fae tale coming to life. Even in the holy book itself, the gods speak with reverence for the horned horses. In the peak of fae times, only a few monoceros ever existed. Not even the Immortals could fully tame the beasts' indomitable will.

The monoceros is a tool of destruction. A powderkeg made flesh. And Sabine rides it with such effortless grace that my knees go weak.

I could kneel to her, now and forever, embracing her as my one and only god.

The breathtaking scene causes a hush to fall over the battle, a shared pause among Volkish and Astagnonians alike. I can only imagine that every one of us will forever have the memory of Sabine riding the monoceros etched into our mortal minds.

She reaches the end of the arena and doubles back into a battle stance. A thrill of victory for her tightens my chest. *Dammit, little violet, you did it.*

Yet, amidst the awe of the beautiful scene, there's a wrath to their dance, a violence in their grace. I might be a warrior seasoned in bloodshed, but even I feel a jolt of electric dread for what's to come.

"Rian." I jerk him by the back of his collar away from the exposed archway. "Get back. Everyone, fall back!"

At my call, our soldiers snap to reason and hustle for the safety of the deeper interior.

The Volkish raiders are slower to piece together what's happening.

A flash of blinding light erupts from the monoceros like a star being born. The sheer force of the light knocks half the raiders to their knees.

From the safety of the archway, I watch in stunned silence as the monoceros's horn catches a ray of sunlight and beams it with the precision of an arrow along the arena's floor. Bluish-silver fey fire blooms wherever the light touches. It melts sand into lines of molten glass that immediately hardens into fantastical shapes.

The fey fire decimates raiders into ash faster than they can blink.

The monoceros lifts his head to adjust the light's angle, and fey fire bursts in a radiant fan across the sky, incinerating every starleon it touches until their ashes fall in a black blizzard over the arena.

The smell of burned flesh mixes with the lingering scents of old iron and black cherries.

The Volkish raiders try to seek cover, but between Rian's sword and my good fist, we flush them out into the exposed portion of the arena, where Sabine circles around on the monoceros, then commands it to cast its fey fire.

In a finger snap, they are ash.

For a brief moment, my gaze meets Sabine's. Her hair has fallen loose from its braid, and she looks like the Wilder-woman herself, as if she is no longer human but a force of nature.

My skin prickles with the uncanny sense that I'm witnessing the birth of a legend that will be written about a thousand years from now.

"She was meant to be a queen, wasn't she?" Rian speaks at my side, voice resonant with awe.

"Not a queen," I rasp, my throat raw. "A goddess."

Rian gives a soft snort. "A queen I can tame. A goddess? Some things are too much for even my ability to handle."

Too much? No. What I feel for Sabine in this moment has nothing to do with games of power; to love her is to dance with the fire of the gods, fearless and forever bound by the heart. A fire I would willingly walk into to be at her side for a lifetime.

I'm not intimidated by Sabine's power—I'm fucking *awestruck*.

A shiver runs up my spine, and I ask quietly and urgently, "What did Sabine mean about a deal with Rachillon?"

Rian coughs into his shirt sleeve, then adjusts the straps of his vest as though they're too restricting. "Hmm?"

My jaw hardens. "She wouldn't have said that Rachillon spoke of a deal if he had not."

"I have no idea what he referred to. They call him the Mad King for a reason."

The surviving soldiers are within earshot, but their attention is fixed on Sabine and the monoceros blasting starleons from the sky. I lower my voice further. "Did you have dealings with the Volkish king I should know about?"

"When exactly was I meant to travel to the forbidden city of Norhelm to scheme with the enemy, pray tell?"

"Rian, tell me if there's something I should know."

He stops fidgeting with his clothes and finally looks me in the eye. "You've only just earned yourself a pardon, Wolf. At the cost of fifteen lives. Don't damn yourself back to the arena for next year's Everlast just yet."

He takes off his crown, rakes his hair back into place, and replaces the circle of gold.

Folke limps up to rest a hand on my shoulder. "Come. We must clear out the raiders hiding in the stands. I don't doubt Lady Sabine's monster could smite them, but to do so, she would reduce the whole stadium to rubble."

Tension still crackles between Rian and me; this discussion is unfinished. I knew a pardon wouldn't wash away all our tumultuous past, and here I am proven right.

Still, I grab a sword from a fallen sentinel and nod to

Folke.

"We should head to the Immortal Box." Folke's rugged face shows a rare tenderness. "Ferra's there."

We sweep through the lower stands methodically, the way we were trained in the army. Folke, with his bad leg, flushes any hiding raiders out into the open, and I stand at the exits to run them through. It's grisly work, but there's always been a dark part of me that loves the fight. The clash of swords. The tang of blood. The spike of adrenaline.

Once a beast, always a beast.

By the time we reach the Immortal Box, I'm drenched in Volkish blood and thirsty for more. Folke and I rush in with swords drawn like heroes from the pages of fae tales, only to pause.

Everything is eerily silent.

The box is a mess: chairs overturned, ashen plague dust covering the platters of plumcakes and sugared berries, one of the curtains torn down. Dead soldiers litter the ground. Dead raiders, too. As well as dozens of bodies of high-class citizens: crystal-studded silk slippers unmoving, gilded jewelry tangled around cold throats.

"Do you see them?" Folke starts.

Pulse pounding between my ears, I use my sight to quickly scan the bodies. "None of the dead are Ferra. Or Suri. I don't know where—"

A rustle catches my ear.

I signal to Folke, and we step over the bodies with swords at alert to a servants' closet tucked away behind a heavy curtain. We trade a look, nodding, and then I pull back the drape.

"Oh! Wolf! Gods in hell, you startled me." Ferra scowls at me as she rests a hand on her ample bosom, dramatically bolstered by her corsetted gown. Her scowl melts into a coy smile when she spots my partner. "Hello, Folke. Look what we caught."

Ferra and Lady Suri, barely a ruffle out of place, have a Volkish raider tied to a chair with a silk tablecloth. Lady Suri points a sentinel's sword against his chest.

"A raider!" Lady Suri beams.

Folke and I, swords still drawn, gape like river guppies.

"You caught a Volkish raider? The two of you?" I echo.

I catch my reflection in a silver serving tray on the floor —I look like a gods damned fool, rushing in to rescue women who have already saved themselves. I have to wipe the shock off my face. I shouldn't be surprised. If Sabine has shown me anything, it's that I need to reevaluate my preconceived notions about what women are capable of.

"My pampered little kitten caught a raider?" Folke sheaths his sword and steps over a dead servant to sweep Ferra into his arms.

"What," she purrs, "You didn't think this cat had claws?" She digs her nails into his arm and he flinches, eyes darkening with lust.

"Oh, I know she does. However, I thought those claws only came out when we were in bed . . ." He nibbles at her neck, and she gasps and pushes him away.

I sheath my sword and do a quick inspection of the raider's binds, tightening some of the knots. "Lady Suri, are there any other survivors among the box's spectators?"

She shifts the sword to her other hand, not lowering it from the enemy's chest. "When the starleons first attacked, guards got most people out of the stadium. Ferra and I ended up trapped here with Brigit and Maximan, but they went back for the Valveres."

Maximan? Sure. But Brigit?

"Brigit went back to *save* the Valveres?"

"She said she knew a safe place away from the pestilence that would hold them all."

My jaw parts, still unsure why anyone would wish to rescue a single Valvere, but I suppose Brigit has a kinder heart than me. Leaving the raider under Folke and Ferra's care, Suri and I cautiously pass back through the Immortal Box.

She holds the sword with an unskilled but determined hand. Now, I understand how she survived so long under Lord Charlin's roof. She's a warrior at heart, masquerading as a sunbeam.

"Lord Berolt?" I call, raising my voice. "Brigit?"

Even with my keen hearing, there is no answer. Only the distant cries of the few remaining raiders running from Sabine and the monoceros, and moans from the wounded in the stands.

But then, I hear a tiny squeak and look down.

Between my feet, that goddamn forest mouse that stowed away in Ma Na Tir Forest wiggles its nose at me.

"You?" I bark at it. "What the hell are you doing here?"

"That's Brigit's pet mouse!" Lady Suri says.

Of course it fucking is. So, I have no choice but to follow the mouse as it scampers over fallen chairs and beneath tables to lead us back to the outer hallway. All seems empty, but the mouse purposefully continues, glancing back to make sure we're following, until it disappears through a rain grate in the floor.

Frowning, Lady Suri and I approach the grate. Amid the smell of brick and runoff, I smell a trace of aloeswood incense.

My jaw hangs open when we discover five people crammed inside, faces peering back up at us.

"Wolf Bowborn!" Lady Eleonora shouts, elbowing Lady Runa in the stomach as she clutches her emerald necklace. "Get us the hell out of here before we end up in the gutters!"

"By the gods," Suri gapes. "I'll fetch some soldiers."

Suri hurries off, and I have to stifle the urge to laugh as I use the pole from a flag post to pry the heavy grate off and, one by one, help them out of their hiding place. Lady Eleonora. Lord Berolt. Lady Runa. Lord Gideon, who does not appear to have been crying very hard over his wife's death. And finally, Brigit, who dusts off her apron and then scoops up the mouse into her pocket.

"Gods help me!" Lady Eleonora wails, collapsing back against a marble column. "That escapade was a journey through the seventh circle of hell. I thought we'd be trapped down there for days, crammed like peasants in a public carriage. Not to mention, the urgency in my bladder is reaching legendary proportions."

"Let me help you to the latrine, my lady," Brigit pipes up.

I stop her briefly. It's hard to believe that a servant girl and a mouse saved the lives of the future royal family of Astagnon. "They'd better hang your portrait in the ballroom for this, girl. That fucking mouse's, too."

Brigit grins shyly.

I continue, "Now go. Help Lady Eleonora, then meet Suri with the soldiers. Take heed. The danger is not ended. Get outside the arena as swiftly as you can."

Lord Gideon and Lady Runa leave with them, taking more care arranging their wrinkled clothes than stepping over their subjects' dead bodies.

Lord Berolt remains. Now that it's just the two of us, I

quietly take Sabine's necklace from my pocket.

Throwing it at him, I spit, "I guess you couldn't control her, after all."

I expect his vitriol, so when he only catches the necklace and laughs darkly, I feel as if I've been kicked by a stallion.

"On the contrary," he says. "Failure is an intrinsic part of experimentation. Essential, even. Now, I know what steps I'll need to take to create a more permanent means to tame her. And mark my words, she will come to obey me. I have big plans for the female you made yourself a lovesick fool over."

His cruel mockery enrages me, but not for the reason he thinks. He can slander me all he likes. But to threaten Sabine?

He's a dead man.

"Mark *my* words," I growl, "You won't get a single more godkissed person on that experimentation table of yours, or it will be you strapped down after I come for you."

He smiles as though I've said something funny, clapping his hand on my back like we're old friends—as though it's all a game to him. Leaning close to my ear, he says quietly, "How badly I wanted *you* on my table, Wolf Bowborn. You have my son to thank for never seeing the inside of my laboratory. But keep falling out with him, and you'll be mine, too."

Fury cuts shards into my skin, but before I can respond, a soldier hurries around the corner, slowing when he spots us. "My lord?"

Lord Berolt pockets Sabine's necklace, flashing me a cold smile, and strides off with the soldier.

Fighting the anger burning through me, I flex my fists a few times, bringing my emotions back into check, then make quick strides back through the Immortal Box to the brass railing.

Lord Berolt isn't my greatest concern right now.

Every moment away from Sabine sends a jolt of worry through my veins like I've left a part of my soul unguarded in the midst of chaos. The thought of her facing danger without me by her side gnaws at me like a hungry beast. I want to be near her, not just to protect her, but to stand with her.

The two of us against any force.

My anger softens when I finally spot her. She and the monoceros have torn up the arena. Beautiful, otherworldly lines of melted glass pool in the sand, evidence of the battle they've fought. Heavy black ash tells of her vanquished enemies.

She spurs on the monoceros to blast its fey fire, and the final starleon falls from the sky in a puff of ash. The monoceros finally slows to a walk. Its fiery mane and tail seem to hover in the air for a beat too long, as does Sabine's own hair, like they're suspended in magic.

My hands curve around the railing, my heart so deeply in love with this woman that I can hardly breathe. I will follow her to the ends of the earth if she asks it of me.

She just defied a king. Damn the fact that he was her own father. This woman is going to change the course of everything.

Then, the spell shatters, and Sabine slumps forward on the fae horse. Her shoulders sag. Her head lolls from exhaustion.

My protective instinct flares to life, as powerful as any fey fire, and I leap over the railing and scale down the stands two at a time, ready to tear through death itself to reach her.

CHAPTER 27
SABINE

My lungs are lead. My muscles scream in rebellion. Blood pours from my shredded hands. I'm bone-tired, every breath a battle in itself.

But the skies? They're clear. No starleons. No plague dust shimmering in the breeze. Warm sunlight bathes my face, and I rip off the cloth mask, gasping in fresh air.

Tòrr, I say. *It's over. We did it.*

Pity, he snorts. *I was having fun for the first time in a thousand years.*

Beneath my thighs, Tòrr's massive muscles ripple from withers to hindquarters. All that effort, and he's barely out of breath. He could have easily continued casting fey fire until the entire city lay in ruins.

But I'm not fae, like him. Red blood flows through my veins. There's a limit to what the human body can endure, and simply staying upright astride Tòrr takes a monumental effort. My legs tremble, pushed beyond their limit to hold on.

As soon as we draw to a halt, Myst comes galloping up to us, her black eyes wide with worry as her muzzle dips into every cranny around the both of us, searching for wounds.

You smell weak, Sabine, she says. *You pushed yourself too hard.*

Black spots flash at the edges of my vision. My body slumps forward over Tòrr's neck. The razor-sharp strands of his mane slice against my forearms, but I can barely feel the pain. The arena spins like a child's top around me.

Basten, I struggle to form the words in my head. *Basten, I need you. Please.*

But in my daze, I forget that Basten can't hear my call in his mind like one of my animals.

"Songbird!"

As my balance shifts, and my body tips over and begins to fall, strong arms suddenly swoop in to catch me. I sink into a man's powerful embrace as he lowers me to the arena's surface, laying me out gently over sand and ash.

Squinting through the starbursts clouding my vision, I see Rian smoothing my sweat-soaked hair off my brow.

Rian? No—it isn't Rian's heart that I need close to mine. Every bone in my body screams out for Basten, a yearning that goes beyond mere desire. It's a visceral need, my soul desperately reaching for its missing piece.

My lips crack, trying to form words. "Where . . . is . . ."

"Quiet now, songbird." Rian runs the back of one knuckle over my left cheek. "You're going to survive this. The Volkish attack is over. You're the reason we're all still standing." He shouts over his shoulder, "Would someone fetch the fucking healer already? I don't care what it takes!

Melt down my crown and sell it for scrap metal, for all I care!"

Dimly, I'm aware of boots running off to seek help. The air is thick with the acrid smell of ash and burnt sand. The sunlight feels heavy on my face, a blanket of warmth, as if giving permission to finally rest.

"Songbird?" Rian says. "Stay with me. The healer is coming. Gods dammit, to see you on that beast was like witnessing a star being born." He murmurs to himself as he traces a line over my cheek, "What was I thinking when I . . . Gods, what have I done?"

His words feel spoken from across a veil as my mind begins to flicker in and out of reality. I try to tell Rian that this isn't his fault. For the first time, he wasn't to blame for the tragedy. It was me, drawing my father here. I don't know how Rachillon found me, but *I* placed the target squarely on Duren.

And now thousands are dead.

"Forgive me, Sabine," Rian murmurs, his voice wavering, as he presses his forehead to the back of my hand.

Heavy footsteps thunder toward us, then Basten drops into the sand at my side.

I could cry, I'm so relieved to see his handsome face. He's breathing as hard as if he climbed a mountain. His hair is sweat-soaked and loose. Blood streaks the tattered remnants of his Vale costume—nothing now but ripped chainmail over his bare chest.

"Sabine." His voice breaks. I can feel how badly he wants to pull me into his arms. I crave it, too. It's a magnetic force between us, making my skin prickle with need.

Instead, he fists his hands in the sand with blanched

knuckles, fighting the urge to touch me. "Gods, I should have been here to catch you. I came as fast as I could."

"I was here." Rian's voice is strangely flat—no malice, simply facts.

"Please . . ." I whisper.

I lift my hand, trying to reach for Basten, but Rian mistakes who I want and takes my hand instead. *No.* A sob forms in my chest, but I'm too exhausted even to cry. Every piece of me screams to be with Basten.

But the wrong man takes me in his arms.

"You'll be okay, songbird," Rian says. "And Volkany will think twice before trying to steal you from me again."

I blink, trying to center my focus on Basten over Rian's shoulder. Twisting my hand in the back of Rian's shirt, kneading the fabric because I can't have the man I want.

Basten runs a hand over his sweat-soaked face with a mangled fist, knuckles broken and bleeding, his eyes never leaving mine.

As darkness unspools around me, our eyes remain locked, because that is the one point of touch no laws can ever force us to break.

In my delirium, strange dreams come to me. The painting on my bedroom ceiling stirs to life again. The cloudfox prances between Immortal Thracia and Immortal Samaur's legs. Immortal Popelin's laughter echoes between my bedroom windows, along with the clink of his ever-present coins. I smell myrrh and fae wine. I'm there with the gods, clinking crystal goblets. Only no laughter graces my lips. Hatred has turned my heart to stone. I loathe each of them—those ten devastatingly beautiful faces, elongated ears bedecked with jewels, wine staining their lips like blood. But serpentine vines coil around my ankles. Heavy golden bracelets shackle my wrists.

I'm trapped in this beautiful fae nightmare.

Tòrr, I scream in my dream. **Burn it down!**

The painting above bubbles as though burning from within. It peels into flecks, a silent snowfall of colored curls falling over my room, erasing the gods to mere paint chips, destined to be swept away and consigned to the flames by Brigit's diligent hands.

I awake with a gasp, still smelling smoke and burning paint. At first, I don't recognize my own bedroom. The walnut dresser. The copper bathing tub. The owl's perch at the window. But then I see the domed painting overhead—perfectly intact, the ten fae frozen in revelry—and everything comes crashing back.

I reach for a water glass with a trembling hand.

How much time has passed? Judging from the slanting light at the window, it's afternoon. But I have no idea which day. The last I remember, I was with Rian and Wolf in the arena. Ashes in the air. Melted chunks of sand. Blood dripping from the stands.

"Oh, gods." My stomach clenches, doubling me over, threatening to be sick. When I close my eyes, all I can picture are thousands of bodies. Their dead eyes glassy from the plaguewing's dust. The raiders' grieving masks. The Mad King's otherworldly face formed out of starleons.

His voice in my head, speaking through the birds: *Daughter. I found you.*

A sob bubbles out of my throat as my body begins to shake. In the next moment, the door flings open.

Basten strides in, immediately gathering me into his arms. His right hand is heavily bandaged. Cuts and bruises paint his face and the parts of his chest that his Golden Sentinel armor exposes. He sweeps his damaged hand around my back, gently touching my right cheek with his good hand, as his eyes volley between mine.

"Little violet. I heard you cry. I've been waiting for you to wake."

"How long have I slept?"

"Two days."

Breathing hard, I loop an arm around his neck and cling to him fiercely as I glance apprehensively at the door. "Where is Rian?"

"It's safe," he murmurs. "We won't be caught. Rian and Berolt are in town with the magistrate, inspecting the damage. We're the only two in the tower at the moment."

I run a trembling hand over the swell of his golden shoulder plate. "I thought Rian would banish you to some distant outpost."

"That was his original plan, but he changed his mind when he was named the king's successor. I'm not your bodyguard anymore—I'm assigned to Rian's own protection team. But it seems most of the servants have a soft spot for our story. Even old Maximan has a heart, if you can believe it. He looked the other way when I heard you wake."

I run my hands over the cuts and scrapes on his handsome face, trying to memorize this new look to him. Finally, the iron fear that's held my heart in a chokehold eases. I rest my head on his shoulder, letting my eyes sink closed, knitting my fingers in his shirt's fabric.

"How bad is the damage?" I ask.

Basten pauses before confessing, "Bad. We're still counting the dead and wounded. The final body count will be near three thousand. Mostly Durish citizens, around a hundred Golden Sentinels, and about the same number of Volkish raiders. Though the raiders' bodies are . . .harder to count. You didn't leave much but ash."

When I look up, he cups my cheek in his good hand.

"It would have been so much worse, Sabine. You saved the city from ruin. If not for you, the starleons would have decimated thousands more. The raiders would have gone into the city to slaughter even more innocent people. Then, they would have—" His voice breaks as his thumb brushes over the hill of my cheek, "—they would have taken you."

Leaning into his palm, I whisper, "It was Myst. She felt my need. She broke down the stall and brought Tòrr."

Basten's brow creases. "Tòrr?"

"The monoceros. I found his name at last. It came to me somehow, almost as if I always knew it and had forgotten."

"And once you had his name, you could control him like the tiger?"

I shake my head hard, though the movement makes me dizzy. "No, not like the tiger. That was something cruel. I forced the tiger to attack against his will. With Tòrr, it was as though our desires were united."

As I speak, Basten's eyes keep tracing over the left side of my face, and eventually, I frown. "What is it?"

He runs his thumb over my cheek. "A deep cut."

"I don't care."

"Rian will. He won't want a queen covered in scars. He'll order Ferra to mend it, just as he did for your hair."

"Rian isn't going to decide my fate anymore." I curl my fingers in Basten's collar, tugging him imperceptibly closer. "He got what he wanted—a weapon. Now, the world knows what Tòrr can do, just as he planned. But Rian's mistake is making *me* realize what I am capable of, too. And if he wants to continue being a player on this gameboard, he's going to have to start listening to us."

Basten shakes his head slowly, his eyes burning. "Gods, little violet. You are a force to be reckoned with."

I tilt my chin toward him, looking up at him through my lashes. I can feel his heartbeat, steady and strong, beneath my palm. All my sharp edges melt away until I'm just a series of curves wanting to fit against his.

"You have no idea how badly I want to kiss you," he murmurs, eyes devouring my sunburnt lips. "And I will, little violet. One day. Damn what the law or anyone else says. You showed me that it's up to us to take our fates into our own hands. Yet, I meant what I said: No more kissing in the shadows for us. Not until I can be your man honorably."

I swallow back a hard lump, fighting the urge to close the distance between our lips. "So you will come to Old Coros with us, spend years as the king's guard just steps away from me, never touching me?"

"Yes, years," he says. "Decades, if that's what it takes. You don't get it, little violet. A love like ours? It's meant to last. But at the end of things, this I swear to you: you will wear my ring. I will serve you on my knees. And we will never be parted until the sky itself falls into the sea."

He takes my hand in his bandaged one and places a single kiss on my knuckles, like the chaste knight in the tale of Lord Blacke swearing his undying devotion to Immortal Alyssantha, though he knew they could never be together.

I grab him by the sides of his face and lock my gaze to his. "You have a king's honor, Basten Bowborn. Fortunately, I'm ignoble enough for the both of us."

I kiss him with all my heart's glow.

A jagged inhale cuts across his lips as he briefly pulls back, the coolness of his breath soothing my burning skin, and then immediately crashes back into me.

His palm anchors around the small of my back, binding his scars and mine. His mouth worships me with the force of a hundred prayers, defiles me with a thousand sins. We cling together as though in freefall, crashing down toward a strange world full of wonder and danger, but as long as we're holding one another, I know we can survive any fall.

CHAPTER 28
WOLF

The constellations shift above, a slow march across the dark sky to mark the passing weeks. Mornings blur into evenings, each day a grueling effort to heal the city after the Volkish attack.

Healers, both godkissed and normal, are brought in from across eastern Astagnon to tend to the wounded. Servants scour blood and fey fire scorch marks off the arena walls. Half the Golden Sentinel army is put on grave-digging duty. The other half stands guard around the city walls in case of another incursion.

There isn't a day that I'm not at Rian's side. Three bodyguards are on him at all times, an equal number on Sabine. We accompany him as he visits the wounded in the Valvere opium dens converted into hospitals. In meetings with his army captains. The many times he convenes with Serenith to make preparations for the upcoming move to Old Coros.

The days are long, the city's mood steeped in grief. For his part, Rian may be drowning in faults, but an inability to forgive is not among them. Since the Everlast, he asks my advice. We spar together in the evenings to work off steam. He includes me in plans for the move to Old Coros. On the precipice of being king, he needs people he can trust.

That he counts on me, of all people, is a perverse irony. It's a grim reflection on his family life that my affair with his bride is only a minor ripple.

I live for the rare, light-filled moments when I see Sabine in my capacity as Rian's shadow. Since she named the monoceros, the change between them is like night and day. Rian and I lean on the railing around the riding ring, watching Sabine ride Tòrr in graceful circles around straw dummies set up as Volkish soldiers. She wears long gloves to protect her hands from his razor-wire mane, and trousers to better grip his sides. Her hair is pinned in an immortal braid, but satin strands slip free to caress the wind as she and the beast gracefully fly from one end to the other.

When word of her taming of a monoceros to defeat Volkish forces spread, the Astagnonian people from Salensa to Old Coros immediately embraced her as their future queen. What they don't know, though, is that she hails from that same enemy nation.

If they find out, they could turn on her.

Call her a spy.

A traitor.

I'll do whatever it takes—beg, steal, kill—to make sure that doesn't happen.

"Reverse," Sabine calls, and Tòrr effortlessly switches direction as he cuts diagonally across the ring. "Now, retreat."

He halts with pinpoint precision, then dances backward with his horn lowered in a defensive battle stance. Truly, it's a wonder to behold. He's a thunderstorm made flesh.

Powerful as a rushing waterfall. Mesmerizing as the abyss of space.

And yet I only have eyes for Sabine.

As she rides, her face is lit from within; cheeks flushed, eyes glowing. Laughter tugs at her soft lips as she and Tòrr move seamlessly together. Since I've known her, I could count on one hand how many times I've seen her truly smile. Joy has been criminally absent in her life until now—and she still faces uncountable challenges.

But today?

Today, her smile is as genuine as a wildflower.

My breath catches, stalled by the spell of her happiness, as if I could sear the image of her joy into my senses. Given the chance, I'd bottle this moment, savor it for a lifetime.

"One day, little violet," I whisper in a soft vow, out of Rian's earshot. "I will find a way to make your smile this bright every day of your life."

"Look, Rian! Look, Wolf!" She holds her hands straight out and uses only her heels to guide Tòrr into a backward lope, weaving in and out of the straw dummies—something I've never seen any regular horse do.

Her hair blows backward over her face, and she laughingly spits it out of her mouth.

I tip a look up at the trap door overhead and ask Rian, "When are you going to let her train with that open during daylight?"

"When I'm convinced she won't immediately incinerate me with fey fire," he mutters wryly.

Despite his sarcasm, something has shifted between the three of us since the Everlast. We've come to an unspoken truce. If not friends, then at least not enemies. Rian is so desperate for both a confidante and a bride that he acts as though our affair never happened.

In turn, he's done well by Duren after the attack, opening the Valvere coffers to rebuild the city, which I know has won a small piece of Sabine's respect.

My heart and my head are at constant war—the desire to preserve the trust Rian and I have rebuilt against the undeniable pull Sabine has on my heart, a love that deepens with each passing moment.

When she finishes for the day, Sabine dismounts, coming over to us with a broad smile and chatter about Tòrr's gait. In kind, Myst trots over to nuzzle Tòrr. She lays the flat of her neck against his, and he rests his chin on her withers. He's twice her size, an otherworldly beast, and yet, like this, he looks like a simple farm horse greeting a friend after a long day's work.

And my heart hurts with the heavy fear that none of us will ever be this carefree again.

~

That night, as Rian and I smoke pipeweed in the leather chairs by his hearth, discussing the move to Old Coros, Sabine knocks at the door.

"You wished to see me?"

"Sabine. Yes." Rian's eyes light up devilishly as he goes to the map table, which holds a wooden box stamped with Hekkelveld Castle's crest. "Wolf, you'll want to see this, too."

Sabine and I share a fleeting, intimate glance as we join him on either side of the table. He rests his palms on the box with a coy smile playing on his lips.

"A messenger arrived today from Old Coros. This box is from the King's Council—the official documentation and supplies for our upcoming coronation in Old Coros."

He opens the box with a hushed sense of curiosity, removes a stack of parchments, then carefully unfolds silk wrappings until his eyes light up. He steps back. "Take a look."

The two royal crowns of Astagnonian royalty rest on satin pillows. They've graced the heads of a long line of kings and queens before them. King Joruun and Queen Rosind. King Byrne and Queen Idarina. Generations back as far as the last Return of the Fae one thousand years ago.

Rian reverently picks up the queen's crown. It's forged from gold from the Golath mines, with nine raised spikes cast to resemble spindly thorns from ancient fae vines. Delicate golden chains hang from the sides, dripping with yellow diamonds cut to throw prisms of light over the queen's cheeks.

"Try it on, songbird," he says.

Sabine's eyes flit nervously to mine, then immediately dart away again. "Surely we aren't supposed to don the crowns until the coronation itself."

"And who will see?" Rian chides. "The closest member of the King's Council is one hundred miles away."

She paints on a smile, bowing her head for him to rest the crown on her immortal braid, but I can hear how her pulse kicks up in her veins. I've come to learn that particular rhythm only happens when she's faced with something unpleasant.

Damn if I don't get a jolt of satisfaction to know that she has no desire to wear a crown. My little violet wants what I want—the forest, starlight, a campfire warming our toes.

Rian brings her to the full-length mirror to admire her crown, whispering promises about how her birthright marks her as a queen.

She's gorgeous in a crown—but I prefer her in nothing at all.

I begin sifting through the mountain of parchment that Rian's secretaries will need to complete before we leave for Old Coros. There are reams of historical records that must be updated with Rian's ancestry. Instructions for when the bloodtaster comes to test Rian's blood to ensure the Kinship Mandate. Copies of the oaths that Rian and Sabine shall recite at their coronation. Pages and pages of etiquette instructions, as well as dossiers on each of the head servants in Hekkelveld Castle.

Topping it all is a letter signed by the ten members of the King's Council, requiring Rian's signature to confirm that he received the coronation materials. My eyes scan over it, uninterested, until the signature line at the bottom catches my attention.

Herewith signed by the successor to the Astagnonian throne, Lord Berolt Valvere of Duren

A chill cuts like ice through my veins, slicing all the way to the back of my neck, where the hair rises.

"Rian." My voice is hoarse, heavy. The letter trembles in my hand. "Have you seen this?"

Rian is so enthralled with spinning Sabine in a circle before the mirror that he tosses me a distracted look. "Later, Wolf."

"Rian, get the fuck over here now!"

He lets Sabine's hand fall, and the billows of her dress collapse as though the wind has suddenly died. Her eyes shoot to mine, asking a silent question. But I can't share the secrets in my mind with her like one of her animals.

"By the gods, Wolf." Rian strides over, acting mildly annoyed, but the sudden hammer of his heart tells a different story. He rips the letter out of my hand and reads it impatiently. "This is simply the official correspondence to say—" His face pales when he reaches the signature line. A beat passes when his left eye twitches. "There has to be a mistake."

Sabine quietly removes her crown and replaces it in the satin box, glancing anxiously from the corner of her eye between me and the letter.

Rian slams the letter on the table, his mouth working anxiously. "It's just as it was before when they mistakenly listed 'Lord Valvere' instead of 'High Lord Valvere.' A clerical error. Confusion over my current title and my father's former one."

I shift my stance, though the heat from the fire does nothing to melt the ice in my veins. "This is no mistaken title—it has his fucking *name*."

Rian's face darkens dangerously. "What, are you suggesting my father has some scheme to steal the crown from his own son?" Although Rian spits the words in jest, as soon as they're spoken, his eyes fill with dread as he realizes just how like something his father would do that sounds. "Fuck!"

He tears through the other paperwork, running his finger down the historical records until it lands on the vacant portion. Teeth gritted, he reads, "To be completed on behalf of Lord Berolt Valvere."

He throws the ream of records on the floor, then tears through the dossier on servants, lips moving silently until he reads aloud, "the number of ladies' maids for the queen shall be the purveyance of the king, His Royal Highness King Berolt, twenty-first ruler of Astagnon . . .*fuck!*"

As he twists toward the fire, dragging a hand down his face, Sabine snatches up a handwritten letter and says breathlessly, "This is from the head advisor, addressed to your father. It reads, 'Congratulations, my lord. We ten are in agreement that, as closest blood relation to the late King Joruun, it is your place to sit on the throne. Given the incursion from our enemy to the north, your decades of experience are necessary to ensure a strong Astagnon. Your son, Rian Valvere, shall remain High Lord of Duren until the time of your death when he shall be named your successor.'"

Sabine looks up, pupils blown with shock.

Rian grabs the letter from her and crumples it in his fist. "This is fucking *bullshit!*"

A tense silence hangs in the air. Sabine's breath comes quick as a chased rabbit, though she tries to hide it. Rian's pulse surges through his veins, thunder-clapping with rage.

"This is a gods damned farce!" he yells loud enough that the candlesticks topple over.

"This was always his plan," I say quietly. "It was no clerical mistake the first time. He intended to let you fight the Grand Cleric for the throne, then take it from you. He used Rachillon's attack as justification—he needed a plausible excuse to get the King's Council on his side, though I would wager they were in league with him all along."

Rian braces his hands on the table, his eyes distant and burning.

My feet begin to pace to master my turbulent emotions. "The deal that Rachillon spoke to you about, Sabine. Could this be it?"

Sabine smooths out the letter to re-read it. "I don't know. He only spoke the name Valvere. I assumed he meant Rian, but he could have been speaking of Berolt."

Rian still stares at a fixed point on the table, his mind elsewhere, the gears churning.

"Rian?" I say.

"Perhaps." Rian's face has gone splotchy. The air grates through his nostrils as he fights to contain his rage. He snatches up the servant dossier. "And this? The reference to a queen? My mother is twenty-eight years dead."

The back of my neck prickles with itches I can't fucking scratch. I thieve a step toward the fire, the tangerine glow focusing my thoughts. In my mind's memory, I hear the tinkling clatter of Sabine's golden necklace as Berolt closed it in his fist on the day of the Everlast.

I return to the map table, steady my hands, bracing myself against the unwelcome fear knotting in my chest. "The queen remains the same—Sabine."

Sabine's hand clutches around the base of her throat, eyes filled with dread.

Rian drills a look into me that could bore out my eyes.

"Even my father would not do such a thing. Steal my throne? Yes, I would believe it. But my bride? He is nearly forty years her senior!"

"And he's taken a keen interest in her since the day she arrived, hasn't he?" My voice rumbles like hot coals, my fury barely restrained. "Her beauty. Her youth. Her godkiss most of all. The necklace he designed to block her powers? That's just his first step in a grand plan to control her. He's gone to such lengths because he intends to have her at his side, not yours."

Sabine plants a hand on her lower stomach, looking green. Her heart is thrashing so hard in her chest that I'm afraid it's going to burst right out.

She tames her disgust, her eyes hardening.

"I believe it," she says in a deathly quiet voice. "On the night of the succession ball, I heard rumors saying the same. Credible rumors."

"I still can't—"

Jaw clenched, she grabs Rian's shirt sleeve. "It's true! You know it is. Your father intends to take everything from you, Rian. We cannot let him win. I'll be damned if another powerful man thinks he can toy with those in his thrall. This isn't one of your fucking card games!"

Rian clamps his hand over hers, trapping it against his forearm. His pulse temporarily falters behind his ribs.

He hisses, "And how am I to stop him? When he has the King's Council behind him? And probably the gods damned Golden Sentinels? My own army captains have been avoiding giving me direct answers about moving to Old Coros and consolidating with the royal army. Now, I know why."

I grab the king's crown from the satin-lined box, fisting it in the air like a torch. "You want to wear this crown? The peaceful days of Old King Joruun are gone. You're going to have to be even more ruthless than your father. A true fucking Valvere."

Rian paces a heavy line across the carpet, turning in tight, coiled steps. As though speaking to himself, he mutters, "I know my father. He won't give up his plans for man or god."

I lean further over the map table, my hair falling in dark lines over my eyes. "I cannot argue that."

Rian bites his thumbnail. "He'd have to be banished to Woudix's underrealm."

Sabine toys with the spires of the queen's crown, pressing her finger against one sharp point until I can smell blood pooling beneath the pad of her finger. Her blue-juniper eyes reflect the firelight, giving her the look of some otherworldly being as she says evenly, "So then banish him there."

The words plant like a boulder between the three of us.

Now, it's out in the open—a dark secret whispered among us, weaving our already tangled fates tighter together like strands in a complex web. And I'd sooner bathe in a sea of arrowwood spiders than ever see Lord Berolt lay a hand on my little violet.

His death? It would give me no greater satisfaction, but the man is as clever as Immortal Meric himself. According to Sabine, he takes a potion to protect himself from poison or venom. He's always surrounded by guards. He'd sense a trap from any direction—except perhaps from his only trusted son.

Rian lowers his head, one hand stroking his jaw. His hands, once steady and sure, now tremble with the weight of his decision. As it finally stills, the silence among us heavy, he lifts his chin and meets our gazes with steel-lined eyes.

"So be it," Rian says.

CHAPTER 29
SABINE

As a child, my mother told me that there would come a day when I had to set kindness aside. Until that point in my life, kindness had flowed like water. My father was often absent, so my days were spent in my mother's loving care, or playing with the chipmunks and kittens and curious crows who would bring me shiny baubles. Even when I was sent to the Convent of Immortal Iyre, I clung to the virtue of compassion like a drowning woman to an oar. Trusting in it. Letting it guide me through dark times.

But today?

Today is the day my mother prepared me for. Lord Berolt plans to steal the crown from his only loyal son, rule my kingdom with a tyrant's fist, and bind me to his side as his unwilling queen.

So, kindness be damned today.

I swear on my mother's grave, Berolt's plan will not come to fruition.

Still, my nerves are jumping as I pace outside Tòrr's stable, the noontime sun burning my cheeks ruddy.

Mother, I mouth silently, *give me the courage to do what must be done.*

"Sabine."

Basten's low voice calls to me from inside the stable, the door rolled open an inch. According to the official logs, Basten is currently out patrolling the town's northern woods, nowhere near the sentinel training camp. We needed the documentation in case Lord Berolt grew suspicious and decided to check on his location.

Glancing at the soldiers stationed nearby, I move toward the door as if to seek the awning's shade. I take out a handkerchief and dab at the sweat rolling down my temples, using it to hide my mouth.

"They're late," I whisper. "I fear something's gone wrong."

Through the crack, I can just make out Basten's handsome profile—his straight nose and cut-glass jaw as perfect as any god's.

"They're coming now," he whispers.

I can't stop myself from glancing at him, surprised. But of course, with his senses, he can hear someone approach long before I can see them. Our eyes lock—a band of light falls on his face, painting him in light and shadow. His chestnut eyes glow. Every muscle in my arm begs me to reach out. One touch. One kiss. Just to know we're together in this.

But I force myself to look away.

"I'm going to climb now," he whispers. "I'll be listening every second from up high. I swear, Berolt won't lay a hand on you."

The band of light catches his throat bob, and I let out a slight moan. My heart batters against my ribs. On impulse, I let my hand fall next to the crack. It's close enough for him to link his index finger around my little one.

My eyes sink briefly closed as a spark from our joined hands travels through me.

Out of the corner of my eye, I spot Rian and Lord Berolt's carriage entering through the training ground's main gate.

"I love you, Sabine Darrow," Basten whispers from the shadows.

I risk meeting his gaze, eyes searching his to memorize every fleck of gold among the chocolate brown. "I love you, Basten Bowborn. Always."

The carriage rolls to a stop, and I quickly unlink our fingers and dab my handkerchief at my face as though I'm flustered by the heat. I pin a bland smile on my face as Rian and Lord Berolt descend, though my teeth are bared just behind it.

The instant Lord Berolt's gaze latches onto my breasts instead of my face, my resolve hardens.

You were right, Mother.

"It's too much money," Berolt snaps at Rian, finishing some conversation from the carriage. "We are not in the business of mercy."

"Aiding Duren *is* business, father," Rian counters. "When word reaches all of Astagnon that we've opened our private coffers to help our people, they will be that much more willing to embrace me as their king. And happy subjects pay their taxes without trouble."

Berolt squints up at the bright sunlight. "Let's get on with this, then. You're certain it's safe to be here during daylight?"

"Quite. The builders ensured no sunlight can reach the riding ring."

Now more than ever, I'm in awe of Rian's ability to hide his emotions behind a balmy mask. Looking at his cool, slightly bored affectation, you would never dream about the dark things he, Basten, and I have schemed over for the last few days.

Even so, as Rian plants a kiss on my knuckles in greeting, there's a slight waver in his kohl-lined eyes.

Fortunately, Berolt's attention is on his pocket watch, which he stuffs into his vest pocket. He eyes me up and down like a pony at auction. "Well, girl? I have many demands on my time. Show me this demonstration you've prepared."

My smile turns scathing as I turn. "Of course, my lord."

I roll back the stable door, letting out the scent of straw and barley, and step back obediently for Rian and Berolt to pass.

Rian's tongue darts out anxiously as he passes me, but when he faces his father, he's all bored arrogance again. "Sabine, bring out Tòrr."

As I go to Myst and Tòrr's stalls, my heart knocks around inside my ribs like a broken bell. When Myst sees the way my hands tremble on the latch, she gives a soft whinny.

She steps out of the stall and nuzzles my shoulder. *You smell of fear, Sabine.*

I spare a moment to press my forehead against hers, closing my eyes to breathe in her familiar scent. *I could borrow a little of your courage today.*

Did you bring a basket to put it in? she asks helpfully.

A gentle laugh softens my chest as I pull back to stroke the velvet hair around her nose. *I didn't. Silly me.*

At Tòrr's stall, a shiver runs through me. Even after all this time, it's impossible to be prepared for his presence. The taste of iron on my tongue. The steam bursting with his every breath. His otherworldly black eyes with their red gleam.

Tòrr, I say as I unlock five of the six latches on his stall, hesitating at the final one. *Today, I need you to trust me. Even if I make a strange request.*

Your requests are never strange, little fae. You do not know what I've done in centuries of life.

Fair point, I think to myself, considering the fantastical, brutal stories in the Book of the Immortals.

I mount Myst, and we move into a slow canter around the riding ring with Tòrr following at our side. As we pass Rian and Berolt, I can make out Rian explaining to Berolt the mechanics of how I use Myst to mount Tòrr, and our plans for constructing a saddle with a retractable extra stirrup so I can mount him directly in the future.

"As king," Berolt objects, "it should be you riding the monoceros against our enemies."

"Of course." Rian rests a boot on the fence's lower ring. "That is the end goal of this training, naturally."

The blood in my veins stirs up to a boil. The gall of Lord Berolt. To lie to his son's face. To think that he might one day, after her steals the throne, he might ride Tòrr himself. As if such a vicious creature would ever deign to let his old, bony white ass sit on his magnificent back.

Tòrr, I'm going to vault onto you now.

As I push to my feet on Myst's back, my legs tremble only slightly. I've built up balance now, and I think I could stand on her back at a gallop if I wanted. Still, the intensity from Berolt's sharp gaze causes my foot to slip as I step onto

Tòrr's back—but I catch myself, and sink into a seated position.

Steady, I remind both him and myself.

Trying to calm my heart, I say to Myst, **Fall back now. Stay at the edge of the ring.**

That isn't part of our usual training, and Myst tosses her head in confusion. **But I—**

Please, Myst.

She whinnies in mild objection but slows to a walk as I nudge Tòrr into a gallop. The wind cools my burning cheeks, the speed and adrenaline strangely comforting, a match to my own racing heart.

Overhead, an iron roof tile groans faintly enough that it could just be the wind.

Don't look up, I order myself. *Don't give Berolt any clues.*

Still, I can't help but wonder how Basten is fairing. It's a climb of thirty feet to the roof; as much as he reminded me that he's scaled my tower countless times, the stable is different. It's built of rough stone bricks with no decorative handholds or ledges. If he falls, there are no bushes to catch him. I don't have his superior hearing; if he were to slip, I wouldn't hear him.

As I circle around again, Rian takes out his Golath dime and dances it over his knuckles.

I draw in a deep breath.

When I drop the dime, Rian said last night, *open the skylight, Wolf. Then, everything is up to Sabine.*

I can only imagine Wolf crouched now over our heads, ears tilted toward the roof, listening for the sound of the falling dime. My mouth has gone as dry as the sand underfoot. My mind feels oddly blank, like I can't hold a thought for more than a fleeting second.

As Tòrr and I circle again, I keep a close watch on Rian's dime, darting my gaze between it and the skylight.

At my signal, I say to Tòrr, *unleash your fey fire on Lord Berolt Valvere.*

I need sunlight, he says.

It will come.

A burst of steam shoots from his snout. *As you wish, little fae.*

My violent-hearted fae horse is not the kind to question me when I have murder in mind. His muscles bunch beneath me, the veins in his neck throbbing in anticipation. As we circle the riding ring's far end, it happens:

Rian drops the dime.

Berolt cocks his head at his son's uncharacteristic clumsiness.

And Basten throws open the—

Overhead, the skylight trap door rattles. The sound of clanking iron echoes in the cavernous stable. It rattles harder. Then something like a fist slams into it.

But the skylight remains closed.

My mind scrambles.

What happened? Why won't the door open? Basten was supposed to throw open the skylight, let in a beam of sun, and Tòrr would do the rest . . .

I draw up Tòrr to a sharp halt, my breath scraping through my lungs. The trapdoor continues to bang ferociously overhead as Basten fights to get it open.

Then, an even worse sound travels through the stable.

Berolt's laughter.

"You witless fool," he scolds Rian. "You did not truly believe I would fall for an invitation here during the day, did you? Without first ensuring the trap door's latch was welded shut?"

My stomach plummets. *Dear gods, no.*

Rian's face goes as slack as if he'd been doused with water. He immediately tries to cover with a laugh. "Father—"

"Couldn't even kill me yourself, eh, boy? Had to have a woman do it for you? Pathetic buffoon. I know that you uncovered the documents meant for me. And you wonder why I plan to take the throne for myself. You never had it in you to be king."

Rian fixates on an invisible speck in the air, his jaw clenched painfully. He seems to war between tactics.

Brush it off. Beg forgiveness. Instead, he draws his sword as he looks up with hatred in his eyes. "Don't I?"

As Rian lunges forward with a thrust, Berolt draws his own sword and blocks the strike. Rian counters with a swing from the left, but Berolt matches it with a deflection, then goes on the offense and slashes at Rian's chest.

Rian parries to the right, slamming into the iron railings, but steps back before his father swings again.

Tòrr rears up. Impatient. Bloodthirsty. He was promised violence and wants his due.

For the first time in my life, I not only feel his bloodlust but crave it, too.

Light suddenly bursts into the stable. Basten, sweaty and scraped, rolls the main door open with both arms, his hair hanging loose in his eyes.

My heart swells. I grip Tòrr's mane, barely able to breathe. So affected by Basten's commanding presence that seems to suck all the air out of the room.

Tòrr, I shout, ***use the sunlight!***

I cannot. He stamps his hoof, as frustrated as me. ***It does not reach.***

I curse inwardly. Of course, when Rian designed the stable, he ensured enough distance between the door and the riding ring that Tòrr wouldn't be able to harness the indirect sunlight.

With a soldier's skill, Basten quickly assesses the situation: Me on Tòrr. Rian and Berolt warring together. Basten has no sword, as it would have hampered his efforts to climb to the roof, and I'm frozen with terror that he'll try to fight Berolt regardless.

Berolt feints a high strike, and when Rian sidesteps, Berolt knocks Rian's sword arm with his hilt. The sword clatters out of Rian's hand, flying to land near a water bucket. Rian and Basten both run for it, but Berolt blocks them with a horizontal slash.

Chest heaving, Berolt shakes his head. "You two have always been at one another's sides, haven't you? One my son. The other a hapless street cur. So alike, ever since you were scrawny little things. And that's still the case: both such terrible disappointments. Fitting that you'll now rot side by side in the dungeon."

Rian and Basten square up on either side of Berolt, glancing at one another with unspoken signals. I've seen Basten fight enough to recognize that look in his eye. His stance. The set of his shoulders.

He's on the verge of unleashing hell.

Sensing this, Berolt adjusts his own stance, guarding his back by standing against the iron railings as he faces off against them.

"Come on, then, boys! Don't think I'll kill my own flesh and blood?"

As I shift on Tòrr, gloved hands twisting in his mane, the air around me seems to thicken with my rage. My heart pounds with a fury that could level an entire forest. The urge to scream, to somehow shatter the invisible barriers that hold me back, is overwhelming.

Tòrr, I say. ***At my signal, gallop.***

I dig in my heels.

Tòrr's muscles spring like a coiled machine, barely able to restrain his anticipation. His massive hooves tear across the ring, flinging up sand, charging the air with an electric current. I remain rooted on his back, calves clamped around his sides, urging on his bloodlust.

Lower your horn.

His neck coils, the glistening solarium horn as long and sharp as a rapier slicing through the bursts of steam from his flared nostrils. He's so fast that Lord Berolt barely has time to turn his head when we are already upon him.

Run him through!

There's a sickening squelch as Tòrr's horn stabs between the iron bars into Lord Berolt's back. Lord Berolt jerks upright, spine unnaturally straight, head thrown back against the railings.

The sword tumbles from his hand.

Tòrr, chest heaving with a well of unspent savagery, rams his horn deeper until it pierces Lord Berolt's chest, erupting out the front of his ribcage. Blood forms rivulets down his torso and back, pooling in his fine leather boots.

Tòrr digs his head in deeper, sliding the horn all the way to the hilt, until a full foot of blood-soaked solarium spike sticks out the other side.

Lord Berolt gargles, blood bubbling out of his mouth to

garble his final words, and then, finally, he slumps forward over Tòrr's deadly horn.

For a few heavy moments, Rian, Basten, and I hold the silence. It isn't until Tòrr steps back, using the railings to pull Berolt's body off his horn, and the body slumps to the floor, that I remember to unclamp my jaw before it shatters.

"And so, it's done." Rian's hand distractedly toys with his Golath dime, his eyes wide and glassy as he stares at his father's body.

The echo of the coin's clinking against his armor rings like a death knell. With each shallow breath, the slight tremor in his fingers betrays the turmoil that the stoic mask of his face refuses to show.

And yet, I see it there, behind the mask—the pain.

Basten scrapes the loose hair back off his face as he stumbles to the iron railing. His broad hands grip the bars, the barrier separating us. When his eyes meet mine, they mirror the same aching relief I feel. My heart still races with adrenaline. Separated by the cold, unyielding bars, I can hardly believe we're both still breathing.

I flex my gloved hand, desperately wanting to hold him instead of Tòrr's mane.

His hand moves along the fence, a touch of tenderness on his face amidst all the scars, and stops in front of me.

He says reverently, "You swore to me once that no man would tame you, little violet. I'd go further than that. I'd say no force on this earth could quell the fire in you. Not with chains, not with cages, not with iron bars. You're going to bring this world to its knees."

CHAPTER 30
WOLF

The slivered moon, which hung like a scythe on the night of Lord Berolt's demise, swells into a circle as fat and bright as a coin before his death is finally declared a heart attack. Rian keeps busy slipping generous bribes into the right officials' hands. Ensuring the body is cremated to hide the killing wound. Paying off soldiers to attest that they witnessed Lord Berolt clutch his heart and collapse.

Fair to say, Berolt was wrong—Rian has exactly what it fucking takes to be king.

On the day of Lord Berolt's funeral, I ride Dare alongside Rian and Sabine's carriage to the Valvere family burial grounds a few miles north of the city walls. The oak leaves are just beginning to turn. It's a golden, late summer day—the kind of day meant for exploring the hedge maze, not a funeral.

But fuck if I'm not overjoyed to see that old bastard's ashes go into the ground. If it's true that Immortal Woudix has a secret door from the underrealm back to the living world, I will barricade it with steel beams to keep Berolt Valvere from ever returning.

After everyone descends from their carriages, Lady Eleonora pokes around the refreshment tent with disdain. "Champagne? Pear tarts? My son is dead. Is this a funeral or a celebration?"

"Why can it not be both?" Rian says, smoothly handing her a glass of champagne. "There is much to celebrate, after all. My coronation documents are nearly complete. Our belongings are already boxed up and sent ahead. In the morning, we leave for Old Coros."

"How good of you to spare an afternoon to put your father in the ground." Lady Eleonora flops onto a velvet cushion, drains the glass, and snaps at a servant to pour her another. Despite her dark humor, she picks nervously at her cuticles. Her wrinkled hands tremble so badly that half the drink ends up on her dress.

If I had a heart, I'd almost feel sorry for the old woman. I *did* conspire to end her son's life. But it's hard to feel sympathy for vipers.

Clearing her throat, she darts a look at Rian. "What remains with the documents? Why are they not yet complete?"

"A trivial formality." Rian lifts his chin as a servant fastens a black grieving ribbon diagonally across his chest. "The King's Council sent the godkissed bloodtaster to verify my parentage. I told him to join us here in the interest of time." He lazily checks his pocket watch. "He should arrive after the funeral prayer."

The tent flap is swept back, letting in golden sunlight. Sabine enters, turning every head as though the sun itself grew legs. She's radiant in wine-red gown of soft velvet. The straps are golden chains that hug her shoulders and drape down her upper arms. The ribbed bodice is decorated with clinking golden tokens that each bear the stamp of Popelin's coins—the Valvere crest. The effect is a walking show of Valvere wealth.

Neither the dress's dark burgundy color nor the black grieving sash belted around her waist can dim her light.

"The priest is ready," she announces.

To everyone else, she must look the picture of Valvere obedience, draped in their golden tokens and chains. But to me? Knowing that my sly wildcat was the one who took Lord Berolt's life does wicked things to my lower half.

The ceremony is blessedly brief. As the priest drones on about Berolt's stature and influence, a warm breeze quivers through the leaves, smelling of damp earth and minerals. An ache circles around my chest and pulls taught.

Gods, I miss the woods.

This is where I'll always feel at home. Where the sights and smells don't assault my senses like a rowdy tavern where someone just offered to buy everyone a round. Here, in nature, everything fits together just as it should. The scents are in balance. The sounds form a quiet symphony.

My chest pools with lead to think about what life will be like in Old Coros. Ten times as many people—and their filth —as Duren.

But to be close to Sabine?

I'd march in a gods damn parade through a holiday market three times a day.

"Grandmother, do the honors." Rian offers Lady Eleonora the gilded box containing Berolt's ashes.

Clutching Rian's arm, she shakily steps on the ramp into

the burial hole. Despite Rian's efforts, her beaded skirt tangles, threatening to trip her.

I leap into the pit, steadying her by her frail arm.

"Take care, Lady Eleonora." I bow my head.

She jerks her arm out of my grasp with a grimace. "You! No, no. I need nothing from you."

The air grows stale in my mouth. It's a battle not to roll my eyes. Still, her scorn is hardly a surprise. The old crow has always despised me.

"I've got her now, Wolf," Rian says.

Combing back my hair, I climb out and take my place beside Sabine—a hair closer than I should.

My skin aches with the overwhelming desire to hold her. I'm inches away, yet the distance feels insurmountable. It's all I can do to keep my eyes ahead as each of the Valvere family members tosses a handful of alder branches into Berolt's grave, then step back to allow servants to fill the hole with soil. My gaze keeps pulling toward her, a moth compelled toward flame even though it knows it'll burn.

I pick up on the vibration of her pulse thumping harder, a beat I could fall asleep to every night. She darts a glance at me, the sound of her eyelashes like fluttering wings.

On our way back to the tent, a carriage emblazoned with the royal crest rolls to a stop. An elderly man in a white healer uniform emerges. His collar is tailored in a half-moon shape to expose his godkiss birthmark.

He bows before Rian, clutching a leather valise.

"High Lord Rian." Next, he bows to Sabine. "Lady Sabine. I apologize for interrupting your grieving to perform my test, but I understand your departure is tomorrow."

"Yes, yes." Rian pops a plump grape in his mouth. "Thank you for meeting us here; I'm afraid time is of the essence. Astagnon has gone too many weeks with its thrones vacant."

"Quite so, my lord." The healer sets his valise on a low table and opens the latch. "All that's left is the formality of verifying your blood tie to the late King Joruun. As a blood-taster, my godkiss allows me to detect ancestry through the blood, in addition to various ailments. I'll need to draw only a small vial."

"Drain me to the dregs, if it means I'll wear the crown." Rian smirks as he rolls up his sleeve to his elbow. The healer prepares a large, hollow needle as thick as a scribe's pen.

"Wait! Put that down, I command it!" Lady Eleonora lurches forward to wrestle the needle from the healer. Her face is splotchy, stricken. The confused healer immediately relinquishes the needle, his bushy eyebrows lifting sky-high.

"My lady—" he starts, uncertain.

"Grandmother, what in Woudix's name has gotten into you?" Rian asks.

"Everyone, out of the tent. I wish to speak to my grand-son." She snaps not only at the servants and the godkissed healer, but also at Lady Runa and Lord Selvig. The family members look affronted, but Lady Eleonora's fiendish scowl sends them scurrying out. "You as well, Lady Sabine."

Sabine starts to leave until Rian grabs her arm.

He scoffs, "Grandmother, whatever this is about, my bride can surely hear it. There are to be no secrets between us when we're married."

"Your bride hates you, as she hates all of us. She'd be the first to use our secrets against us." There's no rancor in her words, only facts. She snaps at Sabine like a dog. "Go."

Sabine's eyes narrow in anger at the command. She doesn't take a step.

Rian rubs his eyes, frustrated, and says, "Sabine, please do as she asks. Wolf, escort Lady Sabine outside."

"No." Lady Eleonora's voice drops like a boulder in the center of the tent. "*He* stays here. He'd hear anyway with those sharp ears of his."

The air is heavy, thick with a scent I can't place. A shiver unfurls down my spine, a dark premonition that has my heartbeat snapping in my veins. I exchange a questioning look with Rian, who appears equally baffled by his grand-mother's behavior.

I say haltingly, "Pardon, my lady?"

She purses her lips. "You heard me, Wolf Bowborn."

Rian gives me a tight shrug as if to say we should indulge her.

Before Sabine leaves, she catches my eye one last time, a soft connection that makes my skin ache for her touch. Then, it's just the three of us in the tent. My muscles tense, picking up on the charged air, like a predator sensing that danger stalks near. I tighten and release my fists to burn through my extra energy.

Rian rests his hands on his hips. "Now what the devil is—"

Lady Eleonora cuts him off with a sharp clap that rever-berates against the cloth walls. She closes her eyes briefly as though pained, then opens them and says quietly, "This is a secret I had hoped to take to my own grave. But Berolt, may Woudix keep his cursed soul, cannot be harmed by the truth any longer. So, I suppose I must now put my efforts toward the living. Toward you, Rian."

She sways, seeming to lose her composure, and steadies herself with one hand on the tent post.

In a thin, wavering voice, she presses on. "Rian, if the

bloodtaster tests you, he won't detect a trace of King Joruun's blood."

Rian strokes his chin, frowning slightly, still humoring her. "I find that improbable, as Joruun and my father were blood cousins."

"That is so." She clasps her unsteady hands, fingers knitting together like warring snakes as she nods a few times. "However, *you* have no blood relation to Berolt."

A sound of surprise tears from my throat before I cup my hand over my jaw, pretending to cough.

In contrast, Rian's face remains impeccably blank as he processes this information. *Talented bastard.* I've never been able to master that card player face.

Not Berolt's son? I eye Rian sidelong. Trying to see Berolt's features in his. They share the same dark hair, the same brown eyes.

But then again, plenty in Duren do.

Hell, *I* do.

Lady Eleonora's eyes shift to me, frosting over with icy hatred. "*He* does."

Wait—*what?*

My heart wallops as my body automatically prepares to fight: my adrenaline surges, my fists ball, my chest tightens. I take a barely restrained step forward, narrowing my eyes. "Excuse me?"

If I know one thing, it's that the hateful bastard we just buried is not my family.

Rian rakes his hand through his hair, huffing as though it's all a joke. "She's gone mad with grief. Wolf, fetch the healer."

I lurch a step toward the door.

"Stop!" Lady Eleonora grips the tent pole, shaking it as

though threatening to pull the whole structure down. "If you wish to be king, Rian, then you'll know when to shut your mouth and listen to a woman who has seen sixty more years than you. Basten Bowborn, though it pains me to admit it, you are the legitimate third son of Berolt and Madelyna Valvere. You were born on the summer solstice twenty-eight years ago, in the southern tower bedroom of Sorsha Hall."

Adrenaline slams into my chest, driving me to pace before I throttle something just for the need to act. I lock eyes with Rian. "Is this true? Did you know this?"

"Of course not! And I don't believe it now!" Despite his outburst, his left eye twitches. Folding his arms, he asks, "So, then, grandmother, who the hell am I supposed to be?"

She sinks into a chair, reaching a trembling hand toward her wine glass. "You were the son of a scullery maid who was around the right age and was close enough in appearance to Berolt to make it believable." She brings the glass to her lips for a long, shaky sip before continuing. "Madelyna saw how hard Berolt was on Lore and Kendan. It wasn't only his temper that drove them away from Duren. Berolt beat them both—he nearly killed Lore, and Kendan fared little better. So, when Madelyna's third baby was born with a godkissed birthmark, as the soothsayer had predicted, she knew Berolt would be ten times as hard on such a child. Berolt always had an unnatural fascination with godkissed people, and Madelyna did not think he would spare his own son from his obsession. She was convinced his experimentation would kill you. So, she came to me."

Listening to this, I can only stare, feeling like I'm hearing a fanciful tale from the Book of the Immortals. But despite

Lady Eleonora's nerves, her body doesn't show any signs of lying.

Steady pulse. Regular sweat.

This damn claim cannot be true.

When she finishes her drink, she says, "I placed Madelyna's infant with a seamstress in Duren. Then, I found the scullery maid's young child and made arrangements to present him as Madelyna and Berolt's baby."

"This cannot be," Rian interrupts in a hollow voice. "I am two years Wolf's senior. No one would believe a newborn infant aged two years overnight."

"The two of you are only six months apart in age," Lady Eleonora explains. "When I placed Madelyna's baby with the seamstress, I instructed her to lie to the child about his age when he was older. Berolt wasn't present for the birth— he was on a long assignment in Old Coros. When he returned some months later, do you think he could tell the difference between a six-month-old and a one-year-old? Ha! He barely even looked at any of his sons until they could hold a sword."

"Stop! Just stop!" Rian pinches the bridge of his nose. "Fuck, I need a drink."

As he guzzles straight from the champagne bottle, I dig my fingers into a chair back and face Lady Eleonora. *My grandmother?* By the fucking gods, it cannot be. If there is one thing on this earth I loathe, it's the idea of having Valvere blood.

Fighting to keep my anger in check, I say quietly, "What happened to the seamstress you gave me to?"

Her watery eyes are still full of ice toward me, though I have no idea why, if we are truly family. "I have no idea. I had no interest in keeping track of the child, for your benefit and ours. She's probably dead."

I grip the chair back so hard the wood splinters. "I grew up on the streets! Fighting for bread! Thinking I was an orphan!"

My outburst doesn't ruffle Lady Eleonora. "You should thank me. Such a life is better than Berolt's special project."

My fingernails dig into the splintered wood as I seethe, "You were always so cruel to me. Why, if you knew I was your true grandchild?"

"I didn't know!" she snaps, then purses her lips. "But I had my suspicions. There are only so many godkissed boys your age who look just like Madelyna. As for cruelty? It's true, I didn't want the secret to come out, so I hoped you would leave our family alone. I was protecting my grandson." She rests a wrinkled hand on Rian's arm.

"This is madness," Rian murmurs, eyes glazed over in shock.

"You *are* my grandson," she insists, the frost in her eyes melting for him. "Blood only matters to the King's Council. What matters is *family name*. You are the child I helped raise, and you are a Valvere."

Rian looks like he might need a bucket to vomit into.

"You had no right!" I yell, smashing my fist against the broken chair.

Lady Eleonora pushes to her feet, eyes flashing, not cowed by my aggression. "When Berolt returned from Old Coros and found Madelyna had given birth to a normal child instead of a godkissed one, as predicted, he flew into such a fury that he strangled her. So, Wolf Bowborn, you want to discuss blood? Berolt was *my* flesh and blood. I owed him a mother's love, but only so far. Madelyna was more like my daughter than he was ever like my son. When he killed her, it only proved me right that I'd done the correct thing. I protected *both* of you." She jabs a finger at Rian. "I gave you the life a servant's boy could only dream of." Then she points to me. "And I spared you death at Berolt's hands—or something even worse."

The strength goes out of my legs. I would sink into the chair, except I've decimated it. I run a clammy hand down my face, trying to pull my emotions together, still feeling as scattered as wheat seed in the wind.

With a curse, Rian tears off his black mourning sash and throws it to the floor. "I'm not mourning an old bastard who wasn't even my father. So, grandmother, what does this mean? That *Wolf* is Joruun's closest blood relation? The rightful successor to the throne?"

There's a chuckle of disbelief on his lips, but Lady Eleonora doesn't laugh.

"Yes," she replies.

Rian's face goes bloodless in the span of a second.

King? Fucking gods, I'm no king.

My body shifts back into fighting mode, heart thrashing, skin prickling. I know what happens to those who get in the way of a Valvere sitting on the throne. Hell, look at what happened to the last two. Berolt's ashes are only an hour in the ground. Grand Cleric Beneveto was humiliated, stripped of power.

"If you wish to be king," Lady Eleonora says to Rian, "then you'll need to pass off Wolf's blood as your own."

A chill worthy of a winter blizzard spreads through the tent. Lady Eleonora's implications are clear enough. There are ways to get both blood and silence from a man, and all of them end with today being my funeral, too.

Rian manages to pull his face back into some form of composure, but he can't hide his pulse. It speeds as adrenaline roars in his own veins. He was a soldier. Like me, he can sense danger.

Because it's a funeral, he wears no sword. But as a bodyguard, I do. He has to know that if it came to blows, I have the upper hand here. Then again, he has twenty guards just outside the tent who wouldn't let me get two feet before cutting me down.

"Do what needs to be done, Rian," Lady Eleonora murmurs, fingers knitting anxiously in the beaded folds of her skirt.

I scowl at her—my biological kin, goading on my death. *What a bloodthirsty bitch.*

The air is alive with crackling tension, the sour-sweet smell of sweat thick around us. Rian and I have been through hell and back together. We've been at each other's throats. We've saved each other's lives. Hell, we're even both in love with the same woman.

Something shifts in the air. Rian turns to me as he rakes back his hair, his eyes full of rage—but not for me. "By the gods, Wolf. Take your hand off your sword. If I wanted you dead, you'd be dead."

He sets his angry glare on Lady Eleonora instead. "I'm not ordering the death of the one person in this world who's stood by my side. He's lied to me, yes. But far less than my own family has."

It takes a second for my tense muscles to ease, to believe that the fight isn't coming. Sweat breaks out on my brow as I hesitantly let go of my sword hilt.

In a shaky voice, I say, "I have no wish to be a king. Or a Valvere. For what it's worth, there is only one thing in this world I desire. You want my blood? I'll give you pints of my blood, Rian, and my sworn secrecy, too. In exchange for Sabine."

Outside, a breeze ruffles the tent. My sharp ears pick up on the not-so-hushed gossip of Lady Runa and Lord Gideon speculating about what the hell is happening in the tent. I can hear Sabine's soft footfalls as she paces in the grass. Of all the scents on the air—freshly turned soil, sweet champagne, incense—hers is the one that sets my heart on fire.

Rian drags a hand down his face, slowly letting out a held breath. I can see the calculations turning behind his eyes. The pocket watch in his vest ticks off the seconds. I can taste the strain in the air, laced with pear tarts and salty sweat.

"My queen or my throne, is that it?" Rian asks tensely.

"Yes."

He laughs to himself, though there's no mirth in it. His eyes fall to his grieving sash, dirtied now under his boots. He stares for a long while, thinking. I get the sense there's something going through his head that I could never be privy to.

"I meant for her to be my wife for life."

"I know," I reply steadily. "So do I."

He turns sharply, pacing, and when he finally looks up, his eyes are resolute.

"Sabine tamed the monoceros. She figured out its name, which is the key to harnessing its power. I don't need her anymore. I only ever wanted her for what she could do for me, and as a beautiful, high-born woman at my side, of course. But I could find another one of those by evening vespers."

His voice is artificially cold.

I don't imagine for a second that Sabine means nothing to Rian more than a means to control the monoceros. But, hell, he can tell himself whatever he wants. I know he loves her, at least on some level. On the other hand, it takes exactly zero stretch of the imagination to believe that he loves his ambition more.

"*Tamarac?*" I say, not breaking eye contact. "You'll really let her go?"

A muscle jumps in his jaw. "Your blood for Sabine. She will be released from the marriage contract. You'll be discharged from service to the Golden Sentinels. The two of you can fuck your way across half of Astagnon as long as our secret never comes out. You will face no threat from me. But I cannot vouch for your safety. Rachillon will still pursue her. If I hand her over to you, Wolf, then she is yours to safeguard. It's on you if anything happens to her."

"Oh, I intend to protect her until her dying days."

He takes a deep breath. "*Tamarac.*"

I nod, a strange, ardent buzz filling my veins as though I'm in a dream. Is this really happening? I feel as if I've won the grand pot in a tournament game of Basel. The throne meant nothing to me, and so it's as easy to surrender as tossing a log on the fire. Sabine is the real prize here. We can live together. Make a life. She'll wear my wedding ring, just as I once vowed to her.

Promise made, promise kept.

May the gods hear my vow that I won't let harm come to a single one of her perfect hairs.

My chest feels tight, unused to the feeling of good fortune. Hell, of any fucking hope at all.

Good things don't happen to people like me.

My mouth parts, dry with disbelief, as I unfasten the

leather arm guard on my left forearm and then roll up my sleeve before Rian changes his mind. "Call in the healer to draw my blood."

Lady Eleonora shoves to her feet and grabs the needle from the table. "Out of the question! The healer cannot know the truth of the blood sample's origin. I'll draw your blood, Wolf Bowborn. You think I don't know how to make men bleed?"

She jabs the needle into my forearm with little care for finding a vein. I grit my teeth against the jolt of pain as she pulls out the needle, which is followed by a flow of crimson blood. She holds the vial against the blood flow until it's full, then corks it.

I wrap Rian's cast-off funeral sash around the wound, then hide it by rolling down my sleeve and replacing my arm guard.

Without warning, Lady Eleonora grabs Rian's arm and stabs him in the same place.

"Ow!"

"It has to appear that the sample came from you." She wastes no time opening the tent flap and snapping at the healer. "Here, bloodtaster. The Valvere blood sample."

Before I leave, Rian grabs my arm, a strange look in his eyes, urgency in his voice. "I mean it, Wolf. Sabine is yours to protect now. And for her sake, I hope like hell that you can."

The small crowd outside the tent whirls around in interest, full of murmured speculation about what was happening within the tent.

But Lady Eleonora ignores the volley of pointed questions.

The elderly healer frowns at the vial. Hesitantly, he says, "You—you needn't have drawn it yourself, my lady."

She scoffs. "Only a fool complains when the work is done for him. Don't just stand there, taste it, and tell me my grandson is fit for the throne. And the rest of you? Shut your painted lips. You're here by the grace of my grandson. If you seek favor with the future king, you'll keep quiet about anything you might have overheard in that tent."

Despite her threat, the crowd can't help but continue to murmur as the bloodtaster pours a drop on his tongue.

My attention, however, is only on Sabine. Her full lips are parted, a thin line cutting between her brows as she looks between me, Rian, and the tent, worry in her eyes about what happened.

Yet when her gaze touches me, her pupils swell in love.

Desire for this perfect woman blooms in my chest, burrowing to my marrow until all I can see is her. Heat prickles along my skin like the first time I felt sunlight after weeks locked in the dungeon. She has no idea how deep my love for her goes—all the way to the underrealm and back.

"Congratulations, High Lord Valvere." The healer's voice buzzes like a far-away beehive in my ear, too distant to be of any threat. "Despite the . . . irregularity . . . of the testing, your blood relation has been verified. All Kinship Mandate qualifications have been met."

I couldn't care less if Rian is named king, if I'm a Valvere, whose ass deserves to sit on a gilded chair in an ancient fae castle. Let him have his crown. Coffers overflowing with coin. Royal balls beneath crystal chandeliers.

My heart craves only one luxury.

I push through the crowd of funeral attendees, eyes fixed on Sabine with a hunter's determination to catch his prize. I take her hand in mine, pausing briefly at the heady rush from the touch, knowing now that not a single day will ever go by that I don't have to hold myself back from her.

Her eyebrows shoot high in alarm as the pulse in her wrist speeds beneath my thumb. Her eyes dart to the watching crowd, wide with fear. "Wolf?"

Gossip flows like wine around us, but I tune it all out.

"Basten. Call me Basten." I place her palm against my chest so that she can feel the pounding of my heart. Quietly, I murmur, "Never call me Wolf again, whether we're being watched or not. From now until the end of our days, I only want to hear my true name on your lips."

On impulse, I run my thumb over the lips in question, then replace it with a kiss.

Tendrils of pleasure hook into me as warmth pours from our kiss, until I can barely maintain control of my desire. I cup my hands around the back of her head, thrusting my fingers through her hair until her braid loosens.

She briefly stiffens, a gasp on her lips. But I swallow her surprise with my mouth over hers. She melts into my hands, kissing me back with soft lips that caress and tease. I anchor one hand on the small of her back, drawing her closer, firmly, so she knows this is no accident.

Our lips meld together, the kiss a seal of our love.

When I finally pull away, both our breaths are ragged. Her hair is mussed. Her lips swollen. She looks more beautiful than a dawn over a fresh snowfall.

Shouts erupt from the crowd.

"Traitor!"

"Betrayer!"

Soldiers' swords ring out as they hold them at the ready to cut me down. There are sharp cries of disbelief that I

EVIE MARCEAU

would ever be so bold as to touch Rian's bride again after having just won my forgiveness.

Rian's voice cuts across the growing buzz. "Stand down, soldiers."

The crowd's voices rise higher now, ripe with confusion. The last time I was caught with Sabine, Rian put me through the Everlast trial, the most brutal punishment. Now, they cannot fathom why he would so easily let us be together.

"High Lord Valvere," a soldier says. "This affront cannot be permitted—"

"I said stand down!" Rian's face reads a wealth of emotion. It's a wash of anger, humiliation, regret, and not a small amount of sadness.

He hasn't just lost Sabine.

He has to know that he's lost me, too.

But you chose the crown, I think.

In a tone that leaves no room for debate, Rian says hotly, "Wolf Bowborn and Lady Sabine Darrow are not to be detained. Let them pass freely. The engagement is over. They are no longer required to serve the Valvere family. You are so hungry to know what we discussed in that tent? Then I'll tell you. My first order of business as the successor to the throne is to give the people what they want. A happy ending for the Winged Lady and the Lone Wolf."

He looks me in the eyes once before looking away—the pain evident.

Tuning out the salacious din from the crowd, Sabine faces me with bafflement in her cobalt eyes as she threads a loose strand of hair back off her face. Her lips tremble as if, at any moment, guards will drag me away again. As though it's all a cruel trick worthy of Immortal Popelin.

414

She echoes what everyone at the funeral is wondering. "What happened in that tent, Basten?"

I rest my forehead against hers, the warmth of our shared breath mingling, the golden tokens sewn into her bodice softly clattering, and murmur, "A pagan finally found his belief in fate."

CHAPTER 31
SABINE

Basten clasps my hand like he never intends to let go as he leads me away from the crowd. My heart tightens in confused bursts as I toss a harried look behind me, still expecting Rian to send his guards to run us through.

My lips taste like Basten: campfire smoke and pine. My lungs strain, still not recovered from the kiss's breathlessness. Has Basten gone mad? Why is Rian letting us go?

Basten doesn't speak. But his urgency, his tight grip on my hand, says everything. I don't need his godkissed senses to pick up on his strained breath. I've seen him afraid, and I've seen him angry, and I've sure as hell seen his lust—this is something new.

The light in his eyes when he glances at me over his shoulder is almost . . .*happy.*

What in the ten realms is happening?

My grumpy, handsome, brooding huntsman is never happy.

He doesn't pause until we're out of earshot of the

416

funeral grounds. The golden tokens on my dress jingle with every step. The smell of incense lifts, replaced by the fresh scent of damp leaves.

A towering oak presides over a winding stream, its ancient roots exposed and serpentine to form nooks where the soil has worn away. Basten leads me to a sheltered alcove between the roots where springy moss underfoot forms a carpet as lush as any in Sorsha Hall.

I gaze up at the dappled light overhead, breaking through leaves just beginning to change into yellows and reds. "It's beautiful."

"Beautiful? No. That word can only ever be used for you." Basten guides my back to the tree trunk and claims my lips with such palpable desire that I could melt into the ground. I wrap my arms around his neck, pulling him deeper into the kiss.

With his lips against me, tasting, sampling, the world tilts dangerously. My heart hammers against my chest, urging me on as my mind screams caution. This is forbidden. Rian could have us hung. Yet every touch of his lips is like a spark that burns through all reason. This kiss, suspended between desire and danger, is a razor's edge.

His tongue slips between my teeth, robbing me of thought until I'm nothing but a puddle of emotions.

Breathless, I lean my head against the trunk, watching the broken light dance over his handsome features. I've never wanted any man as much as I want him. What I thought was love before was a child's game of pretend; the love I feel for Basten burns like a fae candle, never to be put out. It will burn and burn and burn until the world falls.

"No more secrets," I whisper, gazing into his dark eyes.

"No more secrets." He braces one arm on the tree behind

me, leaning close to trace the edge of my jaw with his index finger as though studying an exquisitely carved statue. "Do you remember when I vowed that the next time I kissed you, we wouldn't have to hide?"

My heartbeat falters, afraid to hope because hope has only led to disappointment. "How could I forget?"

His eyes go distant, shifting to focus on a far-away spot. A muscle feathers in his jaw. "The healer required a blood sample to prove a family connection to King Joruun, but it wasn't that straightforward. Rian and I were . . ." His Adam's apple jumps as he shifts his stance, " . . .were switched at birth. *I* am Berolt Valvere's true son. When I was born with a godkiss, my mother feared Berolt's obsession would lead to my death. Lady Eleonora arranged the swap for a normal child. Rian was a servant's child raised in my place. Rian was as unaware of this as I was. Berolt, too."

His words spill out in uncertain drops as though he is still trying to process it himself.

Reality shatters around me like fragile glass under a heavy boot. The ground beneath me might as well be swaying. The revelation sends a jolt of ice through me, freezing me in place.

"Are—are you saying that you are the true heir of the Astagnonian throne?"

He smooths his broad palm over my mussed braid, eyes soft and open now. "That's exactly what I'm saying. I care not for thrones, little violet. I gave Rian a vial of my blood in exchange for you." He lowers his head, lips brushing against my temple as he whispers, "For your freedom. And mine."

My chest goes hollow. Thoughts scatter through my head with the same anxious fluttering as the leaves overhead. *Basten is a Valvere? The rightful king?* It's too much. All at once. A mind isn't meant to contain this many secrets without shattering.

I grasp his hand so hard that my nails dig into his knuckles. "Basten, if that is so, then you're meant to be a king. You cannot give that up!"

His eyes shine with adoration for me as he strokes my hair. "Don't you understand? I would give up every prize beneath the heavens just to win one more day with you. Little violet, you're the dream I dare not wake from. The dream I never thought I could make real."

He cups my face in the shelter of his strong hands. I tilt my chin to meet his gaze. *Holy hell.* He's truly as handsome as a god. A king through and through, even if he won't admit it. The cut of his jaw against the softness of his eyes speaks to his royal blood.

This truth is a shock, yes, but it comes as no real surprise to me. I saw the nobility in him from our first night in the woods, when beneath his coarseness, he showed me kindness, too.

One day, he'll see it in himself, too.

A nuthatch lands on the branch overhead. Two June bugs come to rest on a nearby root. They're jumpy, full of energy.

Drawn by my emotions.

I curl my fingers possessively in the hair at his nape, needing to feel him, to touch him. "It is real, Basten? We're free?"

His breath tickles my cheeks as he brushes me with a kiss. "It's real, little violet. You and me. I'll take you to Salensa to feel the ocean on your toes. We'll buy a little farm bordering the forest, and I'll hunt, and you'll tend to our animals. We'll change our names. Have Ferra alter our appearance. Hide somewhere King Rachillon's men can never find you."

Happy tears flood my eyes, even as my cheeks draw an irresistible smile. I don't bother to wipe the tears away. They mark the end of my struggles. The beginning of a new life.

Leaves rustle gently underfoot as a hayfield snake winds its way toward me, tongue flicking. More birds land in the branches. Bright copper butterflies cover the oak's trunk. From the corner of my eye, I see a buck peer curiously out of a bayberry bush.

A third June bug lands on my shoulder, and with a low snort, Basten flicks it off.

It takes wing, circling the oak tree with a snubbed buzz.

"Basten!" I scold.

"You're mine, little violet. For the first time, truly mine. I want you to *myself*." He curves his hand around the back of my neck to pull me into another kiss.

The air sifts through my lungs, dissipating into nothing. His lips are powerful, possessive. His hands cradle the sides of my skull, thumbs brushing over my silken hair as he deepens the kiss.

I tip my face to him, wanting more. My lips are already growing swollen, but I won't be satisfied until both our lips are bruised. Basten once told me he'd love me the same as a peasant or princess, and now I can say the same. I don't care if he grew up on the streets. I don't care if he's a Valvere by blood. Gods, I don't even care that he's the rightful king.

As long as he's mine.

His tongue asks entrance, and I part my lips for him. He sweeps his tongue along the roof of my mouth in a deep, claiming gesture. I snag his bottom lip between my teeth and bite until he moans.

Pulling back, he trails his lips over my jaw as though every lick, every bite tastes like pure indulgence.

I dig my fingers into the hard ridge of muscle at his waist, just above the hunting knife strapped to his belt. On impulse, I curl my fingers around the hilt and draw the knife.

Breathless, I hold the blade's tip just beneath his chin.

Dark amusement flashes in his eyes. His chest rises and falls hard, roused by the knife's suggestion of danger. "Am I your prisoner, little violet?"

"My heart's prisoner, yes." Sunlight catches on the blade, throwing dancing spots of light around us, like we've stepped into a fae realm marked with hovering glowbugs.

He purrs, "Then I accept my fate gladly."

I take one of his hands and press the knife's hilt into his palm, feeling exhilarated. My heart lurches, a bird poised to take flight. "Cut off my hair."

His eyebrows lift to his hairline. Clearly, this wasn't what he was expecting. Regardless, a wicked smile curls one side of his mouth.

"That is what you want?"

I tug at my braid, feeling almost frantic as I pull out the silver pins and hurriedly comb my fingers through the locks. "You say I am free now? Then I want to be free of these damn chains once and for all. No more men deciding what makes me beautiful. Or trying to weigh me down."

He takes the knife and, with his other hand, twists my hair into a tight rope. It pulls against my scalp in a way that's both painful and exhilarating. He tugs my head back another inch to claim my lips in a charged kiss before resting the knife blade against the strands at shoulder length.

My breath spills raggedly out of my lips. "Do it."

He saws through my hair in rhythmic cuts that match the beating of my heart. With every slice of the blade, the pressure on my scalp lessens. I feel years of heaviness lifting as the strands fall away. My heart feels so light that it could soar. It flutters in my chest, seeking the freedom of the clouds above, yearning never to be held back again.

Basten cuts through the final strands, winds the rope of my hair around his hand, then sets the coil on one of the large roots. I comb my fingers obsessively through my shorter hair, laughing in disbelief when my fingers come away empty at my shoulders.

Tears again dampen my eyes. This can't be real—no one has ever felt this much happiness in a lifetime, let alone a day.

"Damn, you've got a way of shining that makes the night jealous." Basten anchors one hand around my waist, his gaze caressing my face in a promise of what his lips will soon do. "But it's that smile . . .like you're hoarding stars under your skin."

With his other hand, he lightly drags the knife's point along my neckline, so close to my heart that my insides ignite.

Pressing his lips to my ear, he murmurs, "True freedom means no shackles at all. Including these chains."

His deep voice stirs a well of bottomless need in me that flushes my skin from chest to cheeks. With a wicked gleam in his eyes, he runs the knife to my dress's left strap, a golden chain held on by a loop of thread. He frees the chain with one flick of his wrist.

My lips part, unable to hold back my air intake, as I clamp my hand over my dress to keep it from sliding down.

He rubs his thumb over my bare shoulder, then replaces

it with his lips. Everywhere he kisses me burns both hot and cold until I want to scratch off my skin to satisfy the itch. I feel myself growing wet as his hand roughly cups my breast through the velvet bodice. The gown's golden tokens clink like handfuls of tumbling coins.

He presses the knife tip against each golden crest, breaking the threads. They fall one by one. The Valvere crests. Popelin's coins. Everything that marked me as someone else's property.

Once the last token has been severed, the dress hanging on only by the right strap, he circles the knife around and stabs it into the oak tree just above my head.

I jump. The move was swift, almost violent. The sound of the blade stabbing into the tree exciting as much as surprising.

His muscles coil beneath my palms as he bites my bare shoulder hard enough to leave a red mark.

Not just a kiss, but a claiming.

Pain and pleasure alike pierce through me, laden with unspoken promises. As the sunlight catches the embedded blade, sending shimmering light over our faces, he cups my face in his hands, so I fully meet his gaze.

"There—just like that. That's how I want you. Marked only by me."

A whimper forms low in my throat. My fingers twist in his shirt, needing something to hold onto. I'm already so soaked between my legs that I can feel the slickness each time I shift my thighs.

Overhead, more birds flock to the branches, a silent chorus.

Another hayfield snake slinks along the moss, flicking its tongue.

I'm not doing this. Calling them. It's my godkiss going crazy as my emotions pinwheel head first into pure, wicked turmoil.

Basten bites the embroidered edge of my bodice, pulling it down with his teeth until my left breast is freed. The pert nipple jumps, already pebbled.

"Fuck," he moans as he circles his thumb around the nipple, ravenous for it, before taking it in his mouth.

I arch my back as he sucks, drawing out such exquisite pleasure that my vision blurs. By the gods, the things this man can do with his tongue. It leaves my knees weak. But it isn't enough. Not nearly. This is just a taste, and I want everything.

Basten presses the small of my back against the tree with his hips, grinding against me as sweat drips down his brow. "Do you feel that? How badly I want you?"

A moan slips from my mouth. My hips roll against his like waves lapping on the shore. I murmur low, "I want you more."

He groans in response.

I push to my tiptoes to crash my lips to his. My hands fall to his breastplate, fingernails digging urgently at the buckle. He circles one hand around my waist, tugging me nearly off the ground as his tongue captures mine while his other hand fumbles with his buckles. Together, we tear off his breastplate.

"Tell me again that it's real, Basten," I plead, touching his cheek, needing to feel his warmth beneath me.

A part of me still cannot believe it. For so long, my life hasn't been my own. And love? A fantasy. High-born ladies like me don't get to have love matches. The best we can hope for is a husband who ignores us.

At worst? It can be unspeakable. All my life, I wanted to rage against that sad fate. Unleash my inner animal who would claw like a wildcat, bite like a tiger, poison like a spider anyone who tried to stand in my way.

"It's real." Basten melds his lips to my neck, worshiping the long arch of my throat as he unfastens his belt. It, too, falls to the moss, where the snake winds over to explore it.

All the years of rage simmering beneath my skin roll into something very different.

The animal in me takes over. Bursting with need, I tug at Basten's shirt until I can pull it over his head, then bury my face against his bare chest. Breathe in the scent of him that hits me like a gut punch. Earthy. Masculine. A smell that speaks to some primal part of me desperate to lick and kiss and caress every rock-hard inch of him.

A growl rumbles out of him, low and dangerous. He cups my jaw, guiding me back to eye level. His voice is hoarse, brimming with barely restrained need, as he says, "On your knees. I want to look at you."

My heart flutters with a sudden rash of heat.

Pulse jumping, I toe out of my slippers and kick them aside. The moss tickles my bare feet. I sink to my knees, looking up at him sinfully through my lashes.

His eyes are dark, hooded. He purrs, "What a good girl you are. Now sit back. Spread those pretty legs for me."

A deep, primal ache at my core demands attention.

Not breaking eye contact, I sink back on my ass and swing my legs around. Inch by inch, I draw up my skirt until it pools around my waist. The wind ripples over my bare legs, cropping up goosebumps. The moss tickles my feet until my toes curl.

I say low, "I need you, Basten."

He stalks forward, taking his time, gaze locked onto the shadowed crevice between my legs. I rub my palm over the front of his pants as his erection strains against the fabric.

"Fuck, little violet, even your torture is sweet."

He strips off the rest of his clothes, then sinks to his knees on the moss in front of me.

It's just the two of us. Man and woman. Bare as nature made us. A twinge in the back of my mind whispers that this is the true meaning of Immortal Solene's naked ride. To be open. Natural. Guileless. Here, beneath the ancient oak, among the babbling stream and silver wind, I feel a hint of that magic. Not the twisted version that Rian conspired to make me into a spectacle. Real, true magic.

I press Basten's hand against my cheek as I murmur, "I want you every night. No matter where we are. The woods. An inn. Our own bed. I don't think I can go a day without having you touch me now that I know it's possible."

I turn my face to press a kiss into his palm.

Guiding my chin back to face him, he says with a wicked glint, "Just the nights?"

"Basten!"

"How about the mornings?"

As I laugh softly, he sinks his face into my neck, breathing in my scent, letting out a rumbling moan of pleasure.

"Afternoon tea?" I say, tipping my head back to grant him better access.

"And evening vespers." He braces one arm around my back to guide me down to the moss. As I lay flat, his gaze on my body palpable, my skin prickles with anticipation for him to replace the look with a touch.

"Don't forget high noon." My voice is barely a whisper,

all my oxygen needed just to keep my body from burning in this inferno of desire.

The mirth fades from his eyes, hardening into determination as he traces his gaze over my lips, my breasts, and my waist. His throat bobs in a hard swallow.

"I'll make love to you whenever you ask it of me," he vows, hair loose and mussed, eyes just as wild. "At any time of day or night. Being inside you, feeling your heartbeat, hearing your soft little moans, is my reason for living. The only damn one I've ever had."

A line of sunlight breaks through the leaves overhead, blinding me with a golden light that makes everything glow.

"Open for me." Basten watches with a hawk's attention as I part my legs. "Yes—good. You open so well for what I have to give you."

My cheeks flush, but no longer with shyness. That's the old me. The new me devours the look on his face as he studies my pussy, one thumb lazily circling the sensitive outer folds. He swallows as if he can already taste me.

My hips buck, untameable. I growl, "I *need* you."

"You'll have me, little violet, however you want. But first, I need to taste you. It's all I thought about while locked in the dungeon—it's what got me through the damned Everlast."

He lowers his face to my core, breathing in deeply, nose teasing the sensitive bud. My hips writhe, knees falling further open to him. A pebble digs into my back, but the bite of pain only charges me more. I rake my nails down his muscular back. "You're tormenting me."

A dark laugh comes from his throat as he pushes to his elbows, meeting my eyes with a sinful grin. "You're mine now to torment."

Basten's tongue lashes out to lick at my opening from back to front, sending sparks shooting out from my skin. A primal cry rolls out of my throat.

I buck again, the moss tickling my back like feathers, until Basten grabs my hips to hold me steady. He proceeds to devour me. Devoting his time to teasing every inch, every fold, every sensitive crevice, until I'm gushing. As his tongue works, his hand probes between my legs, thumb coming around to press against the sensitive button that drives me wild.

"Basten!" My fingernails rake across his shoulders as I cling to him with a preternatural need.

He speeds his tongue's lashing, driving me off the edge of reason. My hips rise to meet his mouth's caresses, searching for that last rub of friction to make me come undone.

At the last second, he pulls back, wiping his mouth with the back of his hand, and says in a ragged breath, "Not yet, darling. When you come, you're going to come on my cock, so I can watch the pleasure break you apart."

My pussy throbs, so close to release that I care barely find breath. I feel so empty. So ready for Basten to fill me that I grind my hips into the moss, tearing up chunks of it in my fingers.

A hayfield snake slithers against my bare calf, making me gasp.

A spider crawls onto my earlobe.

Called to me by some unspoken force.

Basten wraps his hand around his cock, lining it up against my swollen heat. I give a broken moan, too wrapped up in desire to be able to find words. Basten's voice is nothing but heavy breath, too.

Words aren't needed, anyway. We have the dance of the wind. The trill of cicadas. There's something holy about the way we come together beneath the late-summer leaves, with bees and jumping trout as our witnesses.

He pushes into me an inch, not wrenching his eyes off my face for a second. With my short hair fanned out on the moss, I feel like a woodland sprite from legend. The snake coils itself around one of my ankles like a deadly bangle. One bite means death, but the danger only seems to excite Basten. With the snake and spider decorating my skin, I feel more bedecked by luxury than I ever did with Rian's jewels.

My jewels don't shine—they kill.

Basten pushes in another inch, teeth gritted against the urge to fully sheath himself. His fingers dig into the moss by my head, stirring up earthy smells, as he holds himself back. Wanting this to last.

For once, this is no fast and secretive coupling in a broom closet. For now, and forever, we are free to explore each other's bodies with shameless abandon.

A beetle passes through the moss under my back, and I arch on instinct, rolling against Basten's cock until it slips fully inside my pulsing channel.

"Oh, *fuck*. That's going to make me come." Basten grips me around the waist with bruising fingers as he strains to keep his lust in check. A skylark flies overhead, shadowing the sun from my eyes, and I get a clear view of his perfect features.

In this moment, with his jaw cut hard, he's never looked more like royalty. King of the forest. King of the wild.

I would rule the roots at his side.

I would bow to him in the reeds.

I would crown him with a wreath of ivy vines.

He grips my jaw, fingers framing my face. His thumb digs into my bottom lip before he drags his thumbnail against the hard edge of my bottom teeth. I circle my tongue around his thumb, gently sucking and biting.

"Gods in *hell*." As he pulls out and thrusts into me again, he meets my lips with a kiss. It's somehow both tender and unleashed. Wicked and holy. Smoldering coals and raging flames. I could live in this moment forever, captured like a butterfly under glass.

His lips scorch across mine, drawing moans out of me, until I sweep my tongue along his mouth's seam until he parts his lips, so I can snag his bottom lip and bite down until he groans.

He pumps faster now, our rhythm picking up. I match the thrusts with equal rolls of my hips. I grip him by the back of his biceps, squeezing so hard I'm sure my fingernails break the skin. He cups one hand around the back of my thigh, adjusting me for an even deeper fit.

As his cock slams into me, sparks shoot behind my eyes. Glowing dots that sing like spiders, beautiful and strange. His lips claim mine again and again and again, unrelenting. The sex grows feverish. Frantic. Dragonflies zip around us like shooting stars. He drives himself into me one more time, and my body hums like a star, and then I break apart.

I'm everything and nothing.

I'm the sun, the moon, the stars.

I'm the earth shattering.

As my cry rings out, the birds take flight all at once, hundreds of wings beating into the sky. The buck stomps. The snake writhes. The butterflies flutter their iridescent wings in a spellbinding show.

A second later, Basten comes in me. His body shudders

as he braces himself over me, lips crushed to mine, his cock throbbing deep inside me as it pumps out his essence.

We collapse on the moss bed, spent and pleasure-drenched. Our kiss slows from its fever pitch into a long, languid meeting of our lips.

He rests his head against my chest, eyes sinking closed. For a few moments, we just listen to each other's heartbeats.

"Now that I finally have you," he murmurs, "I'm never letting you go. If I lost you, the seven kingdoms would burn to ash in the wake of my fury. You're my reason for living. My beginning, my middle, and my damn end."

CHAPTER 32
WOLF

I didn't know it was possible to need a woman as much as breath. Sabine has worked her way inside me until it isn't just our bodies that come together to be one, but our damn souls. I don't know what kind of past lives she and I lived, but I can fucking promise that we've found each other in all of them.

I help her clean up, then pull her close with my arm as a pillow for her head as we study the mosaic of leaves against the sky. Our hair is tangled. We're half-dressed, me in only pants, her in a dress with a torn strap. She sighs contentedly, and my heart fucking stops.

To have her in my arms and not care who sees?

It's everything I didn't know I could have.

I press my face against her hair so I can breathe in her scent to the exclusion of all others—because I want my entire world to be her. She snuggles closer, her hand lazily tracing from my navel to my birthmark.

"I'm so incredibly lucky," she whispers as broken

ribbons of sun bathe her face. "I never imagined such riches would fall to me."

"Riches?" I chuckle. "Darling, I hate to remind you of this now, but I gave up the crown."

She rolls over to rest her chin on my chest, grinning at me. "That isn't what I mean. I grew up a lord's daughter. I've dined with silver candlesticks. I guess that to me, wealth never meant money. It meant a full belly. A safe place to rest my head. And—" Her fingernail draws circles on my chest as a pretty shade of pink rises to her cheeks. "—and a love that was my choice."

I take her small hand in mine, running the back of my knuckle along each one of her fingers. Then, I pluck a small, twisting vine from among the moss and wind it into a circle the size of a ring.

For a moment, we both stare at the band of vines.

Unexpected nerves grip my stomach in a punishing hold as I clear my throat, suddenly bashful as a fucking youth.

I start, "I haven't gold or silver . . ."

When my nerves get the best of me, Sabine saves me by plucking the makeshift ring from my hand and sliding it over her ring finger. Our eyes meet with all the soft blaze of overnight coals. Without a word, she bridges the gap, her lips grazing mine with the fleeting grace of a butterfly's touch.

She smiles. Then I smile. Big and goofy, like a fucking dunce. But I don't care. Not even her meddling beasts can bother me now—the snake that's coiled up her calf, the dragonfly perched on her hair like a bow, the polecat that keeps poking up from a hole in the tree roots.

She's mine, and so, hell, I guess they are, too. I not only

get a wife but a gods damn menagerie. And for the love of all that sins, I'm starting to warm up to the idea.

I catch her chin between my fingers, unwilling to let that beautiful smile fade. She laughs softly, flicking a stray strand of dark hair off my forehead. Her fingernail traces aimless patterns on my skin.

"Since we met," she whispers, "my heart has spoken your name in the quiet of night. Now, all I wish is to shout it during daylight until every blade of grass, every bee, every leaf knows your name."

I capture her wandering hand, feeling the pulse of her heart in her fingertips, vibrant and alive. Can a man die of happiness? Because, in this moment, I'm dangerously close to finding out.

The wind shifts, carrying a trace of the scent of old iron.

Faint. Ancient. Unmistakable.

Like a blade to my heart, I sit upright, crushing Sabine against my chest with one arm around her like a shield.

"Basten?" The sudden hard patter of her heartbeat cuts like ice in my veins. Her breath stalls in her lungs. If I could kiss away all her fear, I would. But she might need that fear.

"I smell iron." Granite threads through my voice. "It means a fae creature is near."

Her spine stiffens. She grabs for my hunting knife leaning against a root and hands it to me.

"Take this. I don't need it. I can speak to whatever—" Her thoughts slam to a halt, a strange look crossing her face. For a moment, her gaze is fixed on nothing, her eyes slightly unfocused. Then, they snap to me. "I don't hear any fae animal voices."

A premonition sticks inside me like mud, clogging my ability to think. I've smelled old iron before: around Tòrr, in the Volkish tent that held the goldenclaw. But this scent has a slight variation. A tartness beneath the bite of metal. *Like black cherries.*

About two hundred paces away, out of sight, soft foot-steps shush through the grass, headed for us.

I grip the hunting knife with a sharp-edged ferocity, dragging Sabine to her feet as I push her protectively behind me. My armor is littered on the ground. Strewn among the roots. I'm bare-chested, totally exposed. But I'd put myself between Sabine and danger even if I was faced with every cursed soul in the underrealm, an army of the undead climbing back to life.

"Basten, tell me what the hell is going on!" she says in a loud whisper.

My eyes scour the woods. Tightly, I say, "I've only smelled this once before—when Rachillon commanded the starleons. It isn't the scent of fae beasts, but people using fae powers."

Her pulse leapfrogs over itself. In her eyes, a mist forms, the terror of her father's shadow looming once again. But my brave wildcat squares her stance, not showing an ounce of fear.

She reaches for her slippers in case we need to run—

An odd ringing, like distant unstopping bells, burrows into my ears. I grab Sabine's arm, jerking my chin.

"Ahead."

Her wide eyes follow my gaze fixed on a point across the forest. She shifts from foot to foot, squinting. It's too far for anyone without godkissed vision to see the woman approaching.

She's young—barely eighteen. Her long red hair falls loose around her shoulders in a maiden's style. She wears a cream-colored dress with a deceptively simple cut: no asymmetrical hem, no complicated neckline, though my sharp vision picks up on tens of thousands of tiny, white embroidered stitches in the shape of skeletal keys.

She walks slowly, with the uncanny confidence of a grown man, not a girl. This alone would give me pause, but it's her skin that has me planted to the ground as if my heels have taken root.

Fucking impossible.

At first glance, she was utterly human in appearance. Fair, ivory skin and long auburn-red hair half-pulled back in a braid. But with every step toward us, her skin *changes*.

Glowing fey lines appear from the back of her middle fingers up her arms to disappear under her gown, then reappear along the sides of her neck and face. They give off a faint golden sheen reminiscent of the phosphorescence I saw in the Volkish forest. Her human features shift. The corners of her eyes and eyebrows tilt upward. Her ears come to a point—no pewter caps necessary.

Every bone in my body screams with painful certainty:

This stranger is fae.

Sabine lets out a strangled gasp. The fae woman is close enough now for Sabine to see her glowing form approaching down the path.

The chill coiling up my spine turns to solid ice. My instinct is to use my knife. Everything about this fae's energy says *threat*.

And, dammit, I'm a hunter. Halting threats is what I do.

Still, I'm not fool enough to think bringing down a god is like a deer.

I lift my hunting knife, a clear warning, but it might as well be a daisy for how alarmed the woman seems as she approaches. Thank the gods for my instincts, because I'm starved for thoughts. My mind is a barren field.

Up close, she's so otherworldly that it's like beholding a star fallen to earth. Her features are freakishly beautiful, almost impossibly angular.

Stunned, Sabine and I can do nothing but stare.

The fae takes her time looking at the smooshed moss, the tokens cut off Sabine's dress, and then my armor strewn about the tree roots.

Her gaze locks onto Sabine as she tuts. "You know, little human, chastity is power. When you give a man your body, you give him dominion. Better to dangle the possibility until you've wrung the spirit from him." Her eyes briefly light up, almost kindly. "I could teach you the power of a teasing kiss. A touch in just the right place, with just the right pressure. I've had plenty of practice on human men. We fae can make ourselves look human, you know."

With a wink, she flashes back to her human-looking body for a split second before returning to fae form.

The embroidered keys, the maiden's hairstyle, the lecture on chastity. All of it leads me to one place.

"You're Immortal Iyre." My voice comes from somewhere deep and preternatural inside of me.

"Spare me the honorifics." Her gaze hardens when it slides to me. "I heard your woman's prayers and came to rescue her from the clutches of men."

She extends her hand outward to Sabine, a cool metallic sheen coming from the fey lines in her palm. Her eyes soften when she addresses Sabine—why? Does the Goddess of Chastity loathe all men?

What the hell did I ever do to her?

"Come with me," Iyre says in a lilting voice like a siren's song.

A bee lands on Sabine's bare left shoulder. It tromps anxiously back and forth, fluttering its wings as though giving a warning signal.

"I never prayed to you," Sabine says in a steel-lined voice.

Iyre's gentle smile hardens at the edges. "Perhaps not with whispered words, but all young women pray to me in their hearts. To save them from domineering fathers. Or virulent priests. Or from their betrothed, who want to slowly leech the spirit from them and call it marriage."

As Iyre speaks, the hunter in me takes over, quickly assessing the woods for a means of escape. Sabine is barefoot—we can't run far.

I have a knife. My fists. Sabine can call to her animals for help.

But I'm at a major disadvantage in that I don't know how much of the old fae tales are true. The Book of the Immortals describes each fae's unique sphere of power: Meric controls through pain, Thracia can heal, Woudix can wield death itself.

Legends say that Immortal Iyre's power is in reading truth and memory—hardly a threat against a knife, right?

And yet the pinch in my stomach isn't so sure.

"I don't need to be rescued." Sabine plants her bare feet on the moss with a fearlessness that fills me with both awe and alarm.

Iyre's sympathetic head tilt snaps upright. Her soft voice goes cold. "No? Ah, well, there is more than one way we can do this. In the interest of time, we'll go with the most expedient. He's been looking for you for so long that his patience grows thin."

Sabine's heart contracts sharply, a clench of apprehension, even as her expression remains as impenetrable as tree bark.

I take a step between them. "You mean that bastard king? Rachillon?" A flare of anger tightens my throat. "He awoke you, didn't he?"

Iyre purses her lips, a cryptic light dancing in her eyes, as though I don't even know what I'm asking.

"And, what, you do his bidding?" I scoff, knowing I'm treading on unstable ground. "I never knew gods obeyed humans. Even kings."

If my barb offends Iyre, she hides it well. She merely laughs as though I've said something hilarious, though I don't get the joke.

Sabine rakes her nails through her hair, the shorter length a stark contrast to the traditional, obedient image she never fit into. It seems to remind her of something. A deep-seated strength.

This is the real Sabine Darrow. Her will as sharp as her cut ends.

Sabine's hands curl into fists. "My father knew I existed for twenty-two years and never bothered to search for me— why does he care now?"

"Because you're necessary. Your bond with fae beasts is pivotal to his plans. A great battle is coming between the rising fae and those who do not submit to us. You were at the arena—you heard Rachillon's warning." Her tone darkens as she runs her fingers along her dress's sleeve. "And now, daughter of Volkany, you have no choice but to obey."

She fishes a needle out of her sleeve hem. It's as long as my hand, carrying the smell of pure silver, etched with intricate fae knot patterns. As I watch in wary fascination, she walks to an aspen sapling and pierces the air in front of it.

A beam of light bursts out of thin air. *What the fuck?*

The light is warm and orange, flickering like a fire. Iyre carefully drags the needle in a counter-clockwise circle about as tall and wide as a door.

What happens next is hard to explain. The world simply *falls away* from where she needles the air, as if she's ripping the seams from a curtain that gradually collapses. The view of the sapling and the forest behind it gives way to a different scene, like actors swapping out painted backdrops in a play.

Through her rip in the world, we can now peer into a different forest. This one is bathed in shadows, a thick canopy making it seem like perpetually nighttime. A nearby campfire proves the source of the light. Out of frame, a horse whinnies. I can just make out the edge of a tent made of indigo cloth, marked with Thracia's starburst emblem.

She opened a portal to the fucking Volkish army encampment north of the border.

She's going to take Sabine from me.

The warrior in me roars a bloodthirsty cry. A huntsman? No, not any longer. Not after the screams I elicited from Maks when I drove blades under his fingernails. Not after undergoing the Everlast, putting fifteen bodies in the grave so I could live.

I'm a fucking predator.

And Iyre? She's devoid of weapons, as far as I can tell. She can't hide much more than a needle in that dress. If it were Immortal Artain, gifted with immortal strength, or

Immortal Vale, master of all fae magic, I'd be fucked. But the Goddess of Chastity?

What's she going to do, throw prayers at me?

I toss my knife in the air, smoothly catching it with a backward grip. It's a more brutal, violent hold. Meant for downward slashing, not stabbing.

For *hacking*.

"Sabine stays right fucking here with me."

Iyre calmly slides the fae needle back into her hem, then smooths her sleeve. "I'm taking your lover to the winning side, mortal. You should thank me. In far fewer days than you can imagine, Astagnon will be reduced to ash unless it bows to Volkany."

Sabine seems quiet at my side, but her body tells me differently. I've come to learn that when she communicates with animals in her mind, her lips, tongue, and teeth form the words in nearly imperceptible movements, but *I* can hear their subtle twitches.

And judging by the faint rasp of her lips now, she's already one step ahead of me and my knife.

Out of the corner of my eye, I see the buck step silently out from a silver maple at Iyre's back. The animal moves without noise, the sharp points of its antlers brushing silently against the leaves.

Don't look at it, I tell myself. *If anything, distract Iyre.*

I slam the knife hilt against my bare chest, flexing my muscles. "She isn't going to Volkany, not even at the command of a fucking goddess."

Iyre sneers at me, "When a goddess commands, my handsome mortal, there is no choice but to obey."

Iyre lunges forward with a speed I hadn't expected—not

as fast as the godkissed fighters I've tussled with, but close —and seizes Sabine's arm.

"Call to it!" I tell Sabine.

Sabine braces herself against Iyre's pull as her lips knit in tiny movements, calling to the buck. In turn, it lowers its massive rack of antlers in Iyre's direction.

Everything happens at once. The deer charges. I grab Sabine's other arm, damned if I'm going to let a fae rip her away from me.

Without even glancing at the buck, Iyre sidesteps out of its way as if by magic. The buck loses its balance, tripping on a root, and tips head-first into the portal. It scrambles to its feet, half-in and half-out. The air shimmers like a heat wave.

I'm prepared to play a vicious game of tug-of-war with Sabine, but before I can pull her to me, Iyre twirls toward me as though we're dancers in a three-person waltz, circling until she and I are face-to-face.

With a cruel smile, she briefly taps my left temple before twirling away again—a second before I bring the knife down where she'd been.

My hand swings hard, finding nothing, and I stumble forward.

My head teeter-totters with a sudden rush of vertigo. For a few seconds, everything is a blur. The buck looks strange as it straddles the portal: half here in Astagnon, half in Volkany.

Half dark, half light.

My skin erupts with a rash of heat as though I'm seeing something not meant for me. Something about the buck steals every ounce of my attention: almost as though there's a dream at the edge of my memory, rapidly slipping away. Something I'm so close to reaching out and snatching back.

Something that means everything to me ...

But now, like all dreams, it's gone on the next breeze.

"Basten!"

A woman's voice calls my name. My head feels like I've been asleep for days. I glance around, overcome by a sense of deja vu. Where the fuck am I? I have to remind myself that I'm in the forest, near the Valvere burial grounds, after Lord Berolt's funeral.

More pressingly, why the hell am I only half-clothed?

But I'm tugged away from my confusion when I spot a beautiful woman in a torn velvet dress struggling to get free from another woman's grasp.

I've never seen either of them a day in my life. I sure as hell would have remembered: the woman with honey-blond hair cut to her shoulders is so damn gorgeous that I can barely tear my eyes off her.

She's a stranger, yet my heart tightens with desire.

Both women are young and dressed elegantly, utterly ordinary if not for their attractiveness, and I can only stare, dumbfounded for why two noblewomen would be fighting.

My fingers knit at my hair, a hint of that dream fighting to return ...

"Basten!" the woman with honey-blond hair cries, reaching out a hand toward me. "I need you!"

My heart falters, instinctively wanting to help this woman who is clearly desperate. I take a step forward, haltingly, before stopping.

How does she know my name? Gods, I feel such a strange pull to her. Nothing about this feels right. And as a hunter, I'm always on the lookout for traps.

Regardless, my body urges me toward her as though it's life or fucking death.

The other woman clamps a hand over the first woman's mouth. Something about her face tickles the back of my mind, making me think she isn't as ordinary as she appears. That she's hiding something beneath her skin.

Have I seen her before?

Why does my body react as though she's dangerous?

As she drags the blonde toward an aspen sapling with the strength of a man twice her size, she sneers at me. "Be gone, bandit, before we scream and summon the lord's guards!"

Bandit? Me? *What the fuck?*

There's something odd about the aspen—it shimmers like a lake's reflection instead of the real thing. A buck snorts into the air, also shimmering oddly. Again, I get a crushing feeling that I'm forgetting something important. Something about the aspen . . . Something dangerous and unnatural about the red-haired woman . . .

But as soon as it's in my head, it's gone again.

A wave of confusion threatens to pull me under. Seriously, where the hell is my shirt?

I slowly sheath my knife, holding out my hands nonthreateningly. My instincts still prickle, warning me, but I take a step forward.

The blond woman's eyes lock on me as she gives muffled cries and struggles against the other woman's hold.

"She clearly doesn't want to go with you," I say measuredly, trying to tame my erratic heartbeat to buy time for my memories to return. "I don't know what occurred between you two, but release her, and we'll take this to Lord Valvere to discuss."

The red-haired woman snorts, all her attention fixed on

the aspen sapling. What the fuck does she think she's going to do, climb it to the moon?

The blond suddenly woman sinks her teeth into her captor's hand, who releases her with a sharp curse. The woman immediately cries out, "Basten, I love you!"

My heart pumps faster and faster, trying to prod me into remembering. My fingers flex, innately wanting to reach out to her. My lips part, but I have no idea what to say. This beautiful, desperate woman is a total stranger to me. Her words make no sense.

Love me? She doesn't even know me.

"I'm sorry," I stammer. "I'm so sorry. Who are you?"

"Basten, please!" Tears stream down her cheeks. With her last ounce of strength, she frees a hand and reaches out for me, fingers splayed and quaking. "It's me! Sabine!"

From the bottom of my soul, a voice screams in me to go to her. I don't know what is fucking happening. Maybe this is a trap. Maybe I'm being a fool. But fuck it. Some deep-rooted part of me takes over, trusting this complete stranger.

Gripping the knife, I stalk forward. "Let her go."

The red-haired woman gives a laugh that rings like silver bells as she takes one more step toward the aspen. "Too late, mortal."

In the next instant, the two of them are gone.

Vanished into thin air.

I stare and stare and stare at the aspen sapling, whose strange shimmer returns to normal, and the air seems to let out a collective sigh. The smell of old iron is gone. So is the ringing in my ears.

Now, it's only the sounds of trout jumping in the stream, a dragonfly zipping past my face. In the far distance, I can hear horse tack clanking as servants ready the Valvere carriages to return to Sorsha Hall.

For the life of me, I don't know who that beautiful, mysterious woman with honey-blond hair was—but my heart did.

My palms begin to tingle, memories start to creep back into my head, and I have a bone-deep, soul-shattering feeling that I just lost the one person in this world I love.

Even though I don't know her.

Dare to follow Sabine and Wolf's next steps in the third book in the Godkissed Bride series, *Steel Heart Iron Claws!*